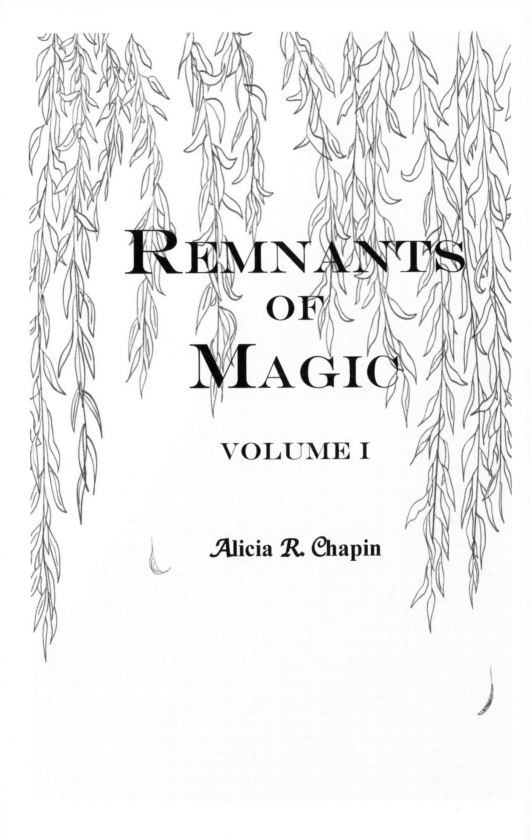

REMNANTS

OF

MAGIC

VOLUME I

Alicia R. Chapin

Remnants of Magic, Volume I
First Hardcover Edition 2021
Copyright © 2012 Alicia R. Chapin
All rights reserved.
ISBN: 978-1-0879-6404-1

Cover design by Cathy Helms, www.avalongraphics.org

For my parents,
James and Diane

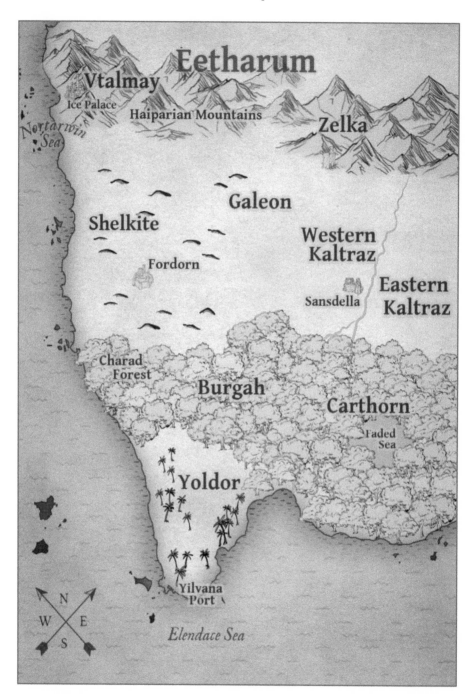

PROLOGUE

The powerful animal's hooves hit the soft beach in the perfect cadence of a full-fledged gallop. The earth churned and sprays of damp sand were cast airborne, leaving the prints to wash away with the crashing waves of the sea. With each stride, the animal's snorted breaths misted in the cool morning air. His eyes wide and alert shone with hope; his long tail floating on the breeze in a ray of silky, iridescent threads. The magical creature's coat was without equal, the purest white, dazzling to the eye, and as sleek as blue ice on the cold bays of the Nortarwin Sea. Nothing thrilled the great beast more than running with the salty winds of daybreak whilst carrying promising news.

As the luminescent sun rose above the watery horizon, his prismatic horn sent all the colors of the spectrum dancing across the beach. He flipped his mane from the pleasure of the warmth on his back and galloped on, returning northward. He was Apollos, an advisor of the country of Shelkite; and he made haste to report to Prince Alkin, who had long awaited him at the castle in the grand city of Fordorn.

CHAPTER ONE

A dark lock of hair fell across Bryan's damp forehead. He swiped it away impatiently and rubbed his brow with restless fingertips. The young warrior bit his bottom lip and felt for the hilt of his sword. His hand found it right where it should be, at his side in its sheath. He exhaled, letting his broad body relax.

The light laughter of a woman escaped from behind the closed door where he stood guard. Bryan's uncommonly bright azure eyes shifted around the corridor, seeking anything abnormal. There was nothing. He started to pace, his black riding boots tapping quietly across the scuffed floorboards. *When is he going to be done?* Bryan rolled his eyes.

Being Prince Alkin's personal guard did have its advantages, but waiting around for him to make social calls was ridiculous. Bryan wanted action, battles, even blood, anything but to tag along with the Prince to visit pretty lady friends of Fordorn.

He let out an annoyed breath and paced the hall quicker. Women! All they ever did was get their skirts in the way. Sure, he had had his fair share of feminine company, but that was all done and over with. No more trouble for him, thanks. Sure, he liked Alkin. He was one of his closest friends, but it was becoming increasingly aggravating that he met with Lady Evelyn every week. She was a beauty known around the city as the Chaos Goddess. And, in Bryan's opinion, she was kind of silly.

The latch clicked on the oak door. Bryan spun around to face it. The handle turned ever too slowly. "Come on," he whispered through clenched teeth. He stood at attention as he heard the Prince say his farewells from behind the door.

The door opened and the blonde-haired Alkin stepped out. The Prince smiled at his awaiting guard, and Bryan nodded his respects as the shapely Lady Evelyn stepped into the threshold.

Alkin turned to face the brunette. "Thank you again for your time, Lady Evelyn." He bowed.

"I'll see you next week, then?" the Chaos Goddess replied.

The sugarcoated words sickened Bryan. While he stood there painfully waiting, she flicked her dark eyes over his broad stature. He clenched his jaw again, growing more impatient with every second.

"Yes, my lady." Alkin took her pale hand and landed a kiss there. He smiled one last time before briskly turning down the staircase to the lobby below. Bryan turned to follow him.

"Goodbye, Sword Bryan," Evelyn said sweetly.

Bryan spun back and politely bowed, "My lady." He smiled the best he could, catching a glitter of amusement in her pretty doe-eyes before she closed the chamber door with a smile. And, letting his gaze linger there for a moment, he heaved another sigh with his eyes turned upward. He then started down the hall to the creaky stairway after his prince, the tip of his sheathed sword clinking on the tops of the steps as he jogged down. He pushed his way through the crowded lobby to the front porch of the inn.

Standing under a weathered sign that read 'Snowed Inn,' he looked up and down the main street of Fordorn City. Those of the city's lower class bustled about, hard at work. Teams of mules and oxen pulled hefty carts loaded with goods through the muddy streets, their drivers disheveled and carelessly spitting out tobacco wads as they jostled by. Cows bellowed and pigs squealed. Women shouted at children causing havoc among the booths, and men hollered orders to their employees.

What a great place. Bryan inhaled the dingy air, happy to be away from the tavern and women.

"Are you coming?" Prince Alkin asked from atop his bay warhorse. The burly horse flipped his black mane, causing the metals of his bridle to clink. Alkin leaned casually on the pommel of his saddle and said, "For acting so impatient, you're not moving very fast."

Bryan smiled at the smirking prince before untying his black mount from the inn's hitching post. He couldn't hide anything from him.

Bryan liked to fancy himself an impassive man; though, when he was impatient it was well known. It was not one of his strengths.

"I'm coming, my prince." He mounted gracefully despite the

bulkiness of his weapons and saddle and reined his burly stallion around to follow the Prince down the road leading out of town.

Bryan and Dragon, his mount, slowly made their way around the bustling citizens. Dragon weaved from side to side of the sloppy road, intent on catching up with his stablemate.

Bryan bumped Dragon lightly when he saw the Prince disappear around a bend. The game horse responded, his huge hooves kicking up clods of dirt.

"Hey! Watch it, dim-wit!" An angry shout came from behind them. Bryan shifted around to see an irate, mud-splattered woman. When she caught sight of him, she bowed, immediately remorseful. "S-sorry, Master Sword, I didn't know it was you!" she apologized, holding her gaze at her feet, which were rapidly disappearing into the muck.

"No, it was my fault. I wasn't thinking." Bryan gave her slight nod and clucked to Dragon to move on.

As they reached the bounds of the city, Dragon drew abreast with the Prince's mount. The stallion gave a loud snort to make known his arrival.

Alkin turned at the sound, his green cloak flowing over the rump of his horse, making him appear regal, even though the Prince was trying to blend in more today by not wearing his usual hue of blue. The people of Fordorn were, for the most part, a friendly and content crowd who knew their prince by face. None-the-less, Alkin hated being ostentatious, something that could possibly cause troublesome attention.

The Prince was softly humming a familiar light-hearted tune native to Shelkitens. He glanced over at his friend as he rode up beside him. "You know your horse has about as much patience as a *real* dragon… And, I fear his master is not far behind," he said, looking up to the next bend in the road, which led them past the last of the city homes.

Bryan snorted. "Humph! We've more important things to do than have tea with the ladies."

Alkin looked at him in genuine surprise. "Really?" he said. "Do you ever recall me stopping by just to make social calls 'with the ladies' in the past?"

"No," the rebuffed Bryan answered slowly.

"Then, maybe you should assume there is more to my visiting Lady Evelyn than just a social call." Alkin heeled his mount into a faster gait.

They rode on, entering the firmer, grassier country roads. The road wended through beautiful, lush landscape, wide-open, rolling fields with crop and livestock farms settled along the way.

Up until the last couple of years, Alkin and Bryan had always been good friends. The Master Swords—a select number of the Prince's elite warriors and advisors—had appointed Bryan two years ago to become a Master Sword and Sword-Guard to Prince Alkin. The necessity of this position was due to an assassination threat to the Prince.

But ever since Bryan's promotion, he and Alkin squabbled more than they ever had as childhood pals. It did not help that Bryan would be happier if he was back training warriors rather than being a Master Sword and a part of the Prince's council. What good was his ability if he could never use it alongside the other warriors? Alas, Bryan worked hard to keep fit and hold his place of high stature.

Moreover, because of his skills and hard work, he had quickly moved up in rank within the Master Swords. He was now the Head-Master Sword. Bryan often thought he should be honored, but he did not feel as such. He felt bored with life, and needed action or something new at least.

Bryan patted his stallion's strained neck as they passed a mare hitched outside the noisy Blue Mermaid Tavern. It was the only decent place a traveler could get a drink for miles until the city. Men from all over assembled there to tell stories of lost sweethearts and distant lands. It gathered quite an interesting crowd. Bryan himself had been there many times.

Dragon nickered but did nothing more than crane his neck to get a better look at the mare. "It's just better off to stay away from those," he said to his horse. "They end up being nothing but trouble." Dragon shook his head and pulled at his bit.

The sun started to dip beneath the hilly horizon. They would not reach the castle until after dark. Bryan nudged his horse to catch up to the now singing prince. Alkin's shoulder-length, blonde hair was down and tousled. The wind lifted it as he turned to him to sing part of the chorus. Bryan smiled and listened to the words that spoke of Shelkite's beloved rolling hills and farmland.

"Sing with me, oh great Master Sword Bryan!" he called over with a joyful air, though his tone held slight mockery at his austere friend.

Bryan stared at him as if he was mad.

"It will pass the time." Alkin smiled at his always-resistant guard.

Bryan cracked a grin. He didn't mind that the Prince occasionally slipped into a child-like demeanor. Alkin was a few years younger than him, Bryan being in his early twenties. The important thing, however, was that Alkin had a good heart and was a clever and fair ruler. No country could ask for more. So, he proudly joined in.

For the remainder of the trek, the two men's voices, Alkin's practiced tenor and Bryan's slightly off-key baritone, resounded clear over the foothills of the Haiparian Mountains.

As they neared the grounds of Shelkite's castle, the men's singing voices died down. Fog began to settle with the night. It flowed milky and vaporous over the dark hills, where it seeped onto the road. They quickened their pace. Some things lurked that even a Master Sword would not want to face.

Soon, through the dusk, formidable stone walls appeared before them.

Alkin gazed at his castle and halted his blood bay, Sapharan, before the gate. His hazel eyes moved over the high walls, thinking of his departed father. His ancestors had built the castle strong. Alkin had only been thirteen when his father had passed away, leaving him the ruler of Shelkite at a young age.

His father had been a demanding, but a just and popular ruler. After his death, the guidance and wisdom of his mother, Adama, had prepared him for the rest of his ruling era.

Bryan sat motionless on Dragon and watched his prince scan the walls of the castle while they waited for the appearance of Lycil, the gateman.

A call shattered the night. "State yourself!"

"It is I, Prince Alkin, returning with Sword Bryan from Fordorn!" Alkin shouted up to the gateman. His breath misted in the rising moonlight, and he held up the Sword of Shelkite to identify himself.

"Ah! My prince, welcome back!" Lycil's now pleasant voice called down.

The chilly damp of the night faded away as Bryan thought of escaping the darkness to the warmth of his chambers.

The two horses stomped their hooves as the gate cranked open. Dragon snorted; a puff of mist sprang into the cool air, and he arched his neck and pranced in anticipation of his dinner. They guided their mounts through the gate and into the flagged-stoned courtyard.

"My prince, I have news!" Lycil called down, holding a torch, the flame high above his head, and looking as if his hair had caught fire. With Lycil's usual luck, he probably *would* catch his hair on fire. Bryan chuckled at the thought.

"What is it?" Alkin answered with a merry note.

"Apollos is back!" Lycil said as they dismounted.

Bryan watched Alkin's features turn dumbfounded. The Prince's most trusted advisor, Apollos, had not been seen or heard from for two years. Apollos been an ally to the crown of Shelkite for many years. Though, the most extraordinary thing about him was that he was not human. He was a unicorn. Unicorns were a rare sight indeed. In fact, other than Apollos, no unicorn had been seen for centuries.

Alkin whispered something inaudible and, looking troubled, he turned and sprinted to the castle's door. Deep in thought, Bryan watched him disappear. He then looked down to the Stable Master's daughter, waiting to take his stallion's reins.

"Thank you, Annelia." He smiled.

"You're welcome, Master Sword." She bowed and gazed at him with admiring eyes, and then led the horses to the stable, speaking softly to them as she went.

Since there were others to help guard the Prince while in the castle, Bryan had been looking forward to a pleasant night in his room away from all disturbances. Perhaps taking a hot bath and reading an old war book. Now, however, unease settled on him.

Why had the unicorn's appearance brought fear into his friend's eyes?

Before Bryan settled in his room, even before his pleasant servant could bring him dinner, he was summoned to the Council Hall. He heaved a sigh, grabbed his knife, slid it back into his boot buckle, and donned his sword. The servant girl gave him an understanding look as she helped him back into his uniform's overcoat. His Master Sword garments comprised of tan trousers, riding boots, a lightweight, white shirt, and a silver-trimmed blue overcoat.

Once dressed, he started reluctantly down to the meeting hall.

He was late. The other eleven Master Swords were already gathered around the massive oak table. It sat in the center of a grand circular room. The thick walls rose high into a domed ceiling, and through a large window on the northeast there was a spacious balcony overlooking Shelkite's precious grazing land.

Murals graced the walls, telling tales of ancient battles. The paintings consisted of hundreds of mystical creatures that had been long forgotten or become extinct. The magical world of Eetharum and its creatures were now of the past. Only a few remnants of it still lingered. The unearthly power that had once ruled Eetharum had waned at a great velocity after the Lost War, which had ended over five hundred years ago. It had lasted a whole century, driven by fear, hate, and bloodlust. A hemorrhaging Eetharum had been left in its wake. Magic and its counterparts had subsided against the multitude of humans. And humans had gone on, no longer bothering to remember their mystical brethren or the power that had once dominated the world. Years of reconstruction had finally healed the land, but some wounds in old enough hearts had yet to mend.

The room, however, was not the magnificent aspect that caught Sword Bryan's eyes. In the far-right, near the balcony, Alkin stood conversing with none other than the unicorn. The creature was like nothing he had ever seen. His coat of heavenly white looked of satin. And when the flickering lights of the hall hit his mane and tail, each single iridescent, pearly thread glimmered one of the colors of the rainbow. His hooves were a shiny copper-gold, and the slender crystal horn shattered dazzling light.

The unicorn bobbed his flawless head and flipped his shimmering mane as he spoke. The Prince, listening intently, nodded and answered in low tones.

Bryan stood, somewhat gawking, for Apollos had left on his mission after Alkin had been threatened and before he had become a Master Sword. Before he had moved to the castle and had nothing to be concerned with other than his everyday life as a warrior in the camp. He'd never seen the mystical creature up close before, for Apollos rarely visited the warrior quarters.

The other Swords spoke quietly, sitting around the table, eyeing Apollos with suspicion. Bryan listened to the older men's murmured gossip.

"Please sit down, Sword Bryan." Alkin strode over. Apollos followed close behind. No sound echoed from the beautiful creature's hooves.

Bryan brushed a lock of dark hair from his eyes and took a seat at the end of the table, bracing himself for the bad news he knew he was about to hear.

Prince Alkin stood at the other end, looking out over his Master Swords. His earlier child-like behavior had vanished into maturity, and he stood now clad in robes of blue, his blonde locks pulled away from his tense features. He looked regal wearing his silver circlet. The Prince placed his hands on the table as the unicorn watched impassively from behind.

He eyed the group. "I've kept a secret from you all."

The Swords looked up, many with a furrowed brow.

"I didn't want to divulge this before I had more facts. So, please forgive me. For it wasn't something I should have spared, after all. But, I have evidence of a threat to Shelkite—as well as Eetharum. King Ret of Zelka has proved he wishes to set himself up as emperor over Eetharum."

He paused so his Master Swords could absorb this, as they glanced around the table to each other.

"I'm not sure if you all know, but King Ret is a wizard…"

Bryan shifted uncomfortably at the mention of the rare, magical race; many of the Swords did, for it was well-known wizards were prone to have an evil nature.

"I'm just going to say this outright. We must stop him. He's a threat to Shelkite and the peace of Eetharum. It could mean an all-out war, but there's still a chance we can stop him before it gets to that. I've learned of his plan from reliable spies in contact with the Chaos Goddess. She's informed me that Ret usurped the throne unlawfully; though, it was done so carefully so as not to be detected by the majority. He wants to dissolve the countries of Eetharum and supplant the rulers with his own men. And that's not half of it… He apparently pledges allegiance to the Arch Demon; and it is known, he has even made sacrifices… This means he'll be using soiled magic against us. We won't be able to fight him with solely manmade weapons."

The Master Swords gazed at him in heavy consternation. The hardy weapons they wielded were all they knew.

"The Chaos Goddess says he has managed to fool many Zelkans into his plan. But he has also somehow recruited some mystical beings. Aside from us, I believe only the country of Galeon is aware of this threat. Our task right now is to inform the rest of the allied countries of Eetharum and ready our military."

"Ready a military ignorant of magic? We'll be slaughtered," Sword Keavin blurted.

Alkin held up a calming hand, "Apollos has just returned from seeking our own magic to fight with. I'm not naïve enough to think that we would succeed without manipulating magic ourselves. But, as you know, magic and its beings are not something we can readily get our hands on anymore. However, Apollos has discovered that there are magical keys—of a sort—we can seek out to aid us in his defeat. The good news is they're in Eetharum, though under watchful eyes."

"What are these keys—or counter-magic?" Sword Xercan asked.

"We don't know. Apollos got this information from the Guidance Naiad."

A moment of surprise passed.

"The legendary nymph? The one that lives in the Faded Sea in Carthorn?"

"Yes. She's real. And, if found, will give the seeker a few

trustworthy words of guidance."

"What if her magic is soiled? How do we know if we can trust her?" Sword Keavin asked.

"Apollos says we can trust her," Alkin said. He took a breath and continued, "Already many Zelkans have died in rebelling against Ret. He's covered up their deaths. He's very clever. And from my own experience, I know he has a likable demeanor, though it is deceiving.

"This is urgent. He might be able to convince other countries to join him. It's our duty to protect Shelkite and our honor to protect our fellow countries. We can't let him cross Zelka's border. And if we can root him out and save Zelka, all the better. I beg you for your pledge to stop him before he destroys the peace and our beloved Shelkite. Can I count on my Master Swords?" The Prince ended with an emphatic plea in his eyes. The Swords looked upon him stunned, voiceless, and breathless.

Bryan gulped down a lump of air. How ironic. This should be enough of an adventure for him. But he would have never wished *this* kind of adventure on anyone. Perhaps he was a little too bored with life, and now it was paying him back. It was as if the buried powers of the world had come to haunt them for forgetting they existed. For Bryan's cautious mind, it was almost unbelievable to think that magic still resided in the present. If it were not for a unicorn standing before his eyes, he would have scoffed at the Prince's insanity. But there, at Alkin's side, a live, magical creature stood.

He rose from his chair. "My service belongs to Shelkite and all it believes worthy," he said.

Alkin gave his friend a sad, appreciative smile. Bryan glanced at the regal unicorn. Apollos gave the slightest nod of approval.

Another Sword stood. "I second that." Two more followed. Then the rest stood. Alkin nodded a cheerless thank you.

"But, here is the main thing." He looked down at his fingers splayed on the table.

Bryan and the others took in a breath. Alkin had not told them everything before they'd vowed? The Master Sword narrowed his eyes, but quickly pushed the angry thought away. He would do his duty anyhow.

"Apollos has learned from the naiad that there's only one person who can control the counter-magic against Ret."

They stared, bewildered. A few mouths opened, ready to question.

"We were told where we could find this individual. She's from Eastern Kaltraz. I'm reluctant to say that we must enter this battle dependent almost exclusively on a single soul…"

The word 'she' echoed in their minds, an endless, resounding word. At least, to Bryan it did. The Swords continued to stare, numb to the world around them.

Bryan was the first to come back. "A woman?" he blurted.

Alkin looked scared. "I'm afraid, it's worse. We must not only put our trust and lives in the hands of a woman, but a girl of just seventeen, a shepherd's daughter."

CHAPTER TWO

A slender figure sat confidently on a white horse in a small assembly making its way across the grassy foothills. The shade of night settled upon the land, but the white animal shone pale in the dusk. The gelding looked petite and fragile compared to the large warhorses striding nearby. But the poised rider knew of the animal's abilities beyond those of the warhorses. The rider flipped her waist-length braid over her shoulder and looked around at the Shelkiten warriors with whom she had traveled across Eetharum's countries. During their time together, the warriors had made sure they took good care of her, though they'd spoken seldom, except maybe to jest about her 'scrawny' horse.

Their journey, which had started more than a month ago, was now nearing its end as the large Shelkiten castle loomed ahead. The young rider knew little about what the Prince of Shelkite wanted with her. She was of the common people. What would royal blood possibly want with a lowly shepherdess? Even her own country's princesses had not known she existed until only recently when she'd received a notice she was to come to the castle of Kaltraz in the city of Sansdella in Western Kaltraz.

From there, she was hurried through an explanation of her somehow aiding Eetharum and how she must go to see Prince Alkin of Shelkite in honor of their countries' alliance. Upon her assent, she'd been rushed away with little more explanation than this. It seemed the warriors would have whisked her away with or without her permission. Nevertheless, though Alexandra was from a family of shepherds and innkeepers, she was ready to meet this head on. As long as she had her faithful mount, Zhan, and her handy bow and arrow at her side.

The group halted in front of the towering stone-mortared walls of the castle. And Alexa could not help but feel excited at being in a new land. She judged from the construction of the castle and the miles of stone fencing she had seen along their way that rocks must be a readily available source of construction material for

Shelkite. It gave the country an inviting atmosphere and was vastly different from the sandstone of Kaltraz.

To the west, the sun slipped behind the rolling hills as if the grass were a sheet for the hot sphere to rest in for the cool night. She watched it set. Her blue eyes glittered in the adventure and the wonder of the moment. She had never traveled this far from her country before.

The castle gates opened for the small procession, and they proceeded to enter the courtyard. Alexa looked around, curious to see how the foreigners lived; or rather, how their prince lived. She then realized *they* were not the foreigners—she *was*. She raised her chin, taking up her guard as a handsome man with dark unruly curls falling over his brow strode from the stables. He wore a uniform of lightweight clothes to enable him to move freely. She presumed he was high in the rankings of the prince's warriors. He was obviously skillful with the sword that hung at his side. Two austere warriors followed in his path. He came to a halt in front of Zhan and her, his bright blue eyes regarding her and her horse suspiciously. He looked cocky. She determined right then to allow no one to get the better of her, especially after having to endure her escorts' impoliteness. She was on her own here. No one would do her any favors.

Sword Bryan strode up to meet the assembly and the girl they had escorted from Kaltraz. For some reason, he felt like starting a grapple. It still irked him that a *girl* was appointed to do the perilous job...and not *him*.

When he approached the waiting lot, he expected to see a petite, helpless lady clad in a white dress riding sidesaddle. However, when he came to a halt in front of the 'redeemer,' he was quite surprised. He saw a young woman. Yes, she was petite, but strangely enough, she looked as if she could pull the horns off a dragon. Unlike the women from Shelkite, who always wore gowns and adornments, she wore dark figure-fitting pants, tall black riding boots, and a light, worn-out shirt and cloak. Slung over her shoulder were a bow and quiver, and a sheathed dagger hung at her side. *A ruffian, not a feminine, girlish charm about her.* He looked her up and down, noting a single raven-black braid falling to the center of her back. Her features were angular and plain, but not unpleasing. Her skin lightly bronzed by the sun that caused a soft sprinkle of freckles to lie across her nose.

Then he noted with alarm her horse. A beast like that was not known around Shelkite. He was too slightly built. His head small, though finely shaped. *He won't last a day of hard riding; no wonder it took them so long to return.* Bryan thought of his burly Dragon with pride.

The girl studied him with vivid sapphire eyes. It seemed as if they saw straight through him, as though *he* was the one being evaluated. He returned the challenging stare.

"Do I not meet your satisfaction, Sir Knight?"

Her tone fell on Bryan's ears like bitter chocolate the tongue. "Master Sword," he corrected. "A Master Sword is not quite the same thing as a knight. We're more superior in many aspects."

"Pardon me, Master Sword. I didn't mean to insult you," she replied, though her inflection betrayed any sincerity.

"You're to meet our prince soon. Why aren't you wearing appropriate clothes? And what kind of animal is that?" Bryan blurted, ignoring her apology. His brash statement even caught him by surprise. The words were over his tongue and out before he realized how very rude they were. It, in fact, did not matter how she dressed. The difference was something like a crisp breath of air to him. However, the horse had to go…

"I'm sorry if you don't approve of the way I look. I am no Duke. This is how most women from Western Kaltraz dress who are under Princess Athena's rule. If you want a girl in a silk gown, I suggest you find one of Princess Livia's easterners. And this is a noble animal, quick-witted and fast. He's bred for the deserts of my country.

"In Kaltraz, women dress and do as they please. And, the horses are high caliber. Isn't that so here?"

"Not exactly. Although nothing is stopping them, they just don't find it proper. It's untraditional. And, as for the horses, they have excellent bloodlines." Bryan gave a smug smile. Sure, she was a cute thing, but a thorn. His lip twitched. Her oddities drew on him, but he resisted it.

"I see, Master Sword." Alexa inclined her head, struggling to hold back a biting remark. Regardless of whether he was a Master Sword and older than her, this man needed to gain a little perspective. "I may be in your country, but I don't plan on changing myself just to make you happy."

"And, we wish it to be that way." A pleasant voice came up from behind the Sword and his silent followers.

Alexa looked up to see a handsome young man stroll up to stand next to the Sword. He was shorter than and not as broad as the Master Sword, but looked fit just the same. His hair was golden blonde and pulled back from his fair features. He smiled warmly. He wore no crown. His conduct and attire were the only indications that perhaps he was royalty.

"Welcome, Alexandra. I'm Prince Alkin. I hope my Head-Master Sword hasn't frightened you." His hazel eyes shone with kindness as he bowed to her. He was not much older than she was.

"Thank you, dear prince. And, I'm not at all frightened by your mighty Master Sword," Alexa said, and in one lithe move, she dismounted Zhan, who eyed the nearby stables and its occupants with interest.

"We're very glad to have you. I'm sure you're tired. You can rest, have dinner, and a tour of my castle before we go over the details. I am sure you are curious as to why we requested your presence."

The Prince took her hand into his and landed a soft kiss there. Alexa smiled at this unfamiliar gesture. His grasp was warm and friendly. She had begun to worry the whole country was going to be unpleasant to her, but he had proven otherwise. He was their leader, and in her situation, that was all that mattered.

They started for the castle's doors. "I hear you're the daughter of a shepherd. Is this true?" Alkin asked.

Alexa followed him down the flagged-stone path, glancing back to see Zhan being led to the stables. The warriors had departed and returned to their business, but the cocky Master Sword followed a few strides behind, just far enough to not intrude on their conversation, but close enough she could sense bitterness flowing from him, masking any other feelings she might derive. However, from the Prince, she felt nothing but sincerity, which gave her confidence.

"Yes, my father's a shepherd and an innkeeper. He's also a wizard. But, he prefers the quiet life of the ranch." She offered the information freely, unabashed of her lineage.

"Really? That's intriguing," the Prince glanced in surprise at her but recovered forthwith, "I can tell by the way you speak that you prize your father highly."

"Yes. He's a good man."

"Well, no more inquiring now. Let's get you settled, and then we can speak some more. I'm sure you're feeling just as anxious as we are to talk."

Alkin's smile widened as they halted in a grand foyer. He called a servant to show her her room. "I'll have Sword Bryan come for you soon. In the meantime, make yourself at home in your chambers."

He bowed and kissed her hand again, and turned to leave her in the servant's care. Sword Bryan also smiled, though it looked forced, and bowed. He then followed the Prince down the corridor.

She watched over her shoulder at the departing Prince Alkin and Master Sword. They intrigued her; the Sword's abruptness, the Prince's calm manner. She quirked her lips with a slight shake of her head. The people here were different from hers, less personable if she had to describe it. She hastened her pace to match the servant's quick steps, all the while wondering why a foreign prince needed her.

She found her chambers decorated elegantly with what she assumed were the latest styles of western Eetharum. Being very fond of the sun, she noted with a sense of glee that the adjoining washroom had large windows facing vast hills. Although at that time, it was not the sun shining through but the moon casting its silvery shadows about the room.

She took it upon herself to soak in the awaiting, soapy, hot water of the tub. Her muscles, tight from the long days of riding, warmed and relaxed. She closed her eyes, relishing the comforts of the castle.

After she had dressed in a clean set of her boyish garments, she re-braided her damp hair, letting the raven plait fall down her back.

While she gazed out across the fields, marveling at the opportunity to see new places, there was a firm knock on her door. Poking her head out, she spotted Sword Bryan, who was trying his best to look his austere part. He didn't fool her. She smiled despite his set face.

"I'm instructed to give the guest of honor a tour of the castle." He bowed and clutched the sword at his side. "Would you like one, Miss Alexandra?"

"You can call me Alexa, or even Lex, as my brothers do. And, I'd love to see the castle." She looked back to her bow and quiver lying on the bed, pondering whether she should bring them. She touched the dagger at her side. If she got into any trouble, it would be enough.

Bryan led the young woman through the castle, making only brief stops to explain murals or various statues. The higher levels of the castle comprised Prince Alkin's personal wing, his family's chambers, and the Master Swords' chambers. The guest chambers were found just below, with the servants' rooms in the southern, lower wing. On the ground level were the ballrooms, dining halls, meeting rooms, throne room, library, and of course, the kitchens and laundry rooms.

He began to lead her down the staircase to meet with the Prince in a dining hall when she caught his arm.

"What's down that wing? You didn't take me down that way." She pointed beyond the staircase to the right.

"That's the Swords' conditioning rooms. I didn't think you'd want to see them," Bryan said, although he thought the girl might have liked them best. They were exquisite rooms, modern for the age.

The girl's eyes lit up. "Can I see them?" she asked, unconsciously clutching his arm.

Bryan gave her a roguish grin, "Of course." He led her down the long corridor to one of the many rooms and took her into the combat one to have a look around. One large window comprised the entire eastern wall. The west wall in the rectangular room was lined with mirrors, and all different kinds of swords, knives, daggers, and other menacing-looking weapons adorned the end walls—lances, maces, battleaxes… Some blades were slim and straight, while others cast a jagged and thick form.

Bryan watched as the young woman looked around entranced. She was unlike girls from Fordorn. Their pleasures were of clothes and jewelry, but she seemed to be enjoying herself quite enough here. He walked down to the weapons and pulled a sword down. She followed him. The two eyed the sharp, glinting metal and delicately designed hilt.

"It's a Galeon sword," Bryan said with admiration. "In fact, all these swords are Galeon made. They're very highly regarded."

"Yes, I've heard of Galeon's impressive sword-makers. Many say the Galeonics are the best smithies and masons in the world." Alexa touched the hilt of the weapon, a sense of awe in her voice. "Though, I've never owned one of their swords myself."

"Yes. But, it still baffles me why a woman would enjoy a warrior's practice room and weapons," Bryan said, a little spiteful. He gazed down at her while she caressed the flat of the blade.

Her head shot up, a glint of blue fire sprung into her eyes, turning her awed countenance into a glare. "Why shouldn't I? And, I could win any fight," she said.

"All right then, Alexandra of Kaltraz." He thrust the sword into her hands and unsheathed his own. "Fight me. I'm the Prince's best. By your fighting, may you represent every woman that believes she's a warrior."

He only meant to challenge her, and maybe irk her a little bit, too. He'd heard and read of many great female warriors fighting in the Lost War and thought highly of them. However, he wasn't about to allow this arrogant girl know his true feelings.

"It's Alexa," she shot back, adjusting her grip on the sword. "I'm my best at bow and arrow."

"So, you lied, then." Bryan grinned. He advanced toward her, holding out his sword. The girl began to back away. "All show, eh?" A mischievous glint was in his eye.

"You're a bitter man." She frowned, taking up the sword. She didn't fear him, but she did not want to fight him either. "Did something happen, *Sword Bryan*? Did some lady snare you on a hook only to throw you back?"

Bryan advanced on her and thrust. She blocked the hard blow.

His features turned sour, and he grimly struck again, his footwork precise. Alexa parried it with a small smile.

The two circled each other in the center of the room. Their eyes fixed for any slight movement. The full moon shone through the liquid dark windows. Sconces lining the walls cast flickering light and shadows across them.

Inside, Bryan seethed. She was a little beast of a girl. He was beginning to wish it *had* been a lady who had come. At least they were governed by protocol, unlike this girl.

He attacked with a series of hard thrusts. She blocked them all, to his surprise. Though, he knew he should not use his full potential on her. It wouldn't be a good idea, considering she was the Prince's guest; and it really would be an unfair fight...

Alexa bit her lip, forced to concentrate more on protecting herself than advancing on him. She could not let her mind at ease, lest he strike. He *was* good. The best she had ever gone up against. She tried to thrust a blow but failed.

"I hit the spot, didn't I? Was she pretty? Did she dump you on your backside? Or did she just outsmart you?" she said through gritted teeth.

Sword Bryan snarled at her and launched a swing. The weapons sang when they connected, and he pressed his down on hers. She strained under his strength, unable to make a move.

Their faces inches apart, the Master Sword shoved. Alexa fell hard, and her sword skidded across the room. He snapped his blade to her throat. She glared up at him, and his mouth twitched into a shallow grin.

"Why do you think you're so clever?" he said through a clenched jaw.

"I don't think I know. I know!" she spat, feeling a bit chagrined. His clear eyes narrowed; she said, "You can't fool me, *Bryrunan!* My father's a full-blooded wizard. I have innate senses." She rushed to rise and the edge of his sword glanced across her cheek. She pursed her lips and gave him an ill-fated look. He was a complete brute.

Bryan stared at the girl's face, now reddened with a scratch. How had she known his birth-name? Very few knew it. He took a step back, bewildered. Her blood was only half-human? What had they gotten themselves into? Wizards lived to be very old, but most had died out. Could this girl possibly be related to, or conspiring with, the wizard in the north?

A figure came to stand in the room's threshold, prying their glares from each other. "Am I interrupting something? Or, do I remember correctly that Alexa is my guest and we were to meet for dinner now?" Prince Alkin said.

The Prince had a notion the two would battle out their strong state of minds eventually, but not so soon. Ever since Bryan had a horrific experience with a former love, the Master Sword held little patience for the female gender, let alone a strong-minded one as Alexandra appeared to be.

"Yes, my prince." Bryan stepped back, now feeling guilt for the scratch, and sheathed his weapon, but any words of apology seemed out of grasp.

Alexa straightened and went to stand next to the Prince, while he replaced the sword she had used. Alkin started down the corridor with the girl in tow.

Bryan slipped up behind her and said in her ear, "How d'you know my real name?"

Alexa grinned and whispered back, "I told you. I have abnormal blood. Be careful what you think. I just might be able to hear you." She gave him an innocent smile and bounded up to walk next to the Prince, leaving the Sword to wonder.

She could, of course, sense feelings because she was part witch, but she had only known his name because it was a common one in the east, albeit an older one. And she had only guessed his bitterness was because of some woman. *It's always a woman...* But perhaps it wasn't. She didn't think Sword Bryan posed any real threat to her, just an annoyance mostly. She would show him up later with her exceptional archery skills. Right now, though, she was eager to speak with the Prince. She would deal with the cocky Sword later.

CHAPTER THREE

"Well, I must say that I'm a little relieved you're a follower of Princess Athena and not Princess Livia." Alkin leaned over the table and smiled at Alexa. "It saves a lot of time and energy to not have to train a lady to fight." He chuckled. The princesses were twin sisters, and Livia was known to be the more refined of the two.

They were seated at one end of a long oak table in a private dining room of the castle. Alkin was at the head. Alexa sat at his left, and Sword Bryan ate quietly at his right. The other Swords had eaten earlier while Bryan had given her the tour.

Alexa smiled at the Prince and then stuffed a ridiculous amount of ham in her mouth. The dinner was a feast for her. Having traveled for so long, the food seemed especially delectable. The servant had set in front of them platters of warm bread, cheese, smoked ham, and sweet potatoes. Her mouth had watered at the sight of it.

"I am still a little confused why I'm here," she said after she'd swallowed. "Why would you have to train me to fight?"

Bryan watched her, disgusted and a little flabbergasted. Why was she jamming so much food in her mouth and, more notably, where did she put it all? She was so slender, she could be a lance. Did she come from a family of heathens? He had to tell Alkin as soon as possible that she had witch blood in her. He was not biased, but it made him uneasy considering the circumstances.

Alkin smiled at Alexa, understanding, and set down his mug with a sigh. "That's reasonable." The Prince searched the girl's face. She had a veiled beauty he figured many men had foolishly overlooked. He could have punched Bryan for being so rude and spoiling his guest's face.

Alexa watched the Prince's features turn from cheery to unsettled, his brow creasing in thought, and she listened with growing trepidation as he explained the situation. He delved much deeper than either of her princesses had. The Master Sword seemed to be ignoring them. He was busying himself munching on a buttered slice of bread and watching a candle's flame.

She leaned toward the Prince, her heart thudding hard and curiosity running wild because of her connection with the wizard Ret... He was her uncle. Her father's estranged twin. But she did not find it wise to mention that just now. She set down her mug.

"So, a nymph gave you my name?" she said.

"Yes, the Guidance Naiad from the Faded Sea in Carthorn. It's the only territory where magic still resides openly. Apollos, my friend, brought this news." Alkin motioned to the entrance of the dining room.

Alexa turned to see, of all things, a unicorn standing in the threshold. Her eyes widened, and she almost choked on her ham. She had only ever heard meek descriptions in children's stories of the beauty of unicorns. This creature surpassed all imagination.

The heavenly animal nodded to her and stepped silently into the room. His lustrous mane and tail shimmered in the light, and her mouth slacked open. The unicorn came and stood next to the Prince.

Bryan stopped chewing to watch the girl; and despite his aversion, he had to smile at her reaction, for Apollos was truly a remarkable sight.

Once Alexa overcame her surprise and noticed that Prince Alkin was grinning at her, she snapped her jaw shut and focused on the task at hand. "I'll do my best to live up to your expectations of finding this magic. But I must admit that, as of right now, I don't know where to begin, though I think it'll come to me...in time."

Bryan snorted from across the table. Alexa, Alkin, and the unicorn turned their attention to the Sword.

"This is absurd. We are to be led by a girl that knows no more about what's going on than the army itself. And! We are asking her to fight against her own kind. Sounds like we have excellent chances." He sat back and crossed his arms, a flicker of flame in his eyes.

Alkin looked down, pursing his lips in thought. Bryan had a point. It did seem like all odds were against them. But he held an unwavering trust in Apollos, and through him, the naiad. Magic was needed to fight the wizard; and here sat a girl with magic bloodlines.

A snort from Apollos broke their despondent thoughts. "Have a little faith, Master Sword," he chided, "Don't act so hopeless." With a toss of his head, he flipped his mane to the other side of his satiny neck. "We're taking the right steps. We're taking the ones we know to take. Patience and good sense are needed. We must plan where to search for the first key, decide where to place the first contingent of troops, and discover with whom we can ally ourselves. We have to do what we can do, first."

"Yes." Alexa perked up. "I'll look for the keys. I wonder what kind of magic they are…"

"But how do we know where to start?" Bryan expressed, "The naiad never said, and she,"—he motioned toward Alexa—"admits she has no clue." His gaze bored into the others.

"We wait until I know…and then we ride. My magical senses give me extraordinary intuition. I am sure it will reveal a starting point. I just don't know when it will," Alexa said, gaining confidence with every assertion. If only her brothers could see her now. They would be so jealous. She smiled at the thought.

"Intuition?" Bryan's eyes nearly bugged out of his head. "We place our lives on your intuition? Foolish! And with that scrawny beast you're riding, you won't get very far," he scoffed.

Alkin sighed. Why did he have to be so difficult? If he were not such a good friend and Master Sword, he would have demoted him at once. However, he knew Bryan's blatant suspicions were all for the best and just a precaution; though, they were exasperating at times.

Heat rose in Alexa's face, and she clenched her teeth. "Magical intuition is different, Master Sword. It can't be defined the same way as a normal person's intuition. And Zhan's a worthier animal than any beast that's bred around here. He's built for speed and distance. He's smart and knows me well."

"His color also stands out more than our horses. It'll draw attention. He'll stand out like a dragon in the city." Bryan sat back again with a thud, feeling pleased with himself, although he had no idea why.

Alkin rubbed his brow in frustration. "I'm sure her Zhan will serve her just fine." He glared at the Master Sword. "And this argument is detrimental."

Alexa gave the Prince a look of approval for using her mount's name.

"His coat is of no matter," Apollos said to Bryan. "I can easily make his coat appear as dark as a raven's feathers. Besides," the unicorn's eyes twinkled, "I can't imagine he'd stand out more than me."

The Head-Master Sword didn't reply.

"Well, that's settled." Alkin smiled. "I still have many things to decide, but as soon as Alexa gives word, we'll send a team in search of the magical keys." He slapped the table and leaned back in his chair, content for the moment. He never stayed in a suppressed mood for long. Things were going as smooth as they could, and he would let nothing get the better of him. He would send out emissaries to the surrounding countries to notify them and advise them to prepare for war and defense. He would also discuss battle plans with his advisors in the coming days. Having a more solid plan eased his tension a great deal.

Alexa looked at the Prince, her senses discerning him. He was such an optimistic young man. Quite the opposite of his Sword-Guard, but she also knew that Sword Bryan was not pessimistic. He was just cautious—realistic...and perhaps a bit bitter.

She turned her attention to Bryan, wanting to discern more of his disposition. The Master Sword sighed and slumped back in his chair, finally relaxing. He was not at all what he appeared. He only played he didn't like her. She could tell he cared for his younger companion and master, the Prince.

Just then, his clear eyes caught hers and his expression dulled; she averted her gaze.

The unicorn nodded his finely shaped head in approval of the plan, a spark of assurance in his eyes.

And Alkin stood, pushing back the heavy chair. The others followed suit. "Oh, one more thing," the Prince said, "Since, Sword Bryan, you're the best of the best, you will be Miss Alexandra's personal Sword-Guard for the time being. It isn't as urgent for me to be protected as it is for her right now." He knew this wouldn't go over well with the Master Sword, but it was the logical thing to do.

Bryan's jaw nearly dropped, but he kept his composure underhand. He'd imagined he would lead the warriors into battle, not follow the girl around…babysitting.

"However, I also hope you will accompany Alexa on the mission, but that's to be decided upon later. I'm putting Sword Xercan in charge of the warriors." Alkin's mouth twitched with a wry smile, knowing Bryan's thoughts. He hated doing the opposite of what he knew his friend wanted, but he had a feeling this was the best place for him.

Alkin looked at Alexa and smiled. She gave him a nod. "Get some rest and make yourself at home. Don't fret too much over knowing what to do. It'll come to you. You were meant for this. And also, tend to your wound. We don't want you ill."

The Prince inclined his head in goodbye and gestured for Apollos to follow him. At the threshold, he added, "You have a guardian now. I won't have to worry about you." Then with a glance at the austere Sword Bryan, he said, "Give him lots of trouble. He likes it." With that, he laughed and left the two.

Alexa chuckled and bowed as the Prince departed.

Dead, awkward silence engulfed the dining room. The two antagonists stood in silence, feeling an invisible barrier grow between them.

"Come on. I'll move my things in the chamber next to yours," Bryan declared and headed out. He must press on and do his duty as much as he despised it.

When they reached her chambers, he stopped at her door as she was entering. "If you need anything, I'll be in there." He gestured to the room across the hall. She turned to face him and he froze as her sapphire eyes gazed straight into his. His nerves unraveled. They had a peculiar and deep penetrating feel. He was certain they were clever bewitchment tools.

Then, surprising even himself, he grabbed her chin and turned her cheek. "I'll send up a servant to care for your cut." He examined the irritated skin around the slash. It was harmless. She would be fine, but he did not feel decent about his part in it.

Annoyed with his sudden, rough contact, she jerked her chin from his grasp. "I can take care of myself, thank you." Her eyes flashed.

"As you wish, but I'll still send a servant. Goodnight." Bryan bowed, annoyed with his own coarse behavior. He couldn't help himself. He couldn't say why he disliked her. The arrogant girl just did all the right things to irritate him.

Alexa watched the tall man stride down the corridor to retrieve the servant. She sighed and a perplexed half-smile curved her lips. Closing the door, she went to undress for bed. Her body felt so weak and worn from the news and travel, and she missed home desperately.

Before she fell asleep that night, she came to the obvious conclusion that it was going to be a long, baffling journey. One, she wasn't quite certain she was prepared for after all.

CHAPTER FOUR

During the next couple of days, Alexa took it upon herself to investigate the castle grounds. She wanted to visit the workers that served under Prince Alkin, in order to see if she could gather any information about this country and its prince.

The castle was certainly a grand one, bigger than Kaltraz's but not quite as exquisite, seeming more utilitarian. Kaltraz's palace was made of red brick, a clay-like substance. It was open to the sun in many places, but cool when inside; its décor enchanting. Glinting, colorful mosaics of the country's history lined the walls and luxurious, cool fountains bubbled among lush gardens around every bend. Alexa had been there only once when she'd been summoned to Shelkite, allowing her her first sight of the Kaltraz palace. She had been awed; and now, she was grateful she could compare the two grand abodes.

Her country was divided into two separate states, Western and Eastern Kaltraz. Eastern Kaltraz was ruled by the Princess Athena, and Western Kaltraz was ruled by Athena's twin sister, Princess Livia. The country had been divided thus upon the death of their mother, the queen. The princesses knew how countries had been torn apart by quarreling twins fighting for the throne, so they settled on mutual power. Instead of declaring themselves queens, the twins crowned themselves princesses, dividing Kaltraz in to two united states. Each princess ruled the best way she saw fit, but any chief decisions were made by the combined councils of both.

A great river sliced through the country, dividing it into western and eastern halves. Therefore, the division had been rather simple, and the people welcomed the idea. The citizens from each state lived in friendly co-existence with each other. They came and went freely between the two states. The currency was the same, but the industrial exports were different. Western Kaltraz comprised many grand cities. Its population full of aristocrats and wealthy merchants, and was well known for its fine cloths and beautiful clothing. Eastern Kaltraz was more rural, and best known for breeding fine horses and raising sheep for wool.

Alexa's family was under Princess Athena's influence. The Princess loved the desert sun. She could often be seen relaxing at many of the luxuriant oases. She attired herself in a red-hooded cloak and traveled with her guards—some of which were rumored to be her lovers. Though the cities were sparse and the countryside consisted mostly of desert, she could often be found traveling through her land, upholding her laws and mingling with the people. However, the more refined and fashionable Princess Livia mainly kept to her palace and left the law upkeep to her trained representatives.

Athena's people were allegedly said to be more of a crude crowd than those of Livia's. Thus, they were dubbed by Livia's followers as the Ruffians. Eastern Kaltrazians referred to Livia's followers, a group upholding etiquette, the Dukes. Alexa was proud to have Athena as her princess. And by all standards, she fit the stereotype of Athena's people to perfection.

Here, among the vibrant green hills of Shelkite, Prince Alkin's castle was vastly different from Kaltraz's. Formidable stone-mortared walls encircled his abode, giving it an aloof feel. Sentries marched atop, holding crossbows aloft, and she guessed the gate was the only entrance in or out, except for a possible secret passageway, as she had always imagined castles to have.

A pleasant courtyard to the right of the main entrance softened the inner grounds. Aside from the castle itself, within the walls, there were cabins to house guards and a decent sized stable with lush, trillium-studded paddocks stretching out beyond.

Alexa paused to view her surroundings as she came from the gloom of the castle into the sunny courtyard. The pleasing sound of the fountain filled the atmosphere. The water sprayed and plopped outside its bounds onto the flagstone walk. She observed some residents collecting their drinking water there and discovered it sat on a freshwater spring and was not just for embellishment.

Surrounding the fountain were walkways lined with flowering bushes and young, blossoming trees that scented the air. Alexa approached the fountain and dipped her hand in the icy waters. The sun glanced off the ripples and plunged her mind into dreamy thoughts.

A moment later, a familiar whinny surfaced her. She looked beyond the garden to the stables, forgetting her silly daydream. Then, cupping her hands with glistening water, she took a sip; and then strode over to the stables, wiping her mouth on her sleeve as she went.

There, she met the Stable-Master and his daughter, and they gushed over Zhan's exquisite features and lively mannerisms. And after exchanging some friendly horseflesh talk, a very pleased Alexa tacked Zhan up and led him out. He wore only a light saddle and bridle, something the stable hands had also marveled over compared to the bulkier designs of Shelkite's tack.

She mounted in the courtyard next to the fountain, and at the sound of heavy hooves clopping across stones and the jingle of metal, she shifted in her saddle to see Sword Bryan ride up beside her. She eyed him a little sourly. "I'm just looking around. Do I really need a guide?" she said. Zhan stretched his neck out and touched noses curiously with Dragon.

Bryan smiled. She would never consent to his authority over her. "Someday, you'll so boldly get yourself in a fix and be glad I am nearby," he said, his azure eyes alight in the sun. "My orders were to take care of you. So that, I will. So, no more sneaking away from me. Come on, I'll show you around."

He had determined he would be nice to the arrogant girl, if only for the Prince's sake. He heeled Dragon forward before the dominant stallion could squeal and strike at Zhan.

Annoyed, Alexa gave Zhan a sharper jab than she intended. Not accustomed to such rashness from his rider, Zhan leapt forward, startled.

Alexa rode ahead; and he could hear her muttering through her gritted teeth, "I don't need a babysitter."

Bryan shook his head, the corners of his mouth curving up slightly. Her vanity would soon get the better of her. "Hey, Lycil! Open the gates!" he called up to the Gate-Master. The day was sunny and beautiful despite the cool breeze, and it raised his spirits. He wasn't in the mood to let anything bring him down. The castle gates creaked open and the horses clopped through.

They had a pleasant ride as they cantered the circumference of the castle. The emerald hills rolled away from them in all directions. Nothing was located for miles except for the nearby extensive warriors' quarters and training grounds.

Alexa scrutinized the towers, walls, and sentries. Bryan rode alongside her, watching her carefully. Every now-and-then, he would impart some history of the castle and Fordorn. When they came around again to the main gate, he stopped his lesson and they halted the horses.

"Everything safe, warden? Where would you like to go next?" he asked. At the sound of a clatter, he glanced up to Lycil. The young gate-master had been resting and humming to himself right before he knocked his mug over with his elbow. Bryan suppressed a grin.

Alexa nodded and turned her eyes back to Bryan from where they too had been on Lycil. "I'd like to see the city. Is that okay?" she asked.

For the first time, the girl sounded unsure. Bryan pondered this. Maybe there *were* some insecurities under that veil of haughtiness of hers. "It's a few miles." He shrugged.

"I'd like to see it."

"All right, then. Let's get started." Bryan glanced down at her. Dragon was much bigger than Zhan and the two horses looked odd alongside each other, like mare and foal.

The Master Sword led the way down the grassy road to the east and Fordorn. "It'll be early afternoon when we reach the city." He turned in his saddle to speak to her. "We can find something to eat at a tavern and then head back. Prince Alkin's mother wants to speak with you later tonight."

Alexa nodded again and flipped her braid over her shoulder, scanning the hilly terrain and farmlands, beginning to find an appreciation for the beauty of the stone fencing.

Sword Bryan picked up the conversation again as she drew abreast with him. He spoke of legends and strange things seen in Shelkite, and also spoke of Prince Alkin and Shelkite's history and a little of the Lost War. The Master Sword seemed very knowledgeable of history, obviously because of a fondness for it. Though, Alexa noted, he veered away from anything personal, his past or anything he did before he had become the Head-Master

Sword. She studied him. He merely looked to the road ahead as he spoke.

Bryan could feel the girl's peculiar prying eyes on him, and he distinctly tried not to look at her as he spoke of the country's supply of crops, including the profitable tobacco plant, and livestock—mainly beef and dairy cattle. He explained how all the surrounding countries depended on Shelkite's agriculture. "We're proud of our farmland and that we can contribute a lot to Eetharum. It gives Shelkitens a sense of pride." He squinted as he looked in approval over the rows of the young, growing crops. The sun shone on them as the wind rippled through the fields, giving an illusion of a verdant ocean.

"What about you, Sword Bryan? Your name isn't from around here. It sounds eastern." She paused and searched his features when he glanced at her. "The real version actually sounds like it's from the Kaltraz region. Why'd you shorten it? Did your family come from the east? Undoubtedly, you'd never admit it…"

The Master Sword scowled and turned his gaze from her when he answered, "For as long as I can remember, I've lived in Shelkite. My parents were farmers. They died when I was very young." He shut his eyes and attempted to clear a single, vivid memory, and then added, raising his chin, "I don't know why my name sounds eastern." He turned in his saddle to look at her. "If I had it my way, it wouldn't." From what he knew of easterners from his travels, they were rude and proud. In his opinion, the west was the pride of Eetharum. He knew this was judgmental, but it'd been his experience.

Alexa bore him with a shallow gaze.

Bryan swallowed and didn't say more. Sometimes his tongue galloped away with him. *So much for trying to get along with her.* He rolled his eyes in exasperation with himself. It bothered him he didn't have a more Shelkiten name, especially being the Head-Master Sword and all. The other Swords seemed to bristle at this aspect too, for whatever reason. It was a sore spot. *She would point that out, wouldn't she?*

They traveled in silence the last miles to Fordorn. With every mile, Bryan seemed to get hotter inside, until he boiled over with irritation. She had no business prying into his life. He was her Sword-Guard. That was all. Not her long-time friend, nor for that matter, even his acquaintance. As far as he was concerned, she was on a need-to-know basis. She asked too many questions. There was something underhanded about this eastern girl. And he wasn't about to let it go.

As they rode out of the farmlands, they neared the city. Fordorn bustled with activity. Amazed, Alexa looked around as their horses carefully made their way through the crowded, cobbled streets. The Master Sword had taken her to an upper-class part of town. Fordorn was so different from the small villages she knew in Eastern Kaltraz. It was large with a mixture of new, grand buildings and some older, quaint buildings lining the main street. Well-kept cobbled roads branched off the main street to lead into fancy neighborhoods and other businesses. They passed by a well-manicured square where some citizens were strolling and enjoying the refreshing afternoon.

They turned down a side street where people, mostly commoners, went about their daily routines. Merchants' carts were set up alongside the road; and they called out to Alexa and Bryan as they passed.

They rode by a rotund man guarding a booth with pearls and other fine jewels. "Hello, beautiful!" The suave man grinned at Alexa and held out a pearl necklace. "Yoldor pearls for that radiant neck of yours? Imported straight from the Elendace Sea. They say *mermaids* grow them." She smiled and declined, although she was drawn to them. The gentleman regarded Bryan with a smile, "Master Sword, why don't you treat your pretty lady friend with a special gift from the deepest, wildest parts of the sea?"

The Sword shook his head and snorted with a scoff.

They continued on, and Bryan maneuvered Dragon around a group of gossiping women. She nudged Zhan to his side. "So, this is Fordorn," he commented, as if the city had lost all charm to him. They halted the horses to let a crowd of people cross. They were now in the working-class part of town.

She looked up and around. Tall apartment buildings towered above them. Women left their laundry out to dry stories above. Young girls hung out the windows to call to their friends below.

Rambunctious boys raced each other, knocking into booths, causing angry merchants to curse them away.

"Marki's Tavern is up the road a bit." Bryan nudged Dragon forward. "I think it'll suit you." He looked over his shoulder at her. "They have great food. I don't usually find too many bugs..." he said, then rode away.

She nodded absently, not losing her zest for the city's sights. He was just trying to agitate her.

They passed more taverns, shops, and inns. A young woman approached Dragon and Sword Bryan as they stopped for another throng to pass. Her pale hand stroked Dragon's dark neck. The stallion craned his head around to investigate the new touch.

"Master Sword," the girl whispered.

Bryan regarded her, his dark locks drooping over his bright eyes. He towered over her atop Dragon. Alexa halted, keeping her distance. The young woman had long, wavy blonde tresses and a small piercing in her nostril. She was not at all homely in her revealing gown. Alexa watched and listened to the encounter with a suspicious, furrowed brow.

The girl spoke for only the Master Sword, "Care to come and savor the last hours of day with me?" She caressed Dragon's reins and laid a gentle hand on Bryan's polished boot.

The Sword's handsome features turned troubled. He studied the girl's brown eyes and said, "No, I don't care to, but here." He dug into one of his overcoat's many pockets and pulled out two silver coins and dropped them into the girl's hand.

Alexa stared in surprise. The young woman's expression turned overjoyed with disbelief.

"Oh! Thank you, Master Sword! Thank you!" She turned and dashed away.

Wordlessly, Bryan moved on.

"A friend of yours?" Alexa said, raising an eyebrow.

Bryan clenched his teeth, looking intently ahead for the worn, painted sign of Marki's, trying to choke his impatience. "No," he replied, then mumbled, "Poor girl."

"Oh," Alexa said with a frown.

"Think I'm the kind to keep company with brothel girls?" He

glared at her.

She shrugged, feinting wide, innocent eyes. "Wouldn't think it was below you," she said as she stroked Zhan's neck. How was she to know? She glanced away.

The Master Sword turned in his saddle to face her, a scathing look in his eyes. "You had better be careful what you say, Miss Alexandra. You've a lot to learn. Remember, *you* are the foreign one here." His words seethed. If she'd been a man, he would have punched her right off that gangly beast of hers and into the mud. "It's my honor and duty to help others. Whether or not they're a brothel girl," he said hotly. "She may be a slave, but she still had more manners than you'll ever have. Maybe if you were in her place, you wouldn't be so vain and we'd all be better off."

Alexa's head snapped up. Bryan glowered at her, his eyes bright and sizzling. She stared back contemptuously, her jaw clenched. Thought he was smart, did he? What a scoundrel! She should curse him. She knew a few. Though, her father always warned her never to use them in anger. But certainly, something good to send Dragon bucking his master off into the mud wouldn't hurt.

Bryan huffed. *Maybe now the self-righteous, so-called Savior of Eetharum will keep her obnoxious trap shut.* What she needed was a good kick in the rear. He knew Alkin would be furious with him if he knew how he was treating her. *But the vain little witch threw her own insult first.* He'd only defended himself.

When they finally reached the tavern, they both had cooled down. The Master Sword heaved a sigh, dismounted Dragon, and tied him to the hitching post underneath the battered wooden sign.

Alexa hopped down from Zhan, her boots sinking deep into the sloppy mud. She screwed up her face and followed the Sword into the noisy tavern.

The two ate mostly in silence. Bryan sipped his drink and watched Alexa stuff food in her mouth. "Does it have your approval?" he asked with a wry, raised eyebrow.

She gave him a vigorous nod and wiped her mouth on her sleeve. "So, what do Shelkitens do for fun? My family's ranch is pretty isolated, so I'm curious."

He set down his mug. "Pretty much the same as anywhere

else, I suppose. They hold dances, have circuses, play games, drink…make love," he said with a roguish smile. She ignored it, and he continued, "Prince Alkin doesn't really care as long as they behave themselves. There's also a fine theatre on the south side of town." He stood and put down several copper coins.

Alexa got to her feet, picking up her much-needed cloak. The air in Shelkite was much cooler and damper than in Kaltraz due to the ocean on the western border.

Bryan waved and thanked Marki as they parted from the tavern.

When they stepped out on the front porch, a curvy woman, holding up her sweeping skirts, came trudging through the mud breathless to greet them. "Oh, Head-Master Sword! I'm so glad you're here!" she called in relief. She went to step on the porch but left a delicate boot behind in the mud. She turned, exasperated, and tugged at the shoe a few times before finally releasing it from the muck. Placing it back on her foot, she said, "I must speak with the Prince at once. Is there a way you could escort me to the castle?"

Bryan nodded and quickly mounted Dragon. "Do you have a mount somewhere?" He reined Dragon around to face Lady Evelyn.

Evelyn shook her brunette curls. "I tried the local stables to rent a pony, but they're all rented out," she said. "My horse," she continued, straightening her stance and looking vexed, "is, unfortunately, missing in action. I'm going to have to have a talk with the innkeeper," she said a little frostily.

"Well, then…" Bryan offered his arm. Evelyn smiled as he hauled her up behind him. If he must do it for Alkin's sake, he would. It was his duty whether or not he liked it. How much worse could it get? He was in the company of two women who couldn't have been more different from each other; and both of whom he despised.

"We aren't seeing more of Fordorn?" Alexa protested from atop Zhan, annoyed with the new company.

"No, Miss Alexandra," he answered. "We have to get back. Remember, Lady Adama wants to meet with you. And now, Lady Evelyn has to speak with the Prince."

Alexa clenched her teeth as Evelyn landed her curious, big, brown eyes on her. Was that a flare of competition in her eye? Well, she certainly had nothing to worry about.

Alexa stared moodily after the departing back of the Master Sword and his warhorse's big rear. "It's *Alexa*!" She muttered under her breath and steered the prancing Zhan to follow him up the street.

As they rode outside the city, Lady Evelyn chatted cheerily. Her words were being mostly wasted, as Sword Bryan didn't answer her often, and Alexa was too busy trying to use her witch senses to discern the woman. She seemed to be a flirt, but of some importance, and wasn't going to see the Prince for personal matters. She was going for a sincere, important reason. The woman seemed to be honest; yet, Alexa sensed dishonesty in her as well. Lady Evelyn seemed like she posed no ill will; though, she obviously had a liking for idle chatter, fine clothes and, from the looks of things, Master Sword Bryan.

As they approached the Blue Mermaid Tavern, Evelyn stopped her chattering. With her magical senses running rampant, Alexa sensed Sword Bryan desiring to make a stop there. He would no doubt return later if he could. There was something bothering him, and she sensed him wishing to drink it away.

When they neared the tavern's sign, swinging and creaking in the breeze, a strange sensation stirred within Alexa, not unlike the odd niggling ones she had felt throughout the day. This one, however, grew to be much stronger. A buzz started in her chest and fluttered to her middle and then tingled out to her fingertips. A quiet, startled gasp escaped her as the magical sensation flooded into her brain. She gazed at the cracked painting on the sign of the bare-breasted and blue-finned, golden-haired mermaid holding up a mug of ale to good cheer. The mermaid beckoned to her. Alexa did a double take at it, eyes wide as she rode closer to the apparently very happy and intoxicated mermaid. When she came within reaching distance of the sign, the magic inside her made a connection, and she knew, all of a sudden, what it meant.

She rode in mute surprise, relief flooding her and replacing the ebbing magical intuition. Craning back around, she blinked at the sign as it swung squeakily in the wind. She had never had such a strong episode of magical intuition before.

The others seemed completely oblivious to her. Evelyn began to chat again, and Sword Bryan would occasionally throw a disgruntled look over his shoulder to see if his responsibility was still riding safely behind.

She allowed herself a small, triumphant smile. The magical key she needed to find for the counter-magic was in the underwater world of the merpeople… If such a place still existed. But she did not doubt the undeniable magic that flowed hotly through her veins.

It seemed her father had mentioned merpeople before, and that they could be found in the Elendace Sea. *"But, the most inhospitable creatures you'd ever come across,"* he used to mutter. She needed to tell the Prince immediately. Zhan sensed her eagerness and hastened his stride, coming up alongside the Master Sword.

Bryan glanced at Alexa from the corner of his eye and was puzzled to see Alexa looking rather satisfied. *What is that all about?* He grumbled to himself. If only he could be back in the camp with the other warriors, sword fighting and training instead of escorting and babysitting these two. He let out a rueful sigh. Alkin would surely give him the rest of the night off… He wouldn't mind a visit to the Blue Mermaid tonight. He just had to get these women off his hands first. Alexa would be completely safe in the castle with another Master Sword to guard her for enough time to have a quick drink. Only, though, if she didn't decide to go off and do something stupid, as was her wont, he suspected.

CHAPTER FIVE

To Bryan's delight, Prince Alkin released him from his duty for the evening, charging Sword Boraz to guard Alexa until his return.

Alkin was overjoyed to see Lady Evelyn. He waved Bryan off and led Evelyn into the library to talk. Alexa, however, huffed out a noisy grunt and strutted away somewhat man-like to her room to retire until the Prince's mother called for her. Bryan gave an unconcerned shrug as he watched the silly girl walk away. He then sent for Sword Boraz and started out for the tavern.

★★★★

Alexa had been raised with eleven older brothers. They lived with their wizard father and human mother in the outer rocky lands of Kaltraz. Though Eastern Kaltraz was known for its horse breeding, her family made their living as shepherds, albeit they had several broodmares. They also owned a well-to-do inn. Most of their customers were travelers, the majority merchants, going to and from the Kalcala Desert. The desert began in Eastern Kaltraz and reached to the far east. Weary pilgrims always welcomed the tranquil shelter and a hardy meal after a trek through the vast, unforgiving land.

Among the family, Alexa was favored as the only daughter and the youngest. Although all her siblings shared the wizard blood, she was the only child their father had begun to teach how to utilize the innate magical powers.

Her father, Erec, had left his magic behind when he had decided to settle down at the age of one-hundred sixty. His love for a beautiful human woman had sparked this change. He and the young woman, Dara, had married and had immediately started a family.

Even though Erec no longer possessed magical powers, he had, over time, decided to teach his only daughter some tricks of his blood. Alexa was glad he had. But she was still a novice at best, and her powers hadn't completely manifested. By wizard reckoning, she was still young and maturing. At this time, she could utilize her senses well, but the innate senses were also something her brothers possessed even without being trained.

Among her siblings, she was the sharpest arrow shot of the family, one of the best at dagger throwing, and the second to best rider. But none of these talents had anything to do with her semi-trained witch blood. She had grown up with a throng of tough, harassing brothers; she had learned how to take care of herself. Her family was competitive among each other, so she had always strived to be better than the boys.

As she lay on her bed, she thought of her best accomplishment—winning the highly coveted Arrow Trophy just last season at the annual archery match in the city of Sansdella. She was proud. Her whole family had been proud.

Alexa rose, splashed cool water on her face, and glared at her reflection in the mirror, wondering just how good she really was. Perhaps she was taking this competition thing with Sword Bryan a little too far. Though, he did seem to think he was the best warrior since the Lost War. She rolled her eyes at the thought of proving herself to the Master Sword. She should be thinking of more important things—like trying to gain an audience with the Prince as soon as possible—than trying to outdo that egocentric pig! Why did it seem so important, anyway?

A knock sounded on the door, and Alexa expected to hear the deep voice of Sword Boraz coming to take her to see the Prince's mother; she snatched up her dagger to strap around her waist, but instead of Sword Boraz, a feminine voice came softly through the door.

"Miss Alexandra?" Another light tap sounded.

"Come in." She finished strapping her dagger and looked up to see a young woman open the door.

The servant was a few years older and held herself with confidence, her bronze-gold hair corralled in a snug plait around her head. She held a tray of steaming food.

"I take it Lady Adama isn't ready for me, yet," Alexa said,

eyeing the food.

The servant shook her head and walked over to set the tray on the small breakfast table. "I'm Melea. I'll be your servant while you're here."

Alexa watched the other woman's brown eyes sweep briefly over her before plopping down in her chair and pulling the tray toward herself, and saying, "Which hopefully won't be long." She took a swig of her drink and discovered it to be Zelkan wine. She wiped her lips with the back of her hand and looked at Melea, who was standing quietly, hands folded in front of her.

"Anything else I can do for you, Miss Alexandra?"

"Yes." She motioned for Melea to take a seat. "Please tell me about Sword Bryan...and Prince Alkin." She would love to learn more about the two men from another's point of view.

Melea's pale cheeks flushed, and Alexa looked at her with a curious, raised eyebrow.

The servant lowered herself across from her. "What would you like to know, Miss Alexandra?"

"Alexa," she corrected, "Oh, would you like something to eat?" she offered, feeling rude for eating in front of her.

"Oh, no thank you. I just ate." Melea gave her a timid but appreciative smile.

"Well, just tell me what you know about Sword Bryan," Alexa said, setting down her massacred chicken bone.

Melea turned a deeper shade of crimson, and Alexa stuffed a mouthful of mashed potatoes in her mouth to keep from snickering at the older girl.

Outside, the sun slipped into its hilly blanket for the night, and pregnant storm clouds began to accumulate, promising heavy rain.

"He's the best of the Prince's men," she began, hesitant, and Alexa nodded, encouraging her to continue. "He's also the youngest of the Prince's Master Swords and an excellent warrior and swordsman, among other things." She paused and raised a suspicious, arching eyebrow.

Alexa took another drink of her wine, knowing full-well the servant thought she was up to no good. But if no one trusted her, how was she supposed to help? She had to get information somehow. So, she prodded, "Was he born in Shelkite?"

Melea straightened in her chair. "Oh! He had to be to be accepted as a Master Sword," she said, a bit defensive. "All the warriors accepted in the school take an oath claiming their blood was born for Shelkite and will die for Shelkite. It's a strict oath, but it's stricter yet if they become Master Swords. They must be pureblood Shelkitens, born on Shelkiten soil. And if they marry, it has to be a woman native to the land—to bear true Shelkiten sons."

Melea paused, and then continued, seemingly warming up to Alexa's curiosity, "Bryan's—I mean *Sword* Bryan's family died when he was a child. It was very tragic." Her brown eyes lowered. "Prince Alkin's father, the late Prince Izsum, found little Sword Bryan and brought him back to live in the warriors' camp. He was taught swordsmanship, war strategy, horsemanship, and other academic studies. He was given more than any commoner child could hope for, and he graduated at the top of his class. Prince Alkin, only the heir at the time, visited the camp often and they became friends. Sword Bryan and he played together and trained together."

Melea was wistful, as if she was retelling a story recounted to her many times. She went on, "When Prince Izsum died, Prince Alkin became ruler, and Sword Bryan began traveling and sword fighting competitively. The two drifted apart after that." She stopped and searched Alexa's face.

Alexa wiped her hands on a linen napkin; her interest in Shelkite's government piqued. "So, you have no kings, no queens, just princes and heirs to the title of prince?" she asked, a little puzzled.

Melea nodded, now at ease with an understanding of Alexa's curiosity. "Yes, the high ruler of our land is entitled prince or princess. After the Lost War, Shelkitens decided 'prince' was less domineering sounding than 'king.' 'The Peoples' Prince' was the idea. They set up the court of councilors for the ruler on the peoples' behalf. Other countries followed our lead. For instance, the rulers of Vtalmay and Yoldor call themselves chancellor and chief and have advisors. Anyway, if Lady Dorsa would have been born first, she would have been the ruler and princess."

"Prince Alkin has a sister?" Alexa said with surprise.

Melea smiled, displaying perfect teeth. "Yes. The power and title go only to the first-born. The current wife or husband of the ruler is the only other allowed to be referred to as either princess or prince," she said with a glimmer of a smile. "Since the Lost War, only a few blood princesses have ruled. In the main hall, there are canvases of all who have ruled. I'll show you if you want to see them," she said, her eyes bright with a possible friendship.

Alexa gave her a small smile. "I would like that. Maybe sometime soon; I'm due to meet with Lady Adama and I really need to speak with Prince Alkin about something... But, tell me, is he a good ruler? Is he well-liked?"

Melea's face broke into a smile, and Alexa could feel the servant's trust growing. "He has a great heart and does his best to rule justly. He holds hearings once a month and keeps track of the regions via the Master Swords, who make regular trips to the cities, and he always treats his people kindly and cares for the poor. Shelkite's relations with other countries are healthy. Prince Alkin is currently working on abolishing the pierced-slave ring. We servants are very fond of him."

"And all the Master Swords like him, too? You don't know of any who are displeased with him?"

Melea's brow furrowed as she thought this over, while outside the walls of the castle, the rush of rain against the windowpanes and a soft rumble of thunder announced the storm's commencement.

"As far as I know, everyone loves the Prince," Melea said. "The Swords are his most trusted companions and advisors. Some of the older Swords served under Prince Izsum. But they're all good-hearted men as far as I know. Sword Bryan is the Head-Master Sword and the youngest of them. I believe he suffers a lot from the other Swords' envy." She sighed and looked out the window, adding wistfully, "All he wants is to be back in the camp training new warriors. He prefers that over being a Master Sword."

Alexa contemplated the young woman for a moment, reading her without using her senses. "You love him," she announced, slouching back in her chair, assured of her conjecture.

Melea looked aghast. "I'm only his servant!"

Alexa grinned and almost laughed. She hadn't called her his

harlot, nor had she meant that. "Of course." She chuckled. "But you can't hide it from me."

Then, using her special senses, Alexa searched the servant's mind and heart. Melea was more than she appeared. She was complex, appearing dainty and naïve, but in reality, she was strong and had courage and a powerful mind. The servant would be a good ally.

Melea sighed, her thoughts still apparently on Sword Bryan. "I suppose so." She narrowed her eyes and leaned forward. "I heard you were half witch and a ruffian. I didn't believe it until now. I didn't know there were any wizards left. But," she added desolately, "I mean nothing to him. I'm just his pleasant servant whom he confides in…sometimes."

Alexa made a sad, and perhaps a somewhat mocking, clicking noise. "I am sorry," she said half-heartedly. Melea would be better off with her sights on someone less grumpy, she thought, and then leaned forward. "Melea, I can tell you're a good person, and I feel I can trust you. Could we be friends?" Alexa wanted the older girl to be sure she could trust her.

"Well, of course."

"I know you thought I might not be trustworthy when you first saw me. But I'm just as worried as everyone else is about all this. I'm only trying to put pieces together. I sense evil here. I didn't want to admit it before. But it *is* here, lurking, and I can't pinpoint it."

Melea had a sudden look in her eyes, as if she had seen a dragon.

"I need a favor."

"Yes," she said, hesitant.

"I want to know more about Lady Evelyn. She seems…not as she is… Could you do some checking for me? Nonchalantly. It'll be easier since you're a servant. What do you know about her?"

"Oh, Lady Evelyn…" Melea faltered. "Not much. She's just a northeastern girl—woman—of some status, I think. She comes and goes from Shelkite on business. I've heard some call her the Chaos Goddess. Prince Alkin visits her often. I don't know anymore. She seems like a dim-witted flirt—I despise those kinds of women," she ended, sulkily.

No doubt, Melea had noticed Evelyn's fondness for Sword Bryan, too.

Alexa bit her lip in thought. Lady Evelyn had to be a spy of some sort, the dim-wittedness an act. She was an intelligent woman. She had sensed the qualities of one in her at once, or at least what she figured were the qualities of a spy. Why was Prince Alkin keeping so much from her? She didn't like being kept in the dark.

A heavy knock interrupted them. "Miss Alexandra, Lady Adama will see you now." Sword Boraz's baritone voice pummeled through the door.

Alexa turned to Melea as they stood. "Friends?"

The servant nodded, a small smile at the corners of her mouth.

Alexa beamed. "Thank you! I'm glad to have found another sincere heart here, aside from the Prince." She then turned to go to the awaiting Sword.

Master Sword Boraz led her up a few levels of stone stairs and down a sconce-lined corridor. The candles flickered, casting shadows along the cold walls. Alexa looked around, evil's presence pricking her heart, but she could not identify it for the life of her. It caused her impatience to speak with the Prince to grow even more so, and Lady Evelyn sidling in before Alexa could announce her intuition frustrated her furthermore.

While she contemplated all these things, beyond the windows, thunder fractured the rush of rain and lightning snapped the halls alight with intense flashes.

With confident strides, she stayed a step behind Boraz, her dagger gently tapping her thigh. The Sword glanced over his shoulder at her and smiled. He was a decent-looking, middle-aged man. She sensed extreme loyalty and evenhandedness in him.

"Lady Adama resides in the west wing of the castle." He stopped in front of an elegantly designed oak door. "Here we are. I'll be right out here if you need me." He took his post beside the doorway.

She knocked firmly on the thick door. A gentle voice beckoned her in. She stepped into the receiving room of the chamber and found herself surrounded by red velvet and black oak décor. A large window on the far wall revealed a spacious balcony outside. A number of chaise lounges and chairs were arranged about the room, and a robust fire blazed in an elaborate stone hearth.

A regal-looking woman sat in a cushioned chair; an older Master Sword stood guard in the shadows a short distance behind. On the lady's proud frame was a gown of shades of purple. Expensive jewelry adorned her neck and fingers, and her soft, frosted auburn locks were piled upon her head in the latest style of high-fashion. The woman smiled.

"Come and sit, my dear." She motioned to a plush chair across from her.

Alexa moved over the threshold, and instantaneously, something cool spilled through her body. Her blood turned to slush, slowing her senses, and a nameless fear crawled over her. Then, just as sudden, a warm calm washed it away.

Alexa gave herself a mental shake, perplexed at the fleeting chill. She remembered to smile and give a polite bow to Prince Alkin's mother. She then took a seat in the chair, settling down somewhat slumped compared to the poised woman.

Her eye caught a canvas above the fireplace. A man, much of the likeness of Prince Alkin, but more matured, peered out into the room from it. Blonde locks of braids fell onto his broad shoulders. His fair face was wreathed with a curious smile, a bit roguish, as if he could see her underclothes or something. She eyed the canvas with a suspicious, raised brow.

"Ah." Lady Adama smiled and regarded the painting. "My husband, Izsum. A wonderful man." She returned her penetrating gaze back to Alexa in silence.

"I'm sure he was," she said, distracted still. She struggled with odd, trapped feelings as she tried to decipher the lady. She found for the first time, she couldn't. Something seemed to be muddling her senses. Was the lady ill? Sometimes when an individual was ill, in either mind or body, it was hard to see into their hearts through the murkiness the sickness created both physically and mentally.

"You traveled far, I hear," Lady Adama said, her voice gentle, but holding an unmistakable tone of authority.

Alexa nodded, feeling uncomfortable in the straight-backed chair.

"Kaltraz is quite warm; you must be chilled here," Adama continued.

Alexa eyed the lady and forced a smile. "The desert nights can get rather bitter."

Adama raised her chin with a slight nod. She peered at her askance, then said, "You appear to be trustworthy, decent for a commoner, and educated somewhat. A bit of a handsome face…but a tad crude in conduct."

Alexa raised an eyebrow and answered tightly, "Do you say this because of my magical blood? My so-called evil heritage? And, what? 'Educated' for a mere shepherdess? My father is an educated man. I may not be wise to all in the world, but he taught me and my brothers well. And my conduct is what *I* want it to be."

Lady Adama leaned forward and flashed her a beautiful smile, and then said with a chuckle, "I can tell you are truly a half-blood. I once knew a wizard. They're such temperamental beings." She cocked her head and looked at her as if she were waiting for another reaction.

Alexa leaned forward, her eyes glinting defiant flames. "Wizards may be descended from evil, but that does not make me so. You can trust me. No need to provoke me for any test."

The lady beamed. "One cannot be too careful around strangers right now." She gestured to Alexa's dagger, referring to her own cautiousness. "I was indeed just testing you," she said, then motioned for her to kneel next to her chair.

Alexa forced a smile. She understood the woman's precautions; even so, she had to will herself to stand and cross over to kneel by the chair. She placed her hand on the armrest and Adama patted it.

"I'm glad my son has someone like you to put his trust in." Her hazel eyes sparkled with gratitude. "Peril awaits us and Eetharum needs capable hands to place its hope into. I see that no hands are as good as yours." Adama's eyes searched her features with pride.

The Lady's praising and mothering demeanor bewitched and

humbled Alexa. No wonder Alkin was such an admired prince. Somehow this soothed a yearning she had for her own mother she hadn't known she'd had.

"Alexandra, Eetharum's deliverer!" the lady said.

"Hardly," Alexa said, but she couldn't hold back a small smile. "I'm intelligent enough to know not to put too much trust in this world and its inhabitants, but in something much more reliable." Was this woman hoping for far too much from her or mocking her?

"But you'll be the one to achieve victory. I know it. I can feel it." Adama reached for a little box sitting on the table next to her and opened it. She pulled out a golden chain. A pendant swung lightly from it. "Here."

Alexa narrowed her eyes to see the small adornment better. It was a tiny golden key. "It's a lovely charm," she said.

Adama unlatched the chain and held it out in her palm. "Given to me by the only full-blood wizard I've ever known. It's a good luck charm, to keep the wearer safe. I want to give it to you."

Alexa stared at the gift, astonished, and Adama carefully latched the chain around her neck. Alexa was not one to wear jewelry, but the necklace was petite and unassuming.

"A key to unlock and hold the intangible. Hope it's useful, my dear," Adama said.

Alexa bowed her head. "Thank you."

Adama smiled. "You go now and get some rest. That was all I wished of you. Take care."

Alexa nodded and then stood and left, closing the chamber door quietly behind her. Sword Boraz greeted her with a smile. Just then, another's presence caught her senses and she snapped her head around to look right.

A young woman came out of a nearby adjacent room. Sunshine-blonde locks curled sweetly around her pretty heart-shaped face. They cascaded down her back, where the curls bounced in cadence with her step. Her jade-colored eyes shone in the lamplight and reflected brightly off her emerald gown.

She whisked down the corridor, smiling at Alexa as she passed and flashing a friendly grin at Boraz. No doubt she was

Alkin's sister, Lady Dorsa. Alexa raised an amused eyebrow at the fashionable girl's back and then strode after the departing Sword, determined from there on out to be all business and to meet with the Prince directly.

CHAPTER SIX

Bryan lifted an over-flowing mug to his lips. He took a slow drink and savored the frothy liquid as it slid down. The Blue Mermaid was a crowded place tonight with the storm driving in unruly wanderers and mercenaries to mingle with the country folk and townspeople.

A loud crash and clatter came from the far side of the tavern. Two men stumbled to sit back down from a minor brawl, and laughter erupted as more and more drinks were consumed.

Bryan sat silently at the bar on a three-legged stool that felt at any moment it might give way. His mind began to wander, wander like many of these patrons did for a living. They were wayfarers, who took up jobs along the never-ending road: some entertainers, some workhands for hire…some with darker purposes. There were times when he thought traveling would be the perfect life: always something new around the next bend…always leaving the past behind.

His mind wove in and about many thoughts as he sipped. He watched the cold rain beat against the windows and the lightning streak the starless night sky. Men on either side of him became merrier as their insides became warmer. Paying no heed to the Master Sword next to them, they often bumped him in their outbursts. He disregarded them and took another swig, draining his mug.

"Master Sword?" a voice hoarse from years of bartending said. It halted his thoughts. "Ya all right?" Binz asked.

Bryan smiled and slid his mug over for the old bartender to fill, "Never better."

Binz filled it. "Jest never seen ya so quiet and thoughtful like. Come to think somethin' was the matter. Ya're usually out there jesting with all the boys, sharin' stories and all that nonsense."

"No worry, Binz." Bryan took another sip. He perched on his stool with such poise and self-assurance one would only have to look at him to think he'd be a force to be reckoned with. But the man to his left let out a booming laugh and slapped him on the shoulder. His meaty hand gripped the Sword's overcoat and gave him a jolting shake. Bryan gazed at him with amused bewilderment.

"No worry?" The man chuckled. His laugh was low and melodious. "Looks to me like this young man has lady problems. I've seen it on many a youngin's face."

Bryan shook his head and gave the older man a crooked smile. It was obvious this man had traveled far. His burly body was covered in weathered clothing. His auburn beard was dirty and now flecked with foam from his drink.

Bryan gazed into his mug and watched the bubbles swim haphazardly. Considering his weighty commitment to Shelkite, perhaps he did have something like lady problems.

He pondered over the recent events. These men knew nothing of the growing threat to their countries and lives. Everything was as it would be on a holiday—merry, without any cares of tomorrow. He had begun to wonder if all the said troubles were true. Life seemed normal. All else felt like an intangible dream— the half-blood witch, the cryptic naiad, the cruel wizard…the sacrifices. It seemed unreal, something that belonged to the past, not the present.

Bryan drained his drink and asked for another. The more he consumed, the more a warmth spread through him, and along with it a plaguing doubt surfaced.

Why should he trust a naiad or a unicorn? Weren't they magic just like the wizard, even if they were of a purer ilk? Or why should he recognize an assassination threat to the Prince as a declaration of war on Eetharum? And what was this nonsense of counter-magic? It all seemed like a bunch of childish tales. His stomach churned; he gripped his mug and took another sip. How could some hidden magic and a young half-witch save Eetharum? It wasn't logical! If it were true, maybe it was time he once again believed in the High Power, the deity he had long ago lost faith in. Where there was evil, there must be good, right?

Bryan shook his head, clearing his thoughts. He was Prince Alkin's Head-Master Sword and friend. If Alkin summoned him to do this job, then no matter how foolish and unrealistic it seemed, he would do it, and would do it not only for his friendship to Alkin and loyalty to Shelkite, but also for gratitude to Prince Izsum. He would not be in his prominent position if it weren't for Izsum. He may have never desired it, but he would honor it.

With another swig, Bryan's glum thoughts about his oath slipped down darker ones of his lineage. How dare that half-witch question his validity? How dare she torment him by bringing up his very un-Shelkiten name? Bryan couldn't remember much of his blood family; and once again, he found himself seeking out old memories in places he had locked away long ago. He had been very young when his parents moved to a little farm on the rolling prairies outside of Fordorn, and he'd called it home for only a short time.

Bryan closed his eyes and took a drink, struggling to bring back vague, distorted images of his blood family. He had had two older sisters. He remembered running through rows of crops with the girls, their gleaming, dark hair flying carelessly around their young faces...

Their mother called to them from their cozy cottage for supper. The oldest girl ran first, calling to her younger siblings. "Come on, Magdalena, Bryrunan, mama wants us for dinner!" The eldest girl's blue eyes sparkle, not unlike the little boy's with whom she held hands.

Bryan tottered alongside his sisters. Bending to his level, the eldest smiled blissfully. "Mama says the land is good here and we're going to stay. No more moving. We'll have a real home!"

Little Magdalena clasped her hands together in joy, "Forever?" she squealed.

"Yes. Forever and ever!" the eldest answered. She picked her sister up for a tight hug and swung her around. They laughed merrily.

"Time to eat!" their mother called again from the doorstep. "Children, go get your father in the barn. I don't think he heard me." The auburn-haired woman's gaze then looked beyond them to land on a tall, muscular, dark-haired man, who appeared from around the house. Worry creased his sun-bronzed brow.

"Riders from the northeast," he said, all the tendons in his

neck tense. His wife looked at him with a question. "Thirty or more coming fast. Get the children inside. I think it's the Galeon warriors that raided Tilicon earlier this month looking for rebels. Hurry," he ordered. She obeyed at once. The dark-haired man stayed outside...

Bryan's limited memory of the tragedy was forever seared on his brain. He remembered a group of men riding onto the property and hearing raised voices, his father's included. He recalled strange noises, screaming horses, the breaking of glass, and the heat of an intense fire. Above all, he remembered the terrified screams of his mother and his sisters and the horrid smell of burnt flesh. He could still hear the clank of metal and rumbling of hooves as Prince Izsum's warriors rode into the fray. Lastly, he remembered being whisked up and carried away, never to see his family again.

The Shelkite warriors had saved him. They had been too late for his father, mother, and sisters. Most of the images of his family were lost and hard to bring up to actual thought, but he could feel them. He knew they were his past, for they forever lingered and haunted him. No matter how hard he tried, he couldn't remember any more than this, nor his eldest sister's and parents' names. It bothered him at times.

The life Bryan had known after that had been as the child of a warrior in the camp of Prince Izsum. There, he had grown to be strong and the best swordsman in all Shelkite. Despite its rough beginning, he had had a good childhood. He didn't feel sorry for himself. In the camp, he had been loved and admired by all, especially by the daughter of the Head-Gate Master...

"Master Sword Bryan." Binz shook the robust Sword. "Ya looked like ya blanked out. Ya feelin' all right?" Binz didn't wait for an answer. "Back to the castle wit ya. The storm is worsenin'."

Bryan rubbed his eyes, clearing his thoughts. "I'm fine," he said brusquely. "But, I should get back...to babysit."

"Shall I send a rider wit ya?" Binz asked.

"I *don't* need an escort." He stood from his stool.

"Of course." Binz left to clean up a mess farther down the bar.

Bryan shoved his wobbly stool in and gave one last grumpy look around the tavern before setting a generous amount of copper coins down and leaving.

Dragon was tethered in a lean-to outside the tavern. He nickered to his master when Bryan neared.

"Hello, pal." Bryan mounted and pulled his cloak tighter around himself, tugging the hood down over his head. He nudged Dragon out into the pounding rain.

The sun had long disappeared. The night had settled like a heavy, black coat on the earth, the dark sky interrupted with periodic glitches of light.

Dragon's strides were steady and sure as he carried his master homeward. They slopped along the road, and Bryan felt for the hilt of his sword. It was there. It gave him a sense of security— completeness. He had been born to carry a sword. He knew he belonged nowhere but clasping a hilt and facing an opponent.

Bitter winds swept over the open fields, and the rain beat down on the Master Sword and his mount. Lightning sliced through the bleak sky and the atmosphere trembled as they rode past cottages alight; the occupants safe and warm from the rampant storm.

The burly horse shook his large-boned head and snorted as the rain stung his eyes. Bryan patted the thick, soaked neck in reassurance and let his thoughts wander from warrior camp to women.

Feeling the cold spring rain bite through his cloak, he nudged Dragon to move into a faster gait. But instead of shifting to a faster pace, the horse suddenly planted his hooves and snorted uneasily, head high and ears alert.

"Come on," Bryan urged. But no amount of asking made Dragon take a step farther. He bumped the horse harder, but the animal snorted and sidestepped nervously. Confused at his horse's odd behavior, he growled, "Don't be such a mule. It's cold out here!" He gave him another decisive bump and Dragon popped forward with a jarring gait and a snort of his opinion. The horse's wide eyes rolled, showing the whites, before he broke into a fast canter. "That's better," Bryan said, satisfied.

All too soon, the Master Sword discovered the explanation for his stallion's hesitance. A beast jumped out of the dark roadside and charged them. Dragon reared, letting out a threatening squeal, and then came down hard to drive the creature's skull into the earth, but the beast skirted aside. The horse swung around to send a hard blow at the creature with his hind legs, giving off a loud battle neigh as he did.

Caught off guard by his mount's sudden shift into battle moves—and feeling his whiskey a bit—Bryan lost his balance. Groping for the slick reins, he caught sight of the creature. *A howler!* Fear jumped into his chest. He bumped Dragon with his heels to escape the dreadful animal. His horse didn't hesitate to go this time.

Howlers were not ordinary animals, but queer creatures that only appeared after dark. They had ghastly sounding calls and were deadly. And where there was one, there were more. They hunted their prey in packs. Though they weren't seen too often in Shelkite, it was enough to cause farmers and savvy travelers to take precautions. Bryan's drink had muddled more than his balance that night; he should have known better.

Bryan careened along on Dragon, and three more howlers came charging out of the hills. Their screeches were terrifying and piercing. He glanced over his shoulder to see snapping fangs and strange, fervent eyes. They looked dreadfully similar to large furless dogs, though their front paws were akin to human hands with long claws. Their bite was deadly, as was their blood if it touched the skin. Two short horns protruded from their skulls. They whined, screamed, and snarled after the rider and horse.

Bryan yelled at the revolting creatures. He feared for his mount as well as for himself. But they paid no heed. Their hairless bodies felt no cold as the rain pounded down on them. They chased vigorously, eager for fresh meat.

Dragon raced along the sloppy road as fast as his hooves could carry his burly body and Bryan. He huffed out heavy breaths and his sleek coat became frothy with sweat, but the game stallion did not let up.

Soon, they were surrounded by a dozen screeching and snarling howlers. With a vicious neigh, Dragon skidded to a halt and reared. He came down, kicking out and flinging his body around in an attempt to ward off the creatures as he was trained to do in battle. Bryan lost control and fell headlong to the muddy earth, thinking ironically as he crashed down that he shouldn't have drank so much. Dragon bolted, drawing the howlers away from Bryan for the briefest moment.

As soon as Bryan hit the earth, a pack of howlers turned on him. Circling and eyeing their prey, saliva dripped from their fangs. Their screeches made him want to clasp his hands over his ears.

But when they attacked, he was ready. His drawn sword swiped at them as each force charged him. Blood poured down on him like rain, the sting of it making him yell out in pain. He was angry. He was furious, far past being logical. How dare these things hunt him! How incredibly stupid of him to be so careless!

Bryan hewed and hacked at the beasts for what felt like hours. His strength began to ebb, but he pushed harder. They hissed and pulled at him with their horrid human-like hands, and lashed at him with thick tails, cautious of their prey's apparent tenacity.

Feeling as if a day had passed, the sound of pounding hooves siphoned into Bryan's dark world like a moonbeam. He had no time to divert his attention to see the source. It came from behind.

A sharp whiz split the air near his ear. A howler shrieked and fell, an arrow piercing its side. A white blur came hurtling out of the darkness, and two more whizzes zipped past; two more howlers fell.

It was the Kaltrazian witch!

Unable to let down his guard at his surprise, Bryan downed two howlers that were attempting to shred his skin, their claws catching in his cloak.

As Alexa let her arrows fly and the Master Sword hacked away at the creatures, beheading as many as he could, the moon broke through the dissipating clouds as if to aid them. And soon, they found they had killed many of the creatures and watched as the rest fled back into the shadowy fields.

Struggling for breath, Bryan heaved in gulps of the moist air, a damp mist sprouting from his lips and nose into the cold night. He stumbled over to a place clear of howler bodies on the roadside and knelt in the stinking muck saturated with howler blood.

Alexa hopped lightly from Zhan's bare back, her near empty quiver still strapped across her back. She stepped over to the kneeling Sword's side and looked down on him. Bryan wiped his sword on the wet grass to clean the blade. His dark hair was in disarray, his cloak painted with gleaming scarlet blood.

"You all right?" she asked, breathless.

Bryan's attention on cleansing his sword, he nodded solemnly, and then stood and sheathed his weapon. He looked up and found himself staring straight into the girl's fiery, sapphire eyes darkened by the night. He shifted his gaze and noted that she must have left in a hurry. She appeared rumpled but poised. She stood tall and strangely elegant for having just survived a battle with howlers.

Bryan then suddenly felt sick, and a great shudder seized him. The places where blood had touched his skin began to seethe. He looked down at the young woman peering at him. His brow furrowed in question, "How d'you—" he faltered as he stepped onto the muddy road.

Alexa, seemingly ignoring his question, turned and whistled to Zhan. The horse trotted over. He wore no bridle or saddle. She turned back to him and answered, "I sensed evil. Have for a while, but couldn't place it until I felt these creatures' intentions."

Bryan looked at her with skepticism. "Dragon?" he inquired.

"Headed for the castle. I shot the howlers after him. He's safe." She placed a soothing hand on the white horse's slender neck.

Bryan nodded in approval. The two then began to trudge through the thick mud. Alexa reached down to pull an arrow from a howler's body, but he grabbed her wrist. She yelled out in pain as the blood seeped from his hand onto hers and pulled her hand away.

"Sorry," he muttered. "But don't take the arrows. They're poisoned."

She glared at him, her jaw clenched in pain. "I know that now."

He scowled at her. "Wipe your hand on the inside of my cloak." He held it out and she brusquely wiped her hand. When she spun away, Bryan's head swam all of a sudden and he stumbled into her.

She caught his arm and refused to yell out as the blood touched her skin again. "You will ride Zhan," she said.

Bryan's thoughts fought through a haze. "I will not ride that…*runt*."

"I've saved you and you insult me?" she shot at him and let go of his arm.

He shut his eyes in pain. He had to get back to the castle. He needed aid for the blistering wounds; his clothes were too saturated with the blood and the rain had ceased, taking away any cleansing it might provide. He started to walk, ignoring her comment and any qualm over his remark.

"You left in a hurry." He gestured to the unsaddled horse as they walked side by side up the road. Zhan followed alongside Alexa.

She turned and looked him straight in the eyes. "Yes," she said, a challenging expression across her features. It was clear she had not yet let go of his insult to her horse.

"I don't understand how you knew."

"I told you, *dear* Sword Bryan." She stopped and held his gaze steady with a futile attempt to unnerve him. "My father is a wizard. My blood isn't all human." Her lips curved into a haughty, half smile.

The Master Sword stared sharply at her for a brief moment and then suddenly felt as if he might buckle over with laughter. She was such a little wisp of a girl; his stature towered over her, but here she stood, unflinching and challenging him in a match of dominance.

He rested his hand on the hilt of his sword, "I see." The corners of his mouth curved into a suppressed grin. Turning, he flipped his hood down over his soaked head and began walking. "But my *dear*, little girl, you left without a guard and without permission." He stopped and turned to face a fuming Alexa. "*Don't* do it again." His voice held all the finality of an ending conversation that only the Head-Master Sword could deliver. He then strode away, feeling her loathe him.

CHAPTER SEVEN

Slopping along the sodden road, Alexa and Bryan soon saw the walls of the castle come into view. Luckily, they had traveled with no other mishaps. Alexa, at Bryan's bidding, rode beside him as he walked. The stubborn Master Sword stumbled over his own feet. His mind had become cloudier and he had trouble remembering what happened. The howlers' blood had begun its evil work. He fought against falling into unconsciousness.

Once they were through the portcullis—Bryan waving away any offers of help from the gatemen—and in the courtyard, Alexa slipped from Zhan's back to assist him to the entrance. His strength began to ebb quickly now, and he leaned on her, his eyes looking glazed and unfocused. Streams of sweat crept down his forehead and dripped off his chin.

Alexa hurried him along the best she could. It had started to rain again, and the pounding droplets impaired their vision. She made her way clumsily through the heavy doors and cried out for assistance. Bryan slipped from consciousness and fell to the foyer's floor in a heap.

Emerging from the large library doors to the left, Sword Boraz's large frame appeared alongside Prince Alkin's slighter form. A woman gasped—Lady Evelyn peered around them.

"Where have you been and what's happened?" Alkin said.

"Ugly…creatures… attacked," Alexa said. Her breath hitched in her chest, and her vision began to swim around her burning eyes.

"Howlers! Sword Boraz, get the Head-Nurse quickly," Alkin ordered.

Boraz dashed out of the hall.

"Alexa, are you hurt?" Alkin asked.

"Not terrible. S-sword Bryan is sick," she stammered. Her hand burned; the blood within her veins seemed to writhe and boil within her.

"Don't worry, we have a salve that may stop the poison before its work is finished."

She nodded, her forehead covered with sweat and eyes twitching. Then her eyes rolled back, and she slumped down next to the Master Sword.

Evelyn let out another gasp and ran to assist, but Alkin held her back. "Evie, don't touch them! The poison will affect you, too. Wait for the Head-Nurse."

A little while later, after the initial treatment, the Head-Nurse dried her hands and said to Melea, "Keep bathing his burns in clean water with the salve. It will help draw out the poison. Hopefully, the fever will break with the draught I've given him. Keep an eye on him and notify me if anything changes."

The stocky woman straightened from leaning over the unconscious Master Sword and looked at the worried prince, giving him a comforting smile. "He needs rest and care. Don't worry. I believe we caught it before it was too late, and the rain helped somewhat." She turned her gaze on Melea, who had been standing quietly in the shadows. "Make sure you stay with him. Howler poison is not to be fooled with. He'll need constant care for at least a night and day. And be sure he keeps drinking this to flush out his system." She held up a bottle of liquid, gave a curt nod, and left the chamber.

Alkin regarded Melea with an encouraging smiled. Then, before exiting the room, he gave Boraz a scolding glance. No doubt, the Sword would be reprimanded for allowing Alexa to slip away.

Smiling weakly, Boraz followed the Prince out.

Melea went to the bedside and knelt, looking at Bryan's pale face. His skin was moist and pasty. The blood from the howlers had burned through the arms of his cloak and onto his skin. His bare hands had borne most of the damage. She took the rag by the bedside and soaked it in the warm salve and water solution. She gently dabbed the raw burns. The poison had already seeped through his skin and begun its deadly journey through the veins.

Sweat covered his forehead. "I don't trust her," he groaned out and attempted to roll over.

She stopped him from moving and watched him, perplexed. Who was he talking about? She dabbed his forehead with a frown.

"Witch…no…good," he foundered.

Melea stopped her caretaking to listen. He grimaced and his eyes flew open. He glanced around the room before spotting her at his side. There was a moment of silence as his eyes dumbly searched her.

"Please, leave," he said flatly.

"No. I can't. You need care."

"I don't. Go away."

"Bryan, don't be stubborn."

"*Sword* Bryan," he corrected hoarsely.

"Him? Be stubborn?" someone said from behind.

Melea spun around at the sound of Alexa's voice. The raven-haired girl stood tall and proud in the doorway, her frame slender and almost queenly. Melea smiled, glad to see her, and even gladder that she looked in better condition than the Master Sword.

Bryan convulsed and then coughed. She turned back to him.

"Prince Alkin sent me when he saw I was better already." Alexa walked to the bedside. Melea looked puzzled. "I can help. I have some healing knowledge."

The servant nodded. But she was hesitant after hearing Bryan's mistrust of the girl. She glanced at Alexa's hands. Linen had been wrapped around one; it was stained crimson. She didn't seem to be affected by the poison. "Are you better?" she asked, her eyes wide with wonder.

"It's not bad."

"It doesn't affect you?"

"I've got something that really helps."

"I *don't* want your help." Bryan came to all of a sudden and glared at the two women. "Leave me alone, both of you."

"What is it?" Melea asked Alexa, ignoring Bryan and still unsure of what she offered.

"Don't worry. It won't hurt him," Alexa replied, moving closer to assist.

Bryan thrust his arm forward to ward her off. "I'll have your hide if you touch me, girl."

"As you wish, Master Sword." Alexa's eyes spit flames and

she glowered at him, then turned and left the chamber.

Melea turned to him. "She was going to help heal you. Why'd you do that?"

"I don't trust her. There's something underhanded about her." His bright eyes beckoned to the servant, and she leaned forward to listen. "Keep an eye on her when I'm not around."

"I don't think she's evil. She asked me to keep a watch on Lady Evelyn," she whispered back, elated by his confidence in her.

Bryan started, and his face turned sour. "Lady Evelyn is loyal to Prince Alkin. But I'm not sure of Miss Alexandra's loyalties yet."

Melea bit her lip undecidedly. She usually trusted his judgment, but she didn't think Alexa wicked. "Look, you have to rest. Forget about your duties for a while." She pushed aside the conversation.

Yielding, Bryan shut his eyes and endured the pain the best he could. He soon fell into a fitful sleep.

Leaving Bryan's chamber, Alexa wandered the halls searching for Prince Alkin. The long corridors were lit by ornate sconces and lanterns that cast eerie, dancing shadows around her. She stopped in the spacious foyer of the castle and paced, biting a short fingernail. Now that the howler poison was underhand, she needed to tell the Prince about her intuition clue, Lady Evelyn present or not.

"Can I help you with anything, Miss Alexandra?" Sword Boraz appeared behind her. He had been close at hand since her return.

She spun on her heel. "Yes. Could you please take me to see the Prince? I have to speak with him."

Boraz nodded, his gaze curious, and said, "He's in the library. In here." He gestured to a double doorway.

Alexa stepped through and immediately found herself in an intriguing atmosphere. Walls of books, plush reading chairs, and lounges surrounded her. She looked up and saw that a second floor with even more books and lavish decorations was tucked beneath a domed ceiling paneled with glass, presenting the gloomy night sky.

Opposite from the doors, a cheerful fire blazed in a large stone hearth.

Prince Alkin and Lady Evelyn stood speaking in low tones by an oak desk in the corner. Alkin looked up. "Alexa!" His fair face broke into a smile. "I'm pleased to see that you're well."

"Yes. Thank you." She inclined her head, and then glanced at Evelyn and said, "I need to speak with you."

Alkin nodded solemnly. There was silence, and then he said, "Anything that you have to say about our big predicament can be said safely in this company." He smiled in reassurance.

Alexa nodded, still unsatisfied, but willing to go on. "Today," she began. She was uncertain how they would react to her story about the mermaid. They would think her crazy. "On the way back from Fordorn, I received an answer to at least one of our problems. I suspect it was my magical intuition. Without a doubt, I know my inclination is trustworthy. I have to go see the merpeople."

Alkin and Evelyn looked at one another for a moment. Alexa stirred, shifting her feet.

"Are there such a people?" Evelyn asked. "I heard that their kind lived a long time ago in the Elendace Sea. Or, maybe it was the Nortarwin Sea. But did the kingdom really exist? And if so, would they still be there? What could they do for us on land, anyhow?"

Alkin was quiet, his face troubled.

"I know it sounds strange, but please believe me," Alexa pleaded. She knew she had to go. The magic pulsing through her veins told her so.

Alkin finally spoke. "I believe there was once an underwater city. Though, the merpeople were rumored to be highly reclusive. It's possible they could be a fabled race. But Apollos is akin to them and the howlers as well. And, too, here stands a young woman that has magical blood." He smiled sadly and looked at Evelyn. "I think there's a chance they existed and are still there. What chances do we have to throw away? If these people can help us, why not make the trip? It's all we have right now."

Evelyn nodded. Wisps of her brown hair fell into her eyes. "Yes, I suppose you're right." She regarded Alexa and studied her.

Alexa noted the woman's face was not as it was earlier in the day, flirty and giddy. She had somehow matured by just a change in her demeanor. She figured Evelyn was at least ten years her senior, and sensed deep intelligence, accompanied with sadness within the woman. Using her senses a little closer, Alexa realized she wasn't prone to wickedness as she had first thought.

Resolved, Evelyn nodded her approval and said to Alkin, "Okay, but I advise you to gather the council for a discussion." She turned to Alexa. "The reason I rushed here today was that my sources tell me there are whispers of multiple assassination plans for the rulers of Eetharum." She looked down at her folded hands, her brown eyes becoming watery. "And, I worry about my people in Zelka left with no one to protect them from his deceit."

Alexa remained respectfully mute, a strong sense growing within her that Lady Evelyn was far more important to all this than Alexa had first understood.

Alkin nodded in agreement, and said, "As soon as Sword Bryan is on his feet again, we'll hold a council." He squeezed Evelyn's hand tenderly. "We'll do all we can to help your people and the rest of Eetharum, hopefully before Ret's reach goes any further." He faced Alexa, his features changing from sympathetic to quizzical. "Tell me," his voice rose with attempted enthusiasm, "How is the Head-Master Sword?"

"I don't know. He looked very ill when I went to help him. He would have none of it."

Alkin heaved an exasperated sigh, and Evelyn turned her head to hide a small smile.

"I don't believe he trusts me," Alexa acknowledged.

Alkin gave her a soft smile and took her hand. "Well, I do, and he's under my orders. Even if he wants to suffer longer than he must, we don't have time to wait around for it. Let's get some of those herbs you used to the Head-Nurse for him. The Master Sword doesn't need to know where they came from."

At that, Alexa's face split into a grin. "Yes, sir."

CHAPTER EIGHT

The next day, Master Sword Bryan sat uncomfortably in the council hall, slouched in his usual chair at the end of the table. Alkin's seat at the head was empty. A trickle of sweat slid down the Sword's face; he was still not entirely well and his blood coursed through his veins with an abnormal heat. However, he was well enough to withstand the meeting.

Today, the council table didn't seat just its usual company of Master Swords. Among the twelve men, there were two women. Alexa sat to the right of Prince Alkin's chair and Lady Evelyn sat to the left.

Bryan eyed Alexa with dislike. She sat slumped, yet proud. Her long, raven hair was braided as normal and rested over her shoulder. She looked preoccupied. Her brow furrowed as she drummed her fingers on the table, staring into space. *Probably amused by a floating speck of dust.* Bryan snickered at his own wit, though he knew it to be quite facetious.

He shifted his gaze to Lady Evelyn. She sat upright and dignified. Her demeanor was quiet and assured, her brown hair down and in soft, wavy locks. Her eyes flicked over and met his; he looked away.

Echoing footsteps came from behind. Bryan peered over his shoulder. Prince Alkin strode in with Apollos at his heels. No sound came from the creature's hooves. All in the room stood and bowed as the Prince took his seat. Apollos stood silently nearby.

Alkin folded his hands together and rested them on the table. All were quiet and expectant. He looked around to each face: the two women, the elder Swords who had served under his father, the Swords he appointed, and to Bryan, his Head-Master Sword and old friend. He thought deeply before he uttered a word, his hazel eyes troubled.

"Soon, we'll all have to set out on missions," he began, solemn. "Tonight, we'll decide what actions to take to carry this out." He paused. "I want everyone to speak their mind freely. Please don't hold anything back." Pushing back his chair, he stood.

The dark blue overcoat he wore and his small silver circlet studded with three simple jewels, a sapphire with two emeralds on either side, made him appear regal and old beyond his years. "I'll go first. It is time I introduced you to this lady on my left, who has been a longtime friend of mine. She came to me in secret two years ago seeking Shelkite's aid. She's a loyal citizen of Zelka. Lady Evelyn is of noble blood and was a close counselor of the former king."

The Swords and Alexa looked around to one another. A few leaned together to hide a whisper.

Alkin cleared his throat. "When she heard of her king's unfortunate and unanticipated death, Lady Evelyn wasn't deceived. She had long been wary of her fellow counselor, Ret, and was one of the few who fled when he overtook the throne. For, as we know, he's not the lawful heir and tricked the sickly king into handing over the crown on his deathbed. But before Evelyn escaped, she stationed behind people loyal to her and the country, and in secret, they've been able to send regular updates to her. She's learned through them of the covert, hostile happenings. We know for a fact that he has used force on any citizens who have opposed him. Lady Evelyn came to me for help because our families are old friends, and because she's the niece of the deceased king and the *rightful* heir to the throne of Zelka. But our foe soon caught wind our meetings, and I received a murderous threat." Alkin looked at Evelyn with a small smile. She returned it with a sad one, looking fondly on him as they shared a memory. "Ret knows we're mobilizing a plan against him, so he is currently preparing for an attack and, I'm told, designing other assassination attempts on Eetharum's leaders."

Alkin regarded Apollos standing a step behind his chair. "Apollos is probably the last unicorn. He has served loyally to Shelkite for many years, as most of you know. After I received the assassination threat, he swiftly left for the territory of Carthorn, in hopes to obtain answers from the Guidance Naiad."

Apollos bowed his head in acknowledgment.

"This brings us to the lady on my right." Alkin gestured to Alexa. "The naiad advised us to seek her help. And, as we have discovered, it is likely because she is the last known witch, half-blood or not... All right...now, Alexa," he petitioned, "I'll let you disclose our first task." He sat down.

Silence reigned in the hall for a long moment, and Bryan fidgeted.

Alexa's eyes flicked over to Sword Bryan and were met by his level gaze. She felt something brewing inside him. It would come out soon, but she pushed it aside, cleared her throat, and spoke with calm confidence. "My first task is to travel south to the merpeople; where I hope, they'll lead me to the counter-magic." There were some surprised murmurs, but Alexa turned to the Prince, "I would like to ask if I could take a small company with me."

Alkin nodded. "Why, definitely, Alexa, I wouldn't send you alone."

Sword Xercan, a broad and warlike man, stood. He was of the old council of Swords under Izsum; his face held weathered lines and his once dark hair was now streaked with gray. "Though we don't have the means to summon mystical creatures like Ret, we can't wait for him to harm more people even while Alexandra is away on her mission. We have to assemble Shelkite's army and go to Galeon. We must confirm the allegiance of Eetharum's countries with us so that we're not unprepared for the impending attack. My prince, while serving under your father, I was in charge of the warriors for many years, so I ask that I may lead the Warriors of Shelkite."

"Yes, Sword Xercan, I had in mind that you would. Prepare the men to mobilize. Every warrior *must* be ready whether he stays to protect Shelkite's borders or goes to Zelka," he commanded. "Lady Evelyn and I have discussed ideas of battle strategy. She's knowledgeable in this area and knows Zelka's terrain. She'll go with you and assist. Her people still loyal will welcome you and join us. They camp just across the southern border of Zelka in Galeon."

Xercan bowed to the Prince and nodded a salute to Evelyn before he sat.

Bryan clenched his jaw in irritation. Lady Evelyn was to go to war? He wanted to be the general of the mobilized army! How did she suddenly become so high in command of Shelkite's warriors?

"Sword Gyqua," Alkin addressed another Sword.

A slender, fair-haired man straightened and acknowledged the Prince. He was the head of Shelkite's Messenger Company.

"Send men as you can spare to Eetharum's countries to warn and gather allies, but first send out scouts. I want to see what countries, if any, are allied with Ret. Send emissaries next to explain the trouble. After you've done this, go to our battlements in Galeon. Your warriors will be used to dispatch messages and keep the battalions in full contact."

Gyqua nodded his understanding, his green eyes sparkling with anticipation.

Alkin continued, "I'm leaving a Sword stationed here to watch over the castle and its warriors. Sword JaVin will stay here to oversee castle duties; though, I give my mother top authority." The Prince turned to regard another older Sword, "Sword Devlon, you will be in charge of the homeland warriors left to protect our beloved Shelkite and its citizens. The rest of my Master Swords shall fall into the army ranks as colonels."

"Where are you going, my prince?" Sword Boraz inquired the question that was on all their minds.

The Prince looked at Alexa. "I feel my place is with Miss Alexandra, as the mission is of utmost importance; and when it is finished, I will go to the Galeon battlements."

There was sudden chaos. Everyone spoke at once, voicing questions and warnings. All the Master Swords advised strongly against his rash idea.

Alexa stared in astonishment at the Prince.

Bryan sat, grinding his teeth, furious. Then he stood with defiance, "How are we to be assured *she* is not in league with this wizard?" His authoritative voice boomed across the room, causing everyone to quiet. "Ret is the same race, isn't he? She's been wandering freely about the castle and grounds, I might add, asking a lot of questions. She's had plenty of time to contrive and send information to Ret! My prince, think of what you're doing." Bryan gazed wildly at Alexa. She stared levelly back at him with a defiant, raised eyebrow.

Alkin opened his mouth, as if he were going to rebuke him,

but Apollos stepped forward and abrupt silence fell. "I came from Carthorn with only the name of this girl for help. My kind knows well of her kind. Our ancestors were fierce enemies and brutally spilled the blood of each other. If you don't trust me or this young woman, as your prince does, then we will fail. Her father may be a full-blood wizard, but he's chosen exile from the evil tendencies of his kind. He's bound by an enchanted, unbreakable promise to the Power. He's taught his daughter the wisdom of integrity. Alexandra is good because she chooses so, you have *my* word. Don't fight each other. We'll most certainly fall if we're divided." He gave them a penetrating stare.

Quiet overcame them. They had listened as if their own lives depended on his words. Even Bryan was humbled at the unicorn's reproof. He sat down, feeling weak with his illness again, and wondered where his place would be. He looked at Alexa. She held him with a strange gaze, and he felt his eyes lock to her features; and for all his wishing, he couldn't remove them. When she let his gaze go, he somehow knew altogether and inexplicably so that she wasn't evil. It was as if she had told him this, by showing him all that was within her, every thought, every motive, every feeling, every hate, and love. Though, he couldn't put a finger on them. She had somehow poured her soul right out through her eyes into him…and persuaded him. *No.* He finally decided. *She's not evil, but she feels no love for me because of my mistrust. It doesn't matter. I don't care much for her either…the haughty little girl.*

Tension clouded the air, and Alkin spoke first, breaking it. "Three of my good warriors shall go with you, Alexa, at your choosing."

She nodded her approval.

"And, as I've said, I'll accompany you. I also implore you to take my advice and pick a Master Sword to come."

Bryan's heart gave a sudden jolt. Where was he in this tale? Surely not with her. He wished to go to battle. That didn't mean he wished to follow this girl over the countryside. Yet, the witch had the choosing. She surely wouldn't choose him for all her loathing of him. Would she?

Alexa looked around the table to the many unfamiliar faces. Who would be the best? Who had what she needed? A fierce loyalty, skill, and everything possessed within that was needed for this journey. She knew who, even before she had to search with her senses. She could feel and see all their hearts. However, she didn't speak of him first. "I would like to ask something else," she began.

All eyes were on her, curious. The Chaos Goddess looked at her with a strong sense of respect. The Master Swords waited on the edge of their seats for her to speak. Alkin watched her closely, while Apollos stood in calm, as if he knew her thoughts.

"That I can be assured that I'll have the right to making every final decision. Even in your presence, sir." She said this without a hint of hesitation. After all, he was not *her* prince.

The Swords were stunned. Evelyn looked at her with grave interest. Alkin just stared blankly; Apollos said nothing and moved nothing but his gleaming tail with a slight flick.

"What for, may I ask? Safety purposes?" Alkin said, perplexed, and a little dazed, but not offended.

Bryan unconsciously leaned forward, greatly intrigued.

"Please don't take me wrong. I don't want to control the company. I just feel that with my senses, I'll be a more adequate decision maker. Everything, of course, will be discussed amongst us first before any decision. It's for your own safety. I believe that since my name was given to help *all* of Eetharum and that I was pulled from my home, I should have at least this," Alexa said. Plus, she felt it necessary to establish her status. She would *not* be overpowered and used. She liked Prince Alkin, but she was still a bit wary of them all and would watch her back.

How bold of her, Bryan thought. She should never speak to the Prince that way. He glanced at the stricken Alkin and sat back with a thump, snorting his disapproval. An older Sword gave him a look of disgust at his child-like behavior. Bryan diverted his gaze.

"As you wish," Alkin stated. "But *everything* must be discussed. And, I'm still acting as the Prince of Shelkite none-the-less."

"Trust me. I don't want any trouble," she confirmed.

"I do trust you," Alkin said, and a genuine smile creased his face for the first time that night.

Apollos spoke, and all ears were sharp to listen to his musical voice. "I'll come, too."

Everyone in the room seemed to take in a breath. Bryan let his boot drop to the floor from where it had been resting on his knee. He received another disgusted look from a fellow Sword. He ignored it and looked at the unicorn gravely.

"You're clever, Miss Alexandra," said the unicorn. "But you've yet to pick your choice of the Master Swords. Who will it be? Tomorrow, you'll choose your warriors, but tonight, a Master Sword must be chosen. One that's skilled, intelligent, and credible."

Bryan held his breath. He had a strange feeling...

Alexa looked up, for her head had been bowed in thought. Her blue, flaming eyes searched each man. They landed on the Head-Master Sword. "I choose Sword Bryan."

"An astute choice," Apollos approved.

Bryan huffed out a pent-up breath, eliciting another scolding glare from the older Sword. It was just as he worried. He smiled weakly at the others, but nodded his acceptance.

"Good," said the Prince, "I was hoping you'd pick him. I didn't want to pressure you. Sword Bryan will continue to be your Sword-Guard until the mission is complete."

Three hours later, when many details had been discussed and debated, Prince Alkin stood and dismissed them. Bryan was the first to leave, but he hid outside the chamber doors in the shadows. Listening, he overheard the whisperings of his departing fellow Swords as they filed out. One in particular was rather vocal...

"...he probably bribed the girl just so he wouldn't have to stay behind. Now, it's my duty. He knew full well Xercan would be general. Mark my words, there's a scam...thinks he's all high and mighty...brash young cock...just because he's the *Head*-Master Sword. He's always strutting around here like he has the biggest— well, you know..."

Bryan glared at their departing backs. Alexa's willowy figure appeared in the threshold; she paused. He stayed silent, attempting to hold his breath. *How childish of me*, he thought, feeling odd.

"I know you're there, my Sword-Guard. Planning to attack

me?" She spoke with a wry air.

Bryan stepped out from behind the door and shadows. Heels together and back tall, he bowed. "No. I've waited to escort you to your room, as it is my duty as your Sword-Guard."

She gave him a curt nod and started at a brisk pace down the corridor. He followed.

After clambering up the flights of stairways and striding in awkward silence down the dimly lit corridors, they finally reached her chamber.

Alexa turned to shut the oak door and nodded a terse dismissal. "Goodnight," she said, but the Master Sword stepped over the threshold and into her room. She glared at him and turned her back to him.

With a calm edge in his voice, Bryan began, "You did that deliberately just to spite me." His words dripped with disdain.

"Of course, I *deliberately* chose you," she spat back. She began to unbuckle her dagger, her eyes zapping dangerously.

"You're a witch. You had to *know* I wanted to go to the battlements." He stood stiffly, but he looked menacing and resolute. His wrath and his want to fight were pent up, boiling, held at bay by some inward dam, showing only through the quivering muscles of his body.

With sudden abrasiveness, she threw her belt and dagger on the bed and strode toward him, her long, fixed strides bringing her quickly to him, where she stood before him, tall and fierce, the top of her head barely passing his nose; a menacing blue fire ablaze in her eyes. She was small but foreboding.

"I'll ask you *once* to never call me that again in such a way," she said through clenched teeth.

Bryan's voice lowered. "As you wish, but I do *not* wish to be your comrade on this little jaunt," he persisted more calmly, but stern.

"Aren't you loyal to Prince Alkin and Shelkite? Then, go for them and not me if that pleases you." She turned and paced with agitation.

Bryan watched, trying to decipher the peculiar girl.

"I didn't pick you to torment you. I had other reasons. You're selfish, Sword Bryan, but very fitting to this. More so than all the rest. You must know that." Her strides quickened. "If blood and battle are what you want, then you won't be deprived of it following me. The end will be a bitter taste for you...and me." She paused reflectively, her brow puzzled, then she looked up at him, adding, "You have no ties. You're free to choose what you want. Your voice must be heard. *You are* the Head-Master Sword, after all. But I've made my decision."

Once again, her gaze upon him was most bewitching and Bryan stared blankly back. But his azure eyes saw a new light and understanding. He pondered for a moment and everything inside deflated. "You're more sensible than you act at times. Forgive me. I'll do my duty now, with no more complaints. I'll protect you as your Sword-Guard until this is over... That's a promise, and my honor." The words had been hard to choke out. But in her eyes, he had seen a fear. He could see the dread of the blackness of death and loss in the depths of her sharp sapphire orbs. He turned to exit. "I'll leave now." He bowed and closed the door firmly behind him.

Pausing in the dim corridor, he attempted to sort through his feelings. He then raised his chin stubbornly, took two strides, and came to his chamber door. He flung it open. Why did she cause him so much inner-strife? She acted so childish at times; and then other times when she opened her mouth, it was as if she were old and wise. She was an enigma.

Troubled with his thoughts, he had expected to walk into an empty room but found Melea standing by the bedside with a steaming teapot. "What're you doing here?" he asked abruptly. "You're to attend Miss Alexandra now." He unbuckled his sword and set it on his bed.

"You're still unwell," she said. She set the pot down on the bedside table.

He turned to face her. "I'm fine now. You can attend to your other duties."

She came to him, placing a soft hand on his brow. "You're still warm. You need to drink this."

He moved from her touch and heaved a sigh. He sat down and began removing his riding boots, first taking the knife from the inner flap. Melea knelt to help.

"I don't need your help," he stated. She raised her face to look at him, and he was surprised to see a troubled set of brown eyes searching him.

"Oh, Bryan!" she suddenly cried, gripping his knee.

He stared wide-eyed at her outburst.

"I know something is wrong. No one has told me anything yet. All I have to do is look at everybody's faces. Please tell me you're not leaving!" Her eyes welled with tears.

He said nothing, but continued to take his boots off with an eyebrow arched.

"If you leave, I'll just die," she said.

Bewildered, he jerked his head up to look her in the eye. What was she talking about? "Don't say that," he demanded, but when Bryan's eyes lighted upon Melea, he seemingly saw her for the first time as a woman instead of his steady servant. She had intense brown eyes and long, dark-blonde tresses that curled softly around her pretty features. A fat tear rolled down her flushed face.

"Please tell me what is going on."

"If you attend to Miss Alexandra like you're supposed to, I am sure she will tell you," he answered softly, turning away.

Another tear slid down Melea's cheek, dripping off her chin and plopping onto his knee. "Could *you* tell me?" she asked.

Dumbfounded at her unforeseen affection, Bryan stared at her trembling figure. She clutched his knee, and he sprang to his feet and began pacing madly about the room. He didn't feel like discussing the situation, or the more surprising situation that was surfacing. "Leave me alone...please."

"Master Sword?" She slowly rose.

"Melea, I said go. Tend to your other duties."

"But, Bryan...I—"

"Master Sword," he corrected stubbornly. He kept his features stern. He then turned his back on her. He didn't want her; she would have to learn that she could not speak to him in a familiar way.

She came to him and placed her hands on his turned back. "I understand why you're doing this...but please don't."

"Just leave."

She tugged at his shoulders and he allowed her to turn him around to face her. "Please, open your heart once again…to me this time. Forget about the past," she pleaded.

He merely stared over her head to the wall and said nothing.

She searched his face for a moment and then lowered her eyes with a solemn nod. "All right." She turned and left without a word or a glance back.

Bryan stared at the closed door in shock. "What in Shelkite just happened?" Then, as if being awoken, he shook himself and went to his washbasin to splash water on his face. He wiped his clean-shaven face dry and grumbled, "That was crazy."

CHAPTER NINE

The next morning, the sun's early rays streamed through the windows in Alexa's chamber, seemingly carrying a new promise. She rolled over to face the light, and a sleepy smile spread across her face as she drank in the heavenly sight. She could just see the sun's pink tip peeking over the vast mounds, spraying golden sunlight upwards. Distant bellows of cattle rolled over the hills, and voices shouted commands to one another. *Shelkite wouldn't be an unpleasant place to live.* If only she had come for another reason.

Hugging the feathered pillow, she shut her eyes and dreamed for a blissful moment, not used to such a soft bed and pillow. Her eyes popped opened when she remembered today would be the day she would choose her warriors. Her journey would start soon. She sat up and mulled over everything that had happened. A light tap on the door interrupted her thoughts.

"Come in." She climbed out from under the warm quilts.

Melea opened the door and entered. "Good morning, Alexa. I have your bath all prepared for you," she said with a bright smile.

"Thank you!" She stretched and gave the servant an appraising sidelong glance. The older girl had quite a different attitude than the one she'd been in previous night.

When Melea had come in, she had been distraught for reasons Alexa could only guess at. But Alexa got a sudden idea. She knew Melea was trustworthy, and she felt there was a strong need for someone to watch things while the Prince was away. So, she asked the older girl to keep a furtive eye out for anything suspicious. She told her to use her own good judgment and make sure everything was running as it should. And, if it was not, then she was obligated to dispatch a rider to the battlements for help. In secret if she must.

The servant had at first demurred, feeling it was going behind Prince Alkin's back. But Alexa assured her it was for his own good.

Now, Melea looked rather buoyant. There was a sparkle in her brown eyes, and she knew the servant felt she had an important job and a purpose now. She would handle her task well.

With Melea now off to attend other duties, Alexa hopped into the lavender-scented waters. She slipped her head all the way to the bottom of the tub and stayed there until she could stand it no longer. She emerged, breathed in deeply and exhaled long, savoring the warmth of the water, for she knew this would be a pleasure few and far between.

★★★★

Gladness flooded Sword **Bryan's** heart as he entered through the main gate to stand in the courtyard of the warrior camp. He was home. The camp was surrounded by large barricades, much like the ones surrounding the castle, was about two miles from the castle, and operated like a small city. The warriors and their families lived here as long as duty required and could come and go as they pleased.

Shelkite's line of princes had always put an emphasis on a good military. So, it was important everything ran smoothly in this town full of warriors. The streets were lined with small diners and shops, mostly managed by the warriors' wives. Almost anything a person would need could be found. When supplies were low, a company was sent out to Fordorn, or elsewhere, to retrieve them; the women often handling the supply trips, shopping for goods ranging anywhere from fabrics to spices. It was a simple life, and Bryan loved it.

Happiness enveloping him once again, he waved at warriors as they passed by. Some called back merrily and others came over to slap him on the back like an old friend, not their superior.

Alexa hung back, waiting for the Sword's next action. She watched him with curiosity. Upon seeing him genuinely smile for the first time, she fell silent and thoughtful. He was a different person here, where he liked it.

After being greeted by more men and women than Alexa would have thought Bryan had the capacity for, his attention returned to the task at hand. With a grin still across his features, he turned to her, "Ready, girl?"

"Yes." A small, intrigued smile curved her lips.

"There's about an hour before the warriors gather on the great field. I'll show you around beforehand." He strode off down the main street. Pointing to his left at a large, domed building, he said, "That's the hall. The top warriors gather there." A light seemed to shine in his eyes, as if a fond memory was embedded there.

Stride for stride, they walked down the way. Immaculate homes and shops lined the well-traveled street. On their right, roomy stables and paddocks stretched to the outer wall. A number of large horses, much like Dragon, hung their heads over the stall doors. Bryan patted a brown, curious nose as he went by. "Look," he said, a spring was in his step as they neared an older looking building, "There's the school. Everything I know, I learned there. That's where the warriors are made."

"Fordorn's School for Young Warriors," Alexa read from the sign in the front of the building. Bryan nodded, a proud smile across his handsome face. They walked by a practice ring where two young warriors, supervised by an instructor, clashed in full combat mode.

As they marched on, they came to a more rural part of the camp. Paddocks lined the roadway on either side with all sorts of animals roaming about. Spotting two small ponies in a field, Alexa pointed, "Brave warrior horses, no doubt," she said good-naturedly.

The Master Sword grinned and gestured farther up the road where two children were riding similar, fat ponies, "Great learning mounts." The children fenced each other from atop their steeds with wooden swords. The ponies, however, had a different idea, and insistently pulled their young riders to greener patches of grass.

Alexa laughed openly. When they passed the playing children and persistent ponies, she noted that one child was, in fact, a little girl. "Ah, the future heroine of Shelkite," she said, making it a point to the Sword.

"Perhaps," was all Bryan said, but his voice held no coldness.

"And where is the great Head-Master Sword taking a lowly

foreigner like me?" she asked with playful sarcasm. There was a slight bounce to her step as she strode ahead, gladly taking in more of the pleasant sights, for the day was bright and the sun shone its favor on the green earth whilst a sweet-scented wind pushed plump clouds across the azure sky.

Stopping in front of a medium-sized cottage, Bryan replied, "Right here." He stepped up to the door and knocked firmly. A moment later, the door creaked open, revealing a middle-aged woman standing there.

"Bryan!" she gasped, her face alight.

A wide grin broke his features, "Hello, Mother."

The woman gave him a tight hug around the neck and called over her shoulder, "Dear, Bryan's home!"

"He is? Well, tell him to get in here," a male voice called excitedly back. "I have so much to show him since he was last here!"

Bryan's mother rolled her eyes. "He's taken up inventing things in his spare time again. The entire camp is wondering when he'll be burning down the house," she said, exasperated. "Well, come on in." She ushered them through the door. Pausing in the hall, she inquired, "So, who is this young lady, Bryan?" A significant look spread across her features.

"This is Miss Alexandra of Eastern Kaltraz. Here on business with the Prince. I am her Sword-Guard." He introduced her with respect and formality. "Alexa, this is my mother, Catha. And my father is around here somewhere, I suspect. Theroe is his name."

"Nice to meet you, Alexandra." Catha smiled and shook her hand.

"Same to you." Alexa inclined her head. "And you can just call me Alexa."

Catha responded with a pleasant smile and nod. She was a small-statured woman, her golden hair tied back into a tight bun, and her kitchen clothes adorned with puffs of flour. She didn't look old enough to be Bryan's real mother. Alexa wondered that the couple must have been very young when they took him in.

Sniffing the air, Bryan asked, "What are you making?"

"Ooo, you're just in time for lunch. Come in. You can eat before you run off again. I'll go get your father." She hurried away, disappearing down the hall.

Unbuckling his sword, Bryan hung it on a hook on the wall. Reluctantly, Alexa did the same with her dagger. She followed him into a modest kitchen with a round wooden table. Bryan took a seat and motioned for her to do the same.

"What're you doing now?" Catha's stern voice rent the air. Alexa started at the sudden outburst. "You'll blow the whole camp up with all that nonsense. Get rid of it, Theroe, now!"

"But, Catha, think of the possibilities!" Bryan's father's voice echoed with enthusiasm.

Looking quite flustered, Catha bustled back into the kitchen. She took up a platter of sandwiches and fresh cookies and placed it on the table. "Thinks he's doing Prince Alkin a favor." She shook her head. "He's trying to start a science program for the warrior school. Pish, I say. Him trying to invent things? We'll all be blown to next year!"

"Oh, you're too critical. Last time I was home, I thought his ideas were great. The school could really use a science program. Besides, the medical program we all thought would fail is up and running successfully. There are already a few students that have specialized in it and have graduated." Bryan served himself some food.

"Yes, well, I thought his ideas were good, too." Catha plopped down in her chair breathless, "Until, some of whatever he was doing decided to blow up in the dead of night, got the whole camp in an uproar. Thought we all were being attacked!" Then abruptly, she turned her attention to Alexa and added, "Eat up, girl. You're far too skinny, I think, for Bryan's taste."

Alexa almost choked on her sandwich and shook her head at Catha with wide eyes. Bryan merely snorted and ignored his mother's comment.

An hour later, the great field was packed with all the top warriors in the camp. The multitude stood at attention, looking crisp and professional. It was magnificent to behold. The Shelkiten warriors were all outfitted in rich green and silver, two of their country's colors.

The Master Swords, who were lined up facing the mass, wore their blue overcoats trimmed in silver. This displayed their higher rank. Sword Bryan stood at the head. Sword Xercan, now Sword-General, stood to his right, and Alexa stood to Xercan's right, feeling quite small next to them. However, she stood proudly, reflecting Sword-General Xercan and the Head-Master Sword's stance: feet braced apart, upright, hands folded in front, and chin high.

Sword Bryan's explanation was brief and to the point. He left out many details. He informed the warriors of the necessity of a select few to join Miss Alexandra on an important mission. The nature of the mission would remain undisclosed until only the men chosen would be briefed. He also gave a succinct explanation of their plans for preparing for battle. Sword-General Xercan would give them a thorough briefing and orders later.

There was tension in the air. Alexa felt it and breathed it. It was suffocating. Sword Xercan leaned over and whispered to her, "How would you like to go about choosing, Miss Alexandra?"

Giving him a sidelong glance, she said, "Let them mingle. I'll just observe. No need to make it like a slave auction." Sword Xercan met Sword Bryan's eyes quizzically. Bryan nodded his confirmation, and Xercan ordered the company to be at ease until further notice.

Alexa and Bryan mingled among and around the various groups of men. She barely looked them over, feeling them out through her senses rather than by sight.

"Him," Bryan gestured toward a muscular, middle-aged man, "He would be good."

She glanced at the man, throwing her senses out as she did, and shook her head. "No. He's not good."

Bryan stared at her, his features hard and obstinate. "What do you mean?" he said through gritted teeth.

"I mean, I like him." She pointed to a young, lanky, dark-haired warrior chatting animatedly with others his age.

The Master Sword looked and then scoffed. "This is *not* a gathering for you to find a beau. He's too young and inexperienced," he said in a hushed tone.

She glared at him with her jaw clenched. "I choose him. The

others you pick are no good."

He let out something like a snarl and hissed in her ear, "I do not need a little wisp of a girl like you telling me who is a good warrior or not."

A clever glint came into her eye and she turned to him and said, "I chose *you.* Remember? Wasn't that the best pick? You of all people should know how it is to be persecuted for being young." She stalked away.

He gave a frustrated growl and followed. "So be it. Warrior Eelyne will be informed."

A bit later, he pointed another out. "What about him?" The man in question was tall and strong looking, with a mop of red, curly hair. "It is Warrior Hazerk."

Alexa took a look and a smile spread across her face. "Very good, Sword Bryan!" she said, as if she was praising a child who had just learned a new task. "I *will* take him on my little outing." Her delighted tone was heavy with sarcasm, a rebuttal for Bryan's earlier remark about beaus, but he nodded his approval.

On they looked.

"One more man," she asserted thoughtfully, "…and, he should do it." She pointed to another warrior, who was giving a forced laugh at a comrade's joke. The blonde-haired warrior was tall, broad, and intimidating.

Bryan glanced his way and nodded his approval once again. "So be it. Our business is done. Warrior Warkan will be the last."

CHAPTER TEN

Darkness obscured their vision. It filled their eyes with the unknown as the newly formed company passed from the lighted courtyard to beyond the gate. South was their path, across the farmlands of Shelkite, through Charad Forest, to tropical Yoldor, and the Elendace Sea, where they hoped to find in the depths of the waves, no matter how unwelcoming, the merpeople. After that, where their road would lead was yet a mystery. Uncertainty and excitement mingled within all their souls.

From atop the stone walls of the barricade, torches threw an orange glow into the chill morning air. Guards peered down to watch the silent group depart, their eyes glistening with wonder in the light.

The company of six humans, cloaked in black, took with them their six mounts and a pack mule. Strange light emitted from the horn of the seventh in the company; Apollos led them off the road and across the grassy terrain. His sleek body shone with a ghostly light and the soft hue of his hooves glistened through the long, shadowy grasses. Fog swirled around the hooves of the beasts as the morning dew wet their legs; the only sounds the soft breaths of the horses and the quiet shifting of the humans.

Alexa sat astride Zhan with her cloak wrapped closely around her and hood drawn up. She glanced over her shoulder to the watchtowers for one last look. Her eyes wandered to the Prince riding alongside her on Sapharan. His gaze met hers. Sadness and worry manifested within him. He had been strongly advised not to join the company, but he refused to listen, stating his place was with them. Turning her eyes ahead, Alexa saw ominous clouds let loose the drizzle of rain they had promised, and she felt the heavy hearts of her companions sink a little lower.

It would take them a number of days to reach the southern border of Shelkite. They then would enter the land of Yoldor, ruled by Chief Bahjahn. They hoped to pass through the country as disregarded travelers in order to reach the seashore on the outer eastern boundaries. Back at the castle, after an adequate amount of time that ensured the company's safe passage through Yoldor, Sword Gyqua would dispatch Shelkite messengers to inform Chief Bahjahn of Ret's intentions. If the Chief turned out to be an ally to Ret, the company would then be safely out of his territory.

Riding in the lead, Sword Bryan kept mostly to himself. He was followed closely by the Prince and Apollos, who were now side-by-side, speaking softly to each other.

Warrior Warkan trailed them, riding a mount nearly as intimidating and austere as the warrior himself. Warkan and his granite-colored warhorse towered over all the company, both wearing constant set scowls. Quick-tempered and one to never take back-talk from anyone, Warkan was a natural leader. But under the Head-Master Sword, he followed orders well.

The light-hearted and witty Warrior Hazerk rode next in line. Like Warkan, he was broad and strong. Though, he hummed a soft tune into the bleak morning. His coppery-colored warhorse arched his neck and had a spring in his step, not unlike his master.

At the tail of the company, young Warrior Eelyne traveled on his sorrel just behind Alexa, leading the sweet-tempered pack mule. As boastful as he must have felt to be a part of such an important mission, he didn't speak of it, knowing he was less experienced than most there. He had an innocent air about him and seemed to have much to prove, but Alexa knew outside appearances were sometimes deceiving. She could see deeper. He was needed here.

The soft, pattering drizzle bounced off the riders' eyelashes and slid down their noses, slowly dampening their cloaks. The low rumble of thunder in the distance promised more severe weather. The riders were quiet. The awkwardness of being thrust into traveling with new acquaintances—practically strangers—had yet to be dispelled.

The silence of the group was much to Bryan's delight. Out in front, he felt as if he was leading a legion off to war. His heart lightened at the thought. However, when he turned to survey his grand army, his fantasy melted away. It was merely a small crew following him, which unfortunately consisted of Alexandra. He rolled his eyes at his thoughts and told himself for the hundredth time that this mission was of extreme importance, probably more so than leading the multitudes; and, he should be thrilled at the opportunity.

Looking to the east, he saw the faint glow of Fordorn in the early morning. The city never completely slept, but the light told that it was awakening from its slumber. As much as he esteemed Fordorn, his heart leapt at the thought of leaving everything familiar behind.

Keeping a steady pace, they stopped only once for a quick lunch in a grove, providing them protection from the rain. They ate mostly in silence, with only paltry attempts at friendly conversation.

Later, pushing his hood aside, Bryan stole a glance over his shoulder to spy on Alexa; to make sure she was in no trouble, as he had not yet enforced his Sword-Guard proximity on her. But his carefully planned glance was met by a steady gaze from her. Startled at seeing her already looking at him, his curious features turned to a cold glower. In return, she narrowed her eyes and stared rigidly at him. From beneath her hood, her wicked sapphire eyes seemed to brighten intensely and pierce him with uneasiness. He turned and gave Dragon a reassuring pat. "Her blood is black," he muttered. "She'll be the death of us."

Prince Alkin perked up. "Did you say something, Sword Bryan?" He rode Sapharan up next to Dragon.

"No."

"Just grumbling, I suppose," Alkin concluded. "You know you should lighten up a bit. Life would be a lot easier."

Bryan grunted, "Tell that to Miss Alexandra."

The Prince gazed at the Master Sword for a moment before replying, "Perhaps, it's more a case of 'you get what you give,' Master Sword?"

Bryan didn't respond.

As the day waned, the thunderstorm came and passed, and the atmosphere filled with a warm breeze that gently brushed their faces. When night fell, the sky cleared into a brilliant, clear midnight blue. The company set up camp at the base of a cluster of boulders. Hazerk took kindling collected from a nearby grove and hummed an upbeat tune as he built a fire large enough to scare anything that may have been lurking and scheming.

For the evening meal, the three warriors sat close to the fire with Prince Alkin. The four laughed and jested, finally breaking the skulking uneasiness.

Apollos stood a distance off, silently gazing at the stars. Alexa watched him from her spot on a rock next to the tethered horses. The unicorn's coat gave off a chilling, ethereal glow. His crystal horn caught the firelight and cast shards of glittering light all around him. He held his head high and moved as if he was counting the stars…or perhaps reading them. He paced through the damp grasses alone and muttering to himself.

Looking over, she spotted the Master Sword sitting on a log by himself, absently shoveling food into his mouth. *I wonder why he separates himself from the warriors if he wants that life so much.* The Sword paused his eating when he spotted her watching. She looked away.

That night, it was cool. Bryan unfurled himself from his blankets and relieved Hazerk from watch. It was quiet. The Master Sword didn't suspect any trouble this early in the trip, yet one could never be sure. He paced around the dimly lit campsite; he found it helped him stay more alert.

In several days, they would come to a forest road. There was a small town just outside of it. They would make a brief stop there. Bryan thought it wise to replenish certain supplies before they started the long trek through the forest.

He looked around to his companions. The warriors were out cold. Alkin was curled up, sound asleep and peaceful. The glow of the fire lit his features almost majestically. Apollos was nowhere in sight, but Bryan felt assured he had good reason to be off by himself. The unicorn could take care of himself. The Sword looked over to the tethered horses and Alexa. He stopped pacing.

The girl looked distressed even in her sleep. Her features contorted while incoherent whispers streamed from her lips. Zhan stood watch over her, and he gave his mistress a gentle nudge with his muzzle, as if he desired to rouse her from her restless sleep.

Feeling as if he should perhaps wake her, Bryan stepped over to where Alexa lay twisted in her blanket. When he approached, Zhan tossed up his head, flattening his ears and snapping his teeth toward the Master Sword. "It's okay, skinny man. I'm just checking on her," Bryan whispered, holding out a hand for the horse to sniff. His reassurance seemed to calm Zhan and the horse allowed him to approach.

Bryan briefly wondered if listening to Alexa's mutterings would help him decipher the enigmatic girl. But he could make nothing of the nonsensical words and placed a heavy hand on her shoulder to give her a gentle shake. She groaned and tossed around. "Wake up, girl!" he urged and tried another shake.

Alexa jerked up, her eyes wide with fear, and sweat trickling down her brow. Locks of her black hair were torn from her usually tight braid.

Bryan, kneeling on the ground, leaned back as she turned on him, her disconcerted features shifting into a smoldering smirk. He narrowed his eyes, knowing exactly what she was going to say before it even passed her lips.

"So, you enjoy watching people sleep, huh?" She untangled herself from her blanket.

"No." Bryan stood.

She stumbled to a stand and straightened herself, finding her composure. Even in her defiant stance, she looked small compared to the Master Sword.

"With all that noise you were making, I didn't want the others thinking we could be…up to something. If you get my drift." He smiled a genuine boyish smile, knowing it would incite her. It just had been too good of an opportunity to pass up.

She snorted and hastily brushed a stray hair from her face. "Not even in your dreams, Master Sword." She stalked off to fetch her water pouch.

"But in *your* dreams." He chuckled and received another murderous glare from her. He let out a loud laugh, then realizing his noise, he stifled it. "What would make you think that *I* would want *you*—a scrawny, little, haughty girl like yourself? That's the funniest thing I've ever heard." With a snicker, he turned to warm himself over the fire. He could feel her icy stare on his back. It shot right through to his fingertips, and they began to ache, as if frostbit. The fire felt like it wasn't providing any kind of heat at all. He shivered; *magic*…

A minute later, Alexa stood by him, holding her hands over the glowing coals as they gazed into the pit. "I'm sorry that you don't like me. You aren't exactly my choice of company either," she said.

Bryan rubbed his hands together, the stinging cold dissipating as Alexa calmed. He sighed resignedly and said, "I think we need to call a truce." She looked up at him, surprise across her narrow features. He continued to talk to the coals, "Whether either of us likes it or not, we have to work with each other. And it looks as if it's going to be for a while…and probably not an easy one at that." He stopped and raised his eyes to look her straight in the face. She stared at him with an arched eyebrow. "We just have to get along," he pressed on. "I don't like you having to do this job any more than you do."

"I do want to do it," she protested.

"I guess, my problem is not so much *you* as it is your smug attitude."

"There you go. *You were* talking about a truce… And I'm not smug," she snapped.

"All right, all right. We work together. I won't harass you…more than required. And you won't be so self-righteous. Sound good?" he said.

"Fine."

They shook hands, briefly.

"Now," Bryan started, "Speaking of dreams, what was all that about?"

"Nothing I prefer to discuss."

"Fine." He let it hang for a moment, and then persisted, "Magical intuition?" She shrugged. There was a moment of silence, and he ventured, "Do you dream like that often?"

"No. Definitely not like that. But, like I said, I don't want to talk about it."

"Do you have an idea what you're looking for?" he asked.

"No."

Then with an accusing edge, he said, "Do you even know

what we're up against? Can you wield this so-called counter-magic?"

"No." She let out an exasperated sigh. "I don't know anything…yet."

"Well, how in all of Eetharum did that naiad pull your name out?" It was meant as a question of puzzlement, but it had come out rather offensive. She turned a pair of cool eyes on him. They glittered dangerously in the firelight. "I mean…just how is someone who knows less than others about this whole ordeal supposed to help?" His tongue tripped over the words in his attempt to reconcile his already forgotten truce.

"I don't know." There was a falter in her voice. "But I was thinking maybe it has something to do with my blood more so than my abilities." She didn't look up at him. She was embarrassed she was allowing him to see she wasn't as strong as she hoped for others to perceive her. Alexa despised weakness, and had always prided herself on her skills, especially because women in Eetharum rarely practiced her fighting techniques. Female warriors were an eastern thing. But some inclination told her it wasn't her being a female warrior that brought her here to do this job, as she had originally thought. It went deeper than that… The dream had led her to believe this much. But, then again, it was just a dream and nightmares often revealed a dreamer's worst fears.

Bryan didn't answer, too deeply lost in thought. He felt relieved in learning that she knew she needed help from others. She would be less apt to fail knowing she needn't do this alone, rather than being too confident in her abilities, for that would have most definitely brought her closer and quicker to trouble. He had thought this was the reckless path she was on, but he suddenly contemplated whether he should change his mind about her… He found, however, he was not ready for that quite yet; though, he would give her the benefit of the doubt for now.

Alexa took the Sword's drawn silence as a subtle hint he did not want the conversation to continue. *Fine.* She clenched her teeth. She didn't feel like talking to him, anyway, and opening up to him would be like throwing herself over a cliff. She shifted her weight and said tersely, "Well, I'm going back to bed."

Bryan straightened his stance next to her and nodded, still

letting his silence reign. But the girl acted reluctant to leave. "All right," he said, then pretended to survey the site in order to pass the suddenly awkward moment. *Why isn't she leaving?* He grew impatient, not understanding her hesitation. She stood next to him, almost fidgeting on the spot, so he turned his steady gaze on her. "Okay," he pressed, in a hurry to pass the weird moment.

"Well…night." Alexa backed away and sauntered over to her staked out spot. Settling herself with her back toward him, she pulled the blanket up to her neck and heaved a sigh. Except for the night creatures' soft sounds, it was quiet.

Her dream had been disturbing. She couldn't bring herself to feel sleepy or even to close her eyes. She stole a furtive glance over her shoulder. Why? She didn't know. The Master Sword moved slowly around the site and was currently on the opposite end. She watched him by the light of the fire as he moved with near gracefulness. Not a sound came from his footfalls. He was so tall, broad, and strong. The metal on the hilt of his sword and scabbard glistened in the low light of the fire. He held himself upright and proud. He was the epitome of what a Master Sword should be.

As she watched, an unbidden thought crept into her mind, one that she immediately regretted. She turned over to look the other way. Feeling vulnerable to her own thoughts, she became furious, as if she had somehow betrayed herself. She absolutely disliked the cocky Sword. Dislike wasn't even a strong enough word. But—she couldn't even bear to think it now—she had just looked upon him with desire. She had admired how soft his unruly, dark curls were in the light; how his square jaw was shaped so perfectly; how his bright azure eyes seemed to radiate when he looked at her. He seemed so *deadly* and *appealing* altogether. She shuddered and glared into the dark, staring unblinkingly at the hooves of the horses tethered nearby. It had only been a childish fancy that had surfaced in her for one split moment. A trait she disliked in other young women her age. One that she never—or would ever—let take over. She refused to be that way; a silly, dumb, flirtatious woman—weak. She was a warrior.

She reached a hand up to pet the lowered muzzle of Zhan to

distract her wandering mind; and, she soon drifted off to a restless sleep, where she dreamt of wielding the mysterious counter-magic.

CHAPTER ELEVEN

Several days after leaving Fordorn, the company's trek through the farmlands had been uneventful and, for that, successful.

They reached a town bordering Shelkite's vast southern forest. Charad forest was uninhabited except for a few secluded woodsmen and a single lumber company located across the eastern border in the small neighboring country of Burgah.

Sword Bryan halted the company just outside the town's boundaries. "There's no need for all of us to go parading down the main street, especially with the Prince of Shelkite. It might cause unnecessary curiosity, or worse, suspicion. I'll pick up the supplies we need quickly so we can be on our way. Warrior Hazerk, you'll join me." His voice held an unquestionable command. Hazerk nodded and guided his big chestnut mount next to Dragon.

"The rest of you stay together and try not to do anything that would bring attention." He stopped and looked at Alkin, a little uneasy. "Of course, my prince, I don't mean to be bossing you around. You can do whatever you wish." Alkin shrugged, a careless smile across his features, and Bryan nodded. "Good. Warrior Warkan and Warrior Eelyne, I'm putting you both in charge of Alexa and Prince Alkin's protection while I'm away. All right, Warrior Hazerk, let's go." He nudged and spun Dragon around.

"Wait," Alexa called.

Bryan sighed and rolled his eyes upward. How did he even think he could get away without her having something inane to say? He turned Dragon back around, lightly bumping Hazerk's mount in the process. "Yes, Alexa?" He tried not to sound exasperated, but failed.

Alexa heeled Zhan to stand in front of the others. Her face held sudden uncertainty upon seeing everyone's expectant features. "I would like to pick up some things of my own," she said with resolve.

"We'll be picking up everything you'll need," Bryan replied, with an inward groan; she was probably just irritated for not being his choice partner to go with him.

Alexa stared at him with a challenging gaze. Dragon tossed his head with a loud snort and stomped one large front hoof as if to show his master's impatience for him.

Everyone waited.

"What?" Bryan huffed. "What is it you need?"

Swiftly, Alexa reached behind her back for her weapon. Surprised at her sudden movement and taking it for an act of violence, Bryan had his sword drawn before she even had a chance to pull out one of her arrows.

"Relax, Master Sword, I'm not going to attack you," she scoffed and held out a slender arrow in her hand.

Bryan snorted and sheathed his sword.

The others stared in shock at them, unable to register exactly what had happened. Prince Alkin blinked and stared at Bryan, dumbfounded. For a moment, he had thought the two of them were coming to blows. It hadn't escaped his notice that they always spoke to each other as if they thought the other was some kind of vermin. He shook away a silly image of two rats with Bryan and Alexa's heads battling each other, and tried to restrain an amused smile, but a confused Eelyne still noticed.

The company watched, speechless, as Bryan reluctantly maneuvered Dragon up next to Zhan.

Alexa handed him the arrow. "I need more of these. I don't want just any arrow. It has to be like this," she said. "I lost a lot of them fighting the howlers."

Bryan examined the arrow. The shaft of it was long and slender and of a peculiar hard, black wood, the blue fletching attached at a precise angle, the tip obsidian and sharpened to a lethal point. "Very nice." He handed it back. "I'll do my best."

"No, you don't understand. I want to pick them out. If they don't have this specific type, I want to choose a kind just as worthy."

He snatched the arrow back. "Like I said, I'll do my best. And I'm not sure why you didn't think of this before." With that, he turned Dragon away from her zapping eyes, which were narrowed with such intensity it was as if they were the only things holding her fury back.

He looked over his shoulder. "You stay," he ordered.

She watched with an angered set jaw as the handsome Master Sword and Warrior Hazerk—with his bouncing red curls that humorously matched his mount's coat—cantered away until they disappeared into the streets of town. She let out a low, frustrated growl.

★★★★

Melea had kept her promise to the peculiar, half-blood witch. Since the company's departure, she went about her daily duties with a clandestine eye open to anything out of the ordinary. So far, everything seemed normal.

The servant let out a tiresome sigh as she flicked some dust off the mantle in Prince Alkin's mother's room. She fluffed the pillows. The castle echoed with emptiness. Most of the Swords were now absent, having gone on missions of their own. Only Sword JaVin was left to watch over the castle, making sure things ran smoothly in Alkin's absence.

She stood in front of the full-length mirror in Lady Adama's room and patted down a stray bronze-gold lock. She rolled her eyes at the thought of Sword JaVin. He was old and grumpy and spent most of his time flirting with the Head-Maid. Not that he ignored his duties, it was just painfully annoying.

Melea leaned in closer to inspect her features. Her face was round and smooth, doll-like. Unfortunate. She turned away in disgust. She wished Sword Bryan thought her attractive, as many seemed to. She missed him a great deal and struggled not to think of him nearly every moment. She threw her duster down in frustration and plopped down on the feather bed, yanking her bootlaces tight. All she wanted was to be near him again, to try again to get him to care for her...to want her.

He never seemed to notice how much time she spent cleaning his room. It meant a lot when he paused his duties to speak with her. Many times, she had wandered into the handsome Sword's bedchamber with a duster or with tea, hoping he would one time take her in his arms. But he never did.

All she had now was an old, grumpy Sword, who liked to boss her around, and a Head-Maid who sent her on pointless errands just to get her out of the way so she and JaVin could be alone. Of course, there were the other servants in the castle. She got along fine with them, but she was by far the brightest and had nothing in common with any of them.

But then, she hadn't thought about her second most favorite person next to Bryan that lived in Fordorn's castle: Lady Dorsa. She was always bouncing around the castle with a friendly smile gracing that perfect face of hers. She was a pleasant girl, and Melea enjoyed the younger woman's company. Dorsa was one of those rare people who were always happy, she—

Melea's thoughts came to a stop. Something *was* awry. Her brow furrowed as she realized she had not seen Lady Dorsa out and about lately. That was unusual.

Melea looked around the room, contemplating. Night had already settled in Fordorn, and the room was flickering with the life of candles, oil lamps, and sconces.

She jolted with a sudden chill of another realization. Lady Adama was not in her bedchamber. Melea stood, her eyes roving in curiosity about the room.

"My lady?" she called, searching the adjoining suite where she had thought she'd been, and found it empty. The servant paused, puzzled. This was odd. Lady Adama never left her room. Never. She ate and slept here, and if she needed to speak with any company, they came to her. It was only on a rare occasion she would leave and eat with her son and daughter. The castle help had concluded that her seclusion was the effect of the great loss she felt from her husband Prince Izsum's death six years prior.

Melea hurried out of the chamber. To be reassured, she would just go find them. She didn't want to seem overzealous about her secret job, and she certainly did not want to seem panicky or paranoid either, but this was something that begged not to be disregarded.

★★★★

"You know it's smarter this way. Better not to bring attention to ourselves nor needless worry to the locals." Prince Alkin was trying to console an irritated Alexa a little while later. He squatted down next to her, where she sat on a rock hunched over, continuously flipping her dagger at a mutilated patch of grass between her feet. She stared at the overturned dirt, ignoring the Prince, her frustration evident. "That will come soon enough if we have to seek civilian recruits…" he trailed off. Then, looking into the hazy, late afternoon horizon wistfully, he added, "But hopefully, we'll be able to resolve this mess before it turns into a full-fledged war, and there will be no need for civilians to fight."

After a moment, he sighed at his failure of eliciting a pleasant response and stood and walked back to Warkan and Eelyne, who were watering the horses in a nearby creek. Eelyne seemed to keep his distance from the older warrior on the count that it appeared he was frightened by him. But even Alkin was a little intimidated by Warkan's size and constant scowl.

The warriors gave a reverent nod as he approached. "Has anyone seen Apollos?" he inquired. Alkin always made it a point to speak to his subjects as equals. It wasn't in his demeanor or ideals to use his royal blood to make others feel insignificant, and the warriors in the company had seemed to take to him quickly because of this.

Eelyne spoke, "He said he couldn't resist a tasty-looking patch of clover nearby."

"Did he say when he'd return?"

Warkan scratched his square chin and turned his austere eyes onto Eelyne.

"He'll meet us at the entry into Charad," the young warrior said, giving his sorrel mount a firm pat. The warhorse turned and nuzzled his master fondly.

Alkin nodded and sighed and began to pace. He was mostly concerned with Alexa's sulky attitude and not the whereabouts of the clever unicorn, but he didn't want to voice his unease with the others. Alexa acted immature sometimes, throwing little tantrums.

And other times she was highly rational, seeming almost otherworldly in her mannerisms. He wondered if he should have given the girl any power concerning the company. However, what would stop them from objecting to her if they decided she was leading them faultily? The Prince hoped it wouldn't come to that— to overriding her. Who knew what she might do? What magic she knew…

Alkin needed her as an ally. He couldn't afford another magical adversary. He knew the history of wizards and witches, and knew they weren't particularly a peaceful or likable lot. And though he trusted Apollos' judgment regarding Alexa, he was feeling apprehensive after seeing her childish, pouting party. He prayed her blood wouldn't turn bad. She was still young and had yet to mature into herself.

He paused his pacing and stared off into the hilly horizon to the north, back toward his home, feeling sad at the prospect of a war. *Well, she'll grow, learn, and no doubt become powerful. Hopefully, we will influence her for the good.* He sighed at his resolution.

He would just continue to trust her as Apollos did. After all, she was only *half* witch. And if a pure creature such as a unicorn could trust a descendant of an ancient enemy, then certainly Alkin could trust her. He *had* to trust her and her witch intuition, as she called it. He had no choice. Or at least, he knew he had to trust he'd made the right decision in listening to the Guidance Naiad.

Alkin glanced at the girl. She continued to pitch her dagger at the dirt and pull it back out with a set scowl on her face. He heaved a sigh that brimmed thick with many unspoken worries.

At twilight, the mounted silhouettes of Bryan and Hazerk appeared, moving leisurely from the southeast. As they approached, the group rose from their places around the campfire to greet them.

Alexa had calmed, and she looked on the forthcoming men with anticipation for her new arrows. Now relaxed, she felt a slight qualm for her behavior earlier. The Prince had always been so kind to her, and she had made a fool of herself, not only for the way she had acted but for forgetting to replenish her supplies. She hadn't apologized, and decided she wouldn't, but would instead settle to kick herself mentally and endeavor to rein in her problematic witch temper better in the future.

Bryan and Hazerk each had a satchel with goods and other supplies strapped to their saddles. Bryan also carried a long, slender object wrapped in a cloth across his lap.

Hazerk steered his chestnut mount to a stop next to Alexa. He dismounted and pointed to the satchel. "Your weapons, my lady." He gave her a slight bow and a devilish grin.

Feeling mocked, Alexa fumbled to open the satchel self-consciously. She drew out a bundle of elegant arrows, much like her own, but not exactly. She examined them, running her fingers over the smooth, black shafts and fingering the sharp-tipped arrowheads, and then eyed the feathers, checking all the angles for any flaw, unaware of the others' keen observation of her.

"Will they work?" Bryan asked as he watched. With her brow furrowed in deep concentration and her head cocked close to the arrows, the girl looked up, startled out of her thoughts. Her features flickered from a serious focus back to her normal countenance. But Bryan thought he caught something in between the transform. His own brows furrowed as he tried to decipher it. Her dark blue eyes, once squinted in scrutiny, had widened. But in one brisk moment, he caught a glint of remorse. Or so he thought. Perhaps it was the breaking of a spirit. Whatever it was, it was gone now, and her wicked sapphire eyes had returned and stared him down with the same acid power they always held.

"They will be fine," she said, then added, "Thank you."

He nodded and dismounted, relocating the slender package as he did.

The others, who had been watching in apprehensive stillness, let out a relieved breath. Alkin, Eelyne, and Warkan sauntered back to the fire as Alexa continued to inspect the arrows. Bryan and Hazerk began to repack the satchels, discussing travel plans and the like.

As the company sat down around the simmering coals and ate their evening meal, the sun set beyond the hills, whispering its goodbye with a lavender-hued horizon. They sat in a companionable silence, letting each have his thoughts, for they all knew the real journey would begin the next morning.

CHAPTER TWELVE

They rose early. The Master Sword was the first up since he had been on watch. They packed and made ready to enter the wood. The Prince and the warriors started single file toward the entrance to Charad Forest, their horses snorting in anticipation of the coming blustery day.

The wind had picked up through the night and now whipped with increasing speed over the grassy plains, rippling the green like a soft blanket. When it reached the outer trees of the forest, it tossed their tops as if they were mere flowers in a breeze.

Bryan waited, holding a prancing Dragon's reins, as he watched a kneeling Alexa fumble around in the small sack she always carried. She was unmindful of the others' missing presence. Zhan stood with her, his head over his mistress' shoulder, curious of her doings. Though, he soon lost interest and tried to spin around in an attempt to follow the others, but it was to no avail; he merely received a sharp reprimand to stand still.

"Misplace your crystal ball?" Bryan asked. Alexa's head shot up, startling an already jittery Zhan. She glared at the Master Sword. He chuckled and held up his hands in submission. "Just joking, relax."

Dragon bobbed his head, his black eyes glinting playfully. He tugged at the reins and flung his head over to whinny to his departing fellows.

"Come on. They're already almost a half a mile up the road." He turned to mount Dragon. The burly horse pranced in place, swinging his hindquarters around, but the Master Sword settled in the saddle with ease.

Alexa glanced up from her pack, "Oh, they are not. Don't be so impatient," she retorted. She fumbled for another second and then finally tied up the bag. Straightening and flipping her long, raven braid over her shoulder, she attached the bag to Zhan's saddle.

Bryan sighed and rolled his eyes lightheartedly. The fine blustery day had put him into a somewhat genial mood. He guided Dragon to face south. The horse pulled at the reins, but he held him, turning in his saddle to regard Alexa, and exhaled, a little exasperated. "Come on, Sand Queen! We're burning daylight!" he hollered above another gust of wind.

Alexa situated her things and prepared to mount. Zhan pawed at the earth and chewed his bit, tossing his silver-white mane as the wind whirled about him. She placed her foot in the stirrup and gracefully swung into the saddle. No more than a second before she hit the leather seat, Zhan sprinted off, neighing loud and clear to alert the others of his coming.

They zipped by the standing Dragon and Bryan in a whirl of light and dark and continued to race down the path. She glanced over her shoulder and cracked a devilish grin at the Master Sword before turning back.

Bryan lingered only a moment to watch the girl's long, raven braid bounce in the breeze and her willowy body move as one with the horse. But before Dragon would allow his master to watch a second longer, he snorted noisily, stomped a large hoof, and shot off after them with his own thudding four-beat gait.

Upon reaching the chatting warriors and prince, Alexa reined Zhan to the front of the company. A moment later, Bryan pulled Dragon down to an exhilarated walk. The horses were puffing with excitement. She looked over to the Sword, who was already looking at her, and said, "If you must know, I was rearranging my herbs."

"Herbs?" Bryan let out an amused chuckle.

"Yes, ones you so naively disregarded when the howlers got the better of you."

He raised an eyebrow. "Oh. So, now the Sand Queen is an expert herbalist…hmm."

Alexa smiled, taking the banter with ease. "I may be from the desert, but it doesn't mean we don't have markets. And don't discredit the desert; many of its plants have amazing qualities. My father believes the best healing comes from the High Power and nature itself. So, he made sure his children knew the basic kinds. I just took it a step further than my brothers and actually applied the knowledge. Anyway, with all the jostling from riding, I didn't want them to mix or even touch. It taints them." She shrugged.

"I see." Bryan looked ahead and gazed at the massive outer trees of Charad Forest.

Prince Alkin trotted Sapharan over. "Sword Bryan, we're entering the forest by the Lumberman's Path. Apollos is supposed to be meeting up with us."

"Yes, my prince."

They rode to the edge and stopped and waited. The wind had not let up; it raced through the trees and tossed them with such exuberance it was almost frightening. However, the clouds overhead were white and fluffy, and the sky a brilliant blue; no sign of bad weather.

"Once we get into the forest, the wind won't be so bad," Warkan said as another gust blasted him in the face. The others nodded.

"Yeah," Hazerk joked, "you're such a lightweight, we were afraid of you blowing away on us."

Everyone except Warkan laughed.

While they waited, Bryan sat alone facing the forest, resting his hands on the pommel of his saddle, deep in thought, far away from the bantering company. He sensed another ride up beside him. Glancing over, he saw Warrior Eelyne hesitantly approach him on his sorrel. He halted his warhorse next to Dragon. The two horses touched noses. Dragon snorted and arched his neck arrogantly. Eelyne stole a wary glance at the Head-Master Sword, who had returned his pensive gaze to the woods.

"What is it, Warrior Eelyne? Something on your mind?" Bryan looked over at the young man and smiled. He watched as some of the unease in him dissipated.

"Master Sword?" he said.

"Yes."

"I was wondering, well, I know it's a lot to ask, especially from a man like yourself, but I was wondering if you could coach me in some swordsmanship tactics?"

Alexa, noting the conversation and curious, rode up within hearing range.

Bryan looked over to Eelyne. "How old are you?"

"Eighteen, Head-Master Sword."

"Just call me Sword Bryan."

"Eighteen, Sword Bryan."

"Well, Warrior Eelyne, you're old enough to have already completed your basic training. At this age, you should already be good at sword handling, if you listened to your instructors."

"Yes, I know." Eelyne fiddled with his reins. "My swordsmanship is good enough, I guess. But your sword tactics are a legend in the camp and all over Eetharum, too. I've heard you could beat Galefen. Just a couple of tips from the greatest swordsman would last me a lifetime." He finished with a more confident air, a hopeful look across his features.

Galefen was a legendary warrior from the Lost War era, his feats so grand, no one knew anymore if he had truly existed.

Alexa stared stunned at Bryan, unable to believe that he was a legend. She'd had no idea, and had never heard of him before, at least she thought she hadn't.

The Master Sword leaned back in his saddle and smiled knowingly, though there was no trace of arrogance. He rubbed his unshaven chin with his fingertips. "First off, Eelyne, let me straighten something out."

Eelyne and Alexa hung on his pause.

"I don't believe a man can be a legend if he's never proven himself where it counts. I've only ever been in contests. It's true I've won from the west coast to the east." He grinned, a trace of conceit now showing. "But I believe that to use the word great, it has to be something deeper than a mere contest. No matter how trying a match is. And Galefen earned that through courage and selflessness. Never forget a war hero for who he is and what he stands for."

"Yes, Master Sword," Eelyne said with understanding.

Alexa continued to stare dumbfounded at the Master Sword. She still could not ever recall hearing his name in contests, and she was certain she and her brothers had attended a highly anticipated sword match in Sansdella several years back...

"Does that mean—" Eelyne began in disappointment.

"No." Bryan smiled. "I would enjoy very much to give you

pointers during our travels whenever we have time."

The younger warrior grinned and patted his sorrel with enthusiasm.

The Master Sword turned to the eavesdropping Alexa, who bit her thumbnail, lost in thought. "And, you." He startled her out of her reverie, and she jerked to attention. "I got you something."

"Me?" she asked, incredulous.

Bryan shifted in his saddle to untie the slender package he had brought the day before from the town. He guided Dragon over to Zhan and handed it to her. She took it, unsure of how to react.

"You need to tame some of that spitfire and learn better sword fighting yourself." He cleared his throat, "Um, because you're in dire need of it." Alexa flashed him an indignant look as she unwrapped the slender weapon. "I'll teach you both. You can practice with each other."

Eelyne could barely contain his excitement. "This is great. Thank you, Master Sword."

Alexa calmly tore the cloth packaging away and looked the weapon over. It was simply made, but perfect. She pulled the long, slender blade from the sheath. A sweet ringing sound issued forth as she drew it. She held it upright in front of her, the silver blade flashing in the sunlight. The sword was lightweight and straight, woman-like in its appearance. The hilt was plain but beautiful in its simplicity. She ran her fingers over it, careful of the sharp edges, marveling at the gift, and felt a warmth grow inside of her. She placed the sword horizontally just below the hilt on her fingers. It balanced out perfectly.

"Excellent craftsmanship," Bryan said.

"Yes," Alexa answered, awestruck. Her fingers were almost caressing the weapon when she abruptly stopped upon seeing a recognizable insignia engraved on the hilt. She looked up to Bryan, astounded. "This is a Galeon sword."

"Yes." Bryan shifted in his saddle. "Don't get too excited. It wasn't the most expensive, but Galeonics never make cheap weapons. Besides, I figured you'd need one. All you have is that bow. What would you've done in close contact battles?"

"My dagger."

"Not good enough." Bryan turned and gestured at Eelyne. "You'll need a Galeon sword to match his when you practice. Isn't that right, Warrior Eelyne? Your sword should be Galeon made. That's all Shelkite outfits its warriors with. Nothing better."

"Right," he confirmed.

"Thank you." Alexa stumbled over the words.

Bryan raised an eyebrow and bumped Dragon, circling the black warhorse to face the other direction. "Oh, don't thank me. I expect to be repaid in full." He clucked to his mount, and the horse trotted over to Alkin, who was now conversing with Apollos, who had reappeared.

Alkin gestured for the group to gather before the forest road entrance. Everyone assembled in a semi-circle facing Apollos. The unicorn stood tall; gusty winds played almost passionately with his opalescent mane and tail, and the sun shone ever-so-slightly through his prismatic horn, causing small color-spots to dance across the waving grasses. His fine, angular face was held high and copper hooves set square; he studied the group with his intent, deep chocolate-colored eyes. The sight of such a magnificent creature rendered them all speechless.

"Just a word of caution before we go," the unicorn began. He waited for a reaction from anyone. When no one stirred, he continued, "Everyone should be aware and on guard while we go through Charad. The main road we'll be using is well-traveled and relatively safe," he paused, and a disgruntled look came over his equine features, "except, of course, for the occasional human scum that pillage travelers." He tossed his mane in his indignation, "But I know you're all good enough warriors to deal with that. We're more in danger from creatures that have siphoned over from Carthorn. Since Charad Forest connects to Carthorn in the east, some strange creatures may lurk about. And I'm not talking about a cougar. Although Carthorn is a wondrous place, it has its dark side. And more often than not, that's what likes to pay travelers a visit. So, just be vigilant. That's all." He stopped and turned away as if there was no need for any response. He began trotting gracefully toward the forest road.

Alexa looked over at her companions. Eelyne and the Prince showed no reaction, albeit Eelyne looked a little apprehensive.

Sword Bryan actually smiled at her; though, it seemed more like a
smirk. Maybe he was hoping something would eat her. She
watched the three follow Apollos. She glanced over at Warkan in
hesitation.

The brawny man rolled his eyes. Kicking his horse into a trot,
he said as he passed, "I wouldn't worry too much about it,
sweetheart."

Hazerk followed close behind. He grinned. "It'd be amazing if
we saw a griffin or something, wouldn't it?" He motioned for her
to follow.

She watched as the others entered the forest and began to
disappear down the furrowed path. Getting a sick feeling in the pit
of her gut, she sighed and puffed out her cheeks to let the air
slowly escape. She wasn't sure if she was ready for this and didn't
feel as confident as she had been, and hated to admit she was
nervous, but despite her reluctant feelings, she squeezed Zhan's
sides, and they followed the others.

They traveled along the wagon-rutted road all afternoon and
well into dusk, progressing deeper and deeper into the heart of the
ancient forest. They rode in relative silence. Each held their own
awe of the forest to themselves—that is until something caught
their eye and excitement seemed to overtake them, and then they'd
break the silence and exclaim, "Look at that!" or "Isn't that
amazing!" or "What in the demon's name is that?"

The monstrous trees towered high over the travelers, their
girths thick with age. Their tops swayed wildly in the roaring wind
but never proved to be a threat. The smells of the wood were
enchanting and brought comfort. The coalescence of cedars, pines,
ferns, and wildflowers made an aroma as calming as a lover's
touch.

Colorful songbirds twittered and flitted around them. Apollos'
presence seemed to have an unearthly effect on the forest and its
residents. The wildlife could not help but to investigate the
unicorn. Handsome foxes paused for a long look, and curious
bunnies, deer, and a bobcat all chanced a glance. Even once, from
atop a branch, a yellowed-eyed panther gazed mildly down at
them. And once, Hazerk swore he saw a phoenix fly low through

the trees—though, the others ridiculed him and told him it was just an eagle. But the forest beasts were not the only creatures engrossed by Apollos. Even the trees seemed to pause their wild wind dancing, so they could have a chance to caress the unicorn's snowy white coat as he passed.

Later in the afternoon, they come upon other travelers making their way north; a single wagon pulled by two stocky oxen. A heavy-set man walked alongside the beasts carrying a walking stick; a peddler, no doubt. His plain-looking daughter rode in the front of the wagon. The two passed the company with no words, just a good-day nod from the man and a smile accompanied with a friendly blown kiss—directed at the blushing Eelyne—from the maiden.

At Apollos' advanced notice, Sword Bryan ordered the Prince and Alexa to put their hoods up and chins down. He didn't feel it necessary for Alkin to show his face in case he was recognized, and wanted to be on the safe side and hide Alexa, too; for it might look a little suspicious to see a young woman riding alone with a group of men.

Apollos made sure he was unseen. Invisible was not quite the word. He could have easily slipped into the woods and waited until they had passed, but he preferred to stay close. So, with just a blue-tinted glint from his horn and a slight flicker, he blended into the background of the forest. He simply faded from sight, taking on the shapes and hues of the objects he passed.

Alexa couldn't outright distinguish him, but if she looked closely, she could see his ever-so-slight movement. Of course, it could have just been the breeze blowing through the forest.

Before dusk, Sword Bryan decided by the aching in his legs and back that it was time to call it a day. Apollos had gone deeper into the woods off the road and found a small clearing that would suffice for the night. They followed his lead, and everyone dismounted with a groan.

"Ahh," Hazerk sighed, cracking his stiff back. "Let's get a fire going, my bum's numb." He and Eelyne set to work, while Warkan took care of the horses, untacking, rubbing down, and graining them.

Once she looked after Zhan, Alexa plopped down next to the

fire and stretched gratefully. "Ah, not so fast, Sand Queen." The Master Sword came to stand over her shoulder. "I think you and Eelyne have your first lesson to get started with."

She stared at him with some disbelief, and then shrugged, "All right." She hopped up, a little too enthusiastic, and went to retrieve her new weapon. "I'm thirsty. Would it be all right if I had a drink first, sir?" she asked with a bit of mockery, as if she was a humble student asking a huge favor of a revered master; which actually *was* the case, although it did not occur to her just then.

Apollos spoke up, "There's a small creek down the way. Alkin and I will get water." And he and the Prince, carrying the water pouches, set off into the dark, the unicorn's natural glow fading into the night.

"All right, pupils!" Bryan clapped his hands together; there was a devilish glint in his eye. Alexa and Eelyne faced him with slightly anxious looks. "Let's get started. No mercy!" He threw his head back and laughed. "This is going to be fun."

So, after warming up, they began. And Sword Bryan indeed proved himself to be unmerciful. They practiced hard, though they were tortured by the smell of dinner cooking and hot tea wafting through their little harbor in the woods. They practiced long after Apollos and Alkin had returned from the creek, and Alexa chanced a curious glance toward Apollos to watch the unicorn dip his horn into the water to purify it. But her peeping proved to be disastrous. She was struck hard on the thigh by the flat of Eelyne's sword. And when the others began to eat, Bryan still didn't stop drilling them until he felt his own stomach give a loud protest.

"All right!" He lowered his sword. "That's enough. I'm getting grouchy. Need to eat," he grunted. He stalked over to the fire and sat, the lesson ending abruptly.

"Humph, getting grouchy?" Alexa mumbled, but no one heard her. She went and sat alongside Eelyne by the crackling fire.

As everyone was hungrily shoving the salted meat into their mouths, Warkan looked up from his meal. "Well, by the looks of things, I certainly hope she doesn't have to face one-on-one combat with this wizard."

"What exactly is that supposed to mean?" she shot back icily.

Everyone paused their eating to stare at Warkan.

"What? I was just saying she's not…well…she's not exactly a seasoned swordswoman," he said.

"She's not *that* bad, Warrior Warkan." Bryan rolled his eyes, but his voice held a slight reprimand, for which Alexa was grateful. Though she didn't think of it at the time, later when she thought back, she felt flattered to have received such praise from the Master Sword.

"Uncalled for," Alkin stated.

"Sorry, Master Sword, my prince, Alexandra. I spoke out of place," Warkan apologized and returned to his plate.

"Also," Alkin said, "I want you all to choose carefully what you say from now on. I mean about the mission because even some trees have ears. Let's not say 'wizard' anymore, as not to prick any unwanted attention."

Once again, Warkan looked up from his meal; this time with disbelief in his eyes, staring at Alkin. "Pish!" he snorted with a laugh. "Forgive me, my prince, but what do you mean *ears?* You must mean the lumbermen are hiding and listening."

Alkin stopped chewing. "No, the trees. They can hear," he said, after he swallowed a mouthful of meat.

Warkan burst with sudden laughter, his face red and eyes squinty. He giggled, almost girlish-like. "Forgive me," he wheezed, "Old fairy tales, that's all that is." He chuckled some more and wiped his eyes.

"No! It's true," Eelyne said.

"Whatever, youngin'." Warkan disregarded him.

"I believe it," Hazerk said.

"Yeah, you would," Warkan mumbled. Hazerk ignored him.

"I heard a tale once of how the trees murdered a man," Bryan said, snatching everyone's attention.

"Trees murdering? They were pulling' your leg." Warkan cleared his throat, adding, "Um, Master Sword."

"Oh!" Hazerk clapped Warkan on the shoulder. "Have a little imagination. Head-Master Sword, I could do for a little story." He looked to his superior expectantly. Bryan ignored him.

"Tree spirits are very old. Some say not very wise, but I knew a few in the old days. They're called dryads," Apollos said. He was lying in a bed of leaves between Alexa and Alkin.

"What? You believe in tree spirits, too?" Warkan was incredulous.

Apollos' eyes glimmered in mischief, "You're asking a unicorn?"

Now, it was everyone else's turn to laugh.

"Well, that's different." Warkan attempted to save himself. "You're living, breathing. You have blood flowing through your veins." He turned to rap on the tree he was leaning on, "Trees don't. They have roots and leaves."

"You're probably safe saying that here," Apollos said, "but I warn you, don't go doing that if you're ever in Carthorn. Most of the trees in Charad have been harvested and planted. So, spirits don't reside in them. They only live in the trees born at the beginning of time. What's left of them are in Carthorn."

Warkan scratched his head. "Well, I don't intend to be waltzing through Carthorn any time soon."

"Apollos?" Alexa broke in.

"Yes."

"How old are you? Do you remember the old time with the magic?"

"Oh." The unicorn sighed, his equine features thoughtful. "Too old to count, or maybe I've forgotten. Even in my lifetime, I haven't known the wonders of the ancient world. When I was a colt, I knew only a few other mystic creatures," he answered, a little wistfully.

"Do you know my father? He's at least two-hundred-years-old," Alexa asked.

"No, I'm sorry to say I've never had the pleasure of meeting your father. I try to steer clear of wiz—I mean magic men, good or bad. Sorry." The unicorn's chocolate eyes sparkled. Alexa gave him a fond smile.

"Why've you never found a female unicorn to keep your race alive," Alexa suddenly—blatantly—asked.

"Unicorns mate for life. I guess I've just never found the right filly." He flipped his silky mane, a playful twinkle in his eye. "That's due to the fact that unicorns are rare. I've lived in Shelkite for centuries. But, I suppose, if I went looking I might find another. Just never have. I've friends in Shelkite. It's hard to be devoted to two things."

"I know this sounds odd," Hazerk said, "but could I touch your coat? It's very intriguing. I mean how it glows and all."

"I could let you, but then I'd have to kill you," Apollos replied.

Hazerk let out a hesitant chuckle, and then seeing Apollos' level gaze, he abruptly stopped. "You're joking, right?" He eyed the unicorn with doubt.

Apollos snorted, a mischievous look in his chocolate-colored eyes. "Only partially," he snickered. Hazerk made a surprised face, and the unicorn continued, "I would just require some of your blood for retribution." He lowered his muzzle to rub it on his hoof casually, as if this was the most normal thing to say. He closed his eyes in satisfaction as he scratched. "Actually," he went on, feeding their curiosity, "there are only two of you here that could touch me with no potential harm."

"I don't understand." Warkan looked confused, and a bit exasperated.

Apollos let them all ponder in silence for a moment, enjoying their puzzlement.

"A virtuous person," Eelyne suddenly said. Everyone's heads popped up out of thought. They all looked surprised except for Alkin, who just smiled knowingly. "Only the innocent can touch you. They can ride you, too. Because you're a creature so pure, nothing soiled can touch you without penalty," he said with growing confidence. "I've read it somewhere. I specialized in magical history and beings at school."

"Right. You know unicorns," Apollos praised him.

"Ha! Well, I guess we all know who those two are," Warkan snickered.

"Oh, I think the answer might surprise you, Warrior Warkan," the unicorn stated.

"Well, I know it's not me." Hazerk laughed, and then stopped, adding, "Although, it's been awhile." The others stared at him with surprised grins. "Anyway..." His cheer faltered.

Apollos tossed his shimmering mane, his horn catching a

blinding light from the dancing flames of the fire, and laughed. "Ah, humans! I'll never understand them." He moved on, directing the conversation away from the improper path it was taking. "But unicorns can be foolish when it comes to the innocent. I know of a time in the past when innocents were used against us. This was far before my time, I might add. But a magic user would use a young girl to convince a unicorn to follow her into a trap. The magic user would then chop off the unicorn's horn and harvest its magical blood. That's the tale anyhow. Because of it, I've always been leery of little girls." Apollos chuckled. He looked at Alexa, "And that gives you the reason why I'm not too fond of magic wielders. Except you, of course."

Alexa gave him a sad smile, ashamed for probably the first time of her heritage.

"Anyways, anyways," Hazerk said, waving a hand, trying to change the subject. "Come on, Sword Bryan, tell us that tree story." He turned to Warkan and added, "Just sit back and shut up, you might like it."

"Who said I wanted to tell it?" Bryan protested. "I can't tell stories. Apollos I'm sure knows it. Let him tell it."

The unicorn stared at him expectantly, playing that he had no idea about the story.

"Oh, all right," Bryan grumbled, "but don't blame me if I get it all mixed up." Everyone nodded and looked at him with eagerness. He took a sip of his tea and began, "Okay, there was this tree—no, there was this *man* once very long ago that—"

"Does he have a name?" Alexa said.

"Yeah, you have to give him a name," Hazerk agreed.

"All right, I'll start over. Apollos, what was the man's name?"

Apollos raised his head, looking surprised, "What? I don't know the story." He stared at Bryan with a devilish glint.

"Okay. Well, once upon a time, long ago, when the forests were still very populated with tree nymphs. There was this young man by the name of DeSont who lived in a cabin by the woods with his family."

"Try Thankeil," Apollos broke in. Bryan shot him a glare, and the unicorn added, "It just sounds better is all." He then started to lip up a mash that had been prepared for him.

Bryan cleared his throat and started once more, "*Thankeil* lived in a cabin by the woods. And he would often go walking into the forest on long summer days. It gave him serenity. He loved the trees and flowers. He loved nature. So, one spring day, while Thankeil was enjoying a walk through the paths in the woods he adored, he came upon a beautiful maiden who had fallen asleep under a willow tree. But she was like no other maiden he'd ever seen before. He stopped, entranced. The maiden was curled up at the trunk, sleeping ever-so-peacefully. Her skin was light bronze and looked as soft as silk, her body willowy and her face so radiant it almost hurt to look at her. She wore a slender dress of sparkling emerald and her long, wavy locks of dark hair shimmered green. Thankeil, completely mesmerized, reached out a hand to touch her, but she started awake. Her emerald eyes opened in shock; she gave a yelp, leapt up, and vanished into the tree. He was left, stunned. A dryad! Humans rarely saw them; they usually shied away.

"But Thankeil had fallen in love with the maiden. So, he stayed and pleaded endlessly to the tall willow for the maiden to come out and speak with him. But it was to no avail. Day after day, he would leave his duties to plead with the dryad to come out and see him. He told her how beautiful she was and how he longed to speak with her, that he would not harm her. He'd bring her gifts and leave them at the base of the tree. And always the next day, when he'd return, they'd be gone. He felt it would only be a matter of time when he would see the maiden again.

"Then, one day, while he was leaning against the trunk, rambling on about his ambitions and himself, like he had so many days, a figure appeared around the corner of the tree. The dryad had come out. He leapt up, speechless. The dryad smiled and placed a soft hand over his heart and said, 'You are beautiful, too, human.' She reached up and touched a yellow lock of Thankeil's hair. 'You are beautiful outside as well as inside. I have listened to all you've said these past months. So kind, adventurous, and wishful; unlike other humans I see tramping through the woods, always with their axes looking for a tree to destroy. Come, I'll show you the wonders of the forest as a dryad knows it.'

"She took Thankeil by the hand and they spent their time

speaking with one another while they walked the golden woods. He returned day after day to see her. He called her Willa, for she was the spirit of the great willow tree. The two soon fell in love. And Thankeil told his family of Willa. Strange as they thought it was, they accepted her. She even braved a meeting with his family at the edge of the forest.

"Thankeil and Willa spent much of their time with one another, and he promised her he'd protect her tree from any lumbermen, and they'd build a house of stone in a clearing near her tree.

"Willa loved him dearly and feared the day when his human life would come to an end. For she would live on, at least until her tree finally withered and died. For the spirit trees born at the beginning of time live to be very old. They knew the danger and hurt that was possible in their future, but they risked it, so they could love each other while they had the chance.

"One night, as they were walking under the canopy of trees by the sparkle of starlight, they heard music and laughter coming from within the forest. Willa paused; a smile spread across her features. She took Thankeil by the hands and said, 'It's the trees; they are merry and dancing, having a Star-Gathering Party. Come, I'll introduce you to the others. They surely will love you as I do.'

"So, they ran hand in hand to find the gathering of dryads. They came upon a clearing in the forest to see many tree spirits dancing and singing in their otherworldly ways. They paused at the edge of the party to watch. It was the most wondrous thing Thankeil had ever seen. Suddenly, Willa grasped his hands and pulled him into the dance among the others. The dancing went on, his presence gone unnoticed for a time.

"Then a dryad stopped and pointed, staring wildly at him. 'A human!' she screeched. The music, the dancing, the laughing, all stopped. Thankeil stared in fear at the dryad who had spotted him. She still pointed a slender, pale finger at him. She was the birch's spirit, her skin alabaster, hair long and straight and rich brown.

"Willa clutched onto Thankeil protectively. 'He's with me. He'll do you no harm, I promise.'

"All the spirits gathered around to stare at the human. But one tall male broke through the whispering crowd. In his hand was a staff with oak leaves sprouting atop it. He was broad. Old, he looked, but his bushy beard and shaggy hair were still a deep brown with leaves and vines intertwined in them. He stared at Willa accusingly. 'How dare you bring a human among us!' he said.

"'I tell you, Oak, he is a friend. His name is Thankeil. He loves the forest,' she replied, still clutching Thankeil tightly.

"The oak's spirit snorted, 'Ha! He is a human, a vile creature that allows and creates the destruction of trees!'

"'He's promised to protect my tree home. I am sure he'd do the same for you all. He can speak to the other humans,' Willa said.

"Then Birch called out again, pointing her finger, 'I've seen them together many times. They spend almost every day together.'

"Oak glared at Willa, 'Tell me this isn't true. You know you're not supposed to be in contact with humans! We forbid it.'

"'It is true. We love each other,' Willa said, becoming angry. The tree spirits began to mumble and speak amongst themselves. Thankeil and Willa retreated farther from the grumbling, unhappy crowd, afraid to leave. She huddled up next to him. And he, fearing for his life, wrapped his arms tightly around her.

"Finally, Oak broke from the crowd; pounding his staff on the ground, he said, 'We've decided we won't allow this relationship to go any further.'

"'Well, you can't stop us!' Willa called back.

"'Yes, we can.' Then Oak, quick as lightning, reached out and grabbed Thankeil, ripping him and Willa apart. He threw him to the other male spirits, who restrained him.

"'No! You can't!' Willa screamed.

"'We've decided,' Oak said arrogantly, 'that this man is going to pay for the evil deeds that his kind has done upon trees.'

"Thankeil was then taken away, struggling and calling out for mercy, while the other dryads restrained Willa. She cursed them to bring him back and screamed for Thankeil. But they ignored her. They took Thankeil and mercilessly threw him over a cliff.

"Willa never got over the premature death of her lover. She cursed the others and secluded herself and cried relentlessly. She never stopped mourning Thankeil. And even at Star-Gathering Parties, which happened each year at midsummer, she would sit out from the dancing and playing, solemn tears rolling down her face. She soon earned the name Weeping Willow from the others. But they never showed remorse or sympathy for what they had done."

Bryan leaned back on his elbows and took a sip of his tea. "There you go." He sighed.

Alexa snorted a laugh, "Where did you hear a sappy story like that? You surprise me, Sword Bryan."

He glared at her from over the fire. "Heard it at the Blue Mermaid. The bard claimed it was true. I don't know if it is or not."

"I thought it was good. Interesting…" Hazerk said, but he seemed a little irresolute. "I liked the detail you put into it…and the animation of the voices. You could be one of those traveling storytellers." He laughed, albeit a little nervously for poking fun at his superior.

Bryan grunted, "See if I ever tell another tale."

"Tale? So, it's not true," Warkan chimed in.

"Yes, it is true." Apollos looked up from his dinner, his muzzle covered with sweet mash. "So, they say. Every legend is based on some sort of fact." He returned to his mash.

"Well, I believe it," Alkin said.

"Me, too," Eelyne agreed.

"Anyway." Bryan stood and brushed his pants off. "I'll take first watch. The rest of you should get some sleep."

CHAPTER THIRTEEN

The heavily cloaked man was indeed very much out of place. But no one seemed to notice him as he slowly made his way about the busy main street of Yilvana Port. It was mid-morning, and the trading boats had docked; the uncouth sailors had begun to unload their goods. The streets were packed with traders' tables and tents, and the buyers bustled in every direction. Horses and carts were jammed in the heavy traffic, and livestock were periodically herded through the throng.

Yilvana was a tropical paradise. The locals dressed light in flowing, vibrant colors. The children ran dirty, barefooted, and merry through the streets. It was the largest trading seaport in all Eetharum. The goods brought to Yoldor from oversea continents were known throughout the world, even as far to the north as the vast country of Sushron, which was not a part of the allied countries.

Sushron, the subarctic and mountainous north, was where the cloaked man had traveled from. It had been where he had resided for the majority of his life. But if anyone ever asked, he would always say it was not his home.

His thick, black cloak was beginning to weigh him down. The heat from the incessant days of summer was breaching him, but he dared not remove his cloak—his sanctuary. No matter how warm it became, he dared not remove the hood which hid his marred face.

Although he felt rather warm, he couldn't remember a time when he had been happier. He had hope again. He was free. He was starting over. This was as far as he was going. He had picked this place as his new home in hopes to find a familiar, lost face among the people. He had brought with him only a small pack of his belongings and a sturdy mare that had traveled with him all the hundreds of miles and, of course, his trusty weapon. When he had left, he hadn't been able to bring himself to part with it, no matter what blood had tainted its name.

Coming out of the busy main street, he paused at the start of another lined with two-story apartments. It was clean and well-kept. He smiled in the shadows of his hood, his coffee-colored eyes alight with hope for the first time in literally centuries.

"Well, Blize, this is as good a place as any," he said to his mare. "I'll board at one of these inns until I can find a small place of our own. Hopefully, out of town…secluded. No one will bother us, and you'll have plenty of room to run."

The grulla-colored mare, Blize, snorted and bobbed her head, pulling gently at the reins held in her owner's hand. She eyed him fondly before nuzzling his shoulder. The black cloaked man smiled once more and clucked to his only friend in the world and began to lead her down the road.

★★★★

After searching the entire castle, Melea returned to Lady Adama's suite. Coming through the threshold, the servant halted upon seeing the lady sitting in her cushioned chair by the hearth.

"What is it, dear?" Adama asked upon seeing her puzzled expression.

"I feared I'd lost you, my lady." Melea smiled, relieved, and then ventured, "Did you take a walk? It was a nice refreshing morning." She attended the lady by fluffing a pillow and placing it gently behind her neck.

Adama sighed and closed her eyes, "I took a ride. It has been so long since I've ridden. I've missed it, but I found it only made me miss Izsum more. We used to go riding on days like this."

"I am sorry to hear that, my lady, but I hope it was refreshing all the same. You haven't been out in a while. It'll have done you good. Shall I bring you tea?" Melea smiled courteously.

Adama nodded. "Yes, thank you, dear."

After she closed the chamber door, Melea paused, touching her fingers to her lips in thought. Something was askew. She couldn't place it, but something just wasn't right regarding Lady Adama. Perhaps she should say something to the Head-Maid or Sword JaVin.

On her way down to the kitchen, she passed a closed chamber door that emitted sobbing sounds from within. She stopped. It was

Lady Dorsa.

Melea knocked lightly on the oak door. She heard a soft snort, a sniff, and some shuffling around before she was beckoned to come in.

She found Dorsa sitting on her large canopy bed, looking quite bedraggled. Her face was red, her eyes swollen, and her nose pink from obvious hard crying. Her usually soft, curly, blonde tresses were frizzed and wild.

"What has happened?" she asked, very much alarmed. "Is something wrong? I went looking for you earlier, but I couldn't find you anywhere. Tell me immediately if something is the matter!" She went to her and sat on the bed by her side.

Big tears welled in Dorsa's eyes. She scrunched up her face and flew down to bury her head in her pillow. "You'll just think I'm being silly!" she fretted, her voice muffled.

"I promise I won't. What is it?"

Dorsa lifted her face and lay back, looking glumly at the ceiling. "I just," she sniveled, "Found out…someone…isn't here." Her face skewed up, but she fought the urge to burst into tears again, and Melea couldn't help but feel a little envious that the girl still was so lovely in this state.

"Who?"

Dorsa sat up and stared at the floor. "It's a secret."

Melea patted her back. "I promise I won't tell… Is it a boy?"

"Yes, but my mother would be so angry if she knew. I'm *seventeen*; I should be allowed to make my own decisions. But she's so upset with me right now."

"Why is she upset? Did you go riding with her today?"

Dorsa nodded and looked away. "That doesn't matter. I won't ever do what she asks," she vowed bitterly. She took her handkerchief and wiped her eyes and nose. "Anyway, I'm crying because he went with my brother and that *girl* from Kaltraz. I didn't even get to say goodbye." She looked over and stared into Melea's eyes, her set of jade-colored ones flaring. "And I know that wherever she's leading them is dangerous. If he doesn't come back… I can't think of it!"

"He's a warrior, then?" Melea sat back and sighed; she understood the girl's feelings all too well. "Well, if my opinion means anything, I don't think you're wrong to love someone your mother doesn't approve of. And I'm sure your warrior is just as broken up about not being able to bid his lady goodbye either. I suppose that when you have a secret love, things like this happen..." She hoped that would console her a bit.

Dorsa smiled weakly, thankful, then frowned. "She'd better not be sweet on him."

"Who? Alexandra? No, I don't think she would. She's a nice person, and I can't believe she'd steal another's beau away. Besides, does he love you?"

"Yes, we wanted to marry...if my brother approved."

"Then you have nothing to worry about. Prince Alkin would surely consent when he returns. And your warrior will be fine, with his own skills to protect him and being with Sword Bryan, the other warriors, and your brother. He'll return safely, no doubt."

Dorsa forced a brave smile through her tears. "Thank you, Melea!" She swung her arms around the servant and hugged her. "I feel a little better. I suppose I overreacted. I know he'll come back to me. It just came as a shock when I found he was gone. I didn't realize he was a part of the company. He wasn't able to contact me in time..."

With a sympathetic smile, Melea smoothed out a lock of Dorsa's blonde tresses. "I know. How about I bring you some tea? I was just getting some for your mother."

"Yes. Thank you."

Melea stood and went to the chamber door. "Nothing else is bothering you then? Something with your mother?"

Dorsa got a bleak look across her features. "Thank you, Melea, but I do not want to talk about it just now."

"All right. I'll be back soon." She shut the door behind her and leaned against it, pondering once more, a little confused. *Oh, how I wish I had someone to talk to.* She thought of Bryan with longing.

★★★★

"I wasn't saying you were a terrible swordsman...woman, whatever. I just meant you might need a little more practice,"

Warkan said the next morning. He was trying to reconcile himself to Alexa as she coldly regarded him from astride Zhan.

"Well," she said, "let's just say I'd take you on in an archery match any day. If you feel so inclined."

"Oh, you think you're that good?" Warkan stared at her in ridiculing doubt.

Bryan, riding abreast with Alkin at the head of the company, had to crack a slight smile. He'd been keeping his eyes on the road, pretending not to eavesdrop. Obviously, Warkan's apology the night before wasn't enough to soothe Alexa's wounded pride. The two traveling companions had been going back and forth about their many achievements for at least a half an hour. Alexa boasted of her archery skills, and Warkan boasted of specializing in combat and winning honors. And frankly, Bryan was getting a little sick of hearing how great they were at this and at that. *Can't really call it eavesdropping, anyhow.* He twisted his lips wryly. They weren't exactly being secretive: they were the only ones talking besides the birds.

The Master Sword had awakened and packed up the camp early, so they could get moving by sunrise. He was intent on getting as fast as he could out of the wretched forest. It made him uneasy for reasons he couldn't explain. He loved trees, but he loved wide-open fields more.

The company had been trotting along at a clipping rate, enough to satisfy his hurry. But for the meantime, they'd relaxed their pace to rest the horses. And consequently, the slower gait had initiated Alexa and Warkan's discussion.

"Well, how about I just show you," she said, her tone assured but not arrogant. Bryan heard the girl shifting in her saddle. He didn't need to look to know she was taking out her bow and an arrow. He huffed out a quiet sigh and made an exasperated grimace. Stealing a glance at Alkin, he noted with surprise that he seemed utterly oblivious to the conversation going on behind them. The young prince was busy looking at the trees and wildlife, softly humming to himself.

"Alexa," Hazerk spoke and rode up between Warkan and her. "We all believe you. Just please give it a rest. Warkan was just being a pig." He turned to the stony warrior and gave him a scowl.

Warkan glared back.

"No. It's fine," she pepped. "I want to settle this."

"Didn't you hear me, you silly girl? You—don't—have—to—prove any—thing," he said.

She smiled and shrugged her shoulders.

"Listen—"

"For the love of Shelkite!" Bryan blurted, cutting off Hazerk's lecture. He halted Dragon, causing the whole company to come to a complete stop. He spun the black stallion around on his haunches to face them. Prince Alkin came back to reality and did the same with Sapharan. The others stared at him in surprise at his sudden outburst and emergence from his usual silent guidance. He regained his composure and cleared his throat. "We will all halt. We will all watch. So that we may go on," he said, and then looked to Alkin for his input.

"Yes, please do. If that'll appease you." He sighed and gave a weary look at Alexa and Warkan.

Alexa beamed, her sapphire eyes glittering, her pleased countenance having a strange, perhaps magical, effect on all of them. "Thank you." She shifted in her saddle and gazed up into the trees, searching for a target. "Okay, see that dragonfly way up there. I'll bet you that I can get that little guy square and dead."

Everyone turned their heads to look up. Bryan squinted, barely seeing a flicker of movement at the top of an enormous maple that was several strides in front of them.

"Uh, Miss Alexandra," Eelyne said.

"Huh?" She set her bow and aimed.

"I don't know if it's a good idea killing things we're not needing to." Eelyne gave Sword Bryan an apprehensive look.

"You know, he may have a point," Alkin said. But Alexa's arrow was already whizzing over their heads.

"Yes," Bryan agreed as he watched the arrow.

"It's just a dragonfly," she said, waiting eagerly.

Right on target, the arrow shuddered, then stopped. The glittering wings of the dragonfly tensed and went limp. The arrow and the quarry began a rapid drop to the earth. They fell to the base of the maple with a small plop.

"Good shot!" Hazerk praised a beaming Alexa, thoroughly impressed. "Wow, but that was a large dragonfly." He squinted over at it.

Everyone nodded in agreement, all a little stunned by the incident.

"Well? See?" She smirked at Warkan.

He shrugged and grunted. "Good shot."

"You know—" Bryan began to comment on the peculiar bug, but a sudden loud buzzing noise cut him off. It came from above. Everyone looked up, perplexed. "What the—" He shaded his eyes from the sunbeams that streamed through the branches. There seemed to be a tuft of cloud hovering over their heads just above the treetops.

"What is that?" Alexa asked.

Everyone shook their heads, speechless, watching the rippling, noisy haze. Then suddenly, the cloud seemed to swarm, maddening like a hive of angry bees; an obnoxious ringing noise emanated from it. Then the realization they were in trouble took effect on all their faces.

"Pixies!" Eelyne broke the confused silence, his face fearful. "You killed a pixie!"

"What?" Alexa said, unable to believe and stricken with sudden horror.

Warkan let out a boisterous laugh, and then stopped short when he saw a wary Eelyne retreat down the road at a good clip, pulling the pack mule right along with him. "You've done it now," he called back, "They're mad."

By that time, Sword Bryan and Prince Alkin had dismounted and walked over to investigate the fallen creature.

"It's a pixie," Bryan said, turning the dead woodland creature over with his boot. "Hmm, this can't be good," he said aside to Alkin. The Prince nodded in grave agreement.

"Ahh! Help! Help!"

The two men swung around to see a swarm of angry pixies attacking Alexa's head. Warkan had withdrawn himself and his horse. He was standing next to Eelyne, farther back down the road. Alexa swatted futilely at the irate pixies. Hazerk had stayed to help, but the pixies didn't seem to be interested in him; all their efforts were in attacking Alexa. He swung at the ones swarming her, yelling, "Get away, you demons! Get back!"

The Master Sword and the Prince looked at each other, horrified. Alexa yelped out some foul curses, covered her head, and attempted to kick Zhan forward, but the pixies would have none of it. They followed, now attacking the horse; he reared, and the distracted Alexa was quickly unseated. The pixies buzzed to the ground with her.

"Get Apollos!" Alkin snatched Zhan's reins when the terrified horse tried to bolt by.

Bryan leapt onto Dragon and galloped up the road, calling out for the unicorn.

Hazerk was now down on the ground, calling the pixies every foul name he knew. He thrashed them with his broad arms, sending hordes of them falling at a time. They began attacking him, full force.

All Alexa could make out were tiny, green-clad bodies, with buzzing, iridescent wings. There appeared to be both male and female present, but it was hard to tell. They screeched at her, though she had no idea what they said, and tore at her face, hair, and any part of her they could get to. And, as if it wasn't bad enough, some of the little beasts had knives! Sharp pricks sprouted across her skin, blood blossoming to the surface. She could only curse them and cry out, "Help! Stop! I'm sorry! I didn't mean to! I didn't know! Oh, blast!"

Bryan found Apollos up the road, where he was doing reconnaissance. The unicorn's voice answered him before Bryan could see him, for he materialized out of the air as he galloped toward him. Dragon gave a slight start at his appearance, but Bryan pulled the stallion to a skidding halt. Apollos met them, worry evident on his features.

"Pixies. Attacking," Bryan said. The unicorn nodded and then shot off toward the catastrophe.

When Apollos reached the catastrophe, he found both Hazerk and Alexa sitting on the rutted road, endeavoring to defend themselves. A very angry Hazerk swatted at the pixies like they were bees, and Alexa sat huddled and cursing.

He stopped in front of the two struggling people and coolly lowered his prismatic horn, aiming at the irate pixies. There was a moment of pure palpable magic in the air around him as he drew forth his power. His beautiful horn took on hues of sparkling pink, like flavored sugar crystals. His coat fluffed to a soft velvet and emitted a stunning white glow. The company caught their breaths at his glorious manifestation of magic.

Small tendrils of translucent, pink-hued lights grew forth from the tip of his horn. They threaded out, thousands of clear pink, glowing strands, all connecting to a pixie and encircling them like a soap bubble. The pixies halted their attack. The awful sound abated as they were enclosed in their prison. Bound by the magical web, their angry faces scowled, their mouths threw soundless insults, and their tiny hands beat against the webs.

Connected to them by the streams of gleaming threads, Apollos lifted his head and moved the pixies away from their quarry. Hazerk stared with his mouth slacked at the unicorn and the cords of light that bound and surrounded the little human-like bodies. Feeling the assault stop, Alexa raised her head and looked around in a daze.

Apollos turned and guided the spellbound pixies, with his horn, to the sky above the trees. With a gusto shake of his head, the glimmering threads broke free and wafted away on the breeze. The pixies stayed encased in the magical nets. Apollos allowed himself a few moments of pleasure in watching the enveloping pink clouds float out of sight, his chocolate eyes holding an amused twinkle.

With a wry snort, he turned back to the two on the forest floor. Alexa, having recovered her awe of the unicorn's demonstration of magic, was grumbling curses under her breath as she searched out all the stinging pricks on her flesh. Hazerk, on the other hand, was staring, mouth agape at the sky, his eyes searching for the lost pixie clouds. Apollos let out a musical laugh, which brought them all back to the present.

"Are you just going to leave them trapped?" Hazerk asked, astonished.

Apollos tossed his mane, a neutral look in his eyes. "They'll get out of it. We should be on our way, out of their territory, lest they should come after us again… And, I should add that perhaps we should not treat *any* other beings so lightly…" Apollos eyed Alexa.

Alexa nodded her understanding, looking away from his reproachful gaze, mute and remorseful, as she and Hazerk stood and brushed themselves off. The others started to regroup. Zhan came up beside Alexa; she gave him a reassuring pat and whispered soothing words.

"What little demons! That's not at all what I thought pixies were like," Hazerk said irritably. "I thought they were giggly, friendly, and airy like." He flitted his hands around, but his eyes held snapping flames.

Eelyne rode up. "Well, she *did* kill one of them. What would you expect?"

"At least you weren't pixilated," Apollos said.

"Pixilated?" The irritation was apparent in her voice and gestures. "*Pixilated!*" she repeated. "I think my skin is shredded like meat in a butcher's shop." She pushed up the sleeve of her slashed cloak and held up her arm for them to see. Her normally smooth skin was inflamed. Her forearm was slashed in all different directions, some cuts so deep that she had carefully folded the skin back over the wounds.

"I'm sure you've got something in that miraculous pack of herbs you carry that's a cure-all," Bryan said as he swung into his saddle.

She turned to him, "As a matter of fact—" Her tone was smart, but then she stopped, mouth open as if she had suddenly forgotten what she was going to say. A puzzled look came over her features, and Bryan stared at her expectantly. She slapped her hand over her mouth and straightened her stance, seeming surprised with herself.

"Well?" he prompted. He was actually kind of curious what it was she had. But then it was his turn to stare at her, puzzled. She shook her head; a lost look glazed over her eyes. Then a very girly giggle escaped her.

Taken aback at her outburst, Bryan couldn't help but let a small, perplexed smile escape him. He wasn't the only one to notice her uncharacteristic laugh either. Everyone in the company paused what they were doing and turned to look at her, everyone but Hazerk.

"Ha!" she belted out, removing her hand from her mouth and pointing at Bryan like something was his fault. "I forgot what I was saying." She let out another giggle that sounded more on the side of insanity.

"Are you all right?" he asked, bewildered at her sudden personality change.

"Uh-huh, yes." She stumbled, turning to put her foot in Zhan's stirrup, and missed it completely, and then began to laugh hysterically. Zhan gave her a skeptical look. Everyone stared wide-eyed at her; worry bordering on alarm across their faces.

"What's wrong with her?" Warkan asked.

"She's pixilated," Eelyne said.

"Pixilated? I am not!" She giggled and dropped to the ground on her backside. Bryan jumped down from his mount and held out his hand to her. "Who are *you*?" she demanded, looking up at him a little dubiously, like he was trying to pull a quick one on her. He laughed.

"Pixilated," Apollos agreed. "It will wear off in several hours. The pixies excrete the dust to confuse whoever gets in their way. They think it's funny. But it's just a pure inconvenience when you're trying to travel and then forget where you are and where you're going, let alone *who* you are."

"She doesn't know who she is?" the Sword looked up, a rare, playful glint in his eye.

"Oh, I do to. But I can't think of it right at the moment..." she said and flopped back to lie on the ground, outstretched. "Let's lie here and wait for the stars." She closed her eyes for a second and then popped them open. "By the way, where am I?"

"A haunted forest. Now, up you go. We've *got* to go." Bryan offered his hand to her.

"No joke!" She stared around the woods, aghast.

"Come on, I'll help you mount, and we can be on our way," he said a little impatiently. The others were all mounted and watched her with some amusement, all except Hazerk, who was digging around in his saddle packs.

"I'm not going anywhere with you. I don't know you," she

said, point-blank.

"I'm your knight in shining armor. I've come to take you home."

"You don't look very shiny." She studied Bryan closely. "In fact, you look grimy—but, I *guess* you're not *that* hard on the eyes." She nodded in approval, a sincere look in her eyes. "I'm sure that under all that dirt you have the potential to be rather handsome…"

"I'm glad you think so," he said, amused. "You could use a bath as well." He held out his hand once more. She took it and hopped to her feet.

"I didn't realize I was waiting for a knight…" she mused while he guided her over to Zhan. "But then again—wow! What an exquisite animal!" Her wide eyes sparkled a dazzling sky blue as she looked Zhan over as if for the first time ever. She went to his head, and he nuzzled her outstretched palm.

"Yes, so you've told us many times. Come on, girl, up you go."

"I don't see how I could. I've never seen him before."

"Do you really think she should be riding in this state?" Alkin inched forward on his mount to stand in front of them.

"Well, hello!" She held out her hand in greeting, a cordial smile lighting her face. "It's so nice to meet you. Is this knight escorting you also?"

"Uh…I uh…"

"No bother. I can ride, for sure. At least, I think I can…or I thought I could…" She looked away, wistful.

Finally, she turned to Bryan, and he assisted her into the saddle. At first, she perched a little wobbly, but then she settled in. She clasped the pommel and held the reins loose like a child; she glanced around, an excited look on her face. "Ready," she announced.

"Okay." Bryan sighed and mounted. "Are we ready? Let's go. Move out!" He started forward. They began to depart the pixies' territory when they heard a call from behind.

"Wait! Wait, gentlemen and fine lady!"

They halted and turned around to see Hazerk stuffing

something back into his saddlebags.

"I'm coming, too!" he called. "I don't know my way out of this haunted woodland." In his haste, he began to mount while his warhorse moved forward. He swung a jerky leg up and over the saddle just as his horse started to trot, exerting much more power than he needed. The company watched in stunned astonishment as Hazerk heaved himself up and clear over his huge chestnut mount to land in a heavy heap on the other side, where he looked rather flabbergasted. The sane people in the group stared at one another, speechless, and Apollos let out an amused snort.

"Great," Bryan breathed through his clenched teeth.

Alkin laughed, and Eelyne finally let out a stifled laugh he'd been holding back; it came out as a snort. Warkan rolled his eyes.

For the next several hours of traveling, which led them well into dark, Sword Bryan, Prince Alkin, Apollos, Eelyne, and Warkan had to endure Alexa and Hazerk's totally confounded state of minds.

The two ambled in the back of the company, laughing loudly—both in untypical Alexa and Hazerk laughs—at anything and everything. They would constantly whisper and snicker behind the others' backs. Which they would cease immediately, both smirking sheepishly, if anyone turned around suspicious of being a target.

When they would tire of jokes, the two would belt out songs. Any songs they knew and even ones they had made up on the spot. They were usually about things they passed or about the others, particularly Warkan, who was never happy when they targeted him. Their songs were never sensible, but no one could deny that listening to them sing nonsense helped pass the time.

CHAPTER FOURTEEN

By the next morning, Alexa and Hazerk had returned to their normal mind-sets and felt only a bit light-headed. They couldn't remember anything while they had been pixilated, except that they had been extremely content the previous afternoon.

The company had risen at dawn and was preparing to set out for another long day of riding.

"You know." Bryan overheard Hazerk telling Apollos as they were gathering up the gear. "Pixies were *just not* what I had in mind when you gave us that warning of certain *risky* things siphoning over." The unicorn flicked his tail and tossed his head with a chuckle.

The Master Sword was on a mission. He pressed the group as fast as he dared, only taking into consideration the horses' welfare. As they moved farther south over the next few days, he noticed a temperature change in the forest. It was warmer, considerably warm for early summer. The horses were sweating visibly, and the company had taken to rolling up their cloaks and stowing them away after sunrise.

As they traveled their days in companionable silence, the forest's ancient trees became sparser, and tiny, well-kept homesteads popped up along the road, and soon small villages sprouted here and there. Any villagers they happened upon were friendly and asked no questions, which contented Bryan.

There was a noticeable change in the vegetation as well. The evergreens and massive deciduous trees were replaced with palm trees and citrus trees of various kinds. Beautiful hanging vines appeared, along with ferns, cacti, shrubbery, banana trees, and even cocoa trees.

The company soon discovered Prince Alkin had a special interest in horticulture. He couldn't contain his thrill at seeing the land transform into a paradise, and he eagerly pointed out and named many plants and trees. He had a surplus of information about them, as well as the country they were traveling through.

"You know, the indigenous people of Yoldor discovered how to make chocolate hundreds of years before now. We've just only persuaded them to give us trading rights for it." He plucked an orchid and handed it to a smiling Alexa.

"I've never had chocolate." She examined the flower and twirled it between her fingers.

"It's good," Eelyne inserted.

"Well, you can thank Prince Alkin for that," Sword Bryan said. "He's the one who convinced Chief Bahjahn not to hoard it. Shelkite now has trading rights with every country in Eetharum for *every* good."

Alexa made an impressed sound, which elicited a smile from Alkin.

"Yes, if I may say so, I'm very happy with my dealings with the chief. We get on quite well. It's a huge benefit to Shelkite. All our fruits, pearls, and chocolate come strictly from Yoldor. We also get first rights to other goods brought into Yilvana Port from other continents." Alkin grinned, pleased with himself.

Soon, the woods came to an end. They entered a pleasant rural area. They pressed on, their pace as sure and as quick as ever. The Master Sword kept them on the main road, which headed straight south and into Yilvana Port on the coast. It was rumored that the merpeople dwelt in a nearby lagoon.

The company traveled this route for a few days, building camp inconspicuously off the road alongside other travelers. The Master Sword planned they would keep to themselves, but not give the citizens and guards of Yoldor any reason to think them shady. So far, they had overlooked them as mere travelers, who perhaps had come to buy goods, as many did, and they had not been questioned. Apollos, however, kept himself unseen, knowing he would attract unwanted attention.

At sunset, several days after crossing the border, they crested a large hill. The sight rendered them speechless. Even Bryan had to pause and appreciate the beauty of the vale below. On the horizon, Yilvana Port rose before them, a massive, bustling city even in the growing darkness. And beyond the grand labyrinth of buildings and homes and streets that weaved serpentine-like through them was the Elendace Sea. To their far right was the setting sun; its rays glistened a dazzling orange on the harbor waters, where countless ships sat docked and bobbing in the placid waves.

"What a beautiful city," Alexa said. She thought of how many inns as grand and grander than her father's inn a city of this size would contain. "I would love to have a warm bath right now and to sleep in a bed," she said wishfully.

"Well, you're just going to have to bypass that wish," Bryan replied, without taking his eyes from the glowing city. "We head that direction." He pointed to the southeast, toward a shore in the distance. "That's where the merpeople are. In a lagoon, a couple days east of the city. We'll camp just outside the city on the shore tonight."

"But—"

The Sword shook his head, his expression firm, and she sensed the company seem to deflate along with her.

"You know, I was thinking that perhaps we should go through the city," Alkin spoke up. "It wouldn't hurt to have a nice rest in an inn just for one night. Plus, it'll give us a chance to scope things out. Just to see or hear of any evidence of corruption among the people."

"You want to chance that, my prince?" Bryan asked. "Some of the higher-ranking guards may recognize you. And what if the chief himself decides to take a jaunt through the city? You'll be hard-pressed to explain why you are wandering around his city in disguise and unannounced. If he is corrupt, then it may turn out to be difficult to leave. I say leave the investigating to your trained spies and the talking to your emissaries. They'll be here soon."

"Oh, come on, Bry—Master Sword," Alexa pleaded, quickly correcting herself after the displeased look he shot her. The others stayed silent, knowing better than to comment, despite their personal desires.

There was a moment of tense silence as he considered. He looked around at the other three men, seeing hopeful looks in Hazerk and Eeylne's eyes; Warkan seemed ill-disposed to express anything. "All right, fine," he resigned. Alexa and the two warriors' faces split into triumphant grins. "One night. And we have to be careful."

They started down the hill, riding along the winding road that led to the city's North Gate.

"Good. I'm dying for a hardy meal," Hazerk said happily to the agreeing Eelyne; Warkan shot them a disapproving look before reining ahead.

It was past dark once they were safely past the guardians of the North Gate and on their way to an inn. They found one at once. The Master Sword didn't feel it necessary to be picky. His first concern was to find a place with good stables and care for the horses.

With the animals attended to, they found enough rooms to accommodate them. The Prince paid the tab. In the tavern, they ate a decent meal with their ears pricked for anything odd spoken by the patrons. But nothing out of the ordinary caught their attention.

While dining, Alexa and Hazerk found it hard to contain their mirth over the natives' peculiar accents. In play, Alexa rudely, but discreetly, imitated the bizarre speech to perfection. Her playful impressions sent Hazerk into fits of wheezing, suppressed laughter and caused Eelyne to have a huge grin plastered across his features. The other occupants of the tavern seemed oblivious to their growing racket.

As the night wore on and they consumed more drinks while joking and talking nonsense, Alexa became sillier. Thanks to growing up with eleven older brothers, she was quick-witted and blatant. One of her sarcastic jokes caused Prince Alkin to snort his drink out his nose, and she even elicited a glimmer of a smile from Sword Bryan. Surprisingly, Warkan also seemed to be enjoying himself: He did not look aggravated once and even refrained from rolling his eyes.

Back in their rooms, Alexa, after succumbing to the fact that she had to share an adjoining room with Sword Bryan, took a long, hot, oiled bath. She took care to scrub herself clean from head to toe with the supplied bar of lilac-scented soap. The others did the like in their own rooms.

As she lay in the steaming waters, feeling quite tranquil, she looked down to the pendant resting lightly on her chest from its gold chain. She lifted the chain and let the key-shaped charm

dangle in front of her eyes. Staring at it as it glistened in the
moisture, a distant thought occurred to her. She took the chain off
over her head and held it in her hand; she turned it over and
examined it for really the first time. The chain was fine and
ordinary. The pendant was small, not even as wide or long as her
baby finger. The key was shaped like any normal skeleton key.
Nothing was engraved on it, and as far as she could tell, there was
absolutely no authentic value to it. She raised it to her mouth and
bit down.

"Ouch!" She rubbed her tooth, and almost immediately heard
Sword Bryan's footsteps in the next room walk to the adjoining
closed door.

"Okay in there?" he hollered through the door.

"Yeah, of course… Just stubbed my toe," she called back, still
rubbing her sore mouth. The footsteps retreated. "Guess I
shouldn't have bit so hard," she whispered to herself, staring at the
key, perplexed. The spot where her teeth had made contact had
chipped off. A black surface showed through. "Hmm," she
pondered, "just a hunk of metal." She closed her wet hand around
it and held it up to her ear as if listening to it. She closed her eyes
and attempted to use her senses to see if the charm revealed
anything. It started in her gut, a slight humming of magic, a feeling
of vibration. It moved through her viscera and spread to her limbs.
She felt herself slip into a trance.

There was a loud knock on her door that startled her back to
consciousness. "Are you still lounging in that bath? Get to bed.
We're not lollygagging in the morning. This isn't your holiday,"
Bryan demanded through the door.

"All right, all right." She dropped the chain and charm to the
floor, feeling an unnatural chill fall away from her, and took one
more dunk under the water to warm herself again. She slipped her
head all the way to the bottom of the tub, staying there until she
could stand it no longer, and then emerged to savor the air.

She climbed out of the tub and dried herself with a towel
heated by the fire. She stared warily down at the necklace. *It's
giving off vibrations. Strange ones, not bad perhaps, but definitely
unfamiliar.* She pressed her lips together in thought and turned to

dress for bed, leaving the pendant in a heap on the floor, not desiring its unnatural vibrations coursing through her as she slept.

The next morning, she sleepily stumbled out of her room into the hallway of the second floor of the inn. Rubbing her eyes, she looked up to see a clean-shaven Master Sword standing beside her, locking his door.

"Good Morning," he said in an abnormally cheerful voice.

"Morning?" she mumbled back. "It's still night." She glanced down to the end of the hall to a window still showing the impenetrable black of night.

Bryan smiled. "It'll get light soon enough."

The door to her left opened and Hazerk stepped out, still buckling his sword around his waist. She noted his unshaved whiskers were still in full effect. She raised an inquisitive eyebrow.

"Oh, I know." Hazerk rubbed his hand over his rust-colored stubble. "I'm going to grow it out."

At that moment, the sound of boots scuffing across the floor filled the soft silence and Eelyne, Warkan, and Alkin came around the curve in the hall from the other end of the building. Like Bryan, they were also clean-shaven. Warkan was sporting a few cuts and looked murderous if anyone dared to mention it.

"All right. We're all here, let's head out. I want to be at the lagoon in under sufficient time," Bryan said in an authoritative tone.

As they began shuffling towards the stairwell, Alexa blurted, "Wait! I forgot something."

"What?" Bryan said wearily as she turned and disappeared back into her room.

She stepped in and paused in front of the tub and looked down to where the mysterious necklace still lay. She bent over and picked it up. Her fingers prickled at its touch as if it were charged with some kind of energy, her senses now tuned with the pendant's curious vibrations since she had opened that door the night before. She considered whether she should wear it, at least until she had more time to examine it closer. Outside, she could hear Sword Bryan's muffled call for her to hurry. She clasped the chain in her hand and turned to leave. It was enchanted to protect her; of course, it would give off some sort of vibration.

In the hall, the men waited a little impatiently. Finally, Alexa appeared, tucking a necklace down the front of her shirt.

"Ready." She smiled.

Bryan looked at her with suspicion. "You better not be stealing anything, or I'll cut your hands off myself."

She glared at him, exasperated. "I don't steal."

Hazerk laughed. "What are you saying? Of course, you do."

Everyone stared at him in shock, Alexa more than anyone, her eyes rapidly changing to a blaze of defense. "What do you…"

Hazerk's grin broadened and he threw his arm around her shoulders, giving her a squeeze. "You stole my heart a while back, my love," he said as if he couldn't believe she didn't know.

Alexa's face relaxed back into a smile. Bryan snorted dryly and turned for the stairs along with Warkan. The others grinned and followed suit.

After gathering their gear and tacking the horses, the pink morning light pierced the inky sky, and Yilvana Port awakened around them. Booths of baubles, food, weapons, fabrics, and anything else one could imagine were opening, and the people were beginning to start their daily routines.

Bryan led the small company toward the East Gate, straight down the main business strip. But before making decent head-way, he noticed the absence of Alexa, and quickly scanning the surroundings, he spotted her at a weaponry booth. "Warrior Hazerk, please go get her," he said with some exasperation, gesturing in her direction. The warrior stalked off after her. But it soon became apparent that Hazerk too had become ensnared by the merchant's wares.

Once they got moving again, this happened twice more, and each time Bryan sent someone new to fetch her, only to become enticed themselves. By the next time around, Bryan stomped back to retrieve her himself, dragging poor Dragon behind; the crowd of shoppers in his wake voicing their annoyance as he went.

Standing at the largest, thus far, of the weaponry booths, Alexa appeared transfixed by a strange, foreign-looking weapon she examined in her hands. Zhan peered over her shoulder as if he was also interested in what the dealer explained.

As Bryan approached, Alexa glanced up, her eyes a brilliant sky blue, and she held up the vile-looking weapon for him to see, its sharply curved blade glinting in the sunlight.

"Look at this! Isn't this amazing? It's from Alidon. It was used in their civil war three hundred years ago. Look what it does." She pulled back her arm as if to throw it, but before she could, Bryan snatched it from her, eliciting an annoyed glare from the merchant. With it now in his hands, the Master Sword stopped briefly to wonder exactly how it *did* work, and Alexa, noting his fleeting, curious look, smiled. "Neat, right? I'm getting it."

Yielding to her enthusiasm, he shrugged, and she pulled out her moneybag and plunked down the amount. The merchant grinned and thanked them in his heavy accent.

"Can you believe it?" she said as they weaved their way back to the rest of the company. "It's a weapon made from across the ocean."

"Yes, I know where Alidon is. I've been there once. Come on," Bryan hastened.

"I wish I could see different lands someday. Alidon sounds wonderful," she said, her heart almost bursting from longing.

Bryan turned to regard her, giving her a puzzled look at her enthusiastic display. It was as if she had not heard of Alidon before. It was part of a larger continent than even Eetharum and Sushron together. Then, much to his surprise, she blushed. "What is it?" he asked.

"I know. I'm a bit sheltered. Living in the desert does have its disadvantages. My father does it to protect us." She lowered her eyes.

Unsure about her sudden, rare self-consciousness, Bryan didn't answer.

"I'm just a commoner. A lot of people think of me as only a dirty shepherdess. New places intrigue me, unlike those of…higher classes."

The Master Sword took pity. He had never thought of her as *below* him. He shook his head. "Different lands and cultures have always fascinated me, too. That's why I took to traveling when I was younger, sword fighting competitively and seeing new places. It was great…most of the time." His eyes darkened to deep cobalt, clouded by a dark memory.

He could feel her mysterious, enchanting eyes on him, making him feel strangely awkward, but he was unable to look at her straight on, being self-conscious of his own reassuring words. He chanced a glance from the corner of his eye as they walked. His pace quickened subconsciously. He caught a small smile from her, and could have even sworn it was bound with a slight shyness. Muscles in his body he hadn't known were tense, relaxed. He let himself crack a small, crooked smile.

Coming upon the awaiting warriors and prince, he was saved from any further uncomfortable conversation. *Thank the High Power.* He rolled his eyes upward in relief.

Re-grouping, he discovered Hazerk had gone off to a booth and was in a flirtatious conversation with a native woman dressed in flowing, vibrant hues. Her brown skin showed a little more scandalously than the women of Shelkite usually preferred, but it was common here among the women to show more of their figures. She was indeed lovely.

"Warrior Hazerk!" Bryan grabbed his warrior's attention. "If you remember, I believe you're already faint with love for Alexandra. Let's get a move on."

"Yes, Master Sword." He promptly stood at attention. After Bryan had turned his back to take up Dragon's reins, Hazerk flashed the woman a boyish grin and shrugged. She smiled, her black eyes glittering, and turned away, flipping her long, glossy hair as she did.

The company continued on to the gate, bypassing all the beautiful sites Alexa was so yearning to see.

CHAPTER FIFTEEN

All morning and afternoon, the castle bustled with people, and Melea felt exhausted. Lady Adama had taken over the monthly hearings in Prince Alkin's absence.

Once a month, citizens from the cities of Shelkite traveled to Fordorn to present their problems and await the verdict from the prince. Normally, this conventional procedure was not difficult. The families and prosecutors of the offender would set up camp outside the castle walls, and any person in question would be guarded in the warrior camp prison.

Each town had their own form of temporary punishment, headed by men graduated from the warrior school, who were required to report back to a Master Sword, who in turn, reported to Prince Alkin on a regular basis. But all final rulings for major crimes were saved for the beginning of the month when Alkin would make the ruling himself. This time, however, while Alkin was still gone, Lady Adama and Lady Dorsa sat in the throne room calling the verdicts.

As Melea flitted in and out of the throne room, she noted the problems were nothing out of the ordinary. They usually consisted of some major spat between families or neighbors, or a stolen horse, or even persons trying to blame another for an accident that had been fatal.

This month, only about seventy people had gathered. But, on this day, they had all found it necessary, because of the stormy weather, to throng in the entrance hall while they waited. Not counting the prisoner guards, there were about twenty warriors around to keep everything in order. Every time Melea entered the hall, she dreaded having to clean it after they dispersed.

Today, and for the rest of the week, her primary job was to keep Lady Adama and Lady Dorsa happy. She brought them tea and snacks during the hearings and a meal when they took the afternoon break.

Everything was going smoothly. As she moved among the people and warriors, she couldn't help remembering how, one time

Sword Bryan, having just returned from a long trip of assessing the cities of Shelkite, had come back with hilarious tales of the stupidity of people. If she closed her eyes, she could still hear his laugh and see his grin. Just the thought of him made her smile at the grim crowd as she walked by.

Holding a tray of hot herbal tea, she paused at the double oak doors; a nearby warrior opened one, bowing as she slipped into the throne room.

At the front of the hall, Adama was sitting straight and tense in Alkin's chair as she regarded a miserable looking young man flanked by two stoic warriors. Melea stopped at the doorway, and suddenly a short fleshy man on her left stood up and shouted.

"Woman! Don't you lie to the lady! Your son's been stealing from my store for over three months!" He pointed an accusing finger at a woman across the room, his face and balding head purple with rage.

"Please, Lady Adama," pleaded the woman. She was accompanied by two children who clung to her. "He's only been taking what he's earned," she said. She turned with a menacing glare to the storekeeper "And you!" she yelled. "If you weren't such a cheat and a liar and a thief yourself, he wouldn't have had to deceive you. The little that he did!"

The storekeeper opened his mouth to retort nastily, but Lady Adama stopped him with a curt wave. "I've heard enough of this nonsense!"

The hall quieted, and Melea looked up to the throne. She noted how the normally serene eyes of Lady Adama were flashing with annoyance. She also noted to Adama's right that Lady Dorsa looked pale and drawn. The young woman sat slumped and looking sickly as her dull green eyes watched the commotion in front of her.

Adama continued, not losing her abrupt tone, "Young man," she regarded the prisoner, "we do not tolerate dishonesty in any part of Shelkite."

The young man nodded solemnly.

Melea watched with wide eyes from behind. From what she heard of the crime, it had not sounded completely terrible. Prince

Alkin would normally have only sentenced a light punishment for this circumstance, on the hope that the young man would learn his lesson and change his ways. And he would, in fact, investigate the storekeeper further. She had no doubts Lady Adama would do the same.

"I'm afraid we've been giving Shelkitens too much free rein, they are beginning to run wild. You will be used as an example. You're sentenced to the amputation of your left hand the morning you return to your hometown," she said, eliciting a murderous scream from the woman and a gasp from Melea. "Now, please take him away."

There was a sudden scuffle, and in a daze, Melea stepped out of the way as the young man was dragged out the doors, screaming at the injustice, and the mother was restrained and taken away.

"My Lady," the storekeeper spoke, his expression now changed to one of disbelief, "the injury to me was not so severe..."

"If you are questioning my judgment, I can also have your tongue amputated." Lady Adama's eyes flashed as she looked down upon him.

"I...I would not question you, my Lady. You are just." The storekeeper bowed, and then turned and left the throne room, his features frozen in a state of shock.

When they had gone, Adama called to the door-guard, "I will not see any more for now." He nodded his understanding and stepped over the threshold to give the announcement.

Melea could still hear the screaming mother as the door closed and then the sudden apprehensive commotion of the awaiting crowd. As she listened, she stood frozen, her eyes wide and mouth slightly agape. *What's going on?*

"Ah, Melea dear, I could use that tea." Adama broke her trance; the lady's voice was its tender self again.

Melea nodded numbly and walked toward the throne, her legs feeling like logs.

"Thank you." Adama took the teacup and exited the hall through a side door, taking the last guard with her. Melea and Lady Dorsa were alone.

Coming out of a daze, Melea looked at Lady Dorsa, who had stood and taken a cup of steaming tea. The young woman gave her a forlorn look. Dark circles had formed under Dorsa's eyes, but she smiled reassuringly as she took a sip. Melea glanced at her fingers wrapped around the drink; a sparkling ice-blue engagement gem caught her eyes. A puzzled look flitted across her features, but she said nothing.

Dorsa, seeing her bewildered face and thinking it was because of the harsh sentence, took pity. "I know," she said, setting the drink on the tray and gently squeezing the servant's shoulder. "Mother thinks it is good to do this. It sets an example, squashing any potential mobs conniving to overthrow. I believe Alkin feels the same."

"Maybe," Melea blurted, "but I believe Prince Alkin would never use a crime such as that as an example. It would be a crime much more deserving. Nor would he give a verdict such as that."

Dorsa suddenly looked stern. "If you were not my friend, I'd slap you for speaking so ill of my mother. She's the one responsible for raising my brother and I so well."

"I apologize, my lady." Melea lowered her eyes.

Dorsa's countenance became sad again, and she sighed. "I must say that I don't agree with the verdict either. But Alkin has given my mother authority while he is away, and she has forbidden me to have any say in this month's hearing."

"Why?" Melea searched the young woman's face in shock, feeling it had somehow matured in the last weeks.

"Punishment for the initial refusal of this." With a dismal air, Dorsa held the large gem in front of Melea's eyes.

"Who?" was all she could manage.

"The new Chancellor of Vtalmay," she said bitterly. "His father has died from an illness, and he's now ruler." Dorsa's eyes glinted with tears. "He's about ten years older than I, and I've only met him once when I was a girl. Alkin and I visited Vtalmay to see for ourselves the beauty of the Ice Palace. It *is* beautiful, but it's so cold. The palace lies right on the shores of the Nortarwin Sea in the mountains." She paused, lost in thought.

Melea waited to see if the young heiress would spill more, and she did.

"He was looking for a woman with noble blood to marry, and

he remembered me. My mother thinks it's a good match." She looked at Melea desperately. "I don't want to live so far away where it's always frozen..." Then she added softly, "Without the person I truly love."

"What has your brother said?" Melea choked over the words.

"Not much. It was only mentioned a little before he left. He had more important things on his mind. He claimed I could marry whomever I wanted and told Mother that he wished she'd please stop pestering us both about marriage. Alkin has never been one to make me do anything I didn't want to. But Mother sent an acceptance to the proposal weeks ago, anyway. A messenger came bringing the ring and the Chancellor's glad words a short time ago."

"When you continued to refuse, your mother became angry. Is that what you argued about?"

Dorsa nodded. "Yes. But I have to go; Mother will wonder where I am."

With that, Melea watched the young woman exit the hall with her shoulders and head held resolutely proud.

Melea was alone. She stared at the floor. A feeling in her gut and her conscious told her that if Prince Alkin were here, he would like none of this. Why was Lady Adama cutting down so strictly and out of the ordinary? This wasn't at all how Adama had taught her son or daughter to act. She had always been a compassionate person. These events weren't adding up right. Why was she forcing Dorsa to marry when Prince Alkin had clearly said no? And more importantly, what was Melea to do about these uncanny changes? She had made a promise; it was now her responsibility.

★★★★

Off the shores of the Elendace Sea, the black-cloaked man sat in a grove before the sandy beach. He sat on a rock smoking a pipe thoughtfully, watching the tide and Blize roam nearby as she munched on the salty sea grasses.

For the few weeks that Kheane had attempted to live in Yilvana Port, his presence hadn't gone unnoticed by the town's guards. Whenever he had ventured out of his small apartment, he was under the close surveillance of at least three Yoldor guards. Although they thought they were completely concealed, Kheane had always known exactly where they were.

How had he thought he would be able to escape his past occupation undetected? His body and soul held shadows of ghosts that exposed too much to the world.

He knew the guards had no idea who he really was, but judging by his clandestine appearance, they had targeted him as some kind of menace. So, Kheane decided to leave Yilvana Port. He settled a few miles east of the city in a crude, abandoned cabin he had found in a grove off the coast. Blize stayed nearby in her own shelter and never wandered far, unwilling to leave her companion.

Lowering his cumbersome hood was a rare pleasure Kheane got to enjoy. But here in the woods, with just the animals and the sea for company, he reveled in that pleasure more than he had in at least two hundred years.

He puffed out a cloud of smoke and side-glanced at his weapon leaning on the door of his home, his ears alert for anything unusual. He heard birds twittering and Blize a few strides away by the stream, pawing at the stones and slurping up the cool, fresh water. But there was something else. He couldn't figure it out. The sound was just hanging there, undetectable to all but him. The years in his previous profession had tuned his senses better than any human; they were almost as keen as a wolf's.

Although he was supposedly retired, he couldn't help being leery. There were many searching for his blood. He peered through the trees. And finally, way off to his right, he saw a small company making their way across the beach from the west—the city. They were only specks in the distance, but Kheane eyed them carefully, his mind calculating subconsciously like it had done so many times.

He lowered his pipe and put it out. He then let out a low, musical birdcall to Blize. The mare raised her head from the stream and silently crept to him. As she came to stand by his side, she raised her head and pricked her ears as she too spotted the unexpected party. Kheane placed his hood back over his dark hair, hiding his maimed face. Only the glisten of his dark, coffee-colored eyes, reflecting the evening sun, could be seen as he peered out to the beach as the group came closer and closer.

After a while, he relaxed, noting they weren't trying to move in stealth. In fact, they were being rather loud. He moved closer to the edge of the woods to where the beach began, but not so close he would be seen. Blize followed. He watched. The party consisted of mostly men, men from a country other than Yoldor, at least most of them appeared to be, and one woman from yet another country. She looked vaguely familiar.

There were five men, four of which he could tell were warriors. The man at the head of the party rode skillfully and assertively, with one hand always gravitating toward the hilt of his sword. Kheane didn't have to see to know he had many other knives hidden on his person. The man that rode next had his face hidden by a hooded cloak. He was quiet and didn't present himself like the other warriors. Next came a stern-looking man, and following him came a blazing redheaded warrior, who was laughing and joking with the two walking behind. The redhead led both their horses and the pack mule tied in a mini caravan.

The two walking, lagged behind. They were both younger, perhaps the same age. And one of the two was the only female. The tall, skinny warrior and willowy young woman were practicing the sword as they traveled along. The girl let out a whoop and holler, and the young warrior grinned devilishly as he landed a play strike. The young woman moved with ease but was still unskilled with the weapon she held in her hand.

Kheane smiled as he watched the girl try to land a blow on the young fellow, her long, braided, raven hair swinging to-and-fro, her stance strong, but not guarded. The young warrior was going easy on her. He had some potential.

He let out a small breath. They were of no harm to him—still, something else pricked his conscious. He could see no more than what was before him, but he sensed another presence. It only bothered him for a fraction of a second before he decided it was none of his business. They weren't out to find him. It would have to remain uninvestigated. He needed to move on and leave his old ways of life behind. But he was having trouble letting go of what had become natural to him. He hadn't been known as the Cold Wolf for nothing.

He rested a reassuring hand on Blize's shoulder, the signal to show there was nothing to fear. She turned and left to return to the sweeter grasses by the stream. He began to turn and forget about the company as well, but when he threw one last glance at the man riding second, the hooded one, he caught a glimpse of his face as he turned from watching the young woman. Kheane halted. He turned back and stared hard at the man's features, his dark eyes wide with shock. It couldn't be who he thought it was? What would he be doing here?

Kheane quickly and stealthily moved to a tree that was closer, and crouched to watch. The company was so close he could now hear their voices clear and strong across the sands. The man spoke with the leading warrior, and Kheane knew for certain that this man was the Prince of Shelkite.

Kheane's brow furrowed, and he thought hard and fast, as was his usual way. He looked back to his small home and to Blize. He had nothing here. He hadn't been able to escape his past, and he hadn't found the person or the hope he had been looking for. He needed to investigate. Just a traveling company was one thing, but a company with the Prince of Shelkite was another.

He moved back to his cabin and began packing his few possessions and food. Blize, noting his haste, stood by her tack and waited as he saddled and bridled her. Grabbing his weapon, he mounted and began to ride through the woods unseen, following the company as they moved east.

CHAPTER SIXTEEN

"He ain't pretty! His face is chiseled from stone! He hates ditties and is married to an old crone!"
Hazerk sang at the top of his lungs about Warkan. He then fell into a boisterous laughing fit along with Alexa and Eelyne. "This is too much fun." He rode up alongside Warkan, who looked rather annoyed. Hazerk gave him a friendly slap on the shoulder. "Just in fun, buddy." He grinned deviously.

"Humph!" Warkan grunted and then turned in his saddle to glare at Eelyne. The younger warrior looked sheepishly back. "I wish you'd never told them about their little sonnets they made up while they were pixilated."

"Oh, I'm glad he did," Alexa said, "Thanks, Eelyne!"

"Me too," Hazerk agreed. Eelyne shrugged, unable to hide a smirk.

"Okay, everyone!" Sword Bryan called back and halted the company. He couldn't contain the smile that appeared across his features that the songs had triggered. "It's fun, but enough singing. We're getting close to the lagoon," he said, all business. He then pulled out the map from his overcoat's inner pocket and studied it. "It seems that as soon as we crest this last dune, we should be able to see the merpeople's lagoon. We'll make camp off the shore, a little way into the woods. I don't want to impose on their space. Then Prince Alkin, Alexa, and I will travel to the sea's edge tomorrow morning to see if we can make contact. It's getting too late to try anything tonight. Agreed?"

Alkin, who was leaning over and studying the map from atop Sapharan, nodded. The others murmured their agreement.

Bryan was about to advance the company one last time for the day, when a voice came out of the air right next to him and startled him.

"Sword Bryan? Prince Alkin? Could I have a private word with you?" Apollos inquired.

"Yes, of course."

They retreated a short distance from the once again bantering company. Standing on the sea's edge, their horses' hooves being wetted by the salty waters, Apollos voiced his concern. "I just wanted to inform you that we're being followed."

Bryan and Alkin stared, shocked, into the air they thought was Apollos.

"What do you mean? I've been keeping an eye out for that." Bryan was unable to keep the alarm he felt out of his voice.

"You?" Apollos said, alarm now apparent in his own voice. "I didn't even notice this person as quickly as I should have. And *I* have magical senses. Alexa obviously didn't notice either. He is good, whoever he is. I dared not go too close to him, because strangely enough, I think he somehow knows I'm here."

"How? You've been invisible the whole time."

"Does he know magic?" Alkin asked.

"No. I don't believe so. He's just a man, a very skilled one at keeping quiet and hidden. His horse must be trained as well."

Bryan looked up and around, careful not to look like he was searching, lest he be seen. Setting his jaw, he contemplated as he stared out over the rippling sea. The water's coloring changed from shades of jade to deep cobalt the farther it was from the shore, the waves small and tide gentle. He looked to the horizon in the west. The orange sun was beginning to sink into the land, sending its colorful rays of pink and lavender skyward. "Well," Bryan broke his reverie, "if he's this good at being unseen, then he must be decent at killing, too."

Alkin looked apprehensively at the Master Sword. Apollos did also, though they couldn't see his features. Alkin sighed.

"Let's not worry about him right now," Apollos finally said. "I'll keep an eye on him. I must say that, so far, he's not giving off vibrations that tell me he wants to do us harm."

"Is he from Yoldor, Apollos?" Alkin asked.

"No. I don't think so."

The Prince seemed to relax a bit. "That doesn't tell us much, though. Let's just keep moving. If he wants to show himself, we'll permit him. If he won't, then by the end of our stay, we'll have to confront him. We just have to make sure he doesn't go anywhere with any information. We don't have much now, but we could."

"Right." Apollos and Bryan both agreed.

"Let's go." Bryan maneuvered Dragon from the water's edge and back to the company.

Alexa, Hazerk, and Eelyne were now practicing their sword fighting two on one, while Warkan looked on.

"Okay, mount up. I want to make camp before dark," Bryan announced. "And maybe we can get in another lesson, too."

After taking a quick glance at the silent lagoon, the company moved inland. It was dusk when they set up camp in a small alcove in the trees. With Warkan tending to the animals and Alkin and Hazerk tending to the freshly caught rabbit roasting over the fire, Bryan gave another lesson to Eelyne and Alexa.

To the sound of the crackling of the fire and swordplay, Alexa watched, sword in hand, as Eelyne took a bout with Bryan. The two men moved swiftly and easily; their attacks administered with precision and their guards never down. Watching them, she felt somewhat useless. She could *maybe* someday be as good as Eelyne, with lots of practice. But, she realized, she could never, no matter how hard she tried, be as good as the Master Sword. If she were asked to explain how he fought, she wouldn't even be able to find the right words. His footwork was flawless, as was his strategy. He could most definitely keep his opponent on their toes, never knowing what move he would make next. He was too quick, too cunning, and he did it all gracefully. She clenched her teeth in frustration. She felt defeated before she even started. She stared at the ground, where the scuffed footprints of the match were.

"Hello? Sand Queen? Your turn now." Bryan waved a hand in front of her to get her attention. He wasn't even out of breath. Eelyne was leaning on a nearby tree, huffing slightly. She raised her sword and Bryan gave her a pragmatic look. "If I'm not mistaken, I think this is the first time I've ever seen you look so beaten. Like you actually believe you *can't* do something," he said, snagging the attention of everyone.

"So?" she shot back. "Maybe I can't do this."

The Master Sword sighed. "Yes, you can. I don't want that attitude while I teach you."

"Warkan's right. My sword tactics are nonexistent. I only know the bow and arrow and some dagger throwing," she said, looking at her sword with wide, unguarded eyes as if she were scared of it.

"Oh, just fight me, girl!" Exasperated, Bryan raised his sword. Alexa reluctantly found her stance. "I'll teach you enough to survive. Contrary to what I think sometimes, you're not dim-witted. You *will* learn. I just want you to be able to stay alive. You don't have to know how to take out an entire regiment single handedly. Stay tough! Don't fall out on me already. No one becomes a master overnight."

Getting a determined look in her eye, she went to strike at him. But before she even thought about moving her sword, he had his blade at her throat. She clenched her jaw and glared at no one in particular.

"Look." Bryan lowered his sword. "You don't protect yourself. You're too worried about trying to figure out how to attack. There has to be an even balance between the two. You can't leave yourself unguarded. You've got to be quicker. At least quicker than your opponent. However, it goes both ways. You can't always be on the run from your enemy either. If you're going to attack—attack! And keep on attacking." Bryan paused for a minute and gazed thoughtfully at her. She now looked rather aggravated, but he continued, knowing it was just frustration. "When Warrior Eelyne and I are fighting, you need to really observe our tactics so you can put them into action. I will guide you as you practice, but observation is invaluable." Alexa gave him a stiff nod. "Also," he looked thoughtful again, "you need to be in better shape. You'll eventually gain the upper strength the more you practice, but I should start making all of you run instead of ride for endurance."

"What? I ain't gonna run," Hazerk piped up from his spot at the fire, sounding a little vexed. "It took me a long time to earn Red Man. I'm gonna ride him."

"Red Man? That's your mount's name? Red Man?" Warkan asked, a derisive glint in his eyes. Hazerk shot him a glare.

"Be quiet," Bryan snapped. "You'll all do what I tell you."

"Oh, yes," Alexa said, her eyes flashing with sudden petulance. "I almost forgot. What was it you were discussing down on the beach earlier today? I thought it was a deal I could know and have final input on everything."

Bryan whipped around and gave her his most menacing glower yet. Alkin even looked up from attending the fire with an indignant look in his eyes.

"We were planning on discussing this with you all later. Now is not the time," Bryan said as if he were speaking to a child. He walked over to Alexa, his body quivering as he towered over her. She held her stance, but suddenly, for the first time, she felt small in his presence. "And for future reference, I'd suggest that you don't speak accusingly to us again," he said, his voice tense and low and his azure eyes spitting bright flames.

"And." Alkin stood and came closer to Alexa, reining in his irritation and speaking softer, "Just so you know. Everything we ever have or ever will discuss has been and will always be for the best of this company. And, as I promised, any major issues will be settled by all of us. And your say, Alexa, will be vital in everything. But, as Sword Bryan already explained, we can't discuss it so openly. We'll speak to each of you aside later tonight, to make it not appear obvious. Let me just say this, keep close to the camp and don't speak of our mission." He went back and sat down.

Everyone in the company glanced at one another in apprehension; even the horses shifted uneasily. Alexa let out a huge, pent-up breath. Her face relaxed, and she looked Sword Bryan and Prince Alkin straight on and said, "I'm sorry. I have a temper like my father. It won't happen again. I promise."

There was a moment of silence.

"Good," Bryan stated, and Alkin nodded his acceptance. "Now let's practice. I'll teach you strategy so it's like a second nature to you." He took up his sword and she followed suit. Everyone went about their business once again.

That night, Bryan took the first watch. As they passed out dinner earlier, he and Alkin had disclosed the presence of their shadow to each in the company in as a surreptitious manner as possible, and Apollos had stepped away to keep an eye on the intruder in his own camp. The Sword felt primed, but not afraid or even uneasy. He knew the unicorn would spear the mystery man through before he could try anything.

As Bryan surveyed the camp, he caught eyes with another, even though it was way past dark. Alexa. She lied awake, watching him as he moved. He gave her a questioning and penetrating stare that asked, 'what's wrong?'

Holding his eyes for only a moment longer, the girl shrugged and turned over to face the darkened woods. The Head-Master Sword brushed it off and continued his surveyance.

Everyone slept safely and soundly for the remainder of the night.

The next morning, Alkin, Bryan, and Alexa made the short trek to the lagoon. When they came to the water's edge, Apollos met up with them, coming out of the woods from their right.

The lagoon's placid waves lapped up on the white sandy shores; its emerald shallows changing to a deep cobalt at its depths. The companions could tell just by looking that the lagoon was practically bottomless, probably filled with caverns and many underwater tunnels.

As the others surveyed the area, Alexa shut her eyes and breathed in the salty air. She listened to the world around her with her senses. She could feel the soft pulse of magic. It was very subtle. The earth around her distressed because of the absence of magic. The land desperately hung onto every last remnant. It yearned for it, so it clung to the pieces that were still there: the merpeople. It was like a widower catching the perfume of his lost wife. Its subtle presence lingered, a painful reminder that magic once dwelled there.

"They're still here," she breathed, almost reverently.

"Yes, I feel the vibration as well." Apollos stood, facing the tranquil waters of the lagoon; the breeze lifted his iridescent mane.

"How do we call them?" Alkin whispered.

Apollos and Alexa looked at one another in thought. Bryan watched them with curiosity, patiently waiting to see what they would decide.

"Well, I could dive out to the center and see if I could beckon them to the surface," Alexa suggested feebly.

"Hmm, something tells me that won't work," Bryan said. "You said they were reclusive. Besides, I don't want you to drown, or worse, get eaten by something."

"That would probably relieve you," she said dryly.

Bryan grunted a garbled response and shifted his thoughtful gaze back over the water.

"Well..." The unicorn began to pace up and down the beach at the water's edge. He lowered his muzzle and sniffed the seawater as the others looked on, lost on what to do.

"Even if we alert them to our presence, which we might have already, we'll probably have a hard time to get them to come out and speak with us. They won't want to be bothered," Alkin said. "You have no intuition clues, Alexa?"

The young woman shook her head regretfully and followed the unicorn down the beach, kicking a seashell as she went.

Bryan and Alkin watched in silence as their two companions slowly circled around to the other side of the lagoon. The morning sun was getting warmer and Bryan was starting to sweat. *Just great; we'll never figure out how to get them to come out. Maybe some fish bait...* He thought with no small amount of amusement.

When Alexa and Apollos reached the other side, Bryan allowed himself to admire the pretty picture they made while they contemplated.

The slender, raven-haired young woman looked almost like a fierce warrior as she gazed out over the cobalt waters. Her stance was strong: a thoughtful scowl set across her features, bow and quiver slung over her back, dagger at her thigh, sword at her hip. And then there was the unicorn, representing the opposite: the epitome of innocence, with his pure white, satiny coat and blazing iridescent mane and tail blowing in the wind. His horn shattered the light across the lagoon. The two figures standing between the vibrant green forest and cobalt waters looked breathtaking. As the Sword gazed, a harsh voice crushed his picture.

"I'm going in!" Alexa shouted across to them.

"We don't know what's in there!" Alkin shouted back.

"I don't feel anything evil," she said, and then started running back around the lagoon's edge toward them. She reached them, a little breathless, and with Apollos cantering at her heels.

"Then, I'm going in with you," Bryan said.

"No, I don't want to anger them."

"Can you swim?"

"Of course."

"How long can you hold your breath?"

"Well…"

"See? It's not a good idea. What if something drags you under? I won't let you," Bryan said firmly.

"Wait! I have an idea," Apollos said, a light in his eyes. They turned to him. "I don't know why I didn't think of this right away."

"What?" they said.

"I'll just lower my horn in the water and give off magical vibrations. That's got to make them curious, and they'll have to come investigate."

"That sounds like the best yet," Bryan said, and then mumbled, "I feel like an idiot that we can't figure out how to communicate. I even studied earth cultures and relations as one of my specialized classes."

Alkin and Apollos gave the Master Sword a remorseful look.

"It wasn't concerning magical beings, though," Alexa said. "This is entirely different. Don't worry. I'll handle it." She turned to Apollos. "Okay, let's try it."

The unicorn lowered his horn into the lapping waters. They all felt a slight tremor in the air as he displayed his magic. His horn lit green as he sent forth silent vibrations that would reach into the bottomless lagoon.

The four of them stared hard at the center of the lagoon, the unicorn watching eagerly as he continued to send forth the call.

They stood there for agonizing minutes and were beginning to lose hope when Alkin looked up and out to open sea, rubbing his neck and sighing. His quick intake of breath caused them to jerk their heads up. "Look!" he said in a hushed, excited whisper.

Past the lagoon, way out to sea, was a rock. Most likely the greatest of its breadth extended to the depths, but the tip jutted above the waves, and on that smoothened tip sat a figure.

Even from a distance, they could see the figure was foreboding; his upper body broad and well-muscled, the lower half a great, glistening fishtail wrapped around the rock. His face was ageless, his features stern as he looked upon them with an inquiring brow. A mane of blonde hair fell to his shoulders, and in his hands, he held an enormous spear.

Feeling choked, the companions moved along the edge of the lagoon to pause at the rim of the Elendace Sea.

Bryan was the first to find his voice. "Hello! We come to you in peace!" he called out to him.

"That's what your Relations studies taught you?" Alexa snickered out of the corner of her mouth.

"What do you suggest?" he looked down at her, his features tense.

She smiled, her eyes sparkling a bright sky blue. "I was just teasing. Relax. The hard part is over."

After being the subject of her bewitching smile, the Sword breathed more easily; and they waited, anxious, as the figure continued to gaze at them in silent austerity.

"We only wish a word with you! If you permit!" Bryan persisted. "We apologize for intruding!"

The merman seemed to consider this, and then he raised his hand in acceptance and called out, "We will speak only to the girl! No weapons!" His voice was powerful. He beckoned to Alexa.

"He wants her to swim out," Alkin said, a little shocked.

"Right," Bryan said through a set jaw, his eyes sparking a flame of irritation.

"What's the matter?" Alexa hurriedly began to take off her dagger, bow, quiver, and sword.

Apollos answered her. "They're asking to speak with the one they think is the weakest and least likely to do harm out of the party."

"What?" She halted her undressing, indignant.

"Right," Bryan repeated tersely.

"I don't like him being armed and not her," Alkin said.

"That wouldn't matter anyhow," Bryan said. "He's asking her to *swim* out to him. What could she do if they decided to attack?"

"Speak to him," Apollos urged.

"We don't want to cause any harm! Will she be safe?" Bryan hollered out to him.

"No harm will come to her if she is honest!" the merman answered.

"I'll be fine," Alexa stated, gazing eagerly out to sea.

The others looked at her, and Bryan received a slap of shock upon seeing her half undressed. He almost reacted by respectfully turning around, but he quickly told himself to grow up.

Alexa stepped to the water's edge. Apollos came to stand beside her. "Be careful," he said. He gave her a reassuring nudge on the arm.

"Thank you, Apollos." She kissed his soft muzzle and grinned. The unicorn bobbed his head. She waded out to her knees. The cool, emerald water swirled around her legs and the soft sand squeezed up between her toes.

"Alexa!"

She turned to see Prince Alkin looking apprehensive and Sword Bryan looking as apprehensive as he would ever. He gave the impression of having stepped on a thorn.

"We'll be here if you need us," Alkin said.

"I know."

"Tell us everything."

"I will." She then waded out past her waist, dove into the water, and began to swim toward the fierce-looking merman.

CHAPTER SEVENTEEN

Whispering, all she ever heard anymore was furtive whispering. Melea would walk the corridors of the castle daily and her sensitive ears would prickle at the sound of hushed, anxious voices escaping from chambers.

She was on her way to the kitchen when she paused by the slightly ajar door to the warriors' and Master Swords' common room.

"Do you know what's going on?" a hushed voice asked.

"No one does. Things are just changing," another voice whispered back.

"I'm worried. This isn't normal. Prince Alkin isn't here. How do we know if these orders are his?" the first voice said.

"I don't know. I don't like it either," the second voice said.

"This isn't at all what is taught in our code. Do you think this is an overturn of power?" the first voice said.

"Hush! Don't speak like that openly, especially in the castle," a third voice reprimanded with a hiss.

The door slammed on Melea's undiscovered presence. She started for the kitchen again, her pace faster. Her stomach gave a lurch inside her. She pressed her hand on it; it sunk with worry.

The castle's atmosphere was a tense, masked worry. She couldn't go anywhere without a warrior or a servant looking upon one another in a lost way.

Her heart pumped her blood ferociously. She was frightened. There was a strange trap weaving its way around them. She couldn't tell its origin, nor could she place what the trap was. But she knew this: most in the castle were innocent, and they would be the first victims.

She whisked by yet another ajar door. A loud voice that spilled through nearly made her jump clear across the corridor. She paused to listen, placing a hand over her heart to calm it.

"Why can't I just wear your wedding dress?" Lady Dorsa's annoyed voice said.

"But dear, don't you want a new one? The fashions have

changed so much. The Chancellor will appreciate it. Let's go pick out new fabric," Lady Adama beseeched.

"No, Mother, I don't want a new dress. I'd rather not."

There was a moment of tense silence, and then Lady Adama said, "This is your wedding. I want to make a good impression."

"Right." Dorsa groaned. Then she said angrily, "Maybe if I could marry whom I actually want to, I would get a new dress. It doesn't make any difference to me if I have to marry the Chancellor."

"Don't get that tone with me," Adama said harshly. "I don't want to hear about this low-class warrior anymore."

"That's no way to speak of Shelkite's warriors!"

There was a spell of silence.

"You are acting ungrateful. I'm sure the Chancellor is a good man. You'll get to know him soon and you'll change your mind." Lady Adama's tone was curt.

"What do you mean?" Dorsa asked, a tinge of worry in her voice.

"The convoy that'll be escorting you is on its way now. It'll be here next week to take you to Vtalmay. I've decided you'll live in the Ice Palace until the wedding at the end of the year. That way you and the Chancellor will have the opportunity to get to know each other during your betrothal. Your brother should be back by then...hopefully."

"What?" Dorsa choked. "You are sending me there now?"

"Yes. The Chancellor agrees with the plans. Don't you want to get to know him? Your father and I did the same before we were married, and it worked out splendidly," Adama said, ignoring her daughter's distress.

"How can you do this to me?" Dorsa cried.

"Do not raise your voice at me."

Dorsa ignored her. "You married Father because you loved him, right?"

"Yes."

"Then, why can't I do the same? I love someone else and you're forcing me to marry this other man! I don't want to get to know him! I don't want to live in a frozen country and I don't want to be a lady of a chancellor!"

"Don't act like a spoiled brat," Adama seethed.

"You're asking me to be a whore for good politics. You're asking me to turn my back on someone who is depending on me to be here when he returns. Alkin hasn't even approved. This isn't Shelkite's way!"

"Dorsa," Adama said more calmly, "it will be fine. I promise. In the future, you'll be happy because of this match. Now, come on, let's have the seamstress make you a beautiful dress. How about using white velvet for the material?"

Melea, fearing her discovery, darted down the corridor, her heart in her throat.

★★★★

Alexa swam with determination toward the merman, her strong strokes slicing her way through the water. He looked on, motionless, watching her with austere, hard eyes and pursed lips. Winded, she focused on the bizarre figure and forced her heart to calm its anxious pounding. She swallowed a gulp of green, salty water on accident and had to choke it down.

The merman was sitting on the right side of the boulder. His magnificent fishtail wrapped around the rock toward the rear. As she neared, she saw the tail was larger than her entire body. It looked extremely powerful, as did the merman's upper body. He was much larger than she had anticipated. His naked chest was broad and robust. His muscles were defined and flexed with his slightest movement.

She swam toward the middle of the rock, far enough not to invade his space. No matter how she looked at it, she was at his mercy. With the ocean surrounding her and mysterious creatures swimming beneath, she was trapped. She clambered up onto the rock and glanced to shore, her eyes showing the slightest need for support from her companions. She spotted their distant shapes: Alkin's slightly lanky physique, Bryan's tall and strong body, and the elegant equine silhouette of Apollos. This encouraged her, and she focused on her present task. She raised her head and locked eyes with the merman for the first time.

She drew in a breath. Aside from Apollos, he was the most beautiful creature she had ever seen. In his hand he held a cold-looking spear upright. His face was an otherworldly handsome. It had an ancient and strange beauty that looked as old as Time itself might look, but he was young in appearance. His skin was a soft, sandy brown. His tail, a brilliant blue-green, glistened with droplets of water. He had strong, well-set features with a mane of sandy blonde hair that fell to his shoulders. His eyes were captivating. They, too, were an extravagant color, changing from blue to green, looking as deep and watery as the ocean he lived in. His gaze upon her stirred the magic inside her, warring with it, as if to break past its barriers.

She couldn't speak, and he was waiting. She sat there, dripping wet on the warm rock as the sun's rays danced on the glassy water. A slight breeze wafted by and chilled her; it brought her mind to life.

"Hello, sir. I'm Alexandra." She bowed her head, attempting to be formal. "It's gracious of you to speak with me." The merman acknowledged her with a slight nod but continued to stare penetratingly at her. "It's very important that I talk with your people. Please, if you consent." She tried her best to act courteous but felt out of rhythm. She was half-dressed, wet, and having trouble using her powers on this wholly magical creature.

"People? There's not many left of my kind, Alexandra," the merman finally spoke, his voice curt and strong. He cocked his head and scrutinized her. "I allow you to speak with me solely because you have a unicorn in your company. My people are and always have been friends with unicorns. Any other creatures, aside from naiads, we don't wish to associate with. We wish to be left alone. What is it you have to say? Why have you brought me out of the sheltered depths? We're a dying race, and I don't desire to speak with a human or half human, as it is, for any length of time."

Alexa closed her eyes and took a breath to relax herself. She began to speak, but the merman broke in first.

"There's no need to worry. I will listen to your words. Whatever you have to say must be important for you to risk your life to say it. You're a half-witch, are you not?" he asked. She nodded. "Go on," he said.

Her courage returned. She was part of his world, too, even if it was just partially. She smiled, subconsciously hoping to impress the handsome creature. Then, she burst into a succinct explanation of Eetharum's predicament. The merman, to her surprise, turned out to be an immersed and concerned listener.

When she had finished, he leaned back and laid the spear over his lap. He heaved a sigh and said, "In the past, this could've been a problem for the merpeople. If there were more than just three of us, I would say this would be a problem worth our power and time to help those above waters. But, as it is, I cannot see how the wizard would even be concerned with us. We are practically extinct. We're best left in hiding, not provoking his attention. There isn't much three of us could do. I'm sorry for your trouble, but the merpeople are powerless and best left alone."

Alexa looked crestfallen, and the merman gazed at her with sad eyes. "That's what you have to say? Eetharum will become under the tyranny of a cruel man—even worse, a wizard. He's recruiting horrid creatures and wicked men as we speak. He's already killed and tortured and plans to do more. We need all the *good* magical power on our side we can get to stop him. Don't you hear me? We can stop him before he reaches further! You won't even give me advice? My father told me you are a wise people and have powers that most magical creatures on land don't possess. I was summoned to help by a power higher than me and then sent to you. Don't tell me I've already failed? Or am I following an evil power? Is that all that's left?" The desperation and terror she felt at her possible failure shadowed her features.

The merman smiled for the first time, albeit it was entwined with sadness. Right then, Alexa felt her magical defenses fall, and despite her indignation, she would have dived into the water and gladly lived with him forever. She struggled for control of herself. Some ancient magic was at work...

"My child," he said with care.

"I'm not a child. I'm a woman—a sorceress," she proclaimed with fire in her eyes.

The merman smiled again. "You say that only because my

presence has a draw on your human blood. Focus on your magic and listen to me and listen well," he commanded, but not unkindly.

Alexa shut her eyes and searched for the magic pieces inside of her. She found them and gathered them up. And then, to her great relief, she felt in control again. Her deceptive longing for him dissipated.

She knew it was from an old curse. The merpeople couldn't control it. If a human looked a merperson in the eyes, it caused them to yearn greatly for them. It was what had eventually destroyed the merpeople as a race—humans desiring them, taking them, and ultimately killing them. The hunger was different for each human: greed, admiration, the want for blood. For Alexa's half-human heart, it was lust.

"The naiad who gave your name is not omniscient. She is a messenger from the High Power, which is far from evil. Aside from my people, there are still many good powers left. They are in hiding and must be sought. You are expected to help if it truly was the naiad who gave your name. Even though you had a choice not to accept, it is honorable you did. The High Power does not expect you to do this alone. The help you seek will be sent."

"Right! That's why I came to you," she broke in.

"Listen! You say your witch intuition sent you to us. I don't know of this intuition. But the merpeople can do nothing. If the wizard knows we still exist, we may be in some danger. But there are too few of us. He knows we wouldn't be able to do any harm. And any power we have would be of no value to him. He would leave us alone. Please don't cause the premature death of the last of my kind."

"You just keep repeating that you want to be left alone so that no harm will come to you. How selfish. All I ask is for advice at the least. You're right; I am *only* a girl. But how am *I* supposed to know what to do to defeat a powerful wizard? I can't ask my father to do it. He's bound by an oath to never do magic. My brothers don't know magic. The others I travel with are more than willing to help, but they don't know any more than I. So, that leaves me and this counter-magic to save Eetharum. It leaves *me* because I'm the *only* sorceress left. The last witch. That's why the naiad spoke my name. It's because magic is needed. But *you,* being a magical creature, won't help. Even though the men standing on that shore,"—she flung her arm out to point—"have no magic of their own to save them, nothing but their own intellect and brute strength to use, and probably the last unicorn in the world, are willing to give their lives because it's *needed.* This world will keep going on when you and I die. But I won't hand it over to be consumed by evil if there is something I can do now that will secure the futures of innocent others. I want to help. And you *know* you must help in some way, even if it's just one thing. My intuition says so. And, let me tell you this. If there is something you have that Ret wants, he'll come and get it and kill you anyway, even if I hadn't brought his attention to you. Now you can be at least warned and prepared. But please tell me there's something you can do."

She had spoken forcefully in her desperation. Oh, how she wished she had been right in believing the merpeople would lead her to the counter-magic. What a waste! What would the others think?

The merman gazed at her in thoughtful sorrow. He didn't rebuke her for speaking to him in such a way, which in old times would have been considered extremely disrespectful on her part. She waited anxiously for him to speak as she searched his features with hope. She now fully understood what her father had meant by the merpeople being reclusive and not liking to be bothered.

"Alexandra," the merman said.

"Yes."

"You must come back tomorrow at the same hour. I'll take you to see my father. He's much wiser and knows more of these things. I will speak to him now. We may be able to help, but I cannot promise anything."

Alexa cracked a smile so fast her cheeks hurt. She had to restrain herself from jumping over and hugging him. "Thank you so much! We're sincerely grateful. I'll come back."

The merman smiled warmly, his brilliant eyes rippling like happy waves. "You're welcome. And please bring the unicorn in the morning, too."

"Yes," she breathed. She began to slide off the rock, but the merman caught her hand, and she looked back in surprise.

"I will guide you to shore. There is a bad spot I don't wish you to swim across alone."

"Oh…" she said, somewhat shocked and curious. But she decided not to question what he meant by 'bad spot' or why he had not offered to guide her in over it.

"Come." He released her hand, and they dove in. She began to swim, the merman close at hand. His fishtail churned the water powerfully. She guessed he was probably not moving as fast as he was capable. She couldn't help but steal a few glances his way. It was amazing to see him swim. When they reached shallow water, he left her with a goodbye smile. Then he was gone from her sight.

Bryan, Alkin, and Apollos were waiting up the shore, watching; the men looking as if their eyes would pop out of their heads. As she waded out of the shallow waters, they all came to her, their faces expressing anxious anticipation.

Apollos reached her first. He stepped in front of her, blocking the breeze, letting the warmth of his body warm her chilled one. His chocolate eyes twinkled as he looked at her. She smiled, resting a hand on his smooth neck. "How did it go?" he asked.

"Well, I think." She shivered in the breeze. The day was warm, but she felt chilled from nerves. Bryan and Alkin reached them and waited before them, squinting in the sun, their hair tousled by the wind.

Alkin removed his lightweight overcoat and stepped around the unicorn to place it on her shoulders. "Here. Keep this until you dry," he said. "So, what did he say?"

"Well…" she started, watching their expressions carefully, "We have to come back tomorrow." The others waited for her to go on, their faces wondering. "He would only speak to me because Apollos was with us. He said at first that they were powerless and would rather be left alone."

"Humph," Bryan grunted but let her continue.

"He says that his father might be able to help, but he couldn't promise anything. It took convincing on my part to get him to just say that." She paused and then added, "He wants Apollos to come tomorrow, too."

"We noticed it looked like you were having a hard time," Alkin said.

"Why?" she asked, puzzled.

Bryan answered, "We heard your raised voice and noted the desperate hand gestures." He grinned.

Alexa laughed incredulously. "I was yelling at him?"

"You did just fine." Alkin smiled.

"You got us a second meeting," Bryan added.

"And whatever you said pressed him out of his unwise choice of ignoring the problem," Apollos praised.

Alexa sighed and looked back at the rock where she had sat with the merman. "I just hope there is something they can do. There are only three of them left, you know."

"We'll see what tomorrow brings," Bryan said. He then motioned for them to head back to camp. "Let's see if our new mysterious neighbor has shown up on our doorstep with a pie."

They began to trek back inland to the camp. Reaching the woods, Apollos flicked his tail and gave a small supportive nuzzle in Alexa's hand before he split off to continue his surveillance of the mystery man. The three companions entered the shade of the trees, with Alkin leading the way a few paces ahead. Alexa fell in step with Bryan.

"Listen," she half whispered, a bit nervous about what she wanted to say. It was outside of her usual nature, and she felt strange.

Bryan looked down at her, curious and waiting for her to continue. The girl fidgeted, shifting her bundle of dry clothes to under her other arm and pulled Alkin's overcoat tighter around herself. He had to force his eyes to veer in another direction from where they were mindlessly wandering—down the neck of the overcoat.

Alexa waited for the Sword to say something that might show his exasperation with her. But he just stared at her, his bright azure eyes wide and curious. "Uh, about last night," she said.

His brow furrowed, and he gazed at her with his undivided attention. "What about it?" he asked in his normal tones. "Why are you whispering?"

Alexa snorted and continued in a hushed voice, "I just wanted to apologize."

"For what?"

"For losing my temper."

"You already did. Forget about it." He brushed it off and began walking faster.

"Wait... Ouch!"

"What is it?" His voice now sounded slightly exasperated. He stopped and looked back at her to see her picking a small thorn out of her foot. "For the love of—here!" He stalked back and dropped her boots, which he had been carrying, at her feet. "You're dry now, hurry and get dressed. Hey! Hold up, Alkin," Bryan hollered up to the Prince, forgetting to address his old friend properly.

Alkin stopped and peered back at them. Realizing the situation, he nodded. He came to take his overcoat back and wait for her to dress so they wouldn't become separated.

When they were on their way again, Alexa attempted to smooth down the escaped hairs from her braid and caught up with the Master Sword, who was now leading.

He didn't look at her, but merely said, "Yes?"

"I just wanted to say I'm sorry I broke our pact. And I promise on my life that I won't act that way again. I want to be as helpful as I can from here on out. I've acted wrongly toward you." She had no idea why she was pressing this issue, nor why she felt nervous. For some unknown reason, it seemed crucial to make *him* understand she was sorry and to have *his* sanction.

"All right." He smiled down at her, although his smile looked a little mischievous. "Is that *all* you were up pondering about last night when you were watching me on my guard?" he added, with a boyish twinkle in his eye.

Alexa narrowed her eyes. "Yes. That's all, Master Sword. Please let the Prince know that it won't happen again." Her reply was curt, and then she stomped up ahead, feeling embarrassed.

Behind her, she heard Alkin say to Bryan, "What's wrong with her?"

Upon returning to camp, they explained the situation to the others. The warriors also reported there had been no sign of their anonymous shadow. Then Alexa and Eelyne had a quick combat lesson. After, they all ate a tasty meal, consisting of more fresh rabbit—a compliment of Warkan's hunting. And they turned in early for the night, each wishing that both morning and answers would come sooner.

CHAPTER EIGHTEEN

The next morning, they dined on fresh fruit from nearby trees. The fruit was so delectable that Sword Bryan had the warriors gather up more for later while he, Apollos, the Prince, and Alexa trekked back to the sea.

They reached the shore a little earlier than they had the day before. They waited. A breeze blew across the turquoise waters, carrying with it the fragrance of wet sand and the potent salty smell of marine life.

Bryan broke the silence, "I think someone needs to accompany her out today."

"I agree," Alkin replied. His brow furrowed as he watched the waves rise and fall with more enthusiasm than the previous day.

"I'll go, since he did say to bring me along," Apollos said. He came to stand gallantly beside Alexa.

"Yes. He seemed more at ease seeing you with us." She shaded her eyes from the sun as she regarded the unicorn.

"Let's go. Take a hold of my mane," Apollos instructed.

Without glancing at the Prince or Sword, Alexa gently entwined her fingers in the silky, iridescent tendrils of the unicorn's mane. He waded into the whooshing, jade-colored shallows. She followed, feeling strength and power emanate from him. It crossed her mind that she was allowing her companions to know she could touch the unicorn without retribution.

Soon, they were in the deeper waters, and the unicorn pulled Alexa along, his legs churning the water beneath her. She was careful not to interfere with his slashing hooves.

"Something lurks," Apollos whispered.

She glanced down into the depths. Her heart skipped a half a beat upon seeing a blurry, but large, shadow moving below. She raised her eyes, deciding not to dwell on it.

"I can't sense it... You can?" she asked, perplexed.

"Yes. My powers can sense a bit beyond the stifling water. Water masks your senses; not completely, but enough. Beware of that in the future," the unicorn advised.

Alexa nodded her understanding. She had never realized this and wondered if she could even sense anything at all in the water, since she was only a half-blood. She bit her lip in thought, tasting the bitterness of the sea.

Apollos guided her safely to the rock. He helped her climb onto it by hoisting her up with his nose. Then he gracefully leapt onto it and shook himself, sending a spray of sparkling water droplets.

Alexa looked down at her attire. She was once again in her undergarments. She had removed her pendent as she had the day before, but, as always, her hair was still corralled in its snug braid. Her mother would be horrified if she knew she was strutting around barely clothed in front of two men. She glanced at the shore to see Alkin and Bryan standing there, shading their eyes, staring out to her and Apollos. There wasn't a doubt in her mind they took the situation serious. *Besides, they've probably seen a woman's body before now;* she had to be realistic. She knew she wasn't anything extraordinary to look at—as far as her figure anyhow— and she didn't think her face completely ugly. But she was skinny and had a humble chest. Her older brothers' constant teasing of her looks had always kept her vanity well-reined in.

"Here he comes," Apollos interrupted her thoughts.

At that moment, the merman from the previous day leapt onto the rock.

"Alexandra," he greeted her, "and noble unicorn." He inclined his head to Apollos.

"My name is Apollos." The unicorn lowered his finely shaped head in acknowledgement. "What do you call yourself, honorable merman?"

"You can call me Nereus. It's a version of my name."

"That's fine," Apollos consented. Alexa nodded in accord, her eyes unmoving from the merman's captivating features.

"Come, let's not waste time. I'll take you to my father, Glyndwr." Nereus turned to dive into the azure waves.

"Wait!" Alexa called, puzzled. "How can we follow? Are you swimming deep?"

Nereus looked back at them and smiled apologetically.

"Excuse me. I'd momentarily forgotten you can't breathe under water."

"I can, Nereus, but Alexa can't," Apollos said. Alexa shot the unicorn a quizzical glance. "My horn empowers me to do so," he replied to her silent question.

"Oh," she breathed, her eyebrows rising. At this, something in her mind seemed to open, and she wondered about Apollos' powers and how extensive and potent they were...

"Here, come stand beside me." Nereus held out his hand for her. She came to the exquisite man's side at the rock's edge—if she could even call him a man—and tentatively took his hand.

Nereus gave her a significant look and raised the massive spear in his hands for her to see. "This spear isn't only used for hunting; it contains its own magic. Hold on to it tight and don't let go. It will allow you to breathe and speak in my world."

Eyes sparkling with a touch of adventure and apprehension, Alexa regarded the spear with awe. It looked cold to touch. But when she wrapped her fingers around it, it was warm, and she could feel the magic flow into her. She took in a breath; it was as if she had awakened from a deep sleep. She looked up and reveled in the bright cerulean sky. The world spun haphazardly about her; she was drunk with the pulsing, foreign magic. Then, suddenly, something pierced her windpipe, and she could no longer breathe. Her hand flew to her throat, and panic fled into her eyes. She gasped for air and found she couldn't speak.

"Come." Nereus took her other hand and jerked her into the crashing waves.

On the shore, Prince Alkin and Sword Bryan viewed the meeting with bated breath. They watched stiffly as the merman disappeared into the sea, jerking an unnerved Alexa with him. Bryan's tense features became hard, and he let out a tetchy mumble.

"Apollos will protect her," Alkin whispered earnestly.

"Yes...but that's my responsibility," he retorted.

Anxious and holding her breath out of habit, Alexa glanced

over her shoulder as Nereus towed her down into the cool waters. She saw Apollos leap into the water after them, diving to swim beside her. She relaxed; while she was mostly confident, she still felt some unease traveling to the unknown depths of the sea alone. It was nice to know Apollos was near.

She discovered the spear was lighter when in water and held it closer to her body. She closed her eyes for courage and took a deep breath of…water? It gushed silkily into her mouth and nose. She could breathe. She opened her eyes and looked around. Everything was bright and clear. Her full confidence flooded back.

They swam out and down; the merman dragging her swiftly along. With wide eyes, she gazed at the surrounding sights. Having thought it was going to be dark and dreary below the sea, like the deep river near her home, she was thrilled to be assaulted by vibrant colors. There was an array of brightly colored fish and a brilliant reef filled with all kinds of plant life and creatures. The sandy bottom was white, the coral a milky cream color. It was a whole new realm. And Alexa intended to ingrain the images in her mind for forever. It was magnificent.

They swam over the reef and down into a wide crevice, going deeper into the sea. It wasn't dark or scary. They took a few turns swimming through tunnels comprising bluish rocks smoothened by years of water brushing them sleek. They swam by many more fish that seemed unafraid of their presence. She noted plants and sea urchins that were arranged decoratively around cave entrances carved into rock facades that looked suspiciously like doorways. They were swimming along an underwater street.

On they swam. The street occasionally opened into beautiful expansive areas that could be nothing other than an underwater park or valley. She couldn't stop her eyes from drinking in all the wonder. There were whales, dolphins, seahorses, and brightly colored sea flowers everywhere.

Finally, the merman slowed his pace, and they turned into a short pathway that led into an underwater town; or what used to be. Homes of all kinds of designs lined the street along with shops and diners, all carved from rock. They were all vacant and lonesome. A purplish light from some kind of stone brightened their path, shining from lampposts along the way. She imagined merpeople thronging in the streets, going about their business, much the same as those above the waters did.

Nereus took her to a beautifully carved rock that looked much like a palace above waters would, except it was smaller. The doorway was embellished with a purple blazing stone and plants that swayed gently back and forth with the current. A menacing looking fish guarded the threshold.

"Move aside, Sunshine," Nereus addressed the yellow fish that was roughly the size of a dog. It immediately stopped baring its crooked, sharp teeth that jutted out from its under bite, and put a congenial, almost fond, look on its face as Nereus stroked him down his back. It gave a warning look at Alexa and Apollos and then swam off at a zippy pace.

Still holding her hand, Nereus guided Alexa through the door, beckoning to Apollos. He paused just past the doorway in what was a large, domed receiving hall, and let her hand go.

Alexa looked around. They were swimming above a polished floor, though the floor and walls were fashionably decorated with flowers, pretty stones, and other various aquatic, homey objects. A smooth pathway—a ramp—sloped up out of the circular room to a balcony above and the second floor. A railing, carved up from the floor, ran up the side of it. Three doorways led out of the room in various directions.

"Wait here. My sister will attend you. My father is out back in the garden. I'll let him know you've arrived," Nereus said with a hospitable smile. He swam out the doorway opposite them.

After surveying the unusual room, Alexa looked over to Apollos bobbing in the water next to her. He was investigating an enormous pink and white flower in a pearl vase sitting just inside the entryway on a round table carved from the stone floor. His muzzle was nestled in the blossom as if he were smelling it. She smiled at the beautiful unicorn that was so strangely out of place in this water land.

She decided she would try out her voice to see how it worked under the spear's magic. "Can you understand him clearly like I can, Apollos?" Her voice sounded odd to her, garbled, and bubbles sprang haphazardly out of her mouth. But Apollos seemed to understand her completely well.

He turned from the flower, his mane and tail floating in billows around him, and said, "Yes." His voice sounded the same as it did above water.

A few moments later, a slender and beautiful mermaid swam into the room, greeting them with a pearly smile. "Hello, friends. Welcome."

"Thank you," they said in unison, Alexa's mouth sprouting bubbles.

"You can call me Vailea," she said. She had the same sandy blonde locks as Nereus, but they were much longer, falling down past her back. They flowed elegantly about her pretty, angular face, rising, falling, and waving with her every move. Her almond-shaped eyes were a vibrant violet and sparkled with life and gentleness. She had long, slender arms, fingers, and torso. Her chest was uncovered, though obscured by her long locks. And, unlike her brother's sandy brown skin, her skin was a soft alabaster, her cheeks rosy, and her lips full and red. Her fins were a different color than Nereus'. Instead of fading in and out from blue to green, her fins glistened violet and scarlet.

Apollos swam to meet her, lowering his head in respect. "I'm Apollos of Shelkite, and this is Alexandra of Kaltraz." He gestured with his horn to Alexa floating nearby, still gripping the spear. "I presume you already know our business?" he asked.

The mermaid smiled and nodded. "Yes, my brother filled us in yesterday. And I'm happy to say we might be able to help."

Alexa and Apollos shared a quick, relieved glance. Alexa's heart lightened a great deal. Her magical intuition had been right after all! She had been so worried she had led the company wrong already.

"Come, I'll take you to my father and brother. They're waiting in the garden. There isn't time to waste if the shores are in as much need as you say." She raised her arm and gestured toward the door opposite them. "Follow me." She swam through.

They hastened to follow.

Vailea guided them through a wonderful collection of underwater trees, plants, and flowers, all growing tall and swaying gently in the current. If Alexa and Apollos were not careful, they could have easily got lost in the vast forest. The mermaid led them through a path that wound its way deeper into the garden's heart. The underwater trees were as tall as trees on land. Alexa paused momentarily to touch the bark. It was smooth.

Seeing Apollos' tail flip around a sharp bend to the right, she swam as fast as her legs could paddle to catch up. She looked around, still awed by this new world. Fish of all kinds brushed up against her skin as if they were as curious of her as she was of them. She swam over a bed of sea clovers, and a herd of seahorses scattered out, swimming up the trail. She followed in the small herd's wake.

They came into a clearing where she found the others gathered around a beautiful collection of pearls. Thousands of pearls, varying in sizes from as small as a bead to as large as a child's toy ball, laid all around them. Their white beauty shed a strange light around the alcove.

"Alexandra, Apollos, this is my father, Glyndwr," Nereus introduced an older merman.

The unicorn and girl acknowledged the old merman by bowing their heads. When she raised her face, Alexa studied him. He appeared younger than he was, but he was by no accounts young, with a shock of long, stringy white hair and a beard just as white and long. He had gentle gray eyes and wrinkled skin. His fins were a subdued blue.

He held out his hands in a welcoming gesture and said to Apollos, "Many years have gone by since we have last seen your kind. We had feared the upper world had lost one of its most beautiful assets—the unicorns."

"No, not completely, albeit I'm probably the last," Apollos replied.

The old merman's face looked troubled. "The shores will be more than a little darker when the magic of the last unicorn passes."

"I could say the same of the merpeople," Apollos said, a sharp edge to his voice.

Alexa shot Apollos a puzzled glance at his tone, but she said nothing. Did he think they could preserve their race whereas he could not his own?

Glyndwr smiled knowingly but turned to Alexa to speak, "My son says there is a war coming to your lands. You have asked for our help because it's not just a war between men but of magic."

"Yes," she said, her eyes pleading.

"As you know, we can't do much, being only three of us, but we have a way to give you information. This will give you knowledge, and knowledge is a weighty key. If one knows of his enemies' plans, then he can learn how he can destroy them."

The old merman looked into Alexa's eyes, seeming to try and detect her reaction. She held his gaze fast, feeling a hot remark bubbling to the surface. Didn't they understand her?

"Yes, but we have our own spies who have told us of Ret's doings. We know he plans to crown himself emperor over all the countries of Eetharum. He plans to enslave the land and force the people to swear piety to the Demon. He's gathered an army of beings and humans. We know this *already*. What we need is good magic to counter his."

The three merpeople stared at her. She couldn't read their expressions, so she glanced at Apollos. He turned away from her, although he didn't look angry but rather amused by her sudden outburst. In remorse, she heaved a sigh; or what would have been one above waters.

"I see you have inherited the hot blood of your wizard father," Glyndwr said, but he smiled widely and forgivingly. "You are a very determined girl. Stubborn and brave, perhaps a little reckless. I also sense a bit of vanity. No wonder you've been chosen by the High Power for this job. You'll need to learn to control that temper and pride of yours better, as well as learn to trust."

Glyndwr studied her carefully, and Alexa felt he could see into the very depths of her heart. *Brave? The other words seem to describe me well enough, even reckless, or so Sword Bryan would say. But not brave.* She felt humbled as well as chagrined by the merman's brutal scrutiny.

"The High Power?" she questioned. It still perplexed her how she was chosen for this extreme task.

"Yes. You do believe in the High Power, don't you? The Master of the Sea? The two are the same. Us sea creatures just refer to the High Power as the Master of the Sea," Glyndwr said.

"Well, yes, of course. But I've never really thought about how it pertains to this," she said, then added quickly, "Other than the naiad's calling."

"If Apollos gained your name from the naiad, then it was indeed the High Power who sent for you. The Master of the Sea has his own reasons for naming you in particular. Only you may someday know the answer to that, and the purpose may not be what you think it is now. But you would do well to acknowledge the call and this chance you've been given to be an instrument. Of course, you always have a choice. But it is easier to ride the tide, than swim against it. It is good you have accepted this calling, and I'll help in ways I can, for my people are faithful to the Master of the Sea." Glyndwr looked at her in a significant way. "But you must understand what I mean by knowledge. You have come to the merpeople looking for some kind of magical weapon we can hand over so that you can fight this wizard. We don't have magic like that. And the war has not yet reached the waters where we live, so we can literally do nothing physically. But, I can give you a vision."

"A vision?" Alexa's brow furrowed quizzically.

"Yes, through this." He gestured toward a shell lying open on a bed of sea flora in the center of the garden. Pearls were arranged decoratively around it. They swam over and encircled it. The inside of the shell was glimmering milky colors of blue, silver, and green—mother-of-pearl.

Alexa gazed at it with curiosity. Apollos did the same. He had kept a respectful silence, but now he said, "This is much like the Guidance Naiad is above waters, isn't it? One beseeches her presence and asks her a question. Then, if she thinks you're worthy, she gives you an answer. Although they're usually a bit elusive, they're trustworthy."

"Yes, Apollos, it's much like that. This shell is the only one like it in all the sea, just like there is only one Guidance Naiad. They're both blessed by the Master of the Sea—vessels. But, this is a little more complicated. It gives visions of your answers. And sometimes, they're much harder to decipher than the mystifying words the naiad gives. The Mother of Pearl will sometimes show what *could* happen in the future, based on a given person's current path. And I emphasize *could*, Alexa." He turned to her and gave her a hard look. "For the future can change its path as easily as an air bubble. Don't make the mistake of believing what you will see is final. Because, I'm positive what the Mother of Pearl will show you is not going to be all sunbeams."

Alexa made a move to touch the seashell, but Glyndwr stopped her. "You must also know that you have only one chance to ask it the right question. Choose your words carefully, because if you do not, you may not get the answer you need. You're allowed only one question ever."

Alexa nodded solemnly and glanced at Apollos. He gave her an encouraging look and nudged her toward the shell. Her mind worked fervently to come up with the perfect words for her question.

"You must place your hand on the Mother of Pearl and ask it loud and clearly what you need," Glyndwr instructed, his gray eyes alight, staring into the glimmering shell. "Apollos, make sure you can also see. Four eyes and two minds are better. You can help her puzzle this through. We will watch, too."

Apollos moved closer to the shell, and Alexa looked anxiously around at the faces in her company. She saw the ethereal beauty of Vailea, the handsome Nereus, the lovely grandfather face of the old merman, and the always breathtaking, kindly unicorn. She gathered her courage. Apollos' chocolate eyes implored her to carry on. She placed her spear-free hand into the center of the Mother of Pearl and said loudly and clearly, emphasizing each syllable, "Show me what I need to know to understand how to defeat Ret the wizard in Zelka."

Instantly, a light glowed from the shell, illuminating their eager faces. Alexa's hand warmed uncomfortably on the shell, but she didn't remove it. Then the light began to swirl like a storm cloud. They leaned forward to peer into the silvery surface. Her eyes widened as a picture appeared. It was of a man…someone very familiar to her. He looked identical to her father. But this man was not her father. This man's eyes held a malice that she had never known her father to show. He had an angular face that narrowed to a sharp chin and pale skin with the luminous sapphire eyes that belonged to all of her wizard-blooded family, and lanky black hair. But he wore upon his hand what she guessed to be the deceased King of Zelka's ring. The wizard Ret. The image changed.

Her homeland materialized—the desert in all its glory, in its own beautiful way. Her family appeared. Alexa's heart gave a jolt, anticipating fearful images, for she saw her mother, father, herself, and her brothers. And then to her horror, but not completely to her surprise, she watched them be kidnapped by evil beings—goblins, harpies, and changers.

The pictures changed to images of war on civilians, an infantry of fiends riding on black, tainted unicorns. They rode, slaying anyone in their path and making bloody sacrifices of innocent people. There was a man who controlled a dragon that mercilessly spewed fire down upon the earth. Another man, on foot, wearing a dark cloak, killed several at a time.

Then faces she knew appeared. There was a careworn Sword Bryan with an image of herself by his side, peering through a thicket, dirt smudging her face. A tired Apollos hung his head as a thick, scarlet liquid dripped from his horn. Prince Alkin, beaten and bloodied, was chained in a cold murky place. She saw Lady Adama holding the key necklace she had given her. And Lady Dorsa stood in a frozen landscape, her eyes full of tears. She wore a brilliant emerald necklace. A sad-looking man Alexa didn't recognize stood nearby, beckoning to her. He wore clothes that separated him as royalty, but blood trickled from his mouth.

Then, to her surprise, she saw merpeople, thousands of merpeople, all swimming in the dark icy waters of the north. Their skin pale as the moon and their hair as dark as night, their eyes like piercing swords. The vision changed, and she saw Sword Bryan with his weapon drawn and his face distorted with rage as he charged a horde of hellhounds and dark unicorns. A fierce Lady Evelyn sat upon a rearing horse with a silver mane. Goblins wielding maces swarmed all around her as she tried to cut them down with her sword. Hazerk and Warkan fought and tended to the wounded, and thousands of other warriors from all countries fought and died.

The image changed, and she saw herself. She lay on a bed made up in black; she was pale and deathlike. Ret stood over her with a satisfied smile.

The next images she could barely stand to watch, but Apollos moved closer to her, his soft body brushing against her. Alexa focused all her attention. She must understand. She watched as the wizard revealed his full plan, and saw her brothers being used and corrupted through their blood to create more wizards, full-blooded wizards... And *she* was to be the shell to harbor the abominations. She could see inside her womb children growing. Her lifeless form on the black bed grew and grew over again and again with child. She saw wizards, female and male, growing. Their innate evil was encouraged and nurtured in their veins by Ret. Ret then sent them out, and they covered Eetharum with blood from wars that saturated the dirt and spilled into the sea, drowning land and sea creatures in its wake. They ruled the lands, minions, under the mighty emperor. Red ships set sail, and the lands over the ocean were saturated with war's blood.

The images went white. Then she saw water, pure, beautiful water. It dripped like teardrops into her cupped hands. Her companions stood around her. There was a beautiful verdant valley in a forest. The trees were in full-bloom with apple blossoms. She saw herself pick a ruby-red apple. Bryan was by her side, his sword drawn protectively. Then flames licked the sky, bursting forth out of a fountain of fire. Eelyne shielded her from the flames as she reached her hand out toward it. Wind swirled above a desert plateau, and she stood bravely alone while it caressed her face and hair. The image changed, and a peaceful summer night came into view. The sky was dark blue and flecked with thousands of twinkling stars. She stood in a field, and the stars fell from the sky upon her, coming down like fiery rain onto her awaiting hands. Apollos stood nearby, gazing into the heavens.

The images changed again, and a beautiful, but terrifying woman she didn't recognize wielded a spear of flame from the sky. Then the woman caused a river to rise and flood. A windstorm of ice and rain was guided by her fingers. The earth trembled and broke open at her command.

Then it ended.

They found they were staring blankly into the silvery bottom of the Mother of Pearl. They were speechless as they let the images sink in. Alexa tried to embed them in her memory. She shut her eyes and struggled, fearing she might forget them. She didn't feel any better about the situation. The magical shell hadn't shown her how to defeat the wizard. Her heart sank. She saw the dreadful plans Ret had in store for her, her family, and the world. But what good would that do if she still didn't know how to stop them? All this had done was to make her more fearful of her task. So much weight was on her shoulders. If she failed, blood would saturate the land. She would become the mother to horrific abominations. *She* would be used to help Ret take over.

"I-I don't understand what I'm supposed to do!" she cried out. The horrendous images had disturbed her greatly. Some were strangely similar to her dream she had had weeks ago while she slept on the ground passing out of Shelkite.

"Yes. Those were unkind images the Mother of Pearl showed," Glyndwr said gravely.

Unkind was hardly the word Alexa was thinking.

"I see now the greatness of it all," Glyndwr continued. "Didn't you see the last images?"

"What? The terrifying woman? Yes, but who is she?" she asked in desperation.

"No, of the elements?" Glyndwr said calmly.

"Elements?" she repeated, her mind's eye straining to remember.

"Yes!" Apollos spoke up, a light in his always gentle face. "The water, the apple trees, the fountain of flame, the windstorm, the stars."

"Correct. I understand what you must do. And I understand what I have to do to help you," Glyndwr said. He swam from the rim of the Mother of Pearl and guided the others away to speak. "In ancient times it was said that if one could gather the purest form of all the elements: earth, fire, water, wind, and starlight, then that person would be extremely formidable. However, only wizards or witches could ever have had enough strength to wield a power so great. Any human would die if they tried. Elemental usage has been heard of in the past, but I do not believe any have succeeded in wielding all of them combined. You see, first, one must gather the elements. But it cannot be just the element; it has to be the element in its pristine form. It must come from a source that still exists from the beginning of time. From when the Master of the Sea created the world and magic was at its pinnacle. The elements are protected by Keepers. The Keepers were set to guard the untainted elements from unfriendly hands, mostly wizards and witches. Because as we all know, wizards first came into being when demons reproduced with humans." He paused upon seeing Alexa's tense face. He smiled and added, "It doesn't mean they are all evil. Wizards and witches began to have children with their own kind as well as humans, and the demon blood lessened over time. And some, like your father, turned away from that path. But the point is, wizards and witches are the only beings powerful enough to control the elements if they ever got their hands on them. In the hands of an evil sorcerer, the elemental power is a dangerous weapon indeed. The Keepers are expecting and prepared to see wizards come searching for the elements. The Keepers have never been known to give up their element easily. The few searchers that managed to gather some of the elements were never able to find all of them in their purest form. But it seems to me you're to go and gather this power, half-blood or not. For the images showed exactly where they are."

"I don't know these places," Alexa said abrasively with clenched teeth.

"You will know. How did you know to come to us? Something is guiding you, and I advise you to listen to it every time it requests. Obey, even if your path ahead is dark. That's how you will succeed; have faith. Just be cautious, know yourself, your friends, and the Master of the Sea, because there are outside wicked powers that will penetrate you and fool you into thinking they are good and will beckon you to follow them. It's to your advantage that you're willing to do this task and will be on guard against wicked powers."

"Who is to wield this power then? That woman wasn't me," she said.

Apollos snorted, and bubbles sprang from his nose. "Ah! I could tell who it was, Alexa."

"Who then? We have to find her. I collect the elements, and she has to wield them. She must be some great sorceress I haven't heard of. I'd thought my family was the last bit of wizard blood left in the world, and I the only woman..." she pondered.

"I've already found her," Apollos stated. She stared at him in puzzlement.

"The woman was you, Alexa," Nereus said.

"Me?"

"Yes," Apollos answered. "You didn't recognize yourself because the elemental power had changed you to your own eyes. But it was you. You're the one to wield the counter-magic as we've called it in the past."

She looked at Glyndwr as if she didn't believe what his son or Apollos were saying. "How can I...I don't..." She let the question hang. It all seemed so far above her. How was *she* to do it?

"It was you, though you're not meant to do it all on your own," Glyndwr confirmed, and Vailea nodded in agreement.

Then it hit her, an understanding, and she suddenly felt calmer. She was called. She was asked. She answered, and now she must be a tool to defeat Ret. She shouldn't worry about doing this herself, for she had a greater power on her side as well as her friends. Then, just as suddenly, new fears surfaced.

"Right. The elements are the counter-magic the naiad spoke about. That makes sense. We have to find them. Okay, but what of the other images?" she asked. She feared the worst; most of them contained her friends and family suffering. She didn't want to mention aloud she was related to Ret, but somehow, she knew the others knew. And they had decided there was no need to speak of it.

"The unclear future. Like I said, this is what the wizard has planned. It doesn't mean it will happen. I can't explain all the images. And I am sure neither my son nor daughter nor Apollos can either. You must keep these images in mind throughout your journey and deal with them as you know and as they come. Always deal with the present, with a regard to the future. It's never good to dwell too much on the future, or the past for that matter. It causes needless worry."

"All right…" she said, her brow troubled.

"You aren't alone, remember that," Vailea empathized. "You have your human companions and Apollos to help you." The mermaid smiled, seeming to connect to Alexa's fears in a way only another woman could understand. "Stay close to them…your friends. You aren't meant to fail, and the Master of the Sea is wise. You just have to trust and obey."

"Now, I've helped you," Glyndwr said. "I've shared my knowledge with you, but there's one more thing that I must do."

"What is that? Do you know who the guardians are?" Alexa asked.

"I don't know who guards them all, but I do know who the guardian of water is."

"It's you, isn't it?" she said with sudden realization.

"Yes. We are called the Water-Keepers. It's a secret among the merpeople. Our tears are the purest form of water. We are an ancient race, so our tears date back to the beginning. And normally we would never give up such a precious thing so easily, but we see the great need, and we will help you," Glyndwr said. He then turned to his daughter and said, "Vailea, would you please fetch me the pearl vial."

The mermaid nodded, and then with a swish of her tail she quickly swam away down the forest path to the house, leaving a trail of bubbles.

"I have one question to ask you myself, Glyndwr," Apollos said. He had a dark glint in his eyes that held accusations once again.

"What is it, my friend?"

"You say you are the only merpeople left and that you can't save your race. Yet the visions showed otherwise. And I also know of another sea that harbors merpeople. It's far to the north, in the cold waters of the Nortarwin Sea. Why don't you seek them out and come together? It would be wise to combine your strength so you're not alone. And you could keep growing as a people."

"We don't speak of our brothers to the north. They're not a part of us. They're different, a more dubious people. We don't commune with them."

"They're prone to wickedness?" Apollos asked.

"I wouldn't rightly use the word wicked. They're a more self-seeking and mischievous people," Glyndwr said.

"Don't you think it would be sensible to go to them before the enemy does and confirm their alliance?"

"Yes, I suppose. But it's a long and dangerous sea to travel between here and there. I don't know—"

"Does it look like our path will be out of harm's way? Does it look like Alexa will have an easy time? Do you think Ret will stop at the shores? If he is intent on creating havoc, he'll not be satiated until everything is entrapped. He'll come sooner or later. You are or will be a part of this whether you want to be or not. You have to do your part to protect yourselves and your future," Apollos said, his whole countenance aflame.

Glyndwr gazed at the unicorn impassively.

Apollos had stated his opinion with such firmness and authority, Alexa wasn't sure if it was proper to speak to the old merman in such a way. But then she realized Apollos was old, too, and wise. Perhaps he was a higher rank in the magical world. The merpeople did seem to place his kind upon a pedestal.

At that time, Vailea returned with a small vial and disrupted the ambiance. She handed it to Alexa. Alexa turned the vial over in her hand. It fit snuggly in her palm. It was carved from one pearl. No ornate designs embellished it, its surface smooth. One small cap snapped shut over the opening.

"A pearl is the only substance that can hold all the elements. You must collect them and hold them in this vial. And when the time comes…you will drink the elements," Glyndwr said.

"Drink them? How can I contain fire? Or wind? I don't understand," Alexa pleaded, frustrated.

"You will. The elements in their purest form are different…magical," Glyndwr explained.

"Where—"

"Do not ask me where the other elements can be found." He cut her off. "I honestly do not know. I am sorry. The Elemental-Keepers all have their own secrets, and for extra protection we don't know much of each other, just of the elemental legend. That's all," Glyndwr said curtly.

"Don't worry, Alexa. We'll help you," Apollos encouraged. He, of course, was speaking of her companions waiting above the waters. "But we should hurry. The others are probably anxious."

"The vial is already partially filled with mermaid tears. Just add the other elements. Be careful not to lose it. Guard it closely against evil. Don't open it once you have them all, at least until you are ready to use it," Glyndwr said fearfully.

"Of course, and thank you." she said, feeling heartened upon receiving the first key.

"You're welcome. And now you must go. Nereus won't accompany you to shore; I've decided we must begin our own mission, as Apollos suggested. He's right. It's not right for us to stay here and do nothing. We'll go to the merpeople in the Nortarwin Sea and convince them to join us, come here and flourish and fight if we must."

"You surprise me, Glyndwr, knowing your kind. But that's a wise decision. You won't regret it. I thank you with my whole heart," Apollos said approvingly, a sparkle in his milky-chocolate eyes.

"You don't know what it means to me to hear you say that. Thank you, noble unicorn." Glyndwr bowed low to Apollos. When he straightened, his eyes held a hurriedness that wasn't there before. "Now, go. You'll be safe on your travels to the surface; nothing that could harm you is in the vicinity. Apollos take her straight to the surface. You'll find you're in familiar territory. Nereus, give Alexandra air so she can make it to the surface. Apollos, you must swim fast." Glyndwr spoke emphatically.

Suddenly, Alexa was in a rush to get to the surface. It was time to get moving, to begin the next step of the mission. She had more knowledge now, and she knew what she had to do. She was *going* to stop those wicked images from coming true.

Apollos swam up alongside her. "Get on my back. They have things to attend to. They can't waste time if they're to convince the northern merpeople."

She slid onto the unicorn's back and felt his legs churn the water around them once again. His hide was as soft as satin, even in the water.

Nereus swam up to her side, and her gaze fell in lock with his beautiful eyes. He placed his hand on her forearm and leaned nearer to her so that they were inches apart.

"Good luck, Alexandra, may the Master of the Sea guide you. Our thoughts will be with you. And know that we will be helping you," Nereus said with affection. Her heart skipped a beat as the merman leaned in and placed his mouth softly on hers. He exhaled long, filling her lungs, giving her air, and then leaned away, taking his spear from a dazed Alexa. He kissed her cheek and said farewell to Apollos.

Apollos rose and climbed through the water. She held on tight, being able to breathe only because of Nereus' magical kiss. As the unicorn ascended, she smiled and waved goodbye to the merpeople, wishing them luck in her heart.

Soon, they were out of sight. Before them was only the great vastness of water. Gradually, through the obscurity, came dim light. She had seized Apollos' mane, her legs wrapped snuggly around his barrel. He swam nearly straight up, as if they climbed a steep mountain. The unicorn's muscles contracted and expanded beneath her legs over and over again.

Then suddenly, she couldn't breathe. Her body went taut with fear and she choked back an urge to inhale.

"Hold your breath, were almost to the surface!" Apollos encouraged.

Time passed, and she felt she might pass out. The water was pressing heavily all around her. She tried to speak, but nothing but garbled mumbles came out. She struggled to fight the instinct to gasp for air. Her underwater vision became blurry. She squeezed her eyes shut.

"Hold on. We're almost there!" Apollos called fearfully. He swam yet harder, straining his body against his own fatigue.

And then, finally, the sun's rays shone brightly. They sliced through the jade-colored waters like dreams slipping into reality. Apollos surfaced with gusto, and Alexa sucked in as much air as she could possibly contain, and never had she been so thankful for it.

CHAPTER NINETEEN

Lady Dorsa paced in her chamber and had a sudden need for fresh air. She ran to her window, struggling against her cumbersome skirts, and threw open the shutters and leaned out as far as she dared, breathing in the clean air, reveling in the soothing effect the breeze had on her rumpled soul and warm cheeks. She let out a pent-up breath with a sigh and leaned on the sill, watching the handsome warhorses crop grass below. A stable boy glanced up and gave her a tentative wave. He blushed, turning a bright crimson when she returned the gesture. When he turned shyly away, Dorsa retreated back into her gloomy chamber and plopped down on her feather mattress. Her hefty traveling trunks sat packed to the brim all around her. There were four of them. They held all her favorite and inseparable possessions.

She sat there slumped, fighting the horrible urge to cry. A lump in her throat was trying its absolute hardest to choke her. She slowed her breathing and tried to calm herself. In a moment like this, Alkin would have told her to take a deep breath and to think things over logically. And her beau would have taken her in his arms and told her everything would turn out all right in the end, and then he would have placed a tender kiss on her cheek.

How would things be all right? And how could she think things over logically? No amount of logical thinking was going to stop her from having to marry a man she didn't love, or for that matter, she didn't even know! She felt betrayed. She was leaving her homeland, leaving her brother and giving up Eelyne forever…

She broke down and fell onto her pillows, letting her hot tears soak her bedding through and through.

The next day, Dorsa settled herself in the main convoy carriage; her escort comprising two Shelkite warriors, her handmaiden, and five Vtalmay warriors. The carriage was a relatively good size, with a small bed and a comfy seat for her during the day.

She fluffed and situated her skirts around her, suffocated by the mass of them. Her gowns were always exquisite, but she couldn't help but remember the free feeling she had had when she and Eelyne had run away for an evening and she'd worn the lightweight uniform of a warrior. It had felt so wonderful to be able to move easily. The simple life of a warrior's wife was so appealing to her. Oh, how she envied Alexandra for being able to wear clothes of her choice and to do what she wished... Eelyne was sure to find the foreign girl's feisty, tomboyish personality appealing, wasn't he? She gave a frustrated huff and glared out the window at her mother's retreating back; she had just given her goodbyes. What did it matter anyway? She was not going to ever marry Eelyne. Yet, she couldn't stop images of him and the unusual Kaltrazian girl from intruding into her mind. She supposed it was just the helplessness of her situation that her thoughts tortured her so. Dorsa knew Eelyne cared deeply for her, but he had no clue what was happening. She desperately wished she could tell him somehow, and that he and her brother could come rescue her.

She wrapped her cloak closer around herself, more for the feeling of security than from a chill. Her fingers brushed the emerald necklace draped around her neck. The jewel hung elegantly there and hovered just above her ample bust, its dark green glitter contrasting with her creamy skin. It had been a combined going away gift and engagement gift from her mother. Dorsa had resisted the urge to throw the beautiful stone down and grind it into the ground with her heel when her mother had presented it. But she had accepted it obligingly—like a brainwashed pawn.

Her escort was preparing to leave. The guards called out last orders. The whole of the castle's help had turned up to wave her off. They stood in the courtyard, waving to her and wishing her luck, unaware she was extremely unhappy with the situation.

A soft rustle of feathers drew her attention from the cheery crowd. She looked at the cage sitting in the opposite corner of her carriage. A handsome falcon sat fluffing his feathers, watching her curiously with his dark eyes. Melea had insisted that Dorsa take the messenger bird and write to her as often as she could. The servant had promised she would write in return, and if she could, she'd send news to the Prince and Eelyne about the engagement. She also promised she would do her best to inform Dorsa of the company's progress. Dorsa was grateful for Melea's apparent concern for her and had asked the servant to watch over the castle secretly while she and her brother were absent. Melea had not even blinked an eye. She had simply accepted the task and didn't even act like it was an oddly suspicious thing to ask a mere servant, especially when there was a lawful person of power left in charge. Dorsa was glad the servant hadn't asked any questions. She didn't want to admit she felt something was very wrong within the castle walls.

The carriage jerked into motion, and she slid the compartment window open and waved cheerfully to the servants, grooms, and warriors. She had to put on a good face. Melea was standing nearby, between the cook and the stable boy; the servant waved sadly and blew her a friendly kiss. Dorsa smiled and returned a tender-hearted goodbye kiss to her friends.

★★★★

Prince Alkin and Sword Bryan paced the white sand in disquiet. They had been waiting for well over an hour in the hot sun. The jade-colored waves of the Elendace Sea crashed on the shore in a soothing, rhythmic manner, but neither man found it calming.

Alkin had finally retreated to the shade of the trees and now sat examining the sharpened blade of his beloved Sword of Shelkite. He glanced up to see his friend still pacing restively near the water's edge, looking out to open sea. *It's not like him to act so unsettled*, Alkin mused. He stood and shaded his eyes against the glaring sun, sheathing his sword. He strode over to the Master Sword, who was staring severely at the sea as if it had done him some sort of wrong. "I hope they're not down there much longer," Alkin said, looking the waves over.

"Yeah," Bryan replied in an edgy tone.

At that moment, something burst out of the lagoon directly to their left. Both men turned and saw the snowy white head of Apollos and a gasping, drenched Alexa emerge from the depths. The men ran along the shoreline to meet them at the lagoon's edge.

"You all right?" Alkin asked anxiously upon seeing Alexa's pale face. Apollos slowly made his way to the bank, dragging the slender girl with him. She hung weakly onto his mane, her body floating out behind her.

The Prince held out his hand. She seized it gratefully, giving an affirming jerk of her head. He heaved her out of the water, and Bryan quickly threw a blanket around the girl's shoulders. Apollos stumbled feebly onto the shore, snorting and shaking his head to clear his nostrils and ears. Alkin moved to touch the unicorn and steady him, but withdrew his hand when Apollos peered at him skeptically from the corner of his eye. "I'm okay, friend," he assured the Prince and then promptly dropped to his knees and rolled in the warm sand, grunting with pleasure.

Alkin smiled briefly at the unicorn and then turned his attention to Alexa. Bryan had wrapped her so tightly in the blanket her arms were plastered at her sides. But the color in her cheeks was returning, and she gave him a meager half smile. Her mouth opened as if to speak, but Alkin held up a hand and said, "It can wait. Rest for a bit."

They trekked to the shade of the waving palm trees and plopped down, all feeling a great amount of relief in some way or another. Apollos joined them and lay down, tucking his legs up beneath himself. His velvety coat had dried, and it shone pleasantly in the sunshine.

Leaning against the tree, Alexa extracted her arms from the blanket and started undoing her braid to run her fingers through her hair and re-braid it again. She sighed as she stared pensively out over the water.

Bryan studied Alexa's angular features, noting her sapphire eyes were gazing worlds away. They had an uncomforting look about them. He glanced at the unicorn; he was watching Alexa closely, too. Now that the girl was back under his vigilant eye, Bryan's anxiety was gone, but his curiosity was now piqued. What had happened down there?

A few minutes later, Alexa burst forth, spewing everything. She rarely paused for a breath and didn't look at anyone, except Apollos to confirm facts here and there. She told them of Nereus, Vailea, and Glyndwr, their world, the Mother of Pearl, the visions she saw, the elements, and of what they had been appealed to do.

Alexa didn't dare look at the Prince or Sword during her explanation. She was waiting to sense out the men's reactions to her not telling them that Ret was her uncle. She explained that Ret was her father's twin and of what he had planned. Though, she didn't tell them of her uncle's plans for her personally. Apollos nodded in approval. He didn't protest when she left out that detail.

She paused for a breath, stopping her report, and tore her eyes from the sea to look at Prince Alkin. He showed no surprise at this last bit of information, lost in his despondent thoughts. With downcast eyes, he absently brushed sand off his black boots. And coming to, he lifted his hazel eyes and met hers with a look of concern. She relaxed. He wasn't angry with her for withholding her relation to Ret.

On the other hand, she didn't have to look at Sword Bryan to know he was shocked. Once again, she sensed an unease and distrust of her flow through him. She could feel the Sword clamming up and becoming tense. She couldn't say why, but it distressed her greatly.

Alkin spoke, disrupting her senses, "Evelyn and I suspected this. In fact, we were pretty sure you must be related to Ret, considering the rarity of magical-blooded people nowadays. Don't worry. It doesn't matter."

Beside her, Bryan clenched his jaw and said, "Why didn't you tell us?"

She turned to him, her eyes flashing in defense. "You already distrusted me, thinking me a spy. Do you think I wanted to reveal to you that this man was a close relative of mine?"

The Master Sword didn't answer, but his features looked resigned. Alkin rubbed his forehead with his fingertips and looked out over the sea in thought.

"But if you'd been straightforward from the beginning, we would've trusted you more," Bryan finally said; his voice was firm but not harsh.

Alexa rolled her eyes. "You're Right. I'm sorry," she said begrudgingly.

Fighting his bitter impulse to mistrust, Bryan merely raised an amused eyebrow and gazed wryly at her.

Alexa took this as a sign of forgiveness. She then decided she would explain her past more, hoping it would rectify herself. "My father, Erec, or Erecin in full, trained me and my brothers only a little in magic. He always said it was dangerous and not something we should let overpower us. We were taught to control our so-called evil blood. My Uncle Ret, or actually Retsin is his full name, is rarely spoken of in our family. My father acts as if he doesn't exist, although he knows of my uncle's whereabouts. At least, he knew he was a counselor on the king's court in Zelka.

"Just before my father married my mother, he and my uncle had a disagreement over something. He's never said about what. They'd been traveling with each other their whole lives. They moved from place to place, never staying anywhere long, doing magic in circuses and things like that: harmless things. My uncle wanted more. He moved to Zelka to elevate his status and become a counselor. My father thought he may have studied and delved into the darker kinds of magic. I guess he was right. But my father didn't want that kind of power. He wanted a family, and that's when he renounced being a wizard."

Alexa looked at the Prince. He nodded mutely, his hazel eyes troubled. Then she glanced at the silent Sword. He showed no emotion but just stared at her attentively. She was strangely heartened that he didn't seem to loathe her anymore. For some unknown reason, it seemed vital he shouldn't think poorly of her.

"I wonder what they argued about," Alkin finally said.

"Yes, I wonder that myself now, too." Alexa gazed at the sand at her feet.

"I wonder if he knew something bad was brewing in that brain of his brother's," Bryan remarked.

"I think he may have," Apollos said. "But there's nothing we can do about that now." He stood up and shook himself, breaking off the conversation. "Let's get back. We're rested now, and the others have to know all this, too."

"Wait, Apollos," Alkin called to the departing unicorn and turned to Alexa, who was brushing herself off. She wrapped the blanket snug around herself, suddenly self-conscious as the Prince gazed kindly into her face. "You told us some startling things. Are *you* all right?"

Alexa lowered her eyes to the ground and shifted her feet bracingly. She *must* tell them about Ret's plans for her, but for some reason, she couldn't just now. It was too horrifying, degrading...personal. It choked her just to think about it. "Yes," she merely said. She looked up and gave the Prince a forced smile. He smiled back and patted her shoulder awkwardly.

Bryan was standing beyond the Prince, waiting to leave with Apollos. Alexa met eyes with him, and, for once, the Master Sword didn't look away. He clenched his jaw and gave her the slightest of encouraging nods and then turned on his heel to follow the unicorn.

When she reached the cover of the forest, Alexa ducked behind a tree to pull on her shirt, trousers, and boots. Apollos appeared at her side. She gave a startled jump. "Don't sneak up like that! You scared me," she scolded as she pulled on her boot, balancing on one foot.

"Sorry, didn't mean to." He reached out his muzzle and steadied her.

"Thanks." Finishing, she paused and looked at the unicorn, who gazed at her strangely. "Do you think I should have told them about..." She pursed her lips.

"No," he said, his tone soft. "Honestly, I wasn't expecting you to tell them right away. That was hard to swallow—to see yourself so. You wait until you're ready to tell them. It's not imperative right now."

She gazed into the unicorn's kind, chocolate eyes. They were so gentle and wise, and yet formidable, too. She nodded. Apollos bobbed his head, sending his silky mane flipping to the other side of his sleek neck. She smiled.

"Just remember." He began walking down the forest path toward their camp. She followed closely at his shoulder. "What you saw in the Mother of Pearl was *not* the future. It was only Ret's plans for the future. Don't think about it too much. That's why we're here together. You, me, Alkin, Bryan, and the others, we're to stop that from being the future."

Alexa nodded glumly and reached her hand over to him. She couldn't resist the urge any longer to touch the unicorn's glossy mane and run her fingers through it. She scratched behind his ears, and he tossed his head in delight. "Right. I know," she said.

"I know for a fact that Prince Alkin and Sword Bryan intend to see you through until this is finished. And the same goes for me. The others, I'm sure, feel the same; they're noble Shelkiten warriors. The Power will take care of us." The unicorn's eyes glittered with confidence.

"I know," was her distracted answer.

A few minutes later, when they could see the backs of Bryan and Alkin ahead of them again, Alexa brought up something that had been troubling her since she saw the visions. "Apollos?"

"Yes."

"I had a dream, if you could call it a dream, it just seemed so real, when we were traveling through Shelkite's fields. It was…very similar to parts of what I saw in the Mother of Pearl. It can't be a coincidence."

The unicorn raised his nose in the air, his eyes thoughtful. "Have you had dreams like this before?"

"No."

"Hmm… I don't think you're prescient. It could have been caused by something magical invading you. It might've given you a glimpse of its origin or something of that nature."

"Like you mean my blood since I'm related to Ret. By that connection, I could have seen what he has planned for me. Does that mean my brothers may have gotten the same warning, too?"

"I don't know," he said, uncertain. "I'll have to think it over." He looked at her fallen countenance. "It might not have been something bad invading you. There's no sense in worrying yourself silly about your family. We're doing everything we know of right now to solve this."

"My brothers don't know of any of this, and my mother is only human…defenseless."

"Right, but they have your father. I'm sure he's a clever man.

Worrying does no good. Prince Alkin and Lady Evelyn, along with the country of Galeon, are doing and will do all they can to stop anything worse from happening to the people of Eetharum," Apollos reassured.

"I know," she acknowledged, her features bound with fret.

CHAPTER TWENTY

When they reached the camp, they found the others gathered around a crackling fire, roasting something delicious smelling.

"Lunch?" Hazerk beamed and held up the game. They nodded and sunk down around the fire, careful not to sit too close in such warm weather. "I could camp like this forever." Hazerk grinned as he offered out the meat.

"So, what happened? You look a little shaken up, girl," Warkan stated. Bryan threw him a scowl but took a seat opposite the stern warrior.

Alexa sighed and dove into an explanation again. By the time she had finished, they had all eaten their food. The men sat staring mutely at her as if they hadn't expected their mission to amount to such a big issue.

This time Prince Alkin noted Alexa's slight hesitance in explaining certain parts of the vision. He stole a questioning glance at Bryan. The Master Sword merely raised a wary eyebrow. He had caught it, too. They would confront her and Apollos about it later.

The others started voicing their concerns. "So, what's this going to do to you? Being only a half-blood?" Hazerk asked, his expression worried. "That, ah…Glendywere merman said the elemental power would kill humans if they attempted to use it."

Alexa shrugged. "I don't know."

"Humph," grunted Warkan.

"It could weaken her a great deal," Eelyne said.

"What do you know?" Warkan shot.

"I specialized in magical beings, remember?" he retorted. He pulled from his sack a fat book and started flipping through it hurriedly.

"You brought a book with you?" Hazerk laughed incredulously.

"Books," mumbled a distracted Eelyne.

Warkan stared, flabbergasted. The others smiled.

"Good, I'm glad he did. Because everyone obviously knows that *I* don't know much!" Alexa said in his defense.

"Don't worry, Alexa. I'll try to find something for you," Eelyne vowed emphatically.

She made a mental note to ask him in private if he could find anything about evil magic invading dreams.

The rest of the afternoon was filled with assumptions, worries, and tentative plans. Alexa voted to go straight through Carthorn and into Kaltraz, where she could meet up with her father so they all could have a conference. Eelyne supported her enthusiastically, knowing Carthorn still held magic he could witness, which would bring his studies to life. Warkan was cynical. He claimed he never heard of anyone coming out of Carthorn alive—until Apollos spoke up and said he'd come out all right. Hazerk announced he would go anywhere, as long as there was food and a potential good fight.

Close to suppertime, Alkin, Alexa, Apollos, and Bryan consulted this proposal in private. The unicorn supported the plan, claiming if there were anywhere the magical elements might be, Carthorn was the place to begin looking. Both Alkin and Bryan agreed. It was settled. They would begin their march to Carthorn in the morning.

Just before dusk, Bryan had Alexa and Eelyne train with the sword two on one. "Eventually, I'll have you fight up to four on one and in teams. But let's not get ahead of ourselves," he said cheerfully.

It was fun when Eelyne was the one defending himself. Alexa's spirits rose to the clouds while she and the Master Sword were a team. Maybe it was possible for her to be a good swordswoman after all. However, her elated feeling didn't last long. Her spirits went crashing to the ground when it was her turn to be on her own. She could sense Eelyne and Bryan's delight in giving her a killing blow every time she turned around. She growled and kept pushing to do her best, but the two men seemed to enjoy hassling her too much.

"Ha! Don't look so foul, Alexa!" Eelyne laughed when they had finished their bout. Bryan was grinning devilishly at her. She merely grunted and kept her face screwed up.

"Okay, now you two against me. Work together," Bryan ordered.

And they did, but to no avail.

The Master Sword couldn't help himself from laughing at their growing frustration. "Okay, we're done," he finally said with a chuckle. The two pupils voiced their relief and went over to the fire, feeling defeated.

As the company sat eating their supper and trying to forget all the pending troubles, Apollos perked his ears in alarm.

Alkin shushed the others. "What is it?"

"Our shadow is approaching," Apollos whispered, his eyes and ears attentive, his head high and tail arched. At that moment, if it wasn't for his horn and the obvious, intelligent look in his eyes, he would have looked like a wild horse sniffing the breeze, catching a predator's scent.

Bryan rose from his spot and quietly drew his sword. Warkan followed suit, silently taking up the battle-ax he always carried strapped across his back. The Prince, Eelyne, and Hazerk took out their weapons. They stood in a half circle facing the shadowy woods where Apollos stared alertly. The silence was tense as they waited. The unicorn had sensed the man in ample time.

"He's close." Apollos lowered his head, trying to decipher the visitor. The others braced themselves.

"I feel him now, too," Alexa whispered.

Bryan was suddenly aware she stood at the opposite end of their half circle, farthest away from him. He clenched his teeth; his charge needed to be right next to him. But he dared not ask her to move.

"He means no harm," Alexa said in relief, as if the man had told her himself.

"How do you know?" growled Warkan.

Bryan moved infinitesimally toward Alexa, as if it would somehow stop her from doing something stupid. He glared at her from out of the corner of his eye, but she was paying him no heed. She looked into the dark forest with interest. *Great!* He was suddenly in a sour mood.

"She's right. Let him approach," Apollos confirmed. He bobbed his head in reassurance. But the others kept their guards up until they saw a dark shape emerge from the shadows.

The tall figure paused just beyond the fire's full light. The glow flickered and danced around his black cloak. The man had the hood drawn over his head, shielding his face in its depths. In the shadows of his hood, his dark eyes glistened from the flame's reflection. He did not speak.

"Who are you to follow us?" Prince Alkin demanded; his voice was crisp and to the point, so unlike his usual congenial demeanor.

"Ah, a unicorn. So, that's what I felt," a raspy voice said from within the hood.

The companions looked at each other uneasily.

"Answer my question," Alkin pressed.

Alexa thought that no one in their right mind would dare disobey the Prince's authority at this second harsh command. But the visitor merely gave a hearty laugh with his hoarse sounding voice. *How arrogant.* She was slightly amused, even though his husky voice sent shivers down her spine. Still, it was strangely alluring. It sounded as if his vocal cords had been scrubbed across coral, as if he had used his voice far too much…or that he hadn't spoken aloud in a long time. She settled on the latter explanation.

She wasn't the only one receiving shivers down the spine upon hearing the stranger's voice. Alkin had, too, but it wasn't for the same reason. It wasn't alluring at all. It was the sudden jolt of fear. He had heard this voice before. But he couldn't bring to mind who it was or when it was. Whenever it was, it hadn't been a pleasant meeting.

"Don't get all up in arms, gentlemen, my lady," the stranger said with a smile in his voice. He approached the fire.

Bryan watched carefully as the flickering light illuminated parts of the man's hidden face. There was no outward show of weapons; his hands were empty. But the Master Sword was intelligent enough to know he had more than one weapon hidden on his person.

"Why are you following us?" Alkin pushed bravely. "We don't wish you any harm. How d'you know about the unicorn? We know you don't have magical blood."

"No." The stranger sat down at the fire. The companions didn't move. They still stood facing him menacingly. "I don't need magic to sense him. I've been around long enough to know these things—I'm sorry, can I sit at your fire and talk business?" he asked with condescension, peering up at them.

"Of course." Alkin sat down sophisticatedly, his royal manners coming back. The others followed suit. Apollos continued to stand protectively but at ease. There was a moment of silence, and then Alkin asked, "Tell us your name, so we can get acquainted."

The shadowy figure turned his head to look behind him into the forest, seemingly ignoring the Prince again. He whistled. Out came a sturdy mare, colored a mousy black-blue. She stood by her master, fully tacked and obedient. She nuzzled his shoulder. "This is Blize." He patted his mare and then regarded the company again. "I'm called many things, but Kheane has been my rightful name for many years."

Bryan narrowed his eyes. He didn't like this man's patronizing air. The Master Sword had marked him from the beginning as an exceedingly dangerous person. And he wasn't far off his assessment.

He glanced at the Prince. Alkin seemed unsettled, but only Bryan, being his Sword, would have noticed, although the stranger seemed to have caught this, too. He then stole a glance at Alexa. The girl was practically gawking at the stranger—Kheane, whatever his name was.

Alkin was about to introduce the others, but Kheane broke in before he could speak. He didn't seem to care to know their names, unless it was that he knew them already. "I was living in a cabin off the coast when I saw your company pass. I came from the north. I'd decided I wanted to retire from my wretched work and pursue unfinished business. But when I saw your company, I couldn't help but wonder what the Prince of Shelkite was doing traveling covertly. And that perhaps this trip you are all on ties to me in some way. I think I can help. I want to help. Let me come with you. I can't run from my past anymore, and the unfinished business will have to stay unfinished."

"How do you know the Prince?" Bryan demanded. His voice was much more daunting than even Alkin's was. The Sword did not like this visitor at all. He didn't trust him, and he didn't want him coming with them.

"Let's just say I'm well-traveled," Kheane replied.

Ignoring his comment, Alkin asked, "What do you know of our trip, as you call it?"

"More than you think, I think," Kheane said.

"If you want to join us, you'd better start answering questions openly," Bryan growled.

"Relax, Master Sword, I respect you. You *are* very good at what you do," he said.

Not realizing this was an enormous compliment, especially coming from the man sitting in front of him, Bryan glowered all the more.

"Look," Kheane said diplomatically, "how about we talk this over in the morning. Let's leave on this note. You all know I'm not trying to do you any harm. And I know you're not trying to do me any harm. You know that I know about your trip. You know I want to help. Hopefully, in the morning, we'll all warm up to the idea a little more."

At this, he stood. No one stopped him. Bending at the waist in a slight bow, he smiled, his eyes did anyway. He then turned to his horse. "Come, Blize." The mare turned and followed him contentedly. "I'll see you all in the morning. Sleep well!" he called over his shoulder. "Don't leave without me." With that, he disappeared into the dark forest.

After his departure, Alexa made a noise as if to speak, but Bryan didn't let her get as far as to say she wanted to add the man to their company. "No," he said flatly.

"Hey—" she shot back, indignant.

"Stop," Prince Alkin commanded. He held up a hand and looked firmly at the two of them. The others stared at each other blankly, not sure what to think of their visitor Kheane. "We will decide on this together," Alkin said calmly. He waited until both Alexa and the Sword nodded in agreement, albeit it looked as if they both had to break their necks to make the gesture.

Alexa wanted to argue that it had been decided at the castle that she could make important decisions. This, she was certain, was important, and she knew they must agree to take Kheane on. However, Bryan looked relentless and Alkin looked doubtful. She bit back the thought. She had also agreed things would be talked over civilly, so she calmed herself.

They talked into the night. Bryan graciously heard Alexa out, and Alexa graciously heard the others out. Bryan didn't like the man's manner. To him, it boded ill, and he felt he was deceiving them. And, he said furthermore, that the name Kheane had an all too familiar ring to it. Not a nice one either. Strangely, both Alkin and Eelyne agreed on that point.

Warkan didn't think one man against the six—he corrected himself at Alexa's evil eye—the *seven* of them were any match. And he would agree to have Kheane join, but he also thought they should watch him closely. Hazerk was completely undecided. He also didn't like the atmosphere about Kheane, but, kind-hearted as he was, felt they should believe him. Alkin still couldn't get over his uneasiness at recognizing that very recognizable voice. He told the others of this concern. Nevertheless, he desperately wanted to trust Alexa and ended up supporting her.

Eelyne, being a fan of Alexa's witch senses, supported her but said he would research the name Kheane in his books. This caused him to swallow huge criticism from Warkan again, who asked sneeringly why a man alive today would be in a history book. However, it didn't deter Eelyne. He was going on the implication of what Kheane had so blatantly stated—that he had been around long enough to be able to notice an invisible unicorn when there was one. And this, to Eelyne, was evidence enough to research.

"All right, all right." Bryan held up his hands in defeat. "We'll talk to him tomorrow morning. If you all still think we should trust him, then I'd be stupid to go against the majority." He looked specifically at Alexa. Her bewitching sapphire eyes sparkled a happy sky blue. He then regarded Apollos, who had been silent throughout the whole discussion. "I value your opinion," he simply said.

The unicorn tossed his mane, his chocolate eyes gleaming

audaciously. "Let's trust him. I felt no ill will in him."

"Okay, it's settled then. All agreed?" the Sword confirmed. Everyone mumbled and nodded in agreement.

They headed to their blankets in a foggy mindset. No one had much sleep that night, and Bryan didn't get any. He volunteered to stay up for the rest of the night on watch. Apollos kept the Master Sword company on and off, as the unicorn didn't need as much sleep as the humans.

During one of Apollos' awake moments, Bryan asked him what Alexa had hesitated in telling them earlier in her report. He didn't ask this accusingly, just curiously. The unicorn studied the Master Sword for a moment before saying what she had withheld was a personal and painful shock to her. And that it was of no detriment to the company right now. She would tell them in due time.

"Alexa's stronger than you give her credit for, Master Sword," Apollos said. Bryan knew that. And the unicorn knew that he knew that. But Apollos went out on a limb and pressed another issue before drifting off to sleep. "You know, I've watched you two. True, you're her guardian, and she needs you, but despite what you may think now, you need her, too. Don't shut yourself away from her just because of your past. She could become a great friend... All other things aside..." Apollos then, with a big yawn, fell asleep, seemingly knowing the stir he had caused in Bryan's chest.

Sitting wide awake beside the snoring unicorn, Bryan pondered out some things. He *was* bitter. Alexa had been right in her assessment when she'd first met him. As the handsome Apollos snored softly on, the Master Sword felt something creep into his chest...dread. Dread on Alexa's behalf. Had she seen her own death? He glanced over at the slumbering girl and remembered the look in her eyes that night in her chamber, after the council, when she had told him she wanted him to be her Sword-Guard. They had had the darkness of loss in their pretty midnight-colored depths. He didn't want anything bad to happen to her. The Sword's body and senses gave a resentful twitch at the foreign feeling that stole over him. It wasn't because he was merely her Sword-Guard that he felt this way. It was because *he*, himself, didn't want anything to happen to her.

With a sigh, he looked up to the pale moon and thought what a wonderful story it could tell if only it could speak. There in the sky, it had seen so many things from the start of time. It had seen the beginning of troubles, as well as the solutions…if there were any. It was a faithful witness at all times. If only it could give him advice. Perhaps it should be that he should again put his trust in what he had been taught to as a child: The High Power.

Bryan stayed awake, pondering all this with a heavy heart in the darkness, until the morning sun sifted through the trees and melted the feelings away.

CHAPTER TWENTY-ONE

The Master Sword woke the others early. The sun had just lit the woods enough to see their camp when he went around and kicked the bottoms of everyone's feet. "Come on guys, get up!"

There were a few resistant groans, but everyone got up and around. By the time they had their horses tacked and were ready for departure, Kheane appeared from the same spot he had emerged from the night before. Blize was tacked and ready. He still wore the obscuring black cloak and hood shielding his face. His coffee-colored eyes still held the same aplomb.

"Well? Do I travel with you?" he said in his raspy voice.

"Maybe," Bryan replied.

"Yes," Alkin intervened. "We've decided to trust you. But give us your word that you're here only to help."

"Good. I give my word. I'll be useful in a fight," Kheane declared, his dark eyes glinting.

"What makes you think we're going to be in a fight?" Warkan broke in.

Kheane turned his attention to the warrior and said knowingly, "It's not hard to tell." He turned to Blize and prepared to mount up, but Alkin stopped him.

"First, we have to tell you it concerns us you know about our undertaking. We'd thought it was confidential. Tell us what you know and how." Kheane stepped down from his stirrup and gave them a scrutinizing look, and Alkin added, "We won't ask to know any more about you personally…right now."

Kheane nodded. "I recognize this girl you have with you. At first, I didn't. She looked vaguely familiar to me, but I know now that she's the only niece of the wizard Ret you're trying to stop. I know you, prince, merely because of the old occupation I held. I was required to know the influential by face."

Alexa butted in, "How do you know Ret?"

"Alexa!" Bryan reprimanded.

But Kheane regarded her and answered solemnly. "He asked me for my help once... I refused. I'm sure he hunts me now."

"Who are you?" Alexa asked eagerly.

"I'm Kheane. You all have nothing to fear from me. Though, my past has a way of popping up from time to time to haunt me. But I want nothing to do with it anymore. All I want now is quiet and the chance to find someone I lost. I can help you. And I'm hoping you'll help me when the need arises."

"If you want quiet, why do you ask to travel with warriors?" Bryan asked curtly. He was slowly warming up to the stranger, very slowly.

Kheane gave him a sharp look, his eyes blazing, and said, "Because to have quiet, a person must work for it first. *You* know that, Master Sword."

"Who have you lost? A woman?" Alexa asked. Bryan and Alkin gave her a warning look. But she kept her eyes on Kheane, who regarded her coolly.

"Maybe," he said. "But I fear it's in vain. The individual is more than likely dead. That's why I ask to come with you. I don't have anything left for me."

"Your quiet," Alexa answered softly. Kheane's eyes smiled at her. Bryan scowled.

"All right." Bryan cleared his throat and glared at the apparently smitten Alexa. "Let's head out. I want to reach Carthorn as soon as we can."

They traveled north from the sea's edge. Carthorn was the northeastern country bordering the peninsula that made up Yoldor. Departing from the sea, they all felt a small loss somewhere in their souls. The waves seemed to say, *stay, stay*, every time they tumbled onto the shore. But slowly, as the company went, they heard less and less of the sea beckoning to them, and their minds turned to the path ahead.

They traveled quickly through the lightly wooded area they had sheltered in. They then crossed a stretch of sand dunes, having to dismount on a couple occasions to ease the chore for their mounts. Later, in a rockier terrain, they passed by an ominous, grumbling and sputtering volcano. They ogled it, and the thought crossed their minds that it could be the fire element. But Alexa assured them it couldn't be. It didn't feel right, and nothing was guarding it as far as she could sense. Apollos agreed.

Kheane fell into the company's rhythm easily. He seemed to belong, so Alexa felt. He traveled silently at the rear, his hard, black eyes forever scanning the vicinity. He never once removed the hood hiding his features. It piqued her curiosity almost to a point of distress; she wondered painfully about this strange man. What did he do? Where did he come from? Why did he hide his face and wear a cloak in the heat of day? Who had he been looking for? How did he know Ret and her?

Bryan rode at the head of the company with Alkin and Apollos, while Alexa rode just a few paces behind where he could get to her easily enough if need be. To his satisfaction, Kheane followed his orders without question. In fact, Kheane hardly said a word, even if he was spoken to. And if he couldn't get around answering, he would merely reply with a curt remark.

The Master Sword would every now and then turn in his saddle to survey the company. He would see Eelyne awkwardly trying to peruse his books astride his sorrel. Hazerk would be staring ahead, giving him a nod of 'all's well.' Warkan would be scowling around at the scenery, and Kheane was always on high alert. To a tiny bit of Bryan's annoyance, he noted that Alexa was constantly craning her neck around to watch the shady man.

They paused sparingly throughout the days they traveled. It was hot and cloudless, the red, glaring sun merciless.

A few days travel from the sea, after dusk, when the bright moon was high in the purple sky, they could see on the horizon the mysterious forest of Carthorn looming. On its outskirts, a lit-up village lay peaceful and dreamlike to their sun worn eyes. Perhaps, Bryan thought, they could find lodging one last night before braving the strange forest. But he feared it would be a stretch to find a place to accommodate them all in such a small village.

They rode down the main street. Some curious children ran over to investigate; even some adults stopped their evening chores to look up. They were friendly and greeted the company pleasantly and then went about their business. The smell of cooking food reached the company's noses as they passed homes with warm light glowing through the windows. A twinge of homesickness pricked Alexa's heart.

A little boy, desperate for a bath and comb, trotted up to them. "Are ya headed for an inn, mister?" He came to Sapharan's side. The boy's head barely reached the warhorse's shoulder.

"Yes, do you have a suggestion?" Alkin said with a warm smile.

"Sure do! My father's an innkeeper. He'll take ya all. We've not had a group this large in a long time. It'll be good for us. It's straight up there to the left. Brant's Tavern is across the way. Ya all can grab somethin' there to eat and drink while we get your rooms ready." With that, he took off up the street, happily calling to his father.

Alkin laughed. "Well, that was easy enough."

"After the trek we've had, a couple of pints sounds good," Hazerk announced.

"It certainly does." Bryan spit some sandy grit out of his mouth.

"I don't think my eyes will ever be the same after all the squinting," Eelyne said, rubbing his eyes.

"I think I'm sunburned." Hazerk gently patted his tender, pink cheeks. "I don't think my face has been this red since my mother smacked me for using dirty language when I was a boy. This fine alabaster skin is not meant for the sun." He grinned.

"Humph," Warkan commented. His own face was more than a little pink.

Alexa just smiled. Her skin was used to the heat, and she glowed prettily from being in her beloved sun all day once again.

They halted and stiffly dismounted at the tavern. The little boy appeared at Alkin's side again. "Ya all go in. We'll tend to your horses," he said.

Alkin handed Sapharan's reins to the boy's eager hands. "Thank you, young man."

"Many thanks to ya." The boy grinned and gestured to his pals to come and get the other horses and mule.

As they headed up the rickety tavern stairs, Kheane spoke, his peculiar, raspy voice cutting the air, "I'll stay with the horses. Just bring me something out."

Bryan paused on the stair step. The idea of Kheane not being watched still troubled him. He raised an eyebrow at Alkin, and the Prince shrugged his shoulders.

"You don't want to be seen?" Alkin questioned.

"That's right."

Alexa, noting the Prince's hesitance, piped up, "I'll stay with him. Just bring me something, too." Her sparkling eyes and rosy cheeks made for a handsome countenance and caused a few blind eyes amongst the men to open.

"No, you won't," Bryan said firmly. He came off the stairway to stand next to her almost possessively. Alexa scowled at him, and he glared back. He would be gutted first before leaving her alone in this man's company. Why was she so eager? Why could she never use her brain?

"She'll be quite safe in my care, Master Sword, no need to worry," Kheane said in his annoyingly patronizing way.

"No, Warrior Warkan can stay." Bryan's voice was gruff.

"Come in with us, Kheane," Alkin said, "It's likely you won't be recognized here. And if you are, we'll take the repercussions, since I said it would be safe." The Prince's manner was sincere as always.

Kheane shrugged his shoulders; his coffee-colored eyes glinted amiably in the half-light. "All right," he consented.

The problem solved, they all strode happily up the stairs toward their dinner.

"It's been a while since I enjoyed a drink with company," Kheane stated when they entered the noisy tavern.

"Good, I'm glad we can assist." Alkin smiled.

By the next morning, they were rested, packed, mounted, and ready to head down the road to the forest. The previous night they had all enjoyed a delicious meal with a drink or two for each. The men had split two rooms between them, and Alexa had enjoyed a room to herself, albeit it was adjoined with Bryan's.

The innkeeper's wife had packed them plenty of fresh food and was seeing them off. Her heavyset form bustled around the big warhorses, making sure everything was packed especially well in all the saddlebags. "I still think ya are all bordering on crazy to enter that uncanny wood," she said for the hundredth time. She was double-checking Hazerk's saddlebag. "The men don't even hunt in there it's so peculiar, too many strange creatures and things happening. Jest be real careful. Hope ya make it to the other side. Ya know, it's no trouble at all to go around the worst of it. It's not that far out of the way."

"Yes, but we're in a hurry," Alkin persisted. He had been trying to convince her since the evening before that they were in their right minds without betraying their mission. It was proving difficult.

"Can't see why is all…jest can't. There's no reason to go in there. We've got roads headed toward Kaltraz. Jest travel a bit to the west, then north, is all. *Around* Carthorn."

"Yes, we do thank you for your advice and most especially for the lodging, the horse care, and the food. It's greatly appreciated. You needn't worry. We'll make it through," Alkin said as the stout woman paused at Sapharan's muzzle.

"We thank you, sir! Ya have helped us out very much." She gave the horse a pat and grinned up at the Prince. The innkeepers didn't know he was the Prince of Shelkite. They were under the impression he was a wealthy merchant on business. Alkin had paid them well over what the expense was. The family was pleased.

"All right, we should be off," Bryan said with authority, although he smiled at the kind woman.

"Yeah, well, if I can't convince ya not to go that direction, then ya must know that there have been rumors of a strange woman that lives in there. Jest be careful. They say she knows magic and has two demon dogs to defend her. Don't want some witch to waylay ya all." With that, the innkeeper's wife smiled and clasped her hands together, apparently done trying to dissuade.

At the mention of a witch, the men looked at Alexa with sheepish grins. However, her eyes danced, and she smiled widely, showing a set of nice teeth as she regarded the woman.

The innkeeper's wife didn't seem to notice the significant smiles amongst them. She glanced at the grinning Alexa and said, "Ya are jest the prettiest thing ever. So slender with your long raven hair and starry blue eyes. I wish I had a girl of my own." She sighed.

"Women must be scarce around here then?" Hazerk asked gravely.

"No," the woman said, puzzled, not comprehending the joke at first. Then she suddenly scowled at the men's chuckles and Alexa's rolled eyes. "Ah! Now that was unkind!" she scolded Hazerk, shaking a finger at him and the others for laughing.

"Aw, it's all right. She knows I'm joking. She's like the little sister I never wanted." He looked fondly at Alexa with bright eyes.

"Right! As if I need another brother." Alexa laughed.

"Well, good luck to ya all. And watch yourself, lassie, with all these men." The innkeeper's wife smiled and waved as they reined their mounts around and headed north. They said their farewells and set to traveling again.

They met up with Apollos at the forest's perimeter. The unicorn was looking lively and well-rested. He held his head high and his tail at an arch, his horn twinkled mysteriously in the early morning light. He tossed his head, snorted in the wind, and greeted them merrily. "All well, humans?" he asked with a mischievous glint in his eyes.

"As well as we can be, considering we're about to march into that," Bryan said as he looked venturesomely through the dark trees of Carthorn.

"Are you going to give us another speech before we go in, Apollos?" Hazerk asked. "Because as long as there is nothing worse than a horde of pixies in there, I think we can handle it." He ended with a throaty laugh.

"I guess there's nothing more to say then," Apollos said, "Although, I can assure you there *are* things much worse than some silly pixies. But I spent almost two years in this forest, and I got out alive. I know its surprises well enough, I hope. But I'm sure it can still pull a good one on us if it wants."

"Two years! Why?" Eelyne said, astounded.

"He came here to see the Guidance Naiad," Alkin answered for the unicorn.

"It took me to wait patiently by the shores of the Faded Sea two years for the naiad to answer my call," Apollos said with a snort of displeasure at the memory.

"You never found another unicorn in all that time?" Alexa asked.

"Not one. But I didn't dare wander far from the sea. I didn't want to miss my chance. I kept safe in a soft bed of moss beneath a hollowed willow at night and stood at the shores by day. Waiting, that was the price. Nothing much happened really to tell of. I did get a visit from a hungry sea-creature once. *That* was a surprise!" the unicorn expressed with wide eyes.

"All right, enough talk. Let's get a move on." Bryan roused his company and put a stopper on any more time-consuming questions. "You guys can talk as we go."

They inched toward the forest, searching for a path. There was none.

"I'll lead the way," Apollos volunteered.

"Right. Prince Alkin, you ride next. Then I and Alexa will follow. Then Kheane and Warrior Eelyne you ride after Alexa. Then Warrior Hazerk and Warrior Warkan will guard the rear of the company," the Master Sword ordered.

"Well, I guess someone has to watch the butt of this outfit. It might as well be Warkan. Better to lose him than the prince or the lady, huh?" Hazerk smiled impishly over at his fellow warrior.

Warkan grunted. "Yeah, it takes real skill to defend you all. You're all in deep trouble if you get ambushed by an army of pixies again, aren't you?"

"Oohoo," Hazerk hollered up to the others, who were just breaching the forest. "I think Warkan made a joke! I'm not entirely sure it was a success, though. I have to think it out…"

The others cracked a grin and a small snicker. They were too busy concentrating on finding a path around the dense branches. Warkan didn't answer.

"I'm just joking, Warkan. We need your expertise." Hazerk changed his tune as they entered the dim woods. "You *did* specialize in weaponry," he said, eyeing Warkan's big pole-ax strapped to his warhorse's saddle and the battle-ax across the big man's back. "Me, I was one of the first to graduate from the medical school. And you see how much of my skill I've used on this jaunt so far..." Hazerk ended with a contemplative air. Warkan looked pleased but said nothing.

Apollos soon found a path to lead them by. Although it wasn't a legitimate one, it worked since they had no specific direction they were headed for, except for north to Kaltraz, eventually.

The atmosphere of the forest was strange. It emitted the sense of deception at every bend. Yet, it was a glorious wonder. Its acidic-sweet life sounded out loudly to the travelers. It was beautiful and sinister altogether. The trees towered above them, blocking most of the sun's rays, although there was enough light to see by. Moss blanketed the buttress-rooted ground, and all kinds of verdant plant life flourished everywhere. Thick vines hung from the trees, and all colors of fungi and mosses grew on the massive trunks.

Odd, unfamiliar noises hounded the company's ears. They knew they weren't passing by unnoticed. Creatures from the trees watched; creatures along the ground watched. Brightly colored birds flew about, squawking, and chattering monkeys hung from trees. Even a couple of lazy tigers lounging on low branches watched warily with their big amber eyes as the company rode by.

The weather was unusual. One moment it was dry, the sun's rays desperately trying to pierce through the canopy of the broad-leafed trees, and then the next minute it was raining a warm, soft drizzle.

The horses were uneasy. But having their own history of grueling war training, they stayed calm at their masters' touch. Zhan, having been trained by Alexa since he was a foal, trusted his mistress readily. The constant comforting murmurs from the riders to the horses were the only sounds the company made for a long while as they went.

"Easy, Lord." Warkan patted his slate gray's sweaty neck. The horse tossed his nose and snorted nervously.

Hazerk whipped around to face Warkan. "What did you just call him?"

"His name is Granite Lord," Warkan replied, giving his burly horse another pat.

"Ha! And you made fun of my Man's name," Hazerk scoffed.

"Red Man is a child's name," Warkan said loftily. "Granite

Lord is noble. Besides, his coat is the color of granite. It's unique."

"Yeah, if you haven't noticed, Red Man's coat is a sizzling red, more so than the normal chestnut, I might add. Matches my hair. We're a team through and through, aren't we, big fella?" Hazerk said proudly. He gave Red Man a firm pat. The warhorse pulled at the reins impatiently and chomped his bit, rolling his brown eyes back to show the whites in excitement.

"You guys both named your horses for the color of their coat; it's the same difference." Eelyne laughed.

"Does that make sense?" Hazerk asked.

"Why? What's your mount's name?" Warkan interjected.

Eelyne's warhorse was a shiny sorrel, a light chestnut coat with a flaxen mane. "I call him Swift Phoenix."

The two men couldn't argue with that.

Up toward the front of the company, Alkin turned around to regard the silent Alexa. "Do you have any witch intuition pertaining to the direction we should go?" he said a little distraughtly. He didn't need to hear her answer; he saw it in her troubled eyes.

Alexa shook her head unhappily, her lips pursed. The Prince gave her a weak smile and turned back around, speaking soothingly to Sapharan. She sighed and clenched her jaw in frustration. Her eyes darted around the forest as if she thought she might see a sign or find an answer. However, she felt nothing. It seemed from the moment she stepped into this mystical wood her senses had plugged. Was it from the strange, wet mist creeping around them? Or was her own slight fear of the unknown masking it? Maybe there was magic hanging heavy in the air, hounding her from all sides, and she wasn't skilled enough to block it out. She felt like something had been cut off from her. Like someone was striving to suffocate her magical senses. She would speak to Apollos about it later. Hopefully, by then, the foggy feeling would clear up. It was an alien sensation for her not to sense the things she normally could. She looked over at Sword Bryan, who was riding alongside her. He rode coolly, looking warily ahead. She couldn't even decipher what mood he was in. How strange!

Bryan glanced over at Alexa to see her watching him, the look on her face nearly startling him. Her sapphire eyes had darkened to a midnight blue and were disturbed, not glittering as usual, and her normally shapely lips were pursed white. His brow furrowed as she looked away without a word. "We'll figure it out," he found himself saying.

She regarded him again, with a curious eyebrow raised. She didn't say anything but gave him a weak, wry smile. And he found he was unable to stop himself from admiring her lips. They were attractive—full and perfectly shaped. He then realized he was gawking, and felt quite ashamed he could not control his thoughts in the path they were headed. He was the Head-Master Sword, and this was his charge; he couldn't think that way. Not to mention that it was Alexa! He clenched his teeth and glared straight ahead, but not after giving her a foul look as if it were her fault he was fond of her lips.

CHAPTER TWENTY-TWO

That evening they stopped earlier than usual. Bryan was aware his company was feeling stressed. A little extra down time would do them good. However, he wasn't about to waste the time. He intended to train Alexa and Eelyne tonight. He hoped it would take the troubles off Alexa's mind.

Alexa's insides were a frazzled mess, and her clothing clung to her from all the anxious sweating; not having any magical senses threw her off balance, and she wished she could take a walk in the forest by herself just to get her senses back in order and calm down. But there was no chance that would ever happen. Lately, Sword Bryan had been watching her like a hawk. It relieved her when he decided to stop early. She was even relieved to hear him announce that she and Eelyne were going to have a lesson. Maybe the physical work might clear her mind.

They found a spacious grove of trees seemingly without anything lurking around. They un-tacked and rubbed down the tired horses. Hazerk and Warkan prepared a fire and began fixing the meal. Alkin plopped down at the foot of a robust, broad-leafed tree. He rested his head against the bark and gazed contemplatively up at the bits of dusky, purple sky peeking through the canopy.

To both Alexa and Eelyne's delight, Bryan let them sit down and relax for a bit. Kheane sat at the fire, silently watching the company. The blue-black Blize stood lazily over his shoulder with a hind hoof cocked.

Alexa had remembered to ask Eelyne about the possibility of evil magic invading her dreams and eliciting visions. He had been diligently trying to find an answer for her since.

As he leafed through one of his books, she sat cross-legged next to him and peered over at the text. Apollos stood above the young warrior's shoulder, so he, too, could read the words. The three of them quietly discussed her dream as they perused.

"There isn't any way it's your blood connection to Ret that gave you your vision. I'm sure of it. It'd be more fitting happening to your father than you—him being his twin," Eelyne whispered in earnest.

Alexa narrowed her eyes and scanned the page. There were many things on prescience and visions, but nothing sounded similar to what she had experienced. There was no chance she was prescient. She had never had visions before, and to discredit the claim that her powers might be blossoming, she hadn't had any since.

Eelyne continued, "The only thing I can figure is that some magical object with an intimate connection with Ret gave you the vision, like it somehow passed on its history to you. If it belonged to Ret, it could expose his plans. And since you're sensitive to those kinds of things, you got the story loud and clear."

"That makes sense," Apollos said. "But, Alexa, you've never met Ret. Do you have anything that might have belonged to him at one time? A family heirloom?"

"No," she said glumly. There was a pause, and then she remembered something; her morose countenance changed to one of realization and excitement.

"What?" Eelyne asked.

"This is a far stretch, but…" She pulled out the necklace that Lady Adama had given her. She held it in her hand for them to see. It glinted in the flickering light of the fire. They stared at it.

And then Apollos snorted in disdain. "That reeks of magic. And I can tell you it's not pleasant. Where'd you get it?"

Alexa's eyes deepened to a midnight blue. "I thought I felt something, but I'm not experienced enough to tell if it is good or bad."

"You should be able to tell with that. It bodes evil." The unicorn was alarmed.

Her brow furrowed, and she leaned in to whisper, "Lady Adama gave it to me. She said it was given to her by the only wizard she ever knew." Alexa growled and clenched her teeth. "I should have realized! How could I be so stupid? My father and Ret are the only two wizards left she could have possibly known…at least in Eetharum. It couldn't have been my father. He's never spoken of knowing her."

"That's interesting…" Apollos said.

"Come to think of it, I think I was bewitched not to feel the evil magic in this thing," she said in an excited whisper. "When I stepped into her room, I *felt* something evil. In fact, I'd been feeling something bad in the air since I had entered the castle, but not after my meeting with Lady Adama. She had a fire going in the hearth. Ret could have sent her something to burn to mask my senses." She ended her theory with her eyes aglitter.

"You're speculating a lot," Apollos said, clearly reluctant to blame Alkin's mother of being a trader.

Alexa gazed at him in thought. And examining her theory, she suddenly realized she was accusing a person of royalty, which could mean her death. "Yes, but…"

Eelyne just stared at her, not daring to utter a word, lest the Prince should hear.

"This is what I figure," Apollos said gravely, "that thing is responsible for your dream. Maybe Lady Adama knows of its origin, and maybe she doesn't. But at any rate, it's been in Ret's care at one time. And now it's found its way to you, and it has either done its job by warning you or it has another, more sinister job we can't openly see. I can't imagine Ret would go through the trouble of cursing an object and making sure it gets to your hands just to warn you of what he's up to. It doesn't make any sense. In fact, I'm sure he probably wasn't planning to warn you. The vision was just a side effect of what it may have done to you."

Alexa stared blankly at the unicorn. "Done to me…"

"I wish you'd shown me that necklace earlier. Get rid of it. I'm afraid it may have done its damage already, but we can't be too sure." Fear was evident in Apollos' normally serene, chocolate eyes.

She threw the pendant to the ground as if it had turned into a snake. The three of them stared at it, and Apollos ground it into the earth with his hoof as far as he could. Alexa stared at the patch of dirt where the necklace had disappeared into, her eyes wide with disbelief.

"What about Lady Adama?" she whispered.

"Don't worry about that now," Apollos said grimly. "I'm reluctant to believe she has done this knowingly. And if she has, then we have an even graver problem than I thought. It means we have a trader, and the Prince, his sister, and Shelkite are in more danger than originally thought. But let's not think of it. We have to work on stopping Ret in the only way we know how right now."

The three of them sat in a bleak silence, their eyes miles away in pensive thought. Alexa was now glad she had been smart enough to have asked Melea to watch over Shelkite's castle. There was definitely a need for it.

Bryan had been watching the discussion between Eelyne, Alexa, and Apollos with curiosity. The conversation looked like a serious one, judging by all their faces. He watched from the corner of his eye as Alexa threw a piece of jewelry to the ground as if it had bitten her, and then Apollos had stomped it into the soft earth while Eelyne looked on, speechless.

The Master Sword stole a glance at the Prince. He appeared not to know of the anxious, whispered conversation only strides away from where he sat. But Bryan knew Alkin was good at pretending. When one was sure he was paying no attention, the Prince was actually listening with rapt ears.

Bryan noted the others paid no heed—all but Kheane. This caused a twist in his gut. This man was hanging around and gathering a ton of information on them. He was always listening and watching, never saying a word, never really proving his allegiance. He was still too shady for the Master Sword's comfort. The interest Alexa showed in the dark man and the idea that Kheane seemed to have knowledge of her bothered Bryan all the more. He was sincerely hoping Kheane didn't mean her or them any harm. Unless he got more answers from the man, he would not trust him alone with even Dragon.

All the secrets agitated him. For some reason, it bothered him a great deal that Alexa was hiding something from him, even more than the whole Kheane situation. What had she held back in her story from him and the Prince? What was she whispering about so candidly with Apollos and Eelyne now?

These boiling questions came to the surface in a hot, annoyed temper. He stood abruptly and ordered for Eelyne and her to get their swords.

The two popped up out of their conversation and hurried to attention for practice.

He had them fight each other one on one for a warm-up. Then he joined in for the two on one routine. At this point, he decided he wanted to make them really work hard, forgetting about his earlier plan of just working them to clear their thoughts.

"Okay, now you're going to have to put in some real effort," he directed. "Warrior Warkan! Get over here and fight on Warrior Eelyne's side with your ax. Alexa and I'll be a team. Then we'll switch."

Warkan snapped out of his lazy position around the fire. He looked devilishly at them, apparently in a good mood and happy the Master Sword was using him as a teacher.

Bryan could smell Alexa and feel the heat of her as she worked relentlessly beside him. She was still a little feeble at her swordsmanship, but she was getting better every time. Her confidence was certainly better. He let them go around this way for a while. He noticed they were getting tired. Eelyne and Warkan were sweating, and Alexa was groaning every time she blocked a heavy blow from Warkan's ax. Her advances and attacks were also getting weaker.

"Okay, stop. Let's switch," he ordered.

They switched to where Eelyne and Alexa were a team. They found Warkan and the Master Sword were quite a tough team to hold off.

Soon, Alexa abruptly halted; resting her sword tip on the ground, she leaned wearily on its hilt. "I need a break!" She glared at Bryan with snapping eyes. Why was he making her suffer when she was sure he knew her mind was already overworked with worries?

The others stopped, too, grateful for her voicing their thoughts, but not wanting the Master Sword to know.

Bryan stared back at her with his own pair of blazing eyes. He clenched his jaw and eyed her as she breathed heavily, bent over her sword. "All right, just a quick one," he consented. What was he planning? To work her to death, to get her to reveal her secrets? He scolded himself. But still in a temper, he said, "In battle, there won't be any breaks you know." He stalked over and plopped down by the fire across from Kheane, wiping his sweaty forehead, and glared into the flames, unaware of Kheane's perceptive eyes on him.

Alexa and the two men shuffled over and sat down. She sat on the far side, giving her satchel an angry shove. It turned over and the Alidonian weapon toppled out. She snatched it up to store it back in the bag, but Kheane broke the tense silence with his coarse voice.

"You know how to use that?" he asked, gesturing at the oddly shaped weapon.

The whole of the company looked up at his voice, curious. Bryan's clear blue gaze eyed Kheane harshly.

"Well...I've never used it. I bought it in Yilvana Port. It's Alidonian. Why? Do you?" Her breathing was still heavy from her exertion.

Kheane's dark coffee-colored eyes smiled in the low light, for most of his face still hid in the shadows of his hood. He reached inside his cloak and pulled a weapon out that was the exact make of the one she held in her hand.

Her eyes widened, and an excited look came over her face. "You have one, too! Can you show me how to use it?"

Kheane chuckled, low and raspy. "Of course," he said with a slight, condescending glance at the Master Sword, who stared back with a lofty, raised eyebrow. Kheane then stood up and walked to the clearing where they had just practiced their bouts. Alexa rose and followed him. "Not tired?" he asked.

"Nope," she answered, breathless.

"All right, watch." He bent his arm back and flung the weapon. It whizzed over the others' heads, making them duck. It turned and came back to its master's hand.

Alexa stared agape. She looked down at the instrument in her hand. It was a sharply curved blade. The hilt was just big enough to wrap one hand around. The blade was broad and extremely sharp. Sharp enough to slice through a man's neck and still travel back to its thrower's hand.

Alexa bent her arm back to have a go, but a chorus of exclamations from the suddenly fearful company stopped her.

"Not over here!"

"Are you trying to behead us?" Hazerk cried with wide eyes.

"Do it that way!" Bryan hollered, amused now and forgetting his anger.

"Oh, sorry." She grinned sheepishly and turned to toss the weapon in the opposite direction. It didn't come back. "Humph…" With a grunt, she moved to retrieve it, but Kheane put out a stern hand to stop her from marching into the forest.

"I'll get it."

He came back a moment later and demonstrated once more how to throw it. To the company's fearful annoyance and a little to their amusement, he sent it whizzing over their heads again.

"Will you stop?" Warkan said icily.

Kheane just chuckled, and to their delight demonstrated a few times more in another direction.

"Wait a minute," Bryan said with realization in a tone that stopped all action. He regarded Kheane with a stony gaze. The others stopped their excited chatter over the talent. The Master Sword marched over to him and faced him. "Hold out your left arm," he ordered starkly.

For a moment, Kheane just stared at him unfalteringly. It seemed he wasn't going to obey. But a yielding look came into his eyes, and he held up his forearm. Bryan shoved back the sleeve of Kheane's cloak and revealed a marking on his skin of a black wolf's head. Blood dripped from its snarling fangs.

"That looks familiar," Bryan said triumphantly and held up Kheane's arm for the others to see.

"Yes!" Eelyne exclaimed and dove for one of his books.

"You need to tell us who you are." Bryan regarded the dark, silent man again. "This is too dangerous for us to allow you to continue to travel with us. Your name sounds familiar, you know of our task, you've spoken to Ret, you know Alexa, and you're obviously a very good killer."

Alkin rose and came to stand with them. "I promise we will consider everything before turning you away, but we need to know the truth," he said.

Kheane didn't speak but eyed the company discerningly.

Then Eelyne spoke up in excitement, "Look, I've found it! I thought the marking looked familiar. It's in this text."

Bryan and the others hastened to look at the picture. There, mid-way through a page, the exact symbol of the wolf baring bloodied teeth was sketched.

"I thought it looked familiar. I'm a history fanatic." Bryan smiled at his finding. "I saw it on his arm when he raised his hand to throw the weapon."

Eelyne summarized the passage with enthusiasm. "It says here the man bearing this symbol is called the Cold Wolf, a lurid assassin from the northern country of Sushron, a man of old Alidonian blood. He rose up two hundred years after the Lost War, when the restructuring of the allied countries was still in progress. It says an infamous assassin's order trained him, but he broke loose and took jobs on himself, becoming the most feared and deadliest man in Eetharum. It says that people, not knowing his true name, named him the Keen Wolf or more commonly, the Cold Wolf, for his callous killings. His taken name, Kheane, derives from the theory he's as keen as a hunting wolf. His blood is sought in Sushron and in almost every country in Eetharum, but he's also worked for many Eetharum royals surreptitiously." Eelyne stopped and stared up at the man known as the Cold Wolf, speechless.

CHAPTER TWENTY-THREE

"I ...I don't understand..." Alexa faltered, apparently
upset this man was not the person she was hoping he
was. "The Lost War ended over five hundred years ago... That
would make you over three hundred years old. Only wizards live
to be that old. You don't look a day past forty," she ended,
perplexed.

Bryan didn't wait for Kheane to answer but stated
knowledgeably, "He's of old Alidonian blood. They're the only
race in the entire world other than wizards to have long lives like
that. But they are dying out fast. If there are any left, they are all in
hiding like Kheane. In Alidon, about three hundred years ago,
there was a brutal civil war. The old Alidonians, the long-lived
ones, had been in slavery for many years by a new breed of
Alidonians that could trace their ancestry back to foreign regions.
There was a rebellion and many of the old race was killed."

"Yes." Kheane's raspy voice caught the company's rapt
attention. "I was only sixteen when the war broke out. I was a
slave to a wealthy family. The land was in chaos. I've never seen
so much gore and hate as I did in that war, even now with all my
years of shedding blood and dealing revenge. If you must know, in
order to trust me, I'll tell you about myself."

Alkin and Bryan looked at each other significantly and then
nodded. The others settled down around the fire to hear Kheane's
tale.

"The family I was owned by was killed. I woke one night to
find the slave homes ablaze and the family strung up by their necks
and burning. I decided at that point I was going to escape Alidon. I
wanted no part of the war. I wanted freedom, but I wanted it in
another world far away from the wretched land that was only a sad
remnant of my ancestors' home. Many of my fellow slaves went to
war, but I had no family and no ties. I went to the shore to find the
merchant ships docked at port. I had many times wandered past
them on some errand or other, dreaming that someday I could sail

away on them to a new world. But the merchants would have nothing of me joining them, though I begged. They didn't want any part of the war, and they certainly didn't want to be caught with a slave aboard their ships. I hid by the bay, watching the ships for days, contriving my plan. There, I met a girl scheming to do the same."

Kheane paused. His black eyes glittered in the low firelight at the memory, and he smiled in the depths of his hood. Alexa noted his eyes were worlds away—centuries away—and she wondered if they were seeing the only beautiful memory in his dark life.

"She was the same age as me and also a slave. Her owners had been killed along with her family. Since we were both orphans, we bonded quickly. We made plans to stowaway on one of the ships. And that's exactly what we did. It took months to travel to Eetharum from Alidon. But in my three hundred years, I have to say it was the best three months of my life. Though we both were always in a state of fear of being discovered, we made plans for the future. We planned to stay together and help each other out. When our journey came close to an end and we were days from docking safely at Yilvana Port, there was a violent storm. The ship was wrecked, and we were separated. I grabbed some scrap to float on. And although I called and searched the waters, I never found her. Many of the men lived from the wreck, and I was sure, and still hope, that she survived. She was strong and smart. It could be that she had only been blown away from the rest of us.

"Well, I and the rest of the men floated to shore. In Yilvana Port, I was taken under the wing of a man who worked for an assassin's order in Sushron. I was forced to leave my lost companion behind. There, I worked and trained for many, many years. I was renamed from my birth name to Kheane. And I earned that reputation you just so rightly read out of that history book.

"Eventually, I wanted to be on my own, and I broke away from the Order at a hard cost. I was the best assassin in the Order, the best in the world. With my weapon I had brought with me from Alidon, I was unstoppable. I took jobs I only wanted to. I did many things I would like to forget. I mostly killed the not so innocent…but sometimes the innocent, if necessary. I told myself it was all only to survive at first, but over the years it became who

I was. I helped out a lot with the reconstruction of Eetharum, doing in people and royals that were still trying to cause problems after the Lost War. That's its rightful name, too. Everyone, blinded by hate, had lost the real reason they were fighting about. It ended in a stalemate. The land went into a dark recession for two hundred years. Eetharum was wounded badly from it. So, hunting down one assassin wasn't enough for the rulers to focus their attention on during that time. I became very good at not being found and doing my jobs quietly."

Kheane paused and waited to hear if his listeners had anything to say. They all waited patiently, completely immersed in the tale, even the Master Sword.

"Well, I can't go through every bit of my history. That would take three hundred years." His voice smiled. "But I will tell you that finally one day I had had enough. And it is true; I don't want to be an assassin anymore. I'm done killing for an occupation. I just want to look for the girl that came over with me. I've kept a vigilant eye out for her all these years during my travels, but I've found nothing. I came to Yoldor in hope to find some evidence of her. But I'm afraid it's in vain. And it seems my past has a way of stamping me as a menace. I can't go anywhere without suspicious eyes prying. But, yes, I was offered a job by Ret at a good price. I thought, even though at the time I had already decided to retire, that it may be worth my while to go and check it out. I traveled secretly to Zelka and met with the wizard. He told me of his plan. He was certain a vile creature such as me would join him. Well, let's say I did agree, and I went to Kaltraz to scout out this young witch I was to capture and bring to him."

Alexa stared open-mouthed at him. But the dark man continued, regardless of the frosty reactions he now received from the company.

"I watched you for days, Alexa. I saw you racing around on your horse and being harassed by your brothers. I watched you shoot your bow, and I saw you with your family in your home. I decided then and there I wasn't going to be a catalyst of a war. I was on the verge of working for the wrong side. And as funny as this sounds, when I was my own master, I only took missions I thought worthy, and this was not one. So, I ran. I ran to Shelkite, the place where my second mission was to take place, given to me by Ret. I was to assassinate the Prince of Shelkite."

At this, Alkin perked up, understanding and recognition evident all over his features. He stood and regarded Kheane, his lean body taut and fists clenched. "It was you! You threatened me. You came into my room that night."

Kheane's eyes smiled slyly.

Bryan jumped to his feet and drew his sword, gazing at the assassin with flaming eyes. *Curse the cold-blooded murderer to hell, anyway!*

Kheane threw his head back and laughed condescendingly, eyeing the weapon Bryan held at his throat. "No offense, Master Sword, but if I'd wanted to, I could have severed your throat before you even drew your sword. I know you're good. I've watched you, but you are no match for me. I've been killing men for three hundred years. I'm sure I could take on all of you."

"Don't be so proud, *Kheane*, or you'll fall into your own pit," Bryan seethed. "So, it seems you're the one who put all this into play. You threatened the Prince; therefore, I was ordered to become a Master Sword, and Apollos was sent away. And *now*, you've put Alexa's life in danger..." He faltered and lowered his sword, suddenly comprehending. "But...it was all necessary." Hearing himself recount everything, he came to understand Kheane's point of view.

"Yes, wisely stated, Master Sword. Forgive my arrogance. You must understand that my past has called for it many times for survival. But don't you see? I was sent to murder your prince, and instead, I threatened his life, giving him a warning to save it, forcing him to take action. And now look, we're all out to stop Ret. If I had just killed you, prince," Kheane regarded the shocked Alkin, "it would've been all over. Ret would be one more step ahead. I did it that way to save myself and prevent an outright war."

"I don't understand. Why me? Solely, I'm unimportant to Ret's plans. How did you breach my castle walls and get past my guards? And now, I finally know why hearing your voice made me shudder. You came to my chamber during the night, cloaked and hooded in black, and said some horrid things."

"Yes, to save you. I warned you of the wizard in an indistinct way to scare you into looking into his affairs. Do you understand my reasoning? I want to help. I want to see quiet amongst people. My entire life has been surrounded by nothing but hatred and bloodshed. I'm done. I want to live in as much peace as possible. To know that life can be kind. But first, more blood must be taken to end the trouble Ret is causing.

"You are an important piece. Ret wants all the countries under his control. Shelkite is strong. He felt you were his biggest threat. Dispatching you would leave the country without an heir. It would have caused discord—an easy in for him. And, as for how I breached your castle, that is centuries of experience. I'll tell you, though; if it had been a hundred years ago when I was desperate and didn't care whether I lived and when I hated others for loving and living happily, I wouldn't have spared a single man in your castle or you. I would have soaked your warm, lovemaking sheets with the blood of you and the lovely woman I caught in your arms. I could have, but I didn't."

The others looked at Alkin with curious eyes, and he blushed under their stares, but the shadows from the fire hid him.

"What woman?" Hazerk teased, momentarily forgetting Alkin was his prince. "I didn't know there was a potential Princess of Shelkite about."

"I don't..." Alkin hesitated, "she...I...it can't ever work out for political reasons." He looked away from the company's interested eyes. *I'm the Prince of Shelkite; what am I doing explaining myself?*

Bryan knew. It had just come to him. The woman was a pretty, cow-eyed brunette with silky, bouncy curls. And she held strong ties with the country of Zelka. He was sure of it. However, he didn't say a word. Alkin's business was his business.

"None-the-less," Kheane started again with amusement at his purposely placed controversial statement, "I've changed. I'm not so much begrudging of others anymore. It took years to change, by the way. And now I want to live happily, if I can, with your help." He stopped there and observed the company's thoughtful faces in the silence that followed. "Well, do I stay?" he asked.

"Yes," Alkin answered. "You saved my life and another's. Not to mention you didn't take Alexa to Ret. Now that we know about you, Kheane, I trust you. You're here to stay and help the company. And we'll protect you because of it. Do you all agree?" He turned and addressed the others for their input. They nodded in consent, even Sword Bryan, who was still smarting from Kheane's earlier remark on his skills.

Kheane regarded the Master Sword. "Do you now trust that I could watch out for Alexa by myself?"

Bryan narrowed his eyes and said dryly, "Yes, but don't ask to again."

"I won't unless you say so," Kheane replied. And then he added with a sly grin that reached his eyes, "Just so you know, you are the best swordsman I've seen in a couple of centuries, other than myself, of course."

The Master Sword raised a wry eyebrow but gave a curt nod in thanks.

"Kheane," Alexa perked up, "what's your real name? The one you came over to Eetharum with."

"It has no meaning anymore. I'm not the same person," he said in a curt, close-ended way.

This didn't deter her. "The orphan girl is the reason you keep going, isn't she? What does she look like? We will keep an eye out for her."

"She used to be. But, like I said, it's useless. She's probably dead," he said with bitterness.

"Can we see your face?" she pried on.

"Alexa, stop it," Bryan scolded. "You have the strangest notions, girl. Leave the man alone."

"I've been burning to ask these questions forever," she countered.

"Well, if you must." Kheane reached up and pulled down the obscuring hood.

They all stared wide-eyed as the reason for it was revealed. A long, raised, purple scar seared across his face. It started at the corner of his right eye and ran down to his lips where the corner of his mouth was deformed. The scar then traced over his chin to his neck and disappeared down into his shirt. On the left side of his face, he had red and purple scars slashed across his cheek as if a beast had swiped at him with claws. His nose looked as if it had been broken a few times over and had been badly set back.

"I stand out too much with a mess of a face like this. And if you think this is bad, you should see the rest of me… Not the soft flesh of a babe." At this, he let out a hoarse, sardonic laugh.

The company was speechless, and Kheane silently placed the hood back over his ruthlessly scarred head. The scars seemed to have reached down past his skin and into the very flesh of his torn soul.

Alexa had a powerful surge of pity for him. She was completely awed by him—his whole story. It was so exotic, callous, and romantic altogether. Upon hearing his tale, she couldn't stop her womanly romantic heart from coming to the surface, an innate sensitivity she had no control over. She usually hated it so much. But this time, she didn't fight the feeling. She desperately wished Kheane could have all the happiness in the world and even secretly envisioned herself with him.

"Alexa." Bryan's voice shot through her imaginings. "I think Kheane's a little too old for you, considering you're seventeen and he's three hundred."

The company all laughed, including Kheane in his luring, cold voice. Alexa started and blushed and then gave her Sword-Guard a deadly glare.

Bryan had been watching her closely. He noted the change in her face, seeing a starry frost come over her eyes. He had to put a stop to it. Although, he didn't like the guilty feeling he had gained from embarrassing her.

"Who said I was interested? I'm not seventeen, anyway. I'm over eighteen." She stood up with as much dignity as she could muster, brushed off her pants, and stalked over to pet Zhan, away from the men's teasing stares, where she could blush crimson all by herself.

"When did that happen? You were only seventeen when we called for you?" Alkin said in good spirits. He had gotten over his shock and had fully forgiven Kheane and now planned to help the tortured man any way he could by clearing his name.

"The day of my birth past while I was traveling to Shelkite," she said, feeding Zhan a piece of dried apple.

"Oh, I see," Alkin said and then turned to Kheane, "Before we turn in for the night, what is it you want from us? You said you wanted our help."

"Just for your royal protection, if you deem it worthy."

"Right. And you will have it. When this is over, I will make sure you have a safe place to live and your peace and quiet," the Prince vowed. Kheane nodded, grateful.

They ate their supper in a comfortable silence. Everyone felt better since Kheane's clandestine life was now revealed. Kheane himself actually felt better than he had in a long time. It was a comfort to have others in his confidence. It was like a wet, suffocating veil had been peeled off his face. He ate his food in a contented state.

The only person feeling a qualm was Alexa. She munched on her food with an unsteady sensation pulsing through her veins. She had come to the point where she needed to tell everyone the purpose Ret intended for her, and she also thought it was important everyone should know about the pendant and that it might have altered her. This was extremely important. This was *her* company. She didn't want to put them in any harm, especially if it ended up being herself who was doing the harm. Besides, she remembered, it was *she* who had let her temper go because Prince Alkin and Sword Bryan were having a private conversation without her.

The notion further bothered her because she had felt Bryan's curious and irritated eyes on her all evening, not to mention the Prince was throwing her suspicious glances, too. She knew they knew she was holding something back from them, and they were uneasy about it. Apollos had said it was fine, so they had accepted her silence. But she realized she was being unfair to them. They needed her to be honest. They were here to help her. She shouldn't keep anything from them. She would tell them everything, even if it meant the Prince would have her hung for heresy.

She swallowed her food and cleared her throat, looking out around the fire at all their faces. Everyone looked up expectantly. Apollos recognized what she was doing and bobbed his head with encouragement, his eyes alight with comfort.

"I…um…haven't told you the whole reason why Ret wants me. I know why Kheane was to take me to him," she said and then added to Kheane, "Do you know why?"

"No. But I'm sure it wasn't for a family reunion. I do know, though, that he's paranoid of wizards becoming extinct. He's obsessed with finding full-bloods."

"Yes. I think he believes he can use me to right that problem."

"Go ahead, Alexa," Alkin prompted gently.

She looked at all their expectant faces and landed on the handsome Sword's. He watched her attentively with his shiny azure eyes. His face held no irritation now, and strangely enough, he looked slightly compassionate. She locked eyes with him, and he didn't turn away.

She then told them everything while she gazed into Bryan's encouraging face. She explained Ret's plan to use her body as a shell to harbor creatures and bring them into the world. She told them of how Ret was planning to use her brothers and her to do this by siphoning out their magic blood. She explained that he wanted to create his own breed of full-blooded wizards. Ones under his power that would help conquer Eetharum and even beyond.

Then, with some hesitance, she explained to them about the pendant she was given. She told of how Apollos and Eelyne had recently discovered that whatever the pendant's purpose was; it was entirely wicked. She dared not look at the Prince when she revealed this detail. She kept her eyes completely focused on the unwavering and emotionless Master Sword, only briefly flicking her eyes to Apollos for certainty.

By the time she ended her account, she noted, with distress, she was trembling slightly. Sitting cross-legged on the ground, she tucked her sweaty palms in her lap to steady them. There were a few agonizing moments of silence as everyone digested her words and their food. Hazerk awkwardly stifled a loud belch.

Kheane spoke first, "Prince," he said to Alkin, "I was going to tell you, from what I could gather in my meeting with Ret, I think there is a good chance someone in Fordorn is assisting him. I'm not saying it's your mother, but I'm sure he has an accomplice."

"Alkin, there's a good chance your mother doesn't know about the pendant's origin," Apollos added in earnest.

The Prince was quiet, his hazel eyes fixated on the colorful, flickering flames of the fire. After a moment, he sighed and looked up at the anxious faces watching him. "Alexa said she claimed a wizard *gave* it to her. I love my mother dearly, but she has changed strangely over the years. She's different from what I remember as a child." He regarded Alexa with an intense gaze, and she sucked in anxious a breath of air. But he merely gave her a sad smile and said, "You're frightened because of what you felt you had to tell me. Don't be. You did the right thing. You told us everything you know. I have no reason to condemn you for your suspicions." He looked away into the fire. "If what you say is true…then, in theory, my people are very much in danger, my home…my sister. I'm positive Dorsa is ignorant to this. She has a heart of gold. I'd thought Shelkite was safe…at least until Ret's armies came for us. But if he has an inside hand, my homeland is in just as much danger as Galeon, maybe more." He groaned and dropped his head into his hands. "What have I done?" he exclaimed. "I've left my castle exposed! My sister is defenseless!"

"Not completely, my prince," Bryan interjected, "The warriors are still there, with the guards and a Master Sword. They are all trained well."

"Not if the problem is eating them from the inside," he lamented. "They will be caught off guard and be unprepared."

"There is one watchful eye," Alexa broke in, still hesitant. "Before I left, I felt something was amiss. And I asked a trustworthy person to be extra vigilant. I made her vow, and I know she'll keep it. I can be very persuasive… It's part of my blood." She gave a sly smile, hoping to hearten the distraught prince.

"Her? Who?" Alkin asked.

"Melea. One of your servants."

"Melea, my servant?" Bryan said with incredulous eyes.

"Yes. She's smart and good. I sensed it in her. I told her to send for help if anything seemed wrong. *Anything*. She was to send for a Master Sword or for you, Prince Alkin, or she was to ride to

Galeon for help."

"She agreed even behind my back?" Alkin gazed at her with a skeptical brow.

"Only because she knew it would be protecting you," Alexa assured quickly.

He heaved a sigh and slumped back. "I'm a horrible ruler... I've deserted my people...my sister, perhaps my mother. If only there was a way to see what was happening back home." Sitting up straighter with hope, he asked Alexa, "Is there?"

She shook her head sadly. "I don't know how. I haven't been taught."

"I guess I'll just have to wait until we reach Galeon for news. But that could be months," he said in resignation.

"We could send someone for news and then rendezvous in Kaltraz," Bryan suggested. "I could go." Alexa's eyes snapped up in alarm to look at him, and he gazed at her thoughtfully. He didn't know why he proposed to go. He knew he had a responsibility here. And he knew he didn't want to leave it. "But I can't. I've pledged to be a Sword-Guard," he said, realizing he was strangely pleased to see Alexa's troubled reaction.

"No, you can't," Alkin agreed.

"I could," Kheane said.

"No. You're needed here." Alkin set his jaw and raised his chin defiantly. "No one will go. Alexa selected this company for a reason. And we're sticking together. I'll have to trust that my land and people are in good hands. I'll send for word immediately once we get where we can." He glanced around at his surroundings.

The dark of the night was complete, though the silvery rays of the moon gleamed through the shadowy branches. A light breeze picked up, and the company shivered as it whispered eerily through the leaves. They were suddenly aware of all the strange sounds emitting from the surrounding forest.

"I think we've momentarily forgotten where we are..." Alkin said a little nervously. "Let's get some sleep and start out early, so we can get going and get out of here as soon as we can." He began to unroll his blankets and situate himself.

"Even in all my years," Kheane said as they settled in their beds around the blazing fire, "I've never ventured into Carthorn."

"Yes," Apollos said, "we can't forget where we are. This forest will pretend to be your friend, but it always undoubtedly turns its back on you when you least expect it. I'll take the first watch."

Alexa settled in her blanket as close to the fire as she dared to without singeing herself. It was a comfort. Zhan crept up behind her to doze protectively over her shoulder. The Master Sword settled as near to her as they both felt comfortable with, and Hazerk slept on her opposite side.

Bryan sensed Alexa tossing around. She flipped around to face him. They were an arm's length apart, but it suddenly felt odd, unlike it had even the day before. He looked over to find her long lashes closed quietly over her eyes. She was breathing easily. He smiled inside. He was glad she had shared her secrets with them. They weren't what he had expected, but it still made his gut churn at the thought of anything that horrid happening to her. And although he had vowed to be her Sword-Guard weeks ago in her chamber back in Fordorn, he promised himself over again he wouldn't let her fate be what she feared.

With eyes closed and trying desperately to drift off to sleep, Alexa listened to the forest's sounds. They were a bit unsettling, but she knew she was safe with her company, especially with Sword Bryan and now Kheane. She smiled, thinking fondly of the men who slept around her. All of them, even the unicorn, were her closest companions. She wished with all her heart that they would be okay in the end.

As she listened to the soft snoring of the company, something pricked her heart, causing sleep to elude her. It was the idea of something or someone, and she couldn't identify it at first. She had been experiencing unfamiliar emotions lately and had struggled with them and tried to snuff them out or hide them away, but they were becoming more untamable. She didn't want to admit to what they might be.

She clenched her jaw and buried her face in her blanket, biting down on the coarse material with her teeth, wanting to shriek in frustration. She realized she was becoming exactly what she detested. Bryan had noted it in her that very night: she had become starry-eyed with silly romantic notions.

Alexa had had boys come around asking for her back at home, but her brothers had always kept them away. And the only one they allowed around was one she heartily wished they wouldn't. They did it as a joke because he was such a nuisance to her. She rolled her eyes at the thought of him.

She had always been satisfied with doing her own thing, not worrying of clothes and pretty things. She had always made sure she was pleasantly presentable, but she had never actively pursued boys like other girls her age did. Sure, she may have kissed at least one handsome young man helping her attend her family's sheep one afternoon... Just for an experiment. But now, her own mind and feelings betrayed her.

Heart thumping, she decided then and there under her blankets to just face the fact and get it over with. On her back, staring through the threads of the blanket to the flickering world outside, she allowed herself to admit that she found Kheane extremely alluring. He was wrapped in a cloak of mystery and danger any woman would be attracted to. But what she couldn't—wouldn't— admit to was what Sword Bryan's eyes had silently rendered to her, and how she felt tremendously delighted about it.

The Master Sword had treated her differently lately. He was no longer looking at her with disdain. His eyes held more depth now when he gazed at her, alluding to sincerity in some feeling toward her. Albeit, she was still aggravated over his comment he had made earlier about her and Kheane. Not to mention she had never forgotten he had called her a scrawny, little girl and a haughty witch... But it didn't bother her as much as she tried to make it bother her. He had said or done other small, more significant things that had replaced those mocking comments. She had an inclination that his bitter remarks derived from some resentment surfacing from his past, and they really had nothing to do with her whatsoever.

She found herself wanting or needing his approval more and more with each passing day. She couldn't figure why it suddenly seemed so important—until now. The answer was plain: she was fond of him. In fact, she had to admit she was more than just fond of him. She had nearly choked when he suggested he should leave the company. Despite this feeling, she wasn't about to tell him. He may have been treating her nicer lately, and he may have had a few appealing looks in his handsome azure eyes when he was watching her, but that sure didn't mean anything significant. Besides, he was a Master Sword, and she was just a commoner. She quickly decided she would ignore the situation. Because more than likely, she was only imagining he might be interested in her.

At this resolution, she rolled over and attempted to get some rest. But Hazerk unexpectedly flung his arm out in his sleep and whacked her hard on the face. She gasped for air and held her smarting nose. Eyes watering, she turned back the other way to face the now slumbering Sword. She sighed desolately upon seeing the fire's light dance across his attractive features. How could she possibly ignore it?

She soon fell asleep, with the sinking feeling that this was only the beginning of all the confused events and emotions she would face in the days to come.

CHAPTER TWENTY-FOUR

Lady Dorsa jerked awake from the worst, most realistic nightmare ever. She sat up and looked around the carriage, her eyes foggy with sleep. The falcon sat snuggly in his cage, sleeping. Everything was as it was when she had drifted off.

She had fallen asleep sitting up. She should've climbed into the bed to nap; the kink in her neck told her so. Sliding back the compartment window, she peered out into the cold afternoon. The bright sparkle of snow dazzled her eyes, and an icy wind blew at her, cooling her creamy pale cheeks.

Her jade-colored eyes moved over her surroundings. Across the glaring snow, towering above the convoy and losing themselves in the clouds, were the cold stone walls of mountains. They were in the Haiparian Mountains—the great chain of mountains that ran across Eetharum from west to east—and just beyond them was Vtalmay. It would take several days to travel through the pass to the frosty country on the other side. There, they would reach their destiny: The Ice Palace and the Chancellor.

Dorsa's heart sank.

They had been traveling for weeks. She was restless, and she was sure her friend the falcon felt the same. Snapping the compartment window shut, blocking out the chill, she pulled her plush blanket closer around her chin and watched the falcon sleep. She had yet to name him; he couldn't be without a name.

Sighing and feeling defeated, she allowed herself to think of the horrid dream she had just had. She couldn't believe she could even possibly dream such a thing; it was so ghastly. She had dreamt she'd murdered the Chancellor in his sleep! Her mind's imaginings while she slept appalled her. It was regretful sometimes that one couldn't control their dreams.

"No matter what I feel about this situation, it doesn't make it right that I murder the poor Chancellor in his sleep," she said aloud to the falcon. "I would never do that."

The bird, with its head tucked under its wing, opened one

sleepy eye and regarded her. She took this as a gesture to continue. She shuddered. "I had a knife, and I just slashed his throat while he slept!" She shivered again and covered her eyes, remembering the vivid image. "I'm sure he's a nice man," she went on. "Everything will be fine… Although, it feels like it would be easier if he was wicked, then I could hate him rightfully."

The falcon made a contented noise as if he agreed with her and then tucked his head back under his wing.

Dorsa's heart fell further into misery.

Her thoughts then turned to Eelyne, and hot, stinging tears rose in her eyes. "Oh, Eelyne, what am I supposed to do without you?" She then began sobbing for what felt like the hundredth time, and curled desolately up in the warm blankets, blocking out the sun and chill, resigning to the fact that the procession moved her ever closer to Vtalmay and away from home.

She woke a couple hours later to the shouts of her guardsmen, and rubbing her red eyes, she tried to decipher the commotion outside. After a few moments of straining to catch the incoherent conversation, she poked her head out of the carriage to inquire.

She found they were preoccupied and stood circled around something in the snow.

She wrapped her cloak around herself, drew up the hood, and stepped out into the deep fluff to investigate. Some of the warriors were still mounted, and others knelt on the ground inspecting whatever it was lying in the snow. She peeked through the men's broad shoulders and saw at their feet a huge snow lion.

It was dead. A pool of crimson saturated its throat and stained the surrounding crystal-like snow.

Dorsa gasped and clutched her hand over her mouth. One warrior, now alerted to her presence, turned and gently took her arm.

"My lady, what are you doing out here? Everything is under control. Don't worry," he said with fervent eyes.

"Wha-what happened?" She stared blankly at the dead creature that she was sure had probably been so majestic in life.

"Well, I think we traveled too close to its den, and it spotted your riding filly. She had pulled loose from the carriage and trotted too close. The lioness came hurling out at us and…well…you see what we had to do," the warrior explained.

Dorsa nodded and looked up and around to see another warrior holding her prancing filly by the lead. The warriors had had the horse tied to the back of the carriage to travel behind, but the high-spirited filly had evidently become bored and torn loose for a fun game of chase.

"Is she hurt?" she asked worriedly.

"No, my lady. She's just as feisty as ever."

"Let me see her." She held out her hands to her pretty liver chestnut mount.

The warrior gladly handed over the rope. She crooned in the fidgeting filly's ear and stroked her, calming the horse down to a standstill.

She then turned to the men and said, "I'll ride her for a while. I need some fresh air, anyway."

"Are you sure, my lady? It's really safer in the carriage," the head-warrior advised.

"Nonsense. Can someone bring me my tack, please?"

Just then, small cries emitted from the den opening, interrupting them. The warriors peered over their shoulders, and Dorsa stood on her toes to see.

Two fluffy white snow cubs tumbled out into the day.

"Oh!" she exclaimed. "You killed their mother."

One of the warriors approached the cubs carefully, speaking softly to them, crouching, and holding out his hand. They bounced on each other and eyed him with suspicion, but after a moment they came to him. The other warriors and Dorsa moved in closer.

"We'll have to dispose of them," the head-warrior stated gravely.

"Why? You won't!" she said, aghast.

"They'll die without their mother."

"And that's your fault. I'll take them," she said a matter-of-factly.

"How will you take care of them? They're wild animals."

"I'll figure it out, and I don't care if the Chancellor likes it or not," she stated, feeling willful. She longed for comfort and companionship. These cubs were so adorable, and they needed her.

"All right, my lady. I'll have the men gather them up." The head-warrior sighed.

Dorsa smiled, pleased. After patting the playful cubs and crooning in their ears, she clucked to her mount and trudged off toward the carriage, towing the filly along.

The dark chestnut horse pranced by Dorsa's side, kicking up the feathery snow and taking playful nips at the lead in her mistress' hand.

"You're a silly girl, Scarlet, aren't you?" she said. The filly flipped her cherry-colored mane audaciously. "We'll all be together... You, me, falcon, and the cubs. We'll have each other now and be a family, and we'll be all right," she said, desperate to convince herself.

★★★★

At dawn, the company rose and started out again. Alexa found to her relief that her senses had seemed to unclog over the night. She had asked Apollos about it the evening before, and he had explained that it was natural for her to feel assaulted at first with all the magic hanging in Carthorn's air.

An enormous weight had lifted off the company; everyone was in everyone's confidence now. And the travelers' moods had improved a great deal toward each other, especially Sword Bryan and Kheane's feelings toward one another.

The company rode in broken silence, ducking under hanging vines and low branches and weaving around marshes laced with mist. They traveled over narrow creeks and around buttress-rooted trees, their trunks massive enough for ten men to circle hand to hand. They heard frequent noises from various unidentified creatures scurrying through the underbrush, but nothing menacing had reared its head yet.

Alexa felt pleased. She had her senses somewhat back and let them wander amongst the group. It occurred to her that this was an invasion of privacy, but what else could she do with all this time?

Sword Bryan rode next to her. He was relatively content for the moment; just some slight worry nagged him. She figured it was merely the normal anxiety one derived from leadership. Her senses couldn't discern that what was actually bothering him was her disturbing future.

Prince Alkin was tangled in distress. She didn't have to guess why. She knew his thoughts were focused on his mother's questionable allegiance.

Kheane, on the other hand, was emitting an almost joyful vibe. The ex-assassin appeared to be feeling better about his life. He was hopeful. She kept an enthralled eye on him for most of the morning.

When her senses landed on Eelyne, she was surprised to discover the normally cool, young warrior was fretting over something, his mind jumbled with questions, doubts, and fears. She could only ever sense emotion and never pinpoint their origins precisely. It was always an educated guess on her part why someone was in a particular mood. However, from her experience, the patterns of his emotions hinted he wasn't thinking about something, but rather someone.

While they were all preoccupied with their thoughts, and Alexa's senses were engaged, the first catastrophe of Carthorn hit them. Unfortunately, neither Apollos nor Kheane sensed it either. Apollos was in a rare moment of deep daydreaming—as unicorns occasionally do; they aren't perfect. And Kheane, feeling content for the first time in centuries, had made the mistake of letting his guard down, something he hadn't done since the beginning days of his assassin training. He, however, was the first to utter a snap warning moments before.

"Something's—Alexa, watch out!" he barked.

Startled and bewildered, she looked at the ex-assassin, and in that moment a gargantuan snake dropped from the branches above.

The creature landed with a vile hiss on top of the unsuspecting Alexa and Zhan, its body so long that only its head and the belly came down to gather up its prey.

The serpent's descending body slammed into Bryan, who had been riding next to her, and Dragon stumbled sideways into a tree, smashing the Master Sword's knee.

Alexa's horrified curses tangled in the forest's atmosphere

with Zhan's enraged squeals. The snake opened its massive maw, showing her its venomous fangs, before entwining its thick body around horse and girl.

"Kill it! For the love of Kaltraz, kill the blasted thing!" Alexa screamed over the stunned hollers of the men and horses.

Bryan jerked out of his shock, drew his sword, and slashed at the swaying serpentine body in front of him. His sword cut into the beast's scales, but barely drew blood. The snake turned on him and snapped menacingly at him with a hiss. Bryan dodged, and Dragon craned out his neck and took an angry bite out of the creature.

"Apollos!" someone cried.

"Help!" Alexa screamed, her arms pinned at her sides, utterly defenseless and beginning to panic. The snake lifted her and Zhan jerkily into the air.

"Get over here!" Bryan roared at the already attacking warriors.

Kheane had drawn his sword and cut gashes in the snake's thick skin, but it caused scarce damage. Hazerk and Eelyne sliced relentlessly at the beast's midsection, and the creature dropped more of its sinewy body, finding the fight harder than it had first presumed.

Warkan had out his battle-axe and whacked at the serpent as if it were a tree trunk. The burly man had only hacked his way into the fleshy outer layers of the hide when the snake flipped its body and pinned him to a tree.

Kheane, giving up on his sword, took out his Alidonian weapon and whipped it toward the beast. The blade cut into the back of the snake's head and lodged there. Hot blood spurted out and rained down on the company with its putrid stink. Alexa caught a gush in the face and gagged. The snake tightened its squeeze, and she gasped for air. Zhan's terrified squeals turned to a meek grunt.

Apollos raced up from the head of the company with his horn lowered and charged full force toward the snake. He leapt lithely up, a vicious glint in his eye, and rammed his horn deep into its flesh. The great snake twisted its body and thrashed, hissing and snapping with its crushing jaws. Apollos tweaked his horn and thrust it deeper. A flash of black radiated when the unicorn let off a deadly vibe of magic. The creature hissed and gave a tremendous shudder, weakened, but not deterred from taking another venomous snap at Bryan, who still engaged the serpent's head.

Alkin, having slid his blade into its neck, jumped off Sapharan and onto its coils, and tugged at Alexa's shoulders. "Hold on!" he encouraged, straining to pull her out by her underarms.

Alexa winced. Her ribs felt as if they would snap any moment. Her vision turned blotchy. *This is it. I'm going to die... At least Ret can't use me now...* She despaired. She couldn't breathe and saw nothing but a white blur before her eyes. Then, waveringly, the world left her.

Warkan tore loose from the snake's hold, the beast being occupied with the others. The brawny warrior jumped up, snatched his poleaxe from his warhorse's saddle and ran up the snake's back to its head. He slipped dangerously in the seeping crimson as he went, but balancing on the writhing creature, he took the weapon in his hands and rammed it straight into its skull with an angry bellow.

The snake shuddered. Its head plummeted to the ground, its body twisting in resistance. Then, after several convulsions, it stopped moving.

Dripping with sweat, Alkin gave a hard tug on Alexa's limp body. She slipped from the snake's coils, and he carried her to the side of the path where he laid her down, gently resting her against the trunk of a tree. He knelt and examined her.

Hazerk leapt off the dead serpent and came to her side, inspecting her health in earnest as Alkin wiped the blood from her face. Bryan and Eelyne, still trying to catch their breath, rushed over.

Seeing the humans, Zhan gave an indignant squeal for attention. The white horse was still trapped under the snake's body. Warkan and Kheane quickly freed him, and he stood and gave himself a robust shake.

"She'll be fine," Hazerk said, breathless from the fight. "Someone get her water," he demanded, still anxiously examining her. He was handed a water pouch, and he trickled some on her face.

Alexa's dark lashes fluttered open. Her blue eyes looked hazily up at the men's worried faces staring down at her. Shaking her head and breathing in deep gulps of air for a few moments, she smiled weakly. "Ugh." She rubbed her ribs. "It felt like I was going to snap in half," she said hoarsely, then fell into a fit of wheezy coughs.

"You *are* a twig. I think you're okay, though," Hazerk said, feeling around her rib cage for any damage. "Can you stand?"

She nodded and slowly got up, glancing at Zhan, who was nibbling on a patch of grass off the path. Seeing her mount was alive, she asked, "Is everyone okay?"

"Yes. We just have a new, pleasant aroma is all," Bryan answered dryly, with a small smile, feeling extremely relieved she was all right. He had fought blindly and with a surprising and piercing fear they would find her dead.

Taking a moment to let the event sink in and to catch their wits and breath, they looked around at the carnage. The chopped body of the snake lay motionless. The creature's bowels were strewn about, the ground littered with its flesh and soaked with blood. Everyone was completely covered in the snake's putrid reek.

"Well, I guess we learned our lesson," Alkin said, wiping his hands and face on his cloak. "We've got to pay better attention. This forest has a way of tricking you into feeling secure and then shaking you up." They all nodded in glum accord.

Apollos snorted his agreement. "It's part of the magic here."

"Right. We should keep moving. Are you okay to ride on, Alexa?" Bryan asked.

Still somewhat shaky, she gazed into the Master Sword's dirty, serious face. His azure eyes were vivid with genuine concern. "Yes, I'm fine," she managed to say, and pulled away from his stimulating gaze to give her face a vigorous wipe, frantic to clean the dirt and blood away—as well as the fluttering feeling he'd imparted on her…

"All right. Come on," the Sword ordered. "Gather the horses and mount up. And keep your eyes open."

Everyone moved halfheartedly toward their mounts. Alexa fumbled her way to Zhan. Bryan reached out a hand and steadied her, knowing she was pushing herself more than she should. She didn't regard him or say anything as he helped her into the saddle. Attentive, he looked into her stoic-set face as she gathered her reins.

Brushing away a lock of escaped hair, she peered down at him. "I could have managed, but thanks," she said stiffly.

Choked, Bryan nodded and went to catch Dragon. The stallion was wandering dangerously close to Blize, who had laid her ears back at him in warning. Bryan swung himself into the saddle and led the company out, leaving the mess far behind.

They rode in silent vigilance now and traveled at an easy but steady pace. Everyone was watchful of their surroundings as they cut their way through the once again friendly forest. The sun shone through the thick canopy of trees, and the colorful birds sang their beautiful serenades.

Several hours after the snake attack, they came to a stream— shallow, cool, and rippling over a bed of smooth stones. As they approached, it looked as if it were materializing from a dream. A light mist swirled around it and among swaying willows, cedars, and ash trees, all leaning over the banks, peering at their elegant reflections.

The company came to the edge, preparing to cross, but Bryan paused and commanded his weary followers to take a break and clean up. They were thankful; it had been a dreadful several hours they had had to endure their own reek.

They washed up and ate in passive silence. Alexa took to herself and washed her hands and face under the cover of the hanging boughs of a willow arched over the stream. She knew she was still under the watchful eye of the company, so she felt no fear. And, of course, if Sword Bryan had thought her doing anything wrong, he would have taken the liberty to say so.

To the rush of water, birdsong, and the gentle wind blowing through the willow, she soaked in the forest's serenity. And taking a seat on the bank, she let the clear water rush over her bare feet and sat and stared contemplatively into the water for a while. Zhan stood by her side, taking long, noisy slurps from the stream, basking in the tranquility, too.

Alexa's body ached from the morning's adventure, but she was recovering fast, inside and out. The forest seemed to have a strange effect on her, as it did on all of them. She tried to decipher it, but it was complicated far beyond her will to understand. It could easily deal out so much grief, yet it was healing, too. It contradicted itself, like it had a life of its own, very unstable, as if it didn't know what it wanted to be. Even the odd assortment of deciduous and tropical trees alongside one another showed evidence of this. She now understood why it was uninhabited by humans.

A short while later, Bryan moved the company out. By that time, they were ready to start again, for the pleasant atmosphere of the stream had changed while they rested. It began to emanate an intense feeling that they were no longer invited. A peculiar silence fell, and the breeze seemed to whisper for their departure.

The company wondered if hidden mystical creatures watched them and if the creatures had the influence to allow them to stay or not. Perhaps the forest and its inhabitants remembered the wedge that had been placed between them and humans during the Lost War, and were feeling not so forgiving.

Later that evening, before twilight, the company's ears perked at the sound of water mingled with vague laughter. The watery sound was unmistakably a waterfall's rush. They quickened toward the alluring sound, hoping to see an awe-inspiring sight.

They weren't disappointed.

They came to the edge of a steamy pool of azure water. The melodious sounds of the cascading fall and joyous birdcalls created an instantly soothing environment. The sight and overtaking mood stole their breath away, rendering them all silent. Not just one mouth fell agape.

A splendid waterfall gushed down into a swirling pool. The white water danced, splashed, and tumbled happily over a stony ridge into the steaming pool. Large boulders blanketed with green, plush moss surrounded the deep blue water. Willows and cedars stood as sentries. The banks thrived with luxuriant beds of forget-me-nots, lilies of the valley, and buttercups.

The pool was nearly perfectly round and appeared bottomless. Opposite of the waterfall, the water trickled down a smaller, narrower fall to become a gently flowing brook. The air was warm and intoxicating with the scent of the woods and flowers. Misty puffs sprouted from the pool: a warm spring—a haven, it seemed.

Arriving at the bank, the company realized they weren't alone. They had accidentally crept up on a gathering of unsuspecting nymphs. The beautiful dryads and naiads were enjoying the pleasures of the warm water. They laughed with otherworldly voices and splashed around in the swirling waves. Some dove playfully from the ridge while others lounged on the soft moss.

The company took in a breath as one, choking back words at the sight. For the nymphs were far more than stunning. This act, however, was enough to alarm the jovial beings; with shouts of fear, they vanished almost immediately. Some dove into the water and dispersed: the naiads. Others fled into the forest and disappeared: the dryads.

"Wait!" called Apollos. But even a mystical brother couldn't stop the frightened beauties from fleeing.

One, however, did pause, infinitesimally as it was. Her rich brown, almond-shaped eyes looked piercingly at a flabbergasted Alexa. Alexa held her breath as she gazed into the eyes of the earth itself. The dryad had long, nut-brown, wavy hair that flowed around her creamy skin. She wore a sheer green, shimmering garment that barely covered her pleasing figure, and glancing at Alexa from the corner of her eye, the dryad gave her a slight nod and the smallest of knowing smiles. Then she bounded lithely over the rocky surface and disappeared into the forest.

Alexa stared, mouth agape, with sudden realization taking a hold of her.

"Wow!" Hazerk breathed. "I don't think I'll ever be able to make love to a real woman again…"

"Shut up, Hazerk," Bryan commanded with exasperation. He glanced from the pool, now empty of nymphs, to Alexa, who was apparently meditating on something big. Her sapphire eyes were a bright sky blue, and she chewed her lip as excitement came over her countenance.

The others waited patiently, anxious for their next order.

"Prince Alkin, I think you just got your intuition wish," Alexa said, an excited tinge in her voice.

"Yes?" Alkin eagerly moved Sapharan next to Zhan.

Alexa still stared with glittering eyes at the waterfall. Apollos came to her side, an understanding look over his equine features. She regarded him, and the unicorn nodded in approval. She moved her eyes from him to the eager Sword and Prince.

"What better creature to be the guardian of the purest form of earth than a nymph? They must be the Earth-Keepers. They're the earth itself."

"Right!" Alkin exclaimed in understanding.

Everyone's spirits suddenly rose. Bryan gave Alexa a wide smile, who returned it happily, her eyes dancing.

"Good job, Alexa, woohoo!" Hazerk hollered and pumped a dramatic, victorious fist into the air.

"What of the Guidance Naiad?" Eelyne suggested, his face alight, obviously thrilled to actually see some of the mystical creatures he had always studied so diligently from a book.

"Hmm... I don't know," she contemplated.

"But, it couldn't be her..." Bryan said with some hesitation and gazing at her for consensus.

The others looked at him with puzzled and skeptical expressions. Alexa stayed thoughtful, not disregarding, as she gazed back at him.

"What do you mean? She's a nympiad or whatever you said they were," Warkan commented.

Bryan shrugged, looking away from Alexa's pensive stare. She apparently didn't realize she was making him uncomfortable. Her eyes were awfully captivating...

"He's right. It's probably not her," Apollos said, realizing where Bryan was coming from.

"Why not? She's a well-known nymph. Like a queen of sorts, right?" Hazerk questioned.

"Exactly," Kheane interjected huskily. "The Earth-Keeper would *not* be known."

"Besides." Eelyne perked up. "She's a naiad."

"A water nymph," Alkin added.

"And we already have the water element," Bryan finished what he had begun to put into words.

"Right." Alexa nodded in accord.

"But maybe we should head in that direction. We could speak with her…" Eelyne suggested, unable to restrain his excitement.

"That took me two years last time. We don't have that kind of time," Apollos stated.

"It wouldn't hurt to head that way, though, since we don't have a clue where to find the element, anyway. What do you think, Alexa?" Alkin inquired to the contemplating girl.

Alexa started out of her thoughts and looked at the Prince. Catching his kind, hazel eyes, she grinned at him. "It's definitely a start. Maybe if we camp near here tonight we could try to communicate with the nymphs here. They could tell us something."

"All right, sounds like a plan," Bryan said. "Let's make camp up a way, on the other side of the pool. It's probably best to not disturb the nymphs' space."

"Good idea," Alkin agreed happily.

"We should take a dip. The water's real warm." Hazerk had dismounted and bent down to touch the steamy water.

Everyone agreed with enthusiasm.

"So tempting… We can in the morning before we head off. We've got to make camp now before dark. I don't want any more surprises when we're not prepared," the Sword said.

The company groaned in disappointment, but everyone nodded in reluctant agreement, knowing that was the smart thing. No one wanted to be caught off guard again.

They took up their reins and guided their mounts over the brook. They traveled about a half a mile down the path from the spring. Apparently, it was a popular place for the creatures of Carthorn: there were paths leading to and from it on both sides.

The company made camp in a grove just as the sun disappeared for the night. By that time, they had a nice roaring fire and sat contented around its warmth and comfortable light, eating their dinner and listening to the horses crunch on their own dinner.

As she ate, Alexa decided she wanted to speak with the nymphs alone. She didn't want the others to know her plan, because they undoubtedly wouldn't approve. She wasn't sure how she was going to do it and would think it over tonight. Perhaps it would be okay if Apollos went with her. Sword Bryan and Prince Alkin would be all right with that. But no, the nymph had definitely looked at *her*. Apollos wouldn't be able to help this time. This was her duty. After all, she was the one called for it.

Alexa smiled to herself when she had made up her mind. She would go in the morning before everyone woke; burning some sleeping herbs in order to sneak past the watch person, then go to the pool to find the nymphs. She delighted in her plan. *Plus, I can get a good bath before the men get there.* Just the thought of swimming in the warm water sent an excited quiver through her.

"Alexa." Kheane's raspy voice broke her thoughts. She looked at him inquiringly. "Let's practice on your usage of the Alidonian weapon."

Bryan straightened his posture from his spot at the fireside. "I was going to give her a break tonight, considering what happened this morning," he said, a little abrasive. He was still not fond of Kheane butting in, for some reason; it was mostly when it pertained to Alexa.

"Have you softened, Master Sword? She has to toughen up if she's to fight Ret and maybe in a battle," Kheane said pointedly.

Bryan cleared his throat. The ex-assassin had a point. And normally he would've made his pupils push on, but he just didn't feel like making Alexa work tonight. Perhaps he *was* softening toward her. He would have to rein that in. "Right. You work with her tonight. Alexa, work on your dagger throwing, too. I'll give you and Eelyne the night off. Unless Eelyne wants to take a bout." Bryan regarded the young warrior, who was leaning lazily against a massive oak.

He grinned, a bit sheepish. "I'll pass tonight, Head-Master Sword."

Bryan shrugged and settled back to watch Kheane coach Alexa on the unusual Alidonian weapon. She was only slightly better than she had been before with her throwing technique. But it surprised Bryan and the others watching the practice session how good she was at dagger throwing. She threw each one with speed, agility, and confidence, hitting her mark almost every time. The Master Sword was impressed. Kheane was pleased too, and told her so, which made the young woman glow with pride.

Soon, the day's earlier troubles were forgotten and a game of competitive dagger throwing started. Everyone participated, even Alkin and Warkan; though, Apollos lounged by the fireside.

The unicorn watched the boisterous, cheerful company fondly with his glistening chocolate eyes. However, he kept vigilant for anything threatening that may have been watching, too. And he had to remind them a few times not to throw the daggers at the trees.

The company played well into the night before exhaustion overtook them and made them come to their senses. They then settled down and fell into a contented sleep, still jesting with each other as they drifted off one by one.

Eelyne took guard duty.

CHAPTER TWENTY-FIVE

Before the first rays of dawn, Alexa woke with a start, her mind full of the plans she had established the night before. She hoisted herself up on her elbows, leaving the warmth of her bedroll, and scarcely daring to breathe, she surveyed her surroundings.

An eerie, warm breeze blew around the dense woods and sent an excited shiver down her spine. The red coals of the fire sizzled comfortingly in the midst of the sleeping company. Even Eelyne, who was supposed to be alert, was sleeping soundly against a tree. She couldn't believe her luck. She smirked. This was good for her, but he was sure to hear about his mistake later.

Eyes alight with mischief, she glanced around to the others. Bryan, lying to her left, had his back toward her and did not stir. Apollos lay curled up like a puppy next to the coals, his soft velvety eyelids closed and his mane glimmering in the low light. Kheane snored faintly, his hood drawn down past his face, while the horses dozed peacefully at their tethers. They all seemed in an enchanted sleep, and their exhaustion now made her plan of burning sleeping herbs unnecessary.

She rose and slung her sack over her shoulder. Alkin muttered something incoherent, and she froze, her heart pounding wildly in her chest. But seeing he was still asleep, she relaxed and smiled down at the Prince. As she crept away, she found herself thinking how fine a person he was and how lucky Shelkite was to have him as a ruler.

She walked in solitude down the rutted path that led to the waterfall, reassuring herself as she went that it was not far and if she needed them, they could be there within minutes. Besides, as always, she carried her dagger and bow.

She strode down the mossy path in silence, and the forest began to awaken with the morning's first light. The sun's rays came shyly down through the trees to sparkle on dew drops scattered over the greenery. The birds began to sing, cooing and twittering in their merry way. And she could soon hear the heady sound of the waterfall, just around the next bend.

Nearly skipping with anticipation, she halted upon seeing a white stag cross the path before her. The magnificent creature paused at seeing the dumbfounded girl, and raising his finely shaped head, pricked his pale ears toward her. His round, black eyes bored into her, and he wore a great crown of antlers that many hunters would have sought after with too much greed.

He gazed at her with his piercing eyes, and Alexa gulped, wide-eyed, unable to move. Her father had told her of the noble white stags. They were said to be unapproachable and untamable, but the wisest creatures the High Power had ever placed on the earth. She had to speak to it. She had to find her voice, but she was entranced beyond words.

The stag had an untamed air about him, yet he seemed to be waiting on her, gazing at her with an imploring expression, and she could only stare stupidly at him. *Oh, I wish you could somehow help.*

The splendid creature blinked and lowered his head, his nose brushing the earth as if he were bowing to her. He then stepped carefully over the path and into the forest's cover.

A breeze caressed her face and ruffled tendrils of her escaped hair. A voice, deep and soft, rode on it, not spoken, but was as if it sifted into her mind: *the breath of the world dawns from the soil of your blood.*

She stood and gazed into the trees where he had slipped away long after he had disappeared, silently absorbing the experience.

Eventually coming to and still puzzled over the words, she made her way to the peaceful azure pool. She delighted in finding the nymphs once again bathing in the steamy waters and basking in the morning light. And once again, before she could utter a word, they screeched and dashed away.

"Wait! I have to ask you something!" she called, helpless, after them.

Yelping, they paid her no heed.

"I need your help; Eetharum does. Wait!" she blundered on, rushing toward a dryad that leapt from the mossy rocks to the forest floor. "I need to know where the earth element is. It's important! There's an evil wizard. I have to save Eetharum!"

But her pleas were futile. The dryads and naiads were gone. She frowned after the departed, finicky creatures and clenched her jaw, putting her hands on her hips. "You stupid, no-brain, frantic beings," she grumbled. She then dropped her sack on a nearby rock covered in plush, green moss, with dainty lilies bowing their pretty heads toward the pool and called, "You all are perfect examples of why men lose their heads!"

With a glower, she looked around the pool. The waterfall was just as enchanting as it had been the day before. Her sapphire eyes glittered as her failed mission sifted from her mind. She would like to climb the rocks behind the waterfall and stand behind the foamy falling sheet of water, but first, she would bathe.

She dropped her quiver and bow to the rock and removed her cloak, then quickly tugged off her boots, unbuckled her dagger, and climbed out of her trousers. She slid her lightweight shirt over her head and discarded her undergarments. And, with a sigh of pleasure, she unbraided her hair. It fell to her waist in raven-colored ripples, and she relished the feel of it flying loose for once. Normally it was straight and silky, but it had many days of hard riding on it—not to mention snake innards—and was in dire need of a washing, as was the rest of her. She pulled from her sack a bar of lilac-scented soap and leapt gleefully into the waters.

The liquid warmth enveloped her. And surfacing, she felt she could not have delighted in it anymore. She quickly washed herself and her hair, and proceeded to take out her newly sharpened dagger and shave off any undesirable hair on her body. She would need to hurry, lest the others woke and noticed her disappearance. She did not want to alarm them, yet she had no desire to have to bathe with them either. They would have undoubtedly acted like a bunch of wild stallions, despite what they said. This was much better. She would just swim around a bit more and enjoy herself. She would even wash her clothes and let the warm breeze dry them. There was still plenty of time; the sun was not yet all awake.

Bryan clenched his jaw as he surveyed the camp. He glowered down at Alexa's empty bedroll. He thought he might explode; he was so angry. Where had she gone? Why hadn't he or Kheane or

Apollos woken at her departure? Letting out a low growl, he looked over to the snoozing Eelyne. And with pursed lips, he stalked over to the young warrior and kicked the bottoms of his boots. Eelyne jerked awake, instantly shocked and ashamed at what he had done.

"She's gone," Bryan growled down at him.

Eelyne's wide, fearful eyes darted over to Alexa's bedroll. The others stirred awake, mumbling inarticulately.

"I—ah—I," stammered Eelyne.

Bryan did not wait to listen. He strode back over to his bedroll and began strapping his sword belt on, not removing his ominous glare from the young man. Eelyne looked away in disgrace, no doubt feeling incompetent.

"Wha-what's going on?" Alkin stretched and yawned and stood up from his bedroll.

"Our little lady is missing in action," Bryan seethed.

"Huh?" The others gasped in unison and looked around as if they might see her hiding in the bushes for a prank.

Apollos stood and shook himself. "She can't be far. She probably just wandered to the pool. I can't sense anything evil."

"You all pack up camp and get the horses ready. I'll go get her," Bryan ordered, his tone not any less severe. At that, he stomped off down the path, scowling as if he enjoyed it.

Feeling he might overflow with fury, he grumbled and mumbled to himself all the way down the path. How could she be so foolish? Why did she take off without telling them? The insane girl! He would drag her back by that wretched black braid of hers!

He came to a stomping halt on a rock banking the azure pool and peered down into the water. A slim shadow moved just beneath the rippling, steamy surface. It was her.

Bryan relaxed; she was at least still in one piece. But he wasn't going to let her get away with what she had done. He had somehow failed. He was supposed to be her Sword-Guard, and it infuriated him beyond sanity she had slipped away unknowingly from him. He made sure he had a set scowl on his features when her head broke the surface of the water.

He continued to glare down at her as she wiped water away

from her eyes with slender fingers. When her sight cleared, she started upon seeing him, but covered her surprise coolly.

"Girl, have you already forgotten what happened yesterday?" he growled at her, his brain hazing over with rage, worry, and relief.

Alexa merely stared at him with placid sapphire eyes.

"You were almost breakfast for a gigantic snake. Are you so daft that you still run off by yourself?" he asked, cross. She didn't answer him, but continued to stare at him mildly. This aggravated him all the more. "Well, Sand Queen? What do you have to say for yourself?" he pressed through clenched teeth.

She gave him a playful, coy look. "Do you want to take a dip, Master Sword? The water is heavenly."

Suddenly, the current situation registered. Dazed out of his anger, Bryan took in the complete picture. He blinked down at the girl floating in the azure waters at his feet. She was undoubtedly fully unclothed, but he could distinguish nothing past her bare shoulders, which were just peeking above the swirling waves of the pool. His eyes involuntarily peered deeper to search out the rest of her, but the pool was too shadowy. An unwelcome heat rose up his neck to his face.

Hoping she had not noticed his fleeting moment of gawking, he managed to mutter a curt reply, "You're changing the subject." He shifted his weight awkwardly, still endeavoring not to stare down into the obscure waters. Alexa gave him a devilish smile, and his heart rate increased. He had obviously failed in covering up his show of attraction.

Then, with resignation, Alexa shrugged her shoulders and said, "I thought I'd try to talk to the nymphs myself." She looked away from his frown, sheepish.

"And?" Bryan implored tersely. He could not help but notice how her eyes seemed to reflect the rippling waters. They glowed such a brilliant azure when they landed on him, it made him uncomfortable.

"They ran off before I could say anything," she finally said with regret. She peered up at him with wide, innocent eyes, trying out her feminine wiles for his forgiveness. Though she was not regretful she had tried, she just craved his approval.

"It was an unnecessary risk and foolish. What if something had happened?" he scolded her, but his tone had less of a sting to it. He was desperately trying not to admire her smooth, sun-bronzed shoulders. The sight of her in this state was softening his cool heart, as was her remorseful countenance.

There was a moment of submissive silence between them. Alexa gazed thoughtfully away at the cascading waterfall, and Bryan took the opportunity to study her, letting his eyes wander and his thoughts ponder. Her long, raven hair floated silkily around her on the water's surface. He had never seen it down before. He found himself wondering what it would look like. It probably fell to her waist, soft and glossy. He suddenly realized he had been feeling more and more enticed by her each day, even with all the dirt and grime. But right now, she appeared more alluring to him than ever. Maybe he had not let himself see her as a person before, only an obligation. He had tried so hard to shut her out for stupid, complicated reasons. Apollos *was* right...

"Well?" Her voice cut into his thoughts, and his mind quickly came back to the present. "Are you just going to stand there and watch me bathe? It's kind of unsettling." She bored him with reproachful eyes.

His eyes narrowed with his scowl. "Well, hurry up and get out of there," he snapped. "We don't have all day to wait on your girlishness."

"Calm your horse, Master Sword. If you'd just give me space, I could finish and get dressed." Her smile was smug as she gave her raven mane a toss.

"Right," he grumbled. "I'll be over there." He jumped down from the rock and crossed over the trickling brook to the other side of the pool. "If you need me, I won't be far," he called over his shoulder.

Alexa swam to the edge, watching him as he made his way into the forest. "I'll be fine. And don't look," she hollered affably after him.

"As if I would want to!" he called back, rolling his eyes, but feeling as if he had just told the biggest lie.

Alexa grinned to herself, her heart beating rapidly. She tried to quell the animated feeling in her chest. He had *without a doubt* looked at her with desire. But it couldn't be true, could it? She smiled happily to herself and dove into the water, plunging herself to the bottom, enjoying the thrill racing through her body. *He's just denying it.* She was hopeful as she whisked along the sandy floor.

Bryan stomped his way into the forest. He stopped a little way down from the pool, but near enough if something might happen. He plopped down on a fallen tree lying off the beaten path, grumbling inwardly. What was happening to him? For a moment there, he felt like he was only sixteen again. She was bewitching him—the little vixen! He rubbed his face vigorously and sighed, resting his chin in his cupped hands. He stared at the ground, trying to clear his mind while he waited. *Ugh, women.* It was unsettling to feel like he was thrown out of character in his own territory: that would be commanding a company with silly distractions such as this!

He sat on the decaying log going over everything, all their conversations, strained encounters, and all his confused feelings. It felt like agonizing hours later when he finally discovered that he actually felt something rather strong for Alexa. This was hard to admit, considering he wasn't sure if *she* had feelings for him. And considering their situation, it was not a good thing. How did he fall into such a pit, especially when he had tried so hard to go around it? *Well, if she's going to act coquettish with me, I'll just ignore it. It's like a woman to do that, anyway; though, I didn't think it was like her... But from how she was looking at Kheane, it's probably him she fancies. She feels nothing for me and is just playing stupid games...*

Finishing her bath and feeling elated, Alexa swam to the rocky edge where the waterfall merged with the pool in a foamy mass. She ducked under the pounding water and hoisted herself up onto the ledge behind the cascading water where a breezeway connected either side of the pool. Squeezing the water out of her hair, she lost herself in dreamy thoughts initiated by the enchanting echo from the water reverberating off the rock wall.

She tilted her head back, breathed in the moist, warm air and smiled to herself. Just then, her senses latched onto something, and a shock of fear sliced through her. She snapped her eyes open and looked over her shoulder, and started upon seeing a poorly clothed, strange man standing behind her.

"Nymph!" the man wheezed in a throaty voice and pointed at her. His wide eyes practically bulged out of his head.

Alexa swallowed a gasp and reined in her escaping composure. The man edged toward her, bent. He was emaciated; his clothes hung on him like rags on a clothesline, and his dirty brown hair was a mass of tangles and grease.

Her eyes darted over to her clothes and dagger lying beyond him. Her heart raced at the inconvenience of the situation. Here she sat naked, with her dagger several strides away.

The man paused his advance and studied her with a crazed look. She stared levelly back at him, raising her chin haughtily, assessing how she was going to take him on. He looked weak, but he was in a strange state of mind. He might be stronger than she figured.

"Who are you?" she demanded, forgetting any modesty and standing up to face him as boldly as she could.

The man smiled, showing a mouth of decaying teeth. His eyes glinted, "You're no nymph. Just a girl." He smirked, giving her a sly look.

Alexa narrowed her eyes and calculated how she could get around him to her weapon. Clenching her jaw and straightening her shoulders, she glared at him with suspicion. "I asked you a question. Who are you? What do you want?" she demanded again, preparing to leap for her dagger.

The man laughed and began walking toward her again, his hand outstretched as if to touch her. He must have gotten lost in the forest and had never found his way out, she concluded. He didn't reply, but reached for a lock of hair draping over her shoulder.

"Stay back!" she growled, her eyes spitting flames. But he merely grinned and kept advancing. Right as he was about to touch her, she dove for her dagger. That same instant, he lunged at her with a snarl, grabbed her hair and yanked her back. Nonetheless, she clutched her fingers around her weapon and unsheathed it in the flurry of warding off his restraining hold. "Get off me, scum!" she hissed.

Paying no heed, he groped for the dagger, and they came into a tangled wrestling match. He twisted her fingers, wrenched her wrists, and clawed at her arms. She aimed solid kicks at him, but he was too wiry.

Then, with a hard knee to her stomach, he grabbed her hair again and wrenched her head. They fell to the ground; the dagger clattering to their side. The stranger snatched it up with surprising speed, and she fought him with fierce determination, her heart racing in fear as he shoved her back to the ground. She fell under him, seeing stars as her head slammed on the rock.

"Bryan! Bryan!" she cried, as the man tried to pin her, a victorious smile spreading across his face.

Sitting on the log, Bryan came out of his quiet ponderings upon seeing something flit by in his peripheral vision. There was a familiar ringing sound, accompanied by a tinkling laugh. He looked around, suspicious, and turned his head back to find himself staring straight at a pixie in front of his nose. It giggled and tugged at the lock of hair hanging down over his forehead. "Hey! Get!" He swatted at her. This only seemed to entice her, and she laughed, buzzing around his head, pulling at his face and hair.

Annoyed and remembering he was in danger of being pixilated, he stood and began walking away, waving his arms at her. "Get out of here," he snarled, but the little creature followed him down the path toward the pool.

Alexa's crying voice rent the air. The Master Sword's head shot up like an animal spotting danger. He began running as fast as he could toward the warm spring, his mind going into full gear and his heart racing with fear for her and anger with himself. How could he have been so stupid to leave her alone?

His throat tightened; he could barely breathe as he charged down the pathway. The pixie pursued, thinking it was a game. She laughed and dashed around his head. Bryan ignored her, but soon became light-headed, and feeling a sudden sense of contentment, he slowed down and tripped over a root and fell flat on his face. Pushing himself up, with a stubborn shake of his head against the pain and dizziness, he gave the pixie one last angry swat and clambered back to his feet. He raced toward the pool again, determined not to be pixilated.

Making it soundly to the spring, he scanned the area and saw through the waterfall two figures wrestling. Alexa's fearful voice called out to him and cursed her attacker. "Bryan, help! Please! Get off me, you scum, get off!" She screamed, and an unfamiliar male voice gibbered.

He dashed around the rocks to the back of the waterfall and found her being attacked by a terribly thin man. They rolled around the ground. The man clawed at her and tried to bite her, attempting to stab her and pin her down. But he had a hard time controlling the feisty girl, for she defended her own skillfully.

At the sight, something roared to life in Bryan's chest. He became utterly enraged. He leapt on the stranger with full force, ripped him from atop of Alexa, and threw him against the rock wall. The man slammed into it with a sickening thud, his head snapping back, and fell to the ground where he didn't move.

Worry and anger renting through his veins, Bryan turned and regarded Alexa with fearful eyes. He panted and shook with anger as he assessed her. She inched away along the ground to rest against the wall, grabbing her shirt to cover herself. Beads of sweat and water dripped down her face, and her chest rose and fell with each rapid gulp of air she sucked in and out. Her normally dazzling eyes held complete horror and relief as they darted from the strange man to the Master Sword.

With a tremble, she clutched her stomach and huddled like a child up against the wall, choking back silent sobs. "Th-thank y-you," she gasped.

Bryan came to her side and knelt. "Are you all right?" he asked with a catch in his voice. His hands trembled slightly as he brushed back locks of hair from her face.

Alexa nodded numbly, staring at the stranger lying face down and motionless not an arm's length away. She grimaced and fought back the stinging tears that threatened to take over. There was the most excruciating pain in her stomach. She had never had such pain before. She didn't think she could bear it. "Is h-he d-dead?"

she choked, weakly eyeing the man.

Bryan glanced at him. "I believe so. If he's not, he's got some explaining to do."

"I th-think he's mad—" she gasped and then coughed. It racked her body with a horrifying pain, and she yelped aloud.

Bryan clutched her shoulders when blood seeped through her shirt. "You're hurt!" He went to yank away the garment, but she held on to it tightly, wanting to cover herself. "Let me see! You're bleeding," he growled as blood soaked her shirt.

"No, I got to get dressed…" She stumbled to stand. Bryan grasped her firmly, helping her. "Help me." She reached for the rest of her clothing with a strained hand, the other clutching her abdomen. Halting and gasping, she gently let off the pressure she was putting on her stomach and lowered her shirt to examine her wound, still concealing the lower half of her body.

A long, deep gash seared across the flesh of her stomach. She gulped and pressed her hand to it, trying to stop the blood flow, but the crimson fluid seeped between her fingers. Tears of pain squeezed through her shut eyelids, and the world began to waver.

Stunned, all Bryan could do was stare wide-eyed. He had never seen a wound so ghastly. Alexa looked pleadingly into his alarmed features, he gazed at her as if in a trance. For once, he was unsure what to do. She held her scarlet-soaked shirt swathed around her waist. Her head bowed so that her long raven locks obscured her face like a curtain, falling over her shoulders and concealing her chest. She wrapped her free arm around her stomach to hold her trembling body.

"Master Sword…" she pleaded, raising her face, bringing him back with her frightened eyes.

Bryan jerked into life and went to gather her things, but found she was swaying on her feet. He caught her before she crashed to the ground. He gathered her into his arms, wincing awkwardly as her hot, wet skin touched his bare hands. She peered at him with dazed eyes, sweat gathering at her brow, and he stared back at her, eyes wide and unguarded with concern. He would not let her die; he ground his teeth with determination.

"Come on," he breathed, wrapping her in her cloak, picking up her dagger, and lifting her carefully into his arms. Alexa heaved a sigh and fell into a semi-unconsciousness; her head rested against his shoulder. Bryan clutched her to his chest and made his way back to the camp, his heart pounding. He had failed again and hated himself all the more for it. He had failed her and had no right to call himself a Sword-Guard, let alone a Master Sword.

He would not—could not—let her die. Something at the sound of her desperate voice calling his name had confirmed the resolution he had come to while sitting on that rotting tree. Her voice and the sight of another hurting her caused a strange pain and anger in his chest he had never thought possible again. If she died, the world would be a void, cold place without her. It was as if not only the mission would come to a complete and devastating stop, but that life—his life—just wouldn't be right without her, like a game of chess with only the king against the horde...

But these feelings could be from his colossal feeling of failure in his duty. Not for her... Right?

Bryan's long strides carried them quickly down the beaten path, his breath working hard with worry. He glanced at her features contorted in pain. Her eyelids flickered and her lips parted in unease. He pursed his own lips upon seeing a trickle of crimson creep out of the corner of her mouth. Her chest rose and fell with each labored, gurgled breath she took.

A lump formed in his throat, so much so that he thought it would literally choke him. He clutched her body more snuggly toward his own and tried to jog down the path. "Hang on, girl. You've got to make it... Please," he breathed in her ear.

To his surprise, her eyes fluttered open, and she gazed into his face. Her sapphire eyes were the darkest blue he had ever seen them. They held an intense but fading flicker, telling him she was fighting.

"Keep awake, Sand Queen. I'll get you help." He managed a tight smile down at her. She only blinked her answer, but her eyes softened before she closed them again. Then she hacked, and blood spewed out of her mouth and splattered his shirt. Her body gave a massive tremble from the pain shocking through her slight frame, and his heart went out to her.

As he held her close, he could smell the clean sweetness of

her. His senses prickled with unsolicited pleasure. And suddenly, never in all his life had he wanted to be in the company of a particular woman as he did right then. With a twinge of guilt, he found himself fancying she wasn't wounded. But it was for reasons far more impractical than her health. Why was he thinking this? Why was he feeling this way about her? He had tried so hard to despise her. Then again, why had he tried to despise her?

He fought an image of him and her on this very path. But instead of running for help, they were evading the others to be alone. They'd find a cozy glade and huddle under one of the ancient trees. It would umbrella them from the world, become a place they could escape to and explore; an island of paradise all their own, where no one could breach the shores.

He shook his head, clearing his thoughts. He was getting too sentimental, or maybe just mental. This is what he meant by being thrown out of his element. She was becoming a complete distraction to him. How was he supposed to do his job? He had never had a problem keeping on track before. Besides, this was Alexa, the arrogant witch he felt nothing for beyond that of his Sword-Guard duty—so he told himself.

Angry with himself and still feeling an enormous amount of apprehension, Bryan came storming into the camp with his face set in a hard scowl. The company rose in alarm upon seeing the two in such an awful state.

"Warrior Hazerk, get over here!" he hollered.

Hazerk leapt up and came to Alexa's side as Bryan gently laid her down on a blanket and carefully wrapped her in another. The others came and gathered around the injured young woman, staring at her in consternation.

"What happened?" Alkin choked, taking in the dreadful, bloody sight.

"I found her bathing in the pool. I left her for a few minutes so she could dress, but then I found a man attacking her when I returned," Bryan explained while Hazerk examined her wound. The warrior's brow furrowed in disquiet.

"Here, keep pressure on it," Hazerk ordered the Master Sword, who was the closest at hand. The warrior got up and retrieved his pack with his medical supplies in it.

The company all looked anxiously on as Hazerk worked. Alexa's head bobbed and lolled as she came in and out of consciousness. Alkin moved around to her side so he could pull her onto his lap and hold her head. Her eyes flickered up at him, and he smiled down at her with encouragement; she returned it with the weakest of smiles.

Bryan fidgeted on the spot. "Well? Can you help her?" he demanded after a few minutes.

Hazerk sat back on his heels and stopped his working. A look of distressed defeat wreathed his face. "I can't do anything," he said.

"What do you mean? Didn't you learn *anything* at the medical school?" Bryan growled, his eyes flashing. The others stared blankly, wondering if the Master Sword was going to punch Hazerk squarely in the face.

"I can't do anything," the dejected warrior said with force. "The wound is too deep and badly placed. She's lost too much blood." Hazerk backed away from the vile look on the Master Sword's face.

Bryan was about to retort, but Apollos appeared over everyone's shoulder and looked calmly down at the girl laying in agony. "I told her to watch out for water. They mask her senses. She must not have felt him approaching," the unicorn said with sad eyes. "I didn't sense him either."

"Apollos, can you do anything?" Alkin asked; his voice held a crack.

"I can try."

"Well, do then," Bryan said impatiently. Alkin gave him a reproachful look. "Please," the Sword-Guard added.

"Alexa?" Apollos addressed her. She looked at him as if through a haze. "I'm going to try to heal you, but brace yourself, it's going to be painful. Are you ready?"

Alexa managed to nod. She raised her chin boldly, watching the unicorn with rigid eyes. Alkin took a hold of her hand and clasped it as Apollos raised his head, closed his gentle eyes, and called on his magic. They all watched in hopeful anxiety.

The unicorn lowered his now brilliant white horn, opened his eyes, and looked steadily at the Master Sword and warriors. "Hold her down. This is going to take a few minutes."

They all gave a stiff nod. Bryan and Warkan took a hold of her legs. Hazerk and Kheane took a hold of her arms. Alkin cradled her head, whispering encouraging words in her ear. Eelyne looked on, too ashamed to say or do anything.

The unicorn lowered his searing horn to inches above her wound, and Bryan glanced wide-eyed to a now fully conscious Alexa and saw a determined yet fearful look in her eyes. He couldn't help but admire her as the unicorn inserted his burning horn into her open wound. She screamed in pain despite desperately trying to refrain.

The men all flinched and watched as the girl ground her teeth and cursed, straining at their holds. Her face became deathly pale and sweat poured from her brow, beading over her skin, making their grips slick.

Bryan watched in anguish as her frantic eyes darted around. They landed on his face, and he held her gaze. She didn't look from him for a long moment, her eyes trapped in excruciating pain.

Apollos continued to hold his sizzling horn at one end of the wound. It snapped and hissed, fire-like inside her gut. Just as Bryan was feeling the unicorn should be done, Apollos thrust his horn deeper and began moving it up and down the length of the wound. The cove filled with such a bright white light, they could barely stand to keep their eyes open to watch.

"Please stop!" Alexa screamed and tried to thrash, but the men held her tight.

Apollos continued this practice for long, agonizing minutes. Bryan watched on, wishing he could take the pain from her. But eventually, she could take no more. She passed out, and her body went lax. The Master Sword clenched his jaw so tight it felt as if it might snap.

Finally, Apollos stopped and gently removed his horn from her stomach. The prismatic light and heat ebbed away to its normal soft glow.

The company looked down at the pallid girl, her eyes closed and her breath still labored, but the wound on her stomach looked nothing like it had minutes before. It looked as it would after years of healing: a mere scar, white and slightly raised, seared across her abdomen.

All the men waited, anxious for her to wake. They watched in silent relief as the color came back into her cheeks and her breathing slowed to normal. Then, finally, she opened her eyes, and they were relieved to see they held a spark of her fire again.

Alexa glanced around to the men and unicorn staring down at her. She cranked her chin to look at her stomach, removing her hand from Kheane's steady hold, to run her trembling fingers along the scar. And, with a sigh of fatigue, she let her head fall back onto Alkin's lap. A weak smile spread across her features as she looked at Apollos and his glittering chocolate eyes.

"Thank you," she croaked to the unicorn. She then looked at the Master Sword with appreciative eyes that said the same but held so much more.

He grinned down at her, feeling so relieved he thought he might faint, although he would have never admitted it.

CHAPTER TWENTY-SIX

Though it had taken days to travel the Haiparian pass, Lady Dorsa and her escorts had had the good fortune of clear weather. They had traveled deep enough into the mountains that snow was a common occurrence even for the warmer seasons. They were, for certain now, out of the beloved territory of Shelkite and on Vtalmay's soil. If one could even find soil beneath all the snow...

Dorsa sat dolefully in the carriage as it bumped and jarred her along the frozen road to the Ice Palace. It wasn't far off. The palace lay just inside the border, nestled high in the Haiparian Mountains and overlooking the cold western shores of the Nortarwin Sea—where Vtalmay was known for its successful fishing. Though the country wasn't incessantly snowy or frozen in lower altitudes, she would be subjected to spending the rest of her days at the Ice Palace, trapped in a cold environment, playing the dutiful alliance-bound wife.

The convoy wound its way down and around one last hill before she could see the front entrance of the Ice Palace and then the Ice Palace itself beyond. Against all her will to stop the procession, her carriage continued to bump its way toward her new home, first passing between two pillars atop of which sat two handsomely carved sculptures of snow lions glaring down at passersby.

Craning her neck to look out her window, she looked at the impressive statues with slight awe and foreboding. She remembered seeing them the last time she was here with her brother and mother, but it was so long ago she had forgotten the strange beauty of this cold place. She stood and climbed onto the bunk, careful not to disturb the sleeping snow cubs, and peered out the window facing west toward the palace.

The palace glittered brightly in the sunlight. Its façade, built elegantly of white stone, melted smoothly into its surroundings, serene yet harsh for its coldness. Beyond the palace, she could see the tumultuous Nortarwin Sea churning violently in the wind.

She swallowed; the lump in her throat nearly suffocated her. She plopped back down on her seat and smoothed out the dark green gown her handmaiden had helped her don just that morning while the convoy took a short recess.

She attempted to clear her mind of all selfish fears, dredging all the propriety and etiquette she had ever learned to the surface. She fiddled with her emerald necklace and let out a breath that softened the lump in her throat. Focusing on her duty and not her heart, she calmed and thoughtfully spun the ice-blue engagement gem around her finger.

Within moments, the carriage halted and someone outside announced her. For one split second, she thought she might faint, but she recovered quickly and put on a stately countenance just as the carriage door opened from the outside.

She took the Shelkite warrior's hand, and he helped her to the ground. The bright sun glared off the snow and dazzled her eyes of all sight.

Momentarily unable to see, she heard a gentle, deep voice greet her; a large warm hand took hers, and by the time the Chancellor's lips were pressed to her hand, she could see the man that stood before her.

She readily took in the stature of her husband-to-be. Chancellor Cheldon was a stately man, who appeared somewhat shy but gentlemanly. He had sweet, unguarded eyes, brown, but not the intriguing dark brown of Eelyne's eyes. He had a broad stature, was taller than she was, but not tall like Eelyne. His hair was a golden-brown, and he sported well-manicured whiskers. His garb was splendid in its richness, no doubt to impress and receive her. He was not a particularly handsome man, but she did not find him unattractive either, to her dismay.

She had been just a girl the last and first time she saw him, and he had only been a young man himself. Only ten years her senior, the Chancellor was hardly old, but the age gap scared her for no reason she could find other than she felt so much like a pawn.

"Lady Dorsa, welcome to Vtalmay. It is most certainly

my and Vtalmay's pleasure to have you." The Chancellor straightened from placing a tentative kiss on her hand.

Dorsa curtsied and smiled a hollow-feeling smile. "Thank you, Chancellor Cheldon. The pleasure I assure you is all my beloved Shelkite's."

He smiled widely and motioned to the flags flapping in the gusty wind on one of the palace's turrets. "Look, my lady, I have raised Shelkite's colors in your honor. I hope you are pleased." He gazed at her in suspense.

Dorsa raised her jade-colored eyes to the sky where she saw the familiar colors of green, silver, and blue flying just below the white and navy colors of Vtalmay. There was a prick of gratefulness in her heart; she felt comforted, yet frightened. "Nothing could give me such happiness. Thank you."

The Chancellor smiled, pleased. "Come, it's chilly out here. I'll show you to your chamber myself." He turned to climb the white steps leading to the palace's courtyard and gardens.

Dorsa and her handmaiden followed while the warriors began to unload her belongings. Reaching the top of the steps, an extravagant view delighted all her senses. Her handmaiden must have felt the same, for she gave out a pleasantly surprised gasp.

Hearing the young women's reactions, the Chancellor turned and smiled. "Yes, it's quite a sight. There are attendants working continuously to keep it as such."

Surrounding the palace as far as she could see in every direction were beautiful, glistening ice sculptures of all shapes and sizes. At her feet, a family of bunnies carved of ice sat munching and frolicking in a grassy field of ice. Alongside the walkway to her left was a life-sized sculpture of two dolphins rising out of a frothy ocean wave; beyond them, a whale flipped his tail in the snow, and to her right, sea lions and seals basked in the cold sun. But most amazingly and abundantly were the sculptures of all types of trees. A woodland of glass encompassed her. And intermingled amongst the ice-forest were sculptures of all manner of creatures, land, sea, and mystical: deer, snow lions, nymphs, winged horses, bears, dragons, merpeople, and even humans, embracing in such ways that made her blush. And as if that weren't enough, she spotted handsome seafaring vessels of ice nestled amongst gardens of icy rosebushes and lilacs. Even an intricate snowflake the size of a carriage flashed and glittered in the cold sunshine alongside the others.

"Do you like them?" Chancellor Cheldon asked, pulling her gaze from her fervent study of the courtyard to his bright smile.

"Oh, yes, I do!" Her eyes sparkled with pure delight. "They're so splendid! I'll have to go for a walk someday and see them all." Her countenance showed her sincere desire.

He grinned. "Then, I'll have one made especially for you." His eyes were unable to hide their pleased sparkle. He then turned and led her up more stairs to the great white doors of the palace.

The inside of the palace was nothing short of magnificent itself. The white stone rose to a high dome, with several elegant chandeliers shining brightly from above, and all along the walls and floors were elegant engravings of alabaster. The ornamental etchings swirled and danced on the white stone, giving the building the illusion of glowing whenever light shone on or flickered over the designs. The palace was relatively warmer than the outdoors, with fireplaces around every bend. However, every so often, in some set-off space along the corridor, it was cooler and there would be an ice sculpture present.

Dorsa could not remember all that the palace had to offer and was enraptured as she was led over plush, white rugs and through alabaster-carved halls to her new chamber. Later, upon reflection, she doubted whether she could remember how to get back to her room from the palace's entrance.

Pausing at a chamber door, the Chancellor led her into her room. It was warm and comfortable; soft, navy and white rugs lined the floors and heavy drapes hung from large double doors and over windows that looked out onto a balcony overlooking the sea.

A place all to herself!

The chamber included two adjoining rooms. The receiving room was spacious and filled with books and things to pass the time, a grand fireplace, and paintings of rolling hills that looked very much like the landscape of Shelkite. She wondered if the Chancellor had had them placed there especially for her. She warmed at the thought.

The adjoining room to the left was her bedchamber, which was just as spacious. There was an elegant canopy bed with white hanging drapes, a handsome wardrobe, a vanity with mirrors, more paintings, another lavish fireplace, and other various necessities. Her bedchamber also had double doors leading out onto the balcony with a spectacular view of the sea.

"I hope you're pleased. I had it redone just for you. I figured you'd enjoy a place to yourself, and the view of the sea is my favorite from this room," he said, waiting anxiously for her approval.

"It's perfect. Thank you for your thoughtfulness. I am very grateful," she said and turned to face him.

"I am glad to hear that. Before I leave you to rest, I have something for you." He reached into his pocket. "I see you already have a very exquisite emerald necklace, and I'm sorry I don't have something different to give you at the moment, but I assure you I'll give you anything you ask for that is within my power, just say the word." At this, he held out a silver, sparkling necklace. A delicate snowflake dangled from the chain.

Dorsa held out her hands; they trembled slightly as he placed the silver necklace into her cupped palms. "Thank you, Chancellor. It's very beautiful."

"Please call me Cheldon. I'll give only you that honor."

"You are very kind."

"Is there anything I can get you at this time, Lady Dorsa?" he asked.

Gently touching the charm of the necklace, she suddenly remembered her animals, her only friends...her family now. She couldn't know how he felt about them unless she asked.

"Yes, there are a couple things."

"What is it?"

"My filly… I just want to know she'll be well-taken care of."

"She will have the roomiest stall and paddocks to roam. My barn hands are excellent; I'm sure she will be spoiled completely,

and you may see her whenever you wish. The Ice Palace is
your home; you can go wherever you wish. I just beseech you
to allow me to take a ride with you sometime on the forest
trails. They are beautiful this time of year."

"Of course. Thank you."

"Anything else?"

"Well, you see… I have two snow cubs."

"Snow cubs!" he said in astonishment. "Where did you
get snow cubs?"

"I rescued them. I was hoping to keep them here with me.
I'll take care of them."

"Well…are you sure they wouldn't be more comfortable
in a stall at the barn? We could put them right next to your
filly," he suggested hesitantly.

"They are so young… All I would need is a warrior to
hunt food for them."

"I don't want to upset you so soon. Of course, they can
stay with you, until you say otherwise." He smiled gently and
then added with a teasing air, "Is there another animal I need
to accommodate?"

"My falcon…"

He chuckled, but not in mockery, his smile genuine. "We
have a very comfortable aviary for him. I'm sure he'll be
happier there."

"Yes, of course, thank you."

"Anything else?"

She smiled bashfully. "No. Thank you, Chancellor."

He grinned. "You're most welcome. I'll have dinner sent
up to you after you settle in." He bowed and took her hand
again and brushed his lips there. "Goodbye."

She watched him leave and then glanced forlornly over at
her handmaiden, who unfortunately had only accompanied her
for the trip. She would soon leave, returning to Fordorn with
the Shelkite warriors, and Dorsa would have new Vtalmay
handmaidens. The servant smiled sadly and then turned and
began to unpack the trunks the warriors had just brought.

Dorsa spun and fled to the doors leading to the balcony,

flung them open, and rushed to the thick stone railing carved with the same alabaster embellishments as the rest of the palace. She leaned over the cold barrier and breathed in the icy, salty air. It stung her throat and lungs. She closed her eyes and a warm tear squeezed free. And listening to the sweet, crashing lullaby of the waves below colliding with the crags on the shore, she whispered into the gusty winds, "Eelyne, I will always love you."

CHAPTER TWENTY-SEVEN

"Who was he, do you think?" Alkin asked.

The men stood at the warm spring, surveying the attack scene. Only Hazerk and Apollos had stayed behind to watch over Alexa. The company gathered around the dead assailant. The thin man's body lay in awkward angles on the ground.

"Who knows?" Kheane bent down and examined the corpse. "He has nothing to identify him... No markings."

Bryan gazed, a little unnerved, at the body at his feet. He had never killed a man before. It was a strange and unsettling feeling to know he had taken life away from another human being. A person only lived once...

Kheane looked up at the frowning Master Sword.

Bryan returned the stare. It was hard to read the ex-assassin's face since his hood still obscured it, but his hard, coffee-colored eyes held an understanding the Master Sword wasn't sure if he found comforting.

"You'll get used to it," Kheane said in his strange, raspy voice.

The Sword studied the Alidonian's confident face and raised a skeptical eyebrow, his frown deepening.

"He was trying to kill her, wasn't he?" Kheane pressed.

Bryan gave a cool shrug; he had a good point.

"Besides," he continued dryly, "who knows what else he had in mind for her. From the way he looks, he was probably deprived of more than just food, and she probably looked appealing having just bathed. He was undoubtedly planning on stabbing her in more than one way."

Bryan's face contorted into a disgusted glare at the ex-assassin, but he said nothing, knowing it to be true. Although, hearing the truth out loud brought another wave of anger over him that made his former uneasiness for killing the stranger to dissipate. He didn't want to dive too far into this new, unwanted desire to protect Alexa's virtue... Well, except maybe from himself. He gave his head a stiff jerk to clear his thoughts.

Kheane's shrewd black eyes watched the Master Sword. Bryan nodded a curt salute and then turned away to investigate what the Prince, Eelyne, and Warkan were now discussing over on the mossy rock where Alexa's quiver still lay.

They debated what should be done with the body. They could just unceremoniously dump it in the woods, or make a pyre, or bury it. They had no idea what the man's origin was; therefore, they didn't know what his tradition was.

"Does it really matter?" Warkan said bluntly.

"No, but—" Alkin hesitated. His good manners were giving him qualms over being so insensitive toward another's customs.

"My prince, there's no way to find out what his custom is. Let's just cover the body and leave it in the woods and move on. Nature will take its course," Warkan pressed.

Bryan joined them. He bent and gathered Alexa's quiver full of black arrows and her well-made bow; straightening, he said, "He's a murderer. He doesn't deserve much of a funeral. Let's bury the body and get out of here."

Warkan shrugged, not caring what they did. Alkin finally nodded in agreement, realizing they had little choice.

Bryan looked to his men. "Okay, let's get this done."

Through the entirety of their surveillance, Eelyne had been silent and had pointedly diverted his gaze from the Master Sword, but he now jumped to the orders with enthusiasm.

"The sooner we get this done, the sooner we can clean up and get moving," Bryan finished in a close-ended way.

After the men had taken care of the body, they indulged themselves in a quick washing in the pool. All clean, they headed back to the camp. They found Hazerk with the camp packed up and Alexa roused and extinguishing the fire. She was dressed in her now clean clothes, although her shirt still had remnants of the bloodstain. She moved around the camp a bit unsteadily, but in better health.

"What are you doing up?" Alkin demanded. He came to her, his features wreathed with concern, and searched her face. She regarded him with an appreciative sparkle in her eye. "Well, you have your color back. Do you feel better?"

"Yes. Hazerk is an excellent caretaker, and Apollos, of course, is watchful. I'm fine, really," she said as robustly as her still waxing strength would allow.

"Well, that's a relief to hear." Alkin smiled and gave her a brief, friendly kiss on the cheek. "Don't scare us like that again." He took up Sapharan's lead to begin tacking him.

Alexa grinned from ear to ear at the Prince's sentiment. Turning, she caught eyes with the Master Sword, who was watching her and the Prince with a keen, conflicted gaze. Her grin faded, but she gave the Sword a small, timid smile, diverting her eyes in shame over what she had done. Surprisingly, Bryan returned her smile with a small nod, and she knew she had been forgiven.

"Alexa, I'm glad you're okay." Eelyne approached her, severing the gaze between her and her guardian. "I blame myself completely for disregarding my duty."

She smiled in reassurance. "How is it your fault? I'm the one who ran off." Eelyne shrugged unconvinced and went to tack up Phoenix.

Alexa moved feebly to her bedroll and lowered herself to her knees, holding her tender stomach, and hoping no one spotted her acting in this pathetic manner. She sat on her heels and rolled up her blankets and packed her things. And upon hearing the crunch of boots on the ground, she looked over to see the tall, black riding boots of the Master Sword. Her eyes followed them up over his form to his face, where her handsome Sword-Guard gazed down at her with a smug look and a raised eyebrow. He held out her quiver and bow. She went to rise, but the sudden movement sent a shock of pain through her body and her head swimming; she crumpled to the ground. Bryan shot out his hand to steady her, and she straightened with his help.

Embarrassed, her eyes flashed. "Come to tell me 'told you so'?"

"Do I need to?" Bryan looked at her with amusement. She lowered her gaze with a slight wince. "Though, I'm not completely blameless either," he added. She raised her chin, her eyes widening with wonder. "I shouldn't have left you," he said in perfect poise.

"Here are your things." He handed over her quiver and bow.

"Thank you," she replied softly and turned to finish her packing, but Bryan stopped her.

"Are you well enough to travel? I would like to get moving, but if you're not feeling well..." He let the sentence hang.

"Yes, Master Sword, I'm sure I can manage to at least stay in the saddle," she said, her usual confidence now recovered.

"All right," he consented, his tone upbeat. Bryan then fidgeted on the spot, wondering whether he should help her pack her things. He decided she would rather not have his help, lest it should hinder her pride. He turned to Hazerk, who was stuffing his things into his saddlebag, and said, "If you and Apollos want to wash up in the spring, go ahead. But we'll be heading out as soon as you've finished."

"Great. I'll be on my way." He collected his reins but then stopped when he remembered his patient. He looked over at Alexa, who moved with care around Zhan. His brow furrowed.

"She'll be fine. I'll make sure of it," Bryan assured.

Hazerk nodded but still approached her. "Okay, Lil' Sis'?" he said in her ear, his hand resting gently on her shoulder. She nodded in reply with a brave smile. This seemed to appease him, and he hollered to Apollos, "Ready for a dip, pal?"

Apollos bobbed his head, and the two made their way down the path.

In a short time, the company was back on the trail again, their destination unclear, but at least they were moving forward, which seemed to quench their anxiety for now. They pressed on for hour after uncomfortable hour and rested for even fewer hours than they desired.

A few days later, Alexa rode near the front of the company with the Prince, Master Sword, and Apollos, who was leading the way. She shifted uncomfortably in her saddle for probably the hundredth time. Zhan turned a confused ear back, no doubt wondering what the matter was with his mistress.

Alexa rolled her neck and winced, and looking upward between the heavy swaying branches to the small patch of sky above, she felt a sense of vertigo. She pressed her hand to her stomach where the wound had been. It seemed to alleviate the ache. Apollos had saved her life, but the pain hadn't yet subsided.

Kheane, who was riding alongside her, glanced at her with a thoughtful eye. "Well, Alexandra, we're bonded souls now," he said.

"Why do you say that?" She looked over at him, making a pained face and holding her stomach.

"You're an initiated warrior now. You've scars to prove it, and be proud of," he replied.

She gave the ex-assassin a weak smile, appreciating his attempt at cheering her. Having the scar didn't bother her, just the pain did.

"More like scars of stupidity." Warkan's wry voice came up from behind.

Kheane turned in his saddle and gave him one of his unsettling stares. "In my experience, sometimes a little stupidity turns out to be a good teacher and therefore turns out a better warrior. Only, of course, if one lives through it."

Alexa flashed Kheane a glowing smile.

The Master Sword, listening to the conversation from ahead, felt his annoyance with Kheane rear its ugly head again. Not because of what he had said, but because he was attempting to bond with Alexa. Bryan forced the feeling away and thought about what the ex-assassin was saying instead. The Master Sword could remember quite a few stupid things he had done when he first began as a warrior. And, yes, the hard lessons he had learned from them hadn't been forgotten. Perhaps this incident would turn out to be a good thing for her.

"So, change of subject," Hazerk spoke up. He rode Red Man up to Alexa's other side. "Eelyne and I were wondering why you don't, or maybe you can't, do all the fancy magic we always hear about in the tales of witches and wizards, like in the Lost War."

Alexa smiled. "Uh, yes, well, I believe a lot of that is legend and a bit exaggerated."

"Oh, you mean like sorcerers tricking unicorns and then sawing off their horns and using their blood for spells. Or cutting out dragons' hearts, or turning people into animals, moving things without touching them, or blowing things up with fire, stuff like that?" he said and then hollered up to Apollos, "Sorry, Apollos, no offense meant!"

"None taken," the unicorn replied.

"Well, some of it is…but," she started slowly, realizing they all strained to hear what she had to say. Perhaps they wanted to see how powerful she was and how leery they should be of her. "You see, my magic has been dormant, like my brothers', ever since I was born. My father made it so. He just recently started to teach me how to awaken it and use it for only good. I suppose it's because I'm more spoiled than the rest." She grinned sheepishly, and the men all let out a wry laugh.

"Well, that explains a lot," Bryan said with a grin.

Alexa tossed her head with poise, carelessly brushing off the snickers. "It could also be that I'm the last witch in the world—or at least in Eetharum. But if I practice, I'll eventually get better and seem more magical. But not in the way you say, especially since I'm half-human. My blood is diluted too much. I'll never be able to create great magic. And what power I have is all about control. I'm still learning to control it. My magic is more apparent when my emotions are intense. Sometimes I don't create magic deliberately, especially if I'm angry. I need to learn to channel that intensity at my will in order to use the power better. The strongest magic I have control over now is my senses. I can sense things, people's feelings and intentions. And, of course, there's my witch intuition. There are many things I'm sure I'll be able to do, but nothing extravagant. I'm not sure of all the powers I'll have. I guess I'll find out as I learn. It's a gradual process. Most of the showy things you hear told in tales that sorcerers do are for evil purposes and take evil magic as a means to gain what they want. Like Ret wanting to harvest the magic out of me and my brothers' blood to create a more pure, powerful magic. I know it's in my heritage to have a dark nature, but I was taught, and I feel, that it's not right. So, I won't have those powers, nor ever be that powerful. I choose not to be evil. Do you understand?"

"Yes, Lil' Sis', don't worry. We were just curious. We don't think you're a demon." Hazerk laughed.

Alexa smiled, her pain momentarily forgotten. "Oh, yes, and I can be awfully persuasive if I want to be."

"Well, any woman can do that if she wants." Prince Alkin chuckled.

"Yes, but it's different." She flashed a mysterious smile.

"Now you have us scared," Alkin added, his brow worried, but a wry smile across his lips.

"Don't worry. I haven't bewitched any of you into doing anything. Or doing something my way… I promised," she reassured the men, who now all stared with wondering eyes at her.

The men returned her grin with uneasy smiles. Each remembering strange feelings they had gained upon looking into her sapphire eyes at some point or another.

"Speaking of sensing things…" Apollos said from the head of the company. He stopped, and they all halted behind him, attentive to him and their surroundings, which, at the moment, seemed normal for the wood.

The unicorn searched the forest floor. Then he raised his head to peer above them. They all followed suit.

A dense, gray fog seemed to seep down among the branches over their heads.

"That's strange," Alkin commented. "The sun is out. I can see it and blue sky through the trees."

"That isn't fog," Alexa said, detached as if she were listening for something, or feeling out something, without the use of her physical senses. She held her head cocked to one side, much like a dog listening to something in the distance.

"Great. What now?" Warkan grunted from the back of the party.

"Quick! We have to move fast," Apollos ordered, his voice urgent. He took off at a canter, crashing through low-hanging branches and underbrush.

"What is it?" More than one company member demanded as they urged their mounts into as fast as a gait as was safe for the footing.

"If it descends on us, and you inhale it, you'll hallucinate your own deaths. Hurry, it's looking for prey!" Apollos hollered.

At that explanation, the company urged their horses for a

higher and more dangerous speed. The warhorses' snorts and the thumping of their hooves on the ground were the only sounds among the harried companions as they fled the pursuing black air. They flew over fallen trees and through a shallow creek and under a garden of low hanging vines before it caught them.

Realizing their hopeless capture, Apollos skidded to a stop, whipped around to face the company, and managed to shout out before it descended on them, "Keep your eyes on me and think of nothing but something worth living for. I'll get you through this. Remember!"

The fear he implanted in their minds showed on all their faces and was something Apollos would never forget. There was an infinitesimal moment filled with pure fright between his words and when the black air seeped into their midst. The company heard one more command from him before they were lost to their own uninvited imaginations, "Follow me. Don't stop."

The next thing Alexa comprehended was the complete, muted silence all around her. It was as if someone had stuffed cloth in her ears. She rubbed her eyes, trying to clear away the black patches forming in front of her, but the act was futile. The black air thirstily sucked up every ray of light and coated the company with its toxin. The afternoon had changed to as if it were the hour before dawn: the darkest part of the day. She closed her eyes and struggled to hold her breath against the oncoming surge. But that also proved to be futile. She had to breathe…and she did. The horses did, too. And the black air gleefully slithered into all their nostrils and pores.

At first, she was surprised. Nothing happened. She opened her eyes. Then she started hearing things. The horses snorted and danced restively. They arched their necks and pulled against their masters' hold. She heard murmuring—the men—and looked around but could not decipher much in the darkness. She could see shadowy silhouettes, but no more. The murmuring turned to fearful mumbles of plea. The horses began to grunt and squeal and toss their heads. Some jerked around wildly and tried to rear. The mumbles turned to calls for mercy and pleas for help and crying out in pain or fear. It was the worst sound she had ever heard. It spilled chill after chill down her spine and raised all the hairs on her body.

Then Zhan threw up his head in fright, nearly knocking her in the nose, and whinnied a horrid, frenzied pitch. She did her best to calm the horse, but he flung his body around, twisting in every direction. She had no control of him. He reared straight up and pawed the air, screaming in panic, his eyes rolling.

Desperate, she looked around and saw all the horses caught in their own web of hallucinations. The half-conscious warriors and prince barely hung on to the beasts as they, too, thrashed and groaned in their own worlds.

"Apollos! Where are you?" she cried out, frantic. The company had come to a halt and was writhing like a dying snake.

"I'm here. I'm here. Look at me! Do as I say and trust the Power!"

Then she saw a light beat back the dark, and a white shape appeared. It was Apollos. He was glowing as if he were the moon. A gentle light emanated from him. And out of his oh-so-wonderful horn came waves of iridescent shimmering light. It attempted to beat back the black air, but the air was pressing ever harder on it as if it had a life of its own.

Alexa watched with hopeful eyes as she saw wave after shimmering wave pulse from the unicorn's horn. He spoke words of comfort to the company and to the horses in their own tongue as his magic slowly filed into the darkness. He was like a creature of heaven, an angel. She kept her eyes on him, but her lips were close to Zhan's ears, murmuring words of encouragement, love, and trust.

Then she heard it: a voice in her mind's ear. The black air had struggled to break through her natural, magical barrier, but now it discovered it could speak its toxin to her. It was a quiet voice, and it hissed in her ear, speaking ever-so-slyly to her, taunting her with words and cruel snickers. She would fail, it said. She would die, it said, and many other frightful things it whispered, all entwined in a raw truth she believed.

She snapped shut her eyes and mind from it. This was something she could handle. *It lies*, she told herself. She only had to concentrate on staying aboard the whirlwind Zhan and will the voice away.

But the voice was relentless, and she spoke to it, imploring it to stop. Nevertheless, it continued. Panic rose inside her. It would soon take over and utterly corrupt her mind. It seemed to know her so intimately, her most inner-fears, and she could not block it.

Then she remembered what Apollos had said. She opened her eyes and focused on the unicorn who still fought the black air. And, as difficult as it was, she endeavored to trust that the High Power was in ultimate control and she needn't fear. She focused on things she lived for, her family and home, and of the company…of Bryrunan.

The cruel voice weakened.

With time, Apollos' iridescent weapon filled their surroundings and blocked out the dark air. The blackness didn't leave without a fight; it roiled and moved like a thundercloud against his magic. But eventually, it retreated to above the trees and drifted away with an unnatural speed for mere air. The horrific sounds of cries of fright and pain died down, and the company slumped with exhaustion.

The warriors and prince fumbled to dismount, essentially falling off their warhorses. They hit the ground and struggled to stand on their wobbling legs. The horses had calmed. They stood with their heads low, noses brushing the ground, and eyes dull.

Alexa sat astride the now settled Zhan, watching the company collect itself. Apollos stood silently by her side, waiting.

"That was the Arch Demon himself," Hazerk finally managed to say in a hoarse voice.

"Derived from him, no doubt, and only defeated by faith and goodness," Apollos answered.

"Tell me that really wasn't happening," Eelyne gasped.

"It wasn't. Though, it would've killed you," Apollos replied.

"That was the worst thing I've ever experienced," Hazerk said.

"Pretty close for me, too," Kheane added, bending over to catch his breath.

"That must be saying a lot from you," the Prince breathed.

"All the snow is gone…" Eelyne said, looking around perplexed. Everyone stared at him in apprehension.

"What snow, Warrior Eelyne?" Sword Bryan ventured.

"Wasn't there a blizzard? I was freezing. I thought I'd die. I couldn't feel my body," Eelyne stated, rubbing his hands together and pulling his cloak tighter around himself.

"No," Bryan answered.

"There were flames everywhere," Hazerk looked up, his eyes recalling his vivid hallucination. "I was burning alive."

No one spoke for several long breaths.

"The forest flooded from the sea. And I was struggling in a maelstrom. I swallowed gallons of water. I thought I'd drown…" Alkin said, his voice and eyes unsettled. "I can still taste the salt." He spat on the ground.

"I was being disemboweled alive," Warkan said. "The pain was…unbearable." He placed a hand on his midsection.

"It was the same for me," Bryan said. "Very real. I could feel myself being hacked into and saw my inners unraveling." He gave a shudder.

There was a moment of silence, and then Eelyne asked, "What about you, Kheane?"

Kheane gave a wry smile. "I felt…utterly forsaken. And then the earth cracked. I fell—endlessly—into the chasm."

"You, Alexa?" Eelyne pressed.

Alexa saw all the men's faces turn toward her. Now becoming habit, she glanced at the Master Sword and held his sturdy gaze with intensity. "I was protected, somewhat, by my magic. I heard voices," she said, still trying to lock the slippery voice far from her memory forever.

They all nodded in silence.

"Let's keep moving. You all rested enough?" Apollos interrupted the unsettled thoughts of the company. They nodded and began collecting themselves, mounting up.

"I wonder what the horses' hallucinations were," Eelyne said as they began to move forward again.

"You spoke to them, Apollos. What did they feel?" Alexa asked, pricking the curiosity of all the company.

Apollos' eyes sparkled. "I can't exchange communication between humans and animals. It's forbidden. Humans were not meant to speak in that way with horses; so, that is how it must be."

"Who forbids it? Come on, Apollos, tell us," Alexa pleaded; the others advocated her plea.

"I can't," he laughed. "Forget it."

They all fell silent as they trekked down the forest path, but it lasted for mere moments before they came to a stop and looked upon two large, black wolves blocking the way with bared teeth and raised hackles.

"What now? Just chase them off, or shoot them with your arrows, Alexa," Warkan grunted.

They received more agitated, low growls from the wolves. The animals stood as still as statues, their amber eyes flicking to each of the humans. The company's horses pranced in place, pulling at their bits.

Apollos stood at the head of the company, his head lowered and his horn pointing at the beasts in defense. His muzzle brushed the ground while his eyes focused on the wolves as if he were communicating with them.

Warkan, who was at Zhan's flank, reached for Alexa's bow and arrow.

"No. Don't hurt them!" She snatched her weapons from his reach, and he shot her an annoyed scowl.

"What shall we do, Apollos?" Alkin asked.

"Wait. They're not possessed, or evil in nature. They're guardians," he replied.

As if it was meant to happen right at that the moment, a human came out of the woods to stand behind the wolves. "Easy, boys," she said to the dogs.

CHAPTER TWENTY-EIGHT

It was a woman; a wild-looking woman, dressed in thick animal skins. She wore knee-high leather moccasins tied on with strings of leather winding up her calves. Leather gloves covered her hands up to her elbows. Piercing gray eyes sat in a pale, dirt-smudged face. And flaming red hair frizzed out in all directions, with bits of leaves and twigs twisted amongst the locks. In her arms, she carried a stack of dry wood. She studied the company with a mixed expression of surprise and suspicion.

"My name is Levaun." Her voice was deep for a woman, but not masculine. She had an unfamiliar accent. "How did a large company like you make it this deep into the forest? I'm surprised. What do you want?" She peppered off the demanding questions so fast the company didn't have time to recover from taking in her eccentric appearance.

Alkin was the first to find his voice, "We wish you no harm, Levaun. We're just passing through and wish to keep our business to ourselves. I'm Alkin, a merchant from the city of Shelport in western Shelkite. These are my traveling companions." He then named off each of the company members, including Apollos, who hadn't made himself invisible.

"I didn't know it was common to have a unicorn as a counterpart in mercantile," she paused, a curt edge to her voice, but continued before Alkin could answer, "You can't expect me to believe you've come to Carthorn for trade. And it's much too far out of your way and dangerous for you to just be passing through." Her gray eyes narrowed a level look at the Prince. "I'm not a fool, my good man." She gave him a small, sly smile.

Her attitude with Alkin stunned the company; though, they knew she did not know he was a prince.

Alkin, however, smiled guilefully at her and bowed his head. "Too true. But as I said, we wish to keep our business to ourselves. However, would you be so kind as to lend us some help?"

Levaun shifted the pile of wood in her arms to a more

comfortable position before she answered; her eyes never left the Prince's. "I can't see why not." She smiled. "I haven't seen a soul in ages. It might do some good to have company for once. How about this? No questions asked; you all come to my cabin by the lake and have some dinner. It's safe and not far from here. By the looks of you, you could use a break. This forest has a way of breaking a person down."

"Would that lake happen to be the Faded Sea?" Alkin asked. She nodded. "Okay then, lead the way."

"Good. This way." She turned on her heel and started down the path at a surprising clip, calling to the wolves, "Come, boys."

The two black wolves bobbed up and down and playfully nipped at each other before charging down the lane after her.

Prince Alkin looked over at Sword Bryan for affirmation. The Master Sword nodded and led the way after the eccentric woman.

Keeping a considerable distance from Levaun, but enough to see where she was headed, the company whispered among themselves.

"Just be careful. We don't know if we can trust her or not. It's strange she has survived by herself in this forest," Bryan told them.

"I didn't feel any magic or any evil in her. She's just a hermit, more than likely. But still, keep a watchful eye," Apollos said.

Alexa was reminded of tales of lost children being mothered by a kind old woman befriending them in the woods, only to find she was leading them into a trap.

"She's the most beautiful creature I've ever seen," Hazerk breathed.

Everyone turned to stare disbelieving at the warrior. He had a starry, glazed look in his eyes as he watched Levaun.

"You've got to be joking! Creature is for sure..." Warkan sneered.

"No. She's absolutely intriguing," Hazerk said, clearly smitten.

"She's not attractive at all. She's clothed in animal skins!" the clearly disturbed Warkan exclaimed quietly, and then continued in disgust, "Her hair needs a desperate brushing. And yuck, bright red hair and pale, freckled skin—"

"What's wrong with freckles?" Alexa interjected huffily.

"She looks scary, Hazerk." Warkan shuddered.

"Does not," Hazerk retorted.

"Now that we all know how Warrior Warkan feels…" Bryan said dryly.

Alkin leaned over and whispered to Alexa with a grin, "Don't worry. Your freckles are very striking."

Alexa gave him a grateful smile, feeling warmth in her cheeks.

"I admit she seems a little rough around the edges," Hazerk stated. "But that's what I like."

"Eeek," was all Eelyne could say as he stared with incredulous eyes at his fellow warrior.

"Okay. Then, are you all in agreement she is nothing you desire?" he asked. Everyone agreed. "Good," he declared happily, "I won't have any competition."

"She kind of reminds me of Alexa," Bryan said, attempting to sound serious, but he gave a roguish glance at his charge.

"Hey!" she hollered, indignant. "I *don't* take that as a compliment."

Everyone laughed.

"Okay, okay." Bryan laughed at her glare and set of eyes spitting sapphire flames at him. "You're not that bad, but I'd say you aren't too far off from becoming that," he teased.

"I am not like that at all," she said firmly, a disgusted look on her face, though her lips quirked into a half-smile at the Master Sword's attention.

"You *are* a bit manly…" Warkan laughed.

Alexa narrowed her eyes at him, and then regarded Kheane in mock offense, "You're just going to let them harass me like that?"

The ex-assassin merely continued to ride in his silent manner, but appeased her when he looked at her with his black eyes twinkling.

"Well, the only girls you like, Warkan, are the ones you pay time for anyway," Hazerk shot at the burly warrior.

Eelyne turned in his saddle and gave Warkan a horrified look, "Really?"

Warkan looked as if he could wallop Hazerk's head off with his ax. "Don't believe a word that red-headed idiot says," he growled.

"I intend to put a stop to that business one of these days," Alkin inserted thoughtfully.

"Well, what kind of women *do* you like? We've been all over the place, and I've never heard you once say that you liked any of them," Hazerk continued snidely.

Warkan made an annoyed face and snorted, "I just like women a little more dignified and feminine."

"Oh, the ones that don't know how to enjoy life…well, for you, that makes sense," Hazerk asserted.

Warkan just scowled.

"Kheane, what kind of women interest you? It seems you'd like the rough type?" Hazerk pried.

"Dead ones," he replied.

The company's conversation came to a shocked halt at his curt answer. Hazerk let out a nervous chuckle, and after a moment, Kheane broke out in a boisterous laugh. His vocal cords sounded as if they had never laughed. It was a harsh and unpleasant sound, making the company uneasy, and leaving them wondering whether they really believed him joking.

"I'm kidding." He laughed.

"Oh. Well?"

"I haven't thought much about it," he groused. "I mostly think of the girl, the orphan girl. I would like a woman like her, at least what I think she'd be like as a woman."

"What about you, Master Sword?" Hazerk turned his attention elsewhere.

Bryan just shrugged, seeming uninterested in the conversation, and oblivious to the fact that Alexa's insides had done a complete flip at the idea of learning what he desired in a woman. Her heart thudded faster; she willed the feeling to go away. This infatuation was getting out of hand, she thought as she strained to hear what he had to say. However, he didn't appease them with an answer at all.

"The Master Sword likes his women dainty and feminine, the all-around damsel in distress type. Very dignified. Isn't that right, Sword Bryan?" Prince Alkin's smile was devilish. "You absolutely love dancing with the ladies at the balls, don't you?"

Alexa cocked her head to get a better look at the Master Sword. She regarded him with an intense curiosity, wondering if it were true. If it was, she was nothing like that. But the Master Sword gave no indication it was true or not. His lips just quirked into a mysterious smile and he shook his head, disregarding his friend.

"And what about you, my prince, if you don't mind me asking?" Hazerk inquired of his ruler.

Alkin sighed as he thought. "I suppose I don't have a certain type. But I like them pretty strong-willed and intelligent." He smiled.

"What about you, Alexa? What kind of women do you like?" Hazerk asked.

"Ha, ha, very smart of you." She smirked.

"What about me?" Eelyne perked up, not wanting to be left out.

"You couldn't get a girl if you wanted to," Warkan jeered.

Eelyne was about to retort when Alexa cut in for him. "Warkan, you're such a bully. Of course, he could. He's smart, handsome, thoughtful, and athletic." The words were out before she realized her mistake. All the men turned and gave her a smug look, all except Sword Bryan, who simply stared at her with an inquisitive brow.

"Hmm, I think we'd better keep Eelyne and Alexa's bed rolls on opposite sides of the fire tonight." Hazerk snickered.

"Hang on now, that's not exactly how I meant it. I was just defending you, Eelyne, you know that," she pleaded for his support.

With a boyish smile, he rescued her. "I know."

"Looks as if we're here," Apollos announced, putting a stop to all the human chattering he could never bring himself to understand.

They came into a small, circular clearing. It was far enough off the shore of the Faded Sea they couldn't see it, but they could smell the watery atmosphere. A one-room log cabin sat snuggled in the glade. Smoke drifted from the chimney, and the scent of pine wafted on the air. A small campfire out front had a spit on it with a fresh rabbit cooking. The only other structure in the clearing was a small shelter containing firewood. Encircling the clearing were torches ablaze, set on stakes every five strides. The sight was inviting to the homesick company.

Turning to face them, Levaun said, "Welcome to my home."

"You live here? Alone?" Alkin inquired in astonishment.

"Yes," she said, "I can't stand people." She gave an apologetic shrug with a wisp of a smile. "I'm originally from a small town on the edge of the forest. The citizens there and I never got on well after I lost my parents. So, I decided to move. I came here. If you're wondering how I've survived, I owe it mostly to my wolves. They're great protectors. My parents also taught me a lot in survival."

"We've a unicorn. How have you protected yourself from the magical elements?" Bryan asked, impressed by her courage.

"There are other forms of protection." She bestowed a secretive smile on them.

"You must be the so-called witch the townsfolk spoke about. One we were to be careful of," Alkin said, suddenly remembering.

Levaun laughed, her deep voice melodious. "No, I'm no witch, just very determined to live here. They're a superstitious crowd. I enjoy being on my own. But you're welcome at my fire. At least until you're rested. Come on, untack the horses and we will eat and talk some more." She gestured for them to come and prepare for the evening.

Later, when the sun had set and the stars were shining boldly in all their glory, the company sat in the clearing, drinking in the sight above the trees. The inky dark blue sky was a brilliant background for the millions of sparkling specks of light. It was breathtaking. There seemed to be more stars here under the wing of Carthorn. But that couldn't be, could it?

"My cabin is located on the north side of the Faded Sea. It's less than a mile from here. I'll take you there if that's where you all are headed," Levaun said while they sat around the campfire eating the delectable rabbit she had prepared.

"Apollos, where was it you stayed when you were by the sea?" Alkin asked the unicorn, who was not joining the others in the rabbit dinner. Considering he didn't have a taste for meat, he was enjoying another one of his warm mashes.

"The southwestern side," he mumbled through a mouthful.

"The lake is vast," Levaun said. "We would have never crossed each other's paths, although if we had, it would've been shocking to me. I've lived here fifteen years and I have not once seen a white unicorn. If I may ask, was it the Guidance Naiad you searched for?"

There was a pause in the atmosphere, and the company all eyed each other with apprehension. They were still unsure whether they could trust her with any amount of information.

The long pause was enough to make Levaun retract her question, "I apologize. We did agree to no questions." She stood and stoked the fire, causing the hot coals to spit, fizzle, and burn more brightly.

After another minute of silent eating, Prince Alkin leaned forward to speak to her. He had a curious and confused look in his hazel eyes. "Why did you say specifically a white unicorn? I've only ever known there to be white unicorns. Isn't that right, Apollos?" He directed the last part to the mystical creature.

Apollos nodded his head and made a gesture equal to a human shrugging their shoulders.

Levaun swallowed her mouthful of food and licked her lips in thought, seeming as if she were contemplating whether she could trust them. "Well, you see, I thought the same thing, too, up until a few years ago." She took another bite of her food, showing no inclination to continue her explanation.

This snagged the company's attention. They waited impatiently for her to explain.

"What do you mean? Are you saying there are other unicorns still alive out there? That I'm not the last one?" Apollos inquired in earnest.

Levaun wiped her mouth on her arm and then settled her eyes on him with a meaningful look. "The forest has been changing more than usual these last few years. And with that, I've noticed a few new creatures that weren't here before. Or rather, I don't even think they existed before... I don't know how to explain it. But

Carthorn has become even shadier than I think it ever was or is supposed to be."

Apollos and the company passed apprehensive looks.

"It's all rather fishy, and I don't like it. Maybe something greater is working here. But it's definitely not something good. The unicorns I've seen, if that's what you could even call them, look exactly like Apollos, except for a few different traits. They are dark. Really dark—a black you almost get lost in. When they're around, your eyes play tricks on you. Their horns are ebony, solid and shiny. Their hooves are the same. They have black eyes, showing red where the whites should be. And the strangest thing, they have sharp teeth, as if they were meat eaters. Oh, but they're beautiful, too. So beautiful. That's how they draw their prey in. I've named them the darkhorns. I've seen several of them. They haven't tried to harm me or the wolves, but I've seen them act violently. The last time I saw them was a few weeks ago. A herd of them was traveling north."

She paused to gaze at the company's shocked, pallid faces. Alkin went to speak, but she silenced him with a raised hand. "There's more. I've seen a higher number of goblins. Before, they mostly hid in their caves and kept to themselves. But they've been out doing wicked things. A few months back, I was hunting and saw them with captives they must have gotten from a village on the outskirts of the forest."

"That's probably where Alexa's attacker came from," Bryan broke in.

"Yes. He must have escaped from them," Alkin said.

The others agreed.

Levaun nodded. "And that's *still* not all. I've spotted manticores. They were extremely rare before, but now I seem to be dodging them more often. You'll need to watch out for them; they're vicious. And I had a run in with a changer the other day. It had me tricked into thinking it was an overly curious and playful monkey. If it hadn't been for my wolves, it would have captured me…and probably stripped me of my flesh." She shuddered.

"Well, it seems meeting you was meant to be," Alkin said. "You've already been a great help to us. You've provided us with vital information and food. We thank you."

"I have more to tell if you wish to hear it. And if I can help in any way in getting you safely through the forest, I will. I may not be fond of human company for long periods of time, but I definitely don't wish you all harm."

"Yes, by all means, if there is more, please tell us. Although, I'm already worried by what you've told us. I hate to think there's more," Alkin expressed, despondent.

"Well, I've run into hatchlings…"

"What kind of hatchlings?"

"Dragon."

Bryan's mount lifted his head from his grazing and nickered at the sound of his name. The Master Sword couldn't help but let a small, amused smile escape him. He turned and gently hushed his friend. The warhorse went back to eating contentedly.

"How would dragon eggs get here without an adult?" Hazerk asked.

"Exactly. They couldn't. That means there must be a full-grown female around somewhere," Levaun answered. "I haven't seen one, though. The thought had crossed my mind just to kill the hatchlings since it was still within my power to do so at the time, but I didn't know what the consequences of that would be. If it meant that an irate female dragon was going to track me down, I decided it wasn't worth it. I've survived here this long, but I'm afraid I have no clue how to fend off a dragon, unless, of course, I had a dragon whisperer. And as far as I know, *I* don't have any dragon whispering talents!"

"What in the demon's name is a dragon whisperer?" Warkan said a little jeeringly.

"Oh, come on, Warkan! Be realistic. You can't tell me you don't believe in the famed dragon whisperers? After all that you've seen now?" Eelyne burst out.

The burly warrior frowned at being chided by his younger counterpart.

"Dragon whisperers were only among certain bloodlines in men," Eelyne explained, eyes alight. "It's said that the men who possessed this innate talent could understand the dragons' language and have them do their bidding. The dragons would do it willingly. It wasn't as if they were slaves. Dragons are fickle creatures by nature. And depending on their master, they could be used for good or evil. In our history records, many battles are recorded where there were dragons on both sides."

"So, you're saying dragons have been extinct, and now they're suddenly turning up again?" Hazerk inquired directly to Levaun.

"I don't think they've been extinct exactly, but dragons have definitely not been seen for hundreds of years, as well as dragon whisperers," Eelyne answered for her. Hazerk gave him a look that told him to back off. Eelyne shrugged.

"Well, this is interesting news," Alkin concluded.

"I know I'm not to ask questions of you," Levaun said, changing the subject, "but out of curiosity, are you searching for the Guidance Naiad? Is that why you've traveled to the Faded Sea?"

"We aren't looking for the Guidance Naiad exactly. But if we happen to meet her, that would be good, because we could use a few answers. However, I know she can be very difficult to contact, so we're not too hopeful," Alkin admitted.

Levaun suddenly looked forlorn. "I'm sorry to disappoint you, but it seems you are out of luck anyhow. The Guidance Naiad has left."

"What do you mean 'left'? She usually comes and goes as she pleases."

"No, I mean she's gone for good."

"What do you mean? This *is* sad news," the Prince expressed.

Levaun's gloomy gray eyes focused on each one of the company's members before she continued. Her pale face, from being under the forest's cover for so many years, shone shockingly in the firelight, and her hundreds of freckles seemed to glow in the low light. "At first I just felt it happening. A few months ago, there was a palpable presence missing here. I've lived so close to the Faded Sea for so long, I sensed it right away. It was like someone had sucked away a piece of heaven. I felt it in my heart—you know, the part that's still attached to that place where all our souls long to be. I felt sad and lost. But it passed, and then she came to me in a dream. I had never seen her before, but I knew it was her. She told me she was leaving Eetharum forever. She was going home now, and I was to tell anyone searching for her that they must not rely on her for guidance anymore. They were to believe and search for their answers in the High Power. She departed saying one last thing. She said the Mother of Pearl will soon no longer be a portal for answers either. I was so shocked, I didn't say a word. I don't know what she means by the Mother of Pearl. I've never heard of it." Levaun ended with a dejected sigh.

The company passed meaningful looks to one another. "Well, we do. Thank you, Levaun, for your information. It's much appreciated," Alkin said. "As you must have already figured out, we aren't just merely passing through. We're on a mission. And it does have a great deal to do with everything you've seen changing around here. We're attempting to find some answers in how to stop something terrible that's happening in Eetharum," he explained, finally deciding it was safe to give her some information. "I strongly urge you to come with us."

The company all passed surprised looks. But after a moment of considering the situation, each one quickly supported the Prince's proposition, pleading with Levaun not to stay in the treacherous forest.

She looked extremely hesitant. "I don't know…" She glanced over to the cozy home she had made and down to the wolves curled up at her feet.

"It's become far too dangerous for you to live here and survive on your own, even with the wolves," Alkin pressed.

"Yes. And the wolves would be more than welcome in our company," Hazerk added.

Levaun gave him a small, sad smile. She reached down to stroke the sleek hair of the wolf closest.

"You could find a nice secluded place and settle there for as long as you wish. You'd only have to put up with us long enough to get out of the forest. What do you say?" Alkin beseeched.

They all waited in anxious silence for her answer. Levaun continued to stroke the wolf. "My place is here," she finally said, looking up. "I will take you to the Faded Sea if that's where you still want to go. And I will help you in every way that I can, but I can't leave here."

"I see. Well, I hope you'll reconsider before we leave," Alkin yielded reluctantly. With that, he stood. "We should rest. We've had a long few days and have our work cut out for us." He gave Alexa a depressed, knowing glance. She nodded grudgingly and stood to make her bedroll. "I'll take first watch," he offered.

CHAPTER TWENTY-NINE

The company decided to rest only one day at Levaun's cabin. They couldn't afford to waste any time. They would leave at dawn the next day and head for a nearby valley to the north. The decision to travel to the valley was made by the company on the account Levaun had given. She explained it was a beautiful, verdant valley filled with scores of apple trees and said it emitted a feeling that distinguished it as old, extremely old. She claimed it might possess magic. Because, strangely, the trees seemed to always be ripe with apples year-round. Levaun had only mentioned the valley in passing among other things she had discovered in Carthorn; she still did not know of their mission.

In private, Alexa and Apollos reminded the others of the vision of the apple trees in the Mother of Pearl. Everyone agreed the orchard seemed like an apt place to check out.

The company took their time off to reorganize their things and give their mounts a little extra resting time. They gave their horses special attention, grooming them until their coats shone, and feeding them fresh carrots they had dug up from Levaun's garden with permission. They also spent the day absorbing all Levaun's stories and information she could offer. And, of course, Sword Bryan spent a good part of the day drilling Alexa and Eelyne in their swordplay.

Mid-morning, Levaun took the Master Sword, Prince Alkin, Alexa, and Apollos to see the nest of hatchlings by the shore of the Faded Sea. Sheltered behind underbrush, the five watched the playful dragonlings in astonishment. Levaun commented that the group of five babies had indeed grown a lot since she last saw them. The little dragonlings seemed oblivious to their watchers. They played much like puppies would play with one another. They yelped, growled, rolled, and snapped at each other. The only difference was their area of play was scorched and smoldering, the effects of their playful spits of fire.

The day turned out to be hot and humid. Alexa could feel the sweat rolling down her back and trickling down between her breasts. Her arms and back ached, as did her still-tender scar. She had insisted she was well enough to swordfight, so the Master Sword had continued on with his usual merciless drilling. Though, now, she was second thinking her choice.

Nonetheless, she resolved to push through the pain.

Eelyne and she had been practicing for what felt like endless hours. She paused her attack on him and made a gesture that meant for him to stop. The warrior was just as pleased to get a break. He plopped on the ground, drained. Alexa bent over the hilt of her sword and tried to catch her breath. Her chest heaved, and she sucked in thick air brimming with the dampness of promised rain. She placed a gentle palm on her scar. The skin and muscles surrounding it throbbed and burned.

"Need a few minutes…" she breathed to Sword Bryan, who was standing nearby with his arms crossed, looking exasperated by their unapproved cease in swordplay.

For a moment, it looked as if he was going to deny them a break, but then he smiled, uncrossed his arms, and said, "Okay, take a quick break. Get some water, and then prepare yourselves to go around in a bout one on three and then four. You've done one on two and two on two. It's time for you to move up."

Alexa stared at him with an evil look in her eye but said nothing. *She* was the dummy who insisted she had felt fine…

She straightened, determined, and pushed a sweaty lock of escaped hair out of her face and went to retrieve her water pouch. She took her pouch and stood by Prince Alkin, who was sitting with Levaun on a bench discussing pathways out of the forest.

"I also found that not far from Orchard Valley is a section in the forest that seems to be impenetrable," she explained, "It's a wall made of thick brush and trees. I've never been able to go around it or through it. It goes for miles and miles east and north. I suggest you pass by it. Just go straight north. Don't try to breach it. I don't know what's beyond it."

"Thank you. I assure you, we'll take your advice into account when we get on the move," Alkin replied.

"You're welcome to all the advice I can think of. I wish you could tell me your reason for this absurd traveling route. I can guess it's much more than you are letting on. But again, it is none of my business…and maybe I don't want to know," she stated.

Alkin patted the woman's hand, which was resting in her lap. "You're correct. But if you still refuse to travel with us, I'm afraid I can't tell you any more than you already know. Just remember to be more watchful from here on out." She nodded with understanding.

"Okay, Sand Queen, Warrior Eelyne! Break's over," Bryan's voice cut through the conversation. He spun around to regard the rest of the group. "I need a few volunteers," he said, smiling impishly. He was answered by silence. "Okay, you all…"

"I'll go a round," Alkin cut him off.

Everyone sat stunned and utterly mute, except for the Master Sword who didn't act fazed at all: he grinned. "Great," he said. He looked around to the rest of them, expecting others to volunteer.

"You don't expect us to actually swordfight with our prince, do you? What if we accidentally injure him?" Hazerk blurted, aghast.

"Prince! You're a prince?" Levaun jumped to her feet from beside Alkin and stared in disbelief at him, a trace of fear in her eyes.

The whole company simultaneously glared at Hazerk, who looked rather sheepish.

Alkin looked up at Lavaun, a reticent though serene look over his features. "In a matter of speaking…perhaps." He then jumped up and said with enthusiasm, "Let's forget what was just said and go around a few bouts. Come on, Warrior Hazerk, Warrior Eelyne, you side with me against Alexa. Warrior Warkan, you come in after a few minutes and join us. And then Alexa and Warrior Eelyne will switch places. The Master Sword will oversee our moves."

They all jumped to action at the Prince's command. Alexa took her stance and grasped the hilt of her sheathed sword, eager for the first blow from one of the three males encircling her. She disregarded her throbbing wound and drew her sword, looking straight into Alkin's eyes. They were kind as usual, but they had a playful, competitive glint she found alluring. She gave the smug-looking prince a sly, half smile, and he gave her a slight nod. He was standing to her left. Hazerk was to her right. She could sense Eelyne standing directly behind her. Her skin prickled with anticipation. She closed her senses to all else around and focused on the armed men, trying to feel out their first move so she would not be struck down right off.

Hazerk was the first to strike. Alkin thrust immediately after. She parried the first and dodged the second, spinning to block a blow from Eelyne. Hazerk swung his large double-handed sword, and she twisted to block the blow, her arm feeling the force and smarting from the strength behind it. A mere infinitesimal second later, Alkin took a mean swipe at her ankles. She leapt, nearly losing her balance, and cried out in the unfairness of the action. She was only answered with a roguish laugh from the Prince and a few more hard-to-block blows from Hazerk and Eelyne.

The foursome went around like this for several minutes. Alexa only had time to parry or dodge. She didn't land a single blow on her adversaries, and her frustration showed. Near the end of the bout, Hazerk swiped at her knees. She leapt high in the air as if she were a schoolgirl playing jump rope with her friends, and she would have landed squarely if it hadn't been for Alkin sending a hard blow at her while she was in mid-air, which caused her to twist and block it, sending her body sprawling in the air off balance. She landed in a heavy heap on her backside. The three men's blades went straight to her throat. All three grinned. Alexa clenched her jaw, glaring at each one from her humble spot in the dirt.

"Good job. Alexa, we'll have to work some more on that, but not bad," Bryan said from the sidelines. "Okay, Warrior Eelyne, your turn to be on your own. Get up, Alexa. Stop pouting and try not to hold anything against your new partners. You're on the same side now."

Pushing aside her pride, she allowed Alkin to give her a hand in standing. And with a loud sigh and an attempt to put aside her agitated feeling, she took her stance beside the Prince. Getting back into focus, she prepared for her first move against Eelyne.

A hair's width from Alkin, the Prince gave her a nudge. She looked over at him to find him grinning at her. To her surprise, her insides melted. Her posture relaxed, and she smiled bashfully back, but, at that same moment, she was blindsided by a blow from Eelyne. The hit knocked her off her feet and back on the ground where she had been moments before. Her body stung from the impact.

There was a scramble amongst the sword fighters to see if their counterpart was okay. They all shoved at one another to reach her.

"Are you all right?" Eelyne exclaimed. "You're lucky I hit you with the side of my sword. I hope I didn't hurt you."

Pushing the men's helping hands away, she slammed her palms down and shot back to her feet. "I'm fine!" she growled.

The men, as well as everyone else in the camp, watched in amused silence as she brushed herself off and took her stance again, acting as if nothing ever happened.

Sword Bryan cleared his throat. "Okay. Now, try not to get distracted this time, Alexa."

She looked over and met eyes with the Master Sword. He was looking rather amused, but grumpy all the same. She gave a curt nod, and he turned from her. She then set to work on the task ahead.

While they teamed up against Eelyne, Alexa often found herself fighting shoulder to shoulder and back to back with the Prince. The brush of his body on hers sent shivers down her spine, which she tried to ignore. But it was hard. Especially since he kept sending roguish grins her way any chance he got. She found herself looking away, realizing she was entering a dangerous zone here, finding herself attracted to and flirting with a prince. It didn't help either that he was excellent at his swordplay. Something she seemed to find irresistible, considering it was one of the things she found pleasing in the Master Sword, too.

Several minutes into the bout, Sword Bryan ordered Warrior Warkan to join on their side against Eelyne. It went rather well, considering everyone was dodging Warkan's wide swings with his battle-ax.

After a while at this pace, Bryan announced, "Okay. That's good for today. Alexa, we'll work more on your three on one practice and then maybe on team practices before adding a hazard such as Warrior Warkan to fight against just you."

Warkan let out a boisterous laugh, while the rest of them laughed a little nervously.

"Thank you," Alexa said, breathless.

Looking glum, Bryan gave a careless shrug and turned from her gaze. His indifference caused a strange jolt to her heart. She shook her head. Why should she care what he thought of her? Had she not decided that he didn't care anything for her and was way out of her reach anyhow?

A bit later, as the evening hours arrived, Levaun prepared a delicious meal for the company. They all sat and conversed pleasantly around the fire. The always silent-observer Kheane caught Alexa's attention and said, "Would you like to work on your skills with the Alidonian weapon again tonight?"

She perked up, happy to have something divert her thoughts from the Master Sword and, now, the Prince. "Yes," she answered.

"Wait," Hazerk spoke up, a sly smile on his face. "Today we all got to see for the first time...*Master* Alkin's sword fighting skills—and if I might say, it was rather awesome. But I'd like to be entertained even further and see Kheane go up against Master Sword Bryan. If you both don't mind? And if Alexa doesn't mind missing a lesson with Kheane."

At this suggestion, everyone in the camp expressed their pleasure at the idea. All except the Master Sword and Kheane, who both just stared at each other. Noting their reluctant silence, everyone pleaded to them to do it. Finally, both men seemed to decide at the same time without a word to the other. They stood and went to a spot where they had plenty of room to bout and faced each other.

All the company and Levaun prepared to watch, an unspoken excitement filling the air. Hazerk moved over to sit by Levaun and whispered in her ear, making her smile. Alexa grinned at him and shook her head. She sat down next to the Prince and glanced at him to find him already gazing at her. He smiled softly, a fond look in his eyes. She couldn't bring herself to look away. But he gestured for her to watch the commencing bout.

She looked to the two men facing each other. Her stomach

gave a flutter at seeing the look on the Master Sword's face. She
found him so handsome, intriguing, proud, and puzzling. His face
was stern and focused. His perfectly formed body flexed a display
of the power beneath. He drew his sword in one fluid movement,
and it came out with a pleasant sing-song sound.

Kheane was just as daunting and captivating in all his
clandestine darkness. His hand was inside his cloak; the observers
barely heard him draw his sword. He held it out. It was long and
slender.

A split second later, the two men clashed into the throes of the
match.

True to Hazerk's guess, it was quite something to behold. Not
all the competitive matches in the world set up for the
entertainment of the public could compare to the match taking
place here. It was a beautiful dance of death. Each man was precise
in every move, in every thought, and motive. The two were not
playing around either; the spectators began to fear for the men's
lives as the match progressed.

Alexa watched as if in a trance. Something new arose inside
her and came to life, something foreign, but not unpleasant or
unsolicited. For as long as she could remember, she had never
desired something as badly as she did at that moment. Every move
he made, every face he made, every sound escaping his lips, was
like air to her. She needed it. She longed for it. And she breathed
it. She drank it up like water to quench a lethal thirst. It took every
ember in her being and self-control not to run to him, pull him
from his match, and take him away to give herself to him. Seeing
him now, dissipated all girlish affections she had held for the
Prince and Kheane. Her eyes locked on every move the Master
Sword made, confirming and forwarding all her feelings toward
him. If only he could see how she felt. How she wished the pairing
was even possible! Her feelings were nearing a dangerous
infatuation, way beyond just a mere fondness for him now…

She tore her eyes from the two men, desperately trying to
redirect her thoughts. She pretended to watch the match along with
the others, but her eyes looked over their heads into the distant
woods. And she kept them there until the wonderful match was

over and she could trust herself to look upon the Master Sword like a normal person again.

Kheane and he were laughing and shaking hands. It had ended with Kheane the victor. Bryan took his defeat with grace, saying casually, "Can't win them all."

The ex-assassin merely replied, "You did well."

They came to sit around the fire and talk merrily with the others, exclaiming over the intense match. Alexa couldn't help but watch the features of the happy Master Sword. He smiled and laughed loudly, something she rarely saw him do. Her insides jumped when he glanced at her with a wide smile. She grinned back, albeit it was cloaked with a yearning she couldn't conceal any longer, and he gave her a puzzled, thoughtful look at her strange display before turning to laugh again with Kheane, whose coarse voice sounded so strange, laughing as it never had before.

At twilight, the company refreshed themselves in the warm waters of the Faded Sea. They washed away the stickiness and sweat the hot and humid day had left them. Levaun had wished to stay back to prepare and pack food for the company's departure in the morning.

Alexa sat on an elevated bank overlooking the waters of the lake. The white half-moon shone brilliantly above. Surrounding the lake were grassy, rolling knolls, stretching from the bank to meet the thick, encompassing forest. A light mist appeared and undulated around them. It swam over the knolls, gently creeping over the quiet waters to kiss the half-clothed bodies of the men. The air had distinctly cooled from the earlier mugginess. And Alexa longed to jump into the warm water and join her company. However, she thought it best she stay-put where she was and enjoy the nice scenery the men provided.

She gazed down on the company from atop her pedestal of rock and dirt, a small smile tugging at her lips as Apollos rolled in the shallow water and then leapt up to paw in it playfully. She studied the men while they waded around with bare chests, their trouser legs rolled up. They refreshed themselves by splashing water over their torsos, faces, and hair.

She openly admired the bodies of her company. Every one of

the men looked as if they could have been the subject of a sculpture to depict one of the gods of old. Their muscled torsos flexed pleasingly to the eye as they moved about. Even Kheane's heavily scarred chest was taut and nicely chiseled. If Alexa had run into him in the dark, she would have been frightened to death, for he had removed his cloak, and all the horror of his scarred face and torso stood out menacingly. But now, to her, he seemed as gentle and kind as a kitten.

The leaner builds of the Prince and Eelyne were just as pleasing. Although they were slenderer than the two other warriors and Master Sword, their muscles were well-formed, too.

Deciding to speak, she said with wry satisfaction, "Ahh, I feel like I'm surrounded by the gods." She said this in play, but she was having serious trouble tearing her eyes away, especially from the Master Sword's tall, broad body.

The tantalizing Sword, however, was apparently ignoring her. While the others chuckled merrily and perhaps a tad vainly at her comment, he showed no sign of hearing her. He merely kept scrubbing grime away.

Grinning, Hazerk waded over to her. He placed a hand on her bare foot where it dangled down from atop her perch and gave it a playful tug. "You have it all wrong, Lil' Sis'. I'm afraid we're just the mere attendants of a goddess."

Alexa threw her head back and laughed, most enchantingly with the moonlight on her dark hair.

"Too true," Prince Alkin chuckled, admiring her pretty silhouette openly.

"Maybe the goddess of war," Warkan said with an attempt at being funny.

Bryan's head shot up in amusement along with the others to peer at Alexa's reaction to this jab. Everyone knew that the goddess of war was the least beautiful of the goddesses. The men snickered, waiting for her to explode.

She simply said with a laugh, "I'll take that as a compliment from you, Warkan."

The men smiled, and Warkan shrugged, a lazy grin across his lips.

Alexa studied his stature. He was by far the biggest of all the men. He was broader, stronger, and taller, and also looked rather disproportioned. Then, knowing full well he could crush her between his thumb and finger if he wanted, she said, "At least my head isn't freakishly too small for my body."

Everyone burst out laughing. Even Warkan cracked a grin. He turned and splashed a heap of water at her. She laughed openly, surprised at his uncharacteristic show of playfulness.

The group quieted down. And after watching the Master Sword for a moment longer, Alexa stood and turned away. She needed a change of scenery. Her thoughts were tormenting her with visions of herself entwined in his capable arms and snuggled against his strong chest. She longed to run her fingertips across his skin. How would his lips feel on hers? And, what of that intriguing trail of hair starting at the bottom of his belly and disappearing into his trousers...?

So annoyingly tantalizing! She clenched her teeth. She had to leave.

"Okay, Alexa, it's your turn! Come on, strip down. Get cleaned up." Hazerk's mischievous voice cut into her fancies.

She turned back to face them with a knowing grin, "Nah-ah." She shook her head and looked at all their impish faces with skepticism. "The last time I stripped down a crazy man attacked me. I'm not about to be caught in that situation again." She laughed.

"Wow, Master Sword! I didn't realize you felt so strongly about Alexa," Hazerk teased, giving his superior a playful nudge with his elbow.

"Ha!" Bryan snorted with a wry scoff.

"You're going to get pretty rank smelling if you don't," Eelyne jumped in, playful, hoping to persuade her. They all gave her a boyish smile. Even Kheane had a small grin across his always-sober features.

"Nice try. At least my stench will keep you wild stallions at bay. Now, stop trying to convince me to undress in front of you. I'm not a showgirl for your entertainment."

"I'm sure your stench isn't the only reason men stay away," Warkan added as one last good-natured jeer when she turned her back. She chuckled and waved his comment away.

"He's insulted you twice now! I'll take him out for you if you want," Hazerk called, and he made a playful combative move in Warkan's direction.

She shook her head, smiling. When she went to turn away again, she was stopped short by the Master Sword's firm voice. "Alexa, don't you walk away alone, again," he called. "Sit back down and wait until we can go with you."

She sighed reluctantly. Oh, why did his voice bring chills to her like a god whispering her name? Even when he was being contrary… Well, she decided, if she was going to have to endure his presence, she would at least clean up, fully dressed, of course. She would just wash up the best she could amid all the distractions.

She then slowly made her way down the steep bank and joined the now cat-calling males.

Early the next morning, they said their goodbyes to Levaun. She still stubbornly continued to turn down all of Prince Alkin's beseeching for her to accompany them. She did, however, generously help them prepare to leave. She also drew up a crude map of where the apple orchard was located. The company was grateful for all the assistance and information she had provided. They told her so, though no one more so than Hazerk. He had scarcely left her side since they had arrived. And now he whispered in her ear, eliciting a smile from her before he mounted Red Man to leave.

Having the company all mounted and ready to begin their journey to the orchard, Sword Bryan knelt down and gave the two wolves an affectionate pat goodbye. Wagging their tails in delight, the animals bounced on their front paws, pushing each other out of the way, each envious for attention. The Master Sword smiled fondly at them, remembering his childhood dog, his best friend. With one last nod at Levaun and a quick glance around at his company to ensure its order, he mounted Dragon. Then, once again, they promptly set off down one of Carthorn's many mysterious paths.

The path Levaun sent them on was steep, narrow, and full of

roots emerging from the ground and low hanging branches. The roots threatened to trip the horses. The branches threatened to unseat the riders. And the journey threatened everyone's peace of mind. Nevertheless, the company had no other troubles than those minute obstacles in reaching the apple orchard.

They arrived at the bottom and end of the path by midmorning, unscathed save for a few scratches. The thick woods came to a sudden stop and opened into a great vale before them. They blinked from the bright sunshine until their eyes adjusted from the gloominess of the forest. The company filed from the narrow path onto the lush, grassy terrain and drank in the beauty around them.

The vibrant colors and overall loveliness of the valley were a pleasure to their senses. The forest set a circumferential boundary around the expanse of the valley. The valley itself possessed hundreds of fruitful apple trees; all filled with red, succulent, plump apples. The green of the trees' leaves was as vivid as the red of their apples, their trunks stout, gnarled, and ancient. But one only had to look to know they were strong.

Weaving between the trees, northeast to southwest, was a rushing, glossy river. Its breadth was not narrow nor too broad, its depth waist deep. The emerald grass was thick and smoothly blanketed the small dips and rises of the valley terrain. It was highly tempting to the horses. A sweet, apple-scented breeze wafted gently at their faces, causing stomachs to grumble with hunger and tongues to water with craving.

Looking farther into the center of the valley, Alexa spotted the tallest and oldest looking apple tree. The magic in her core hummed in recognition. She pointed at the tree, breaking the company's fervent study of the valley, and said, "That's where we have to go."

CHAPTER THIRTY

Lady Dorsa grasped a parchment in her gloved hands and looked up to gaze out the aviary window to the icy blue, cloud-free sky. A chill breeze gusted through the window, and she shivered beneath her heavy, fur-lined cloak. To think it would still get much colder for the winter months...

The parchment was a letter from Melea. It revealed little, speaking of only mundane daily things and asking about her health and whether she found Vtalmay and the Chancellor pleasing, with no word on the company's progress. But Dorsa could read between the carefully written lines. Something was still awry back at home. Something was awry with her mother.

It had been a couple fortnights since she had arrived at the Ice Palace, and she'd felt despondent for the whole of it. She had, of course, immediately sent out a courteous, aloof letter to her mother, notifying her of her safe arrival. She did not feel compelled to act friendly toward the woman who'd subjected her to this unwanted life.

With a resigned sigh, she folded the parchment up and stored it in the inside pocket of her cloak. She had to be making her way down to the stables, as she was due to take a pleasure ride through the forest with the Chancellor this afternoon. She glanced at her falcon perched in his cage, dozing now, exhausted from his long journey.

"Rest well, Stormy," she said tenderly. The falcon lifted his head sleepily and eyed her for a moment before tucking it back under his wing. She gave her pet a small smile before turning to exit the aviary.

A little while later, she was atop her feisty Scarlet and squinting through the glittering snow-covered grounds to the shady forest path before her. Chancellor Cheldon was astride a strapping bay next to her. He smiled warmly at her, his brown eyes twinkling as he gazed at her.

Dorsa wore her curly locks in a long, snug braid down her back; a style more suitable to ride with. She rode side-saddle, attired in a warm, blue velvet gown, with her white cloak wrapped closely around her. Her jade eyes sparkled in the sunlight as Scarlet danced beneath her.

"Are you ready, Lady Dorsa?" Cheldon asked, unable to hide his great pleasure of the upcoming outing. He was an outdoorsman and thrilled to be out for a ride on a beautiful day with the prettiest woman in the world.

"Yes, I think my filly won't wait for a second longer." She couldn't help but smile at Scarlet's excitement for the ride. The filly pulled at the reins and tossed her cherry-colored mane.

"I see. Let's not cause her any more distress, then." Cheldon grinned and heeled his mount forward into the shaded pathway adorned with sweet-scented evergreens.

They trekked for a while in silence. The snow and thick evergreens around them muffled the sounds of the forest, and Dorsa breathed in the cool, fresh air, feeling a rare sense of contentment. She glanced over at the Chancellor and found him studying her. She gave him a small smile, and he returned it with a beaming one, his teeth white against his golden-brown whiskers.

"I normally find pleasure in hunting these woods. But now I see I will have to mend my ways if I'm to have your hand in marriage. I'm sure an animal lover such as you wouldn't want a husband that enjoys hunts," he said conversationally, but there was a hint of uncertainty in his voice.

"No need to change yourself for me, Chancellor. I do love animals, but as long as their meat is not wasted, I have no qualms with hunting. Everyone must have some way to find relaxation to escape the pressures of life. I wouldn't want you to lose that." She smiled at him and found herself strangely pleased he would give up something he enjoyed just for her sake.

He smiled, his eyes unguarded and shy. She studied him for a moment. The Chancellor was very tuned into others, attentive in a sincere way. At least she knew she would always be cared for. This heartened her a bit, but she was still sad for her uninvited fate.

While she gazed into his brown eyes pondering this, the horrifying image from her nightmare flashed before her eyes, and she flinched, feeling along with it a very intense, unbidden hatred towards the Chancellor. Cheldon's features became concerned.

"What is it?" he implored.

Dorsa looked away and closed her eyes and tried to clear her mind of the vivid image of her standing over his still body, holding a red-streaked knife. She could actually see the blood oozing down the hilt to drop thickly onto her pale hands, and could see his wide, brown eyes staring sightlessly up at her as the crimson liquid spilled from his throat to soak his beard and shirt.

"Oh, nothing," she finally said once she managed to clear the image. The harsh feeling accompanying it dissipated along with it. Befuddled, she focused on a brightly colored bluebird chirping in an evergreen ahead on their path. Was she going insane?

"Are you unhappy here? What haven't I done to make your stay more comfortable for you? Tell me so that I can change it for you." He leaned so far over in his saddled it was as if he wanted to jump over to hers and comfort her immediately.

She put a gloved hand to her temple and scolded herself for having such a thought again. Raising her eyes, she softened them upon seeing his concerned countenance. "You have been nothing but wonderful, Chancellor. I just suddenly feel very exhausted. Forgive me." She tried to sound convincing, but he didn't appear convinced.

"You must still be stressed from leaving your home and being all alone here. Let's return to the Ice Palace so you can rest. I'll have some servants bring you something warm to drink. You can spend some quiet time with your snow cubs."

Once again, Dorsa was overly pleased by the Chancellor's gentle and understanding demeanor, and she felt a sudden, sharp pang of guilt for having treacherous thoughts toward him. "But we just began our ride. I wouldn't want to cut short your recreation."

He waved a nonchalant hand. "There will be plenty of days we can go riding. Your well-being is more important. I'll make sure your filly gets turned out, so she can stretch her legs. Come on, now." He pulled up his bay and reined the horse around to face the trail back toward the palace.

She halted Scarlet, but the filly resisted, indignant to have to perform a downward transition rather than an upward one. Dorsa hesitated for a moment, worried she might have upset the Chancellor and he was concealing it. But after a moment of his earnest insisting, she turned the filly around and they headed back toward the palace, leaving a ruffled trail through the fluffy snow.

Despite everything, she was extremely grateful toward Cheldon and felt she needed some time alone to sort through her growing bewildered feelings.

At sunset, she stood out on her balcony, overlooking the gray, churning ocean. The air was cooling quickly as the sun sent its last orange-colored rays over the watery horizon and skyward. Wrapped snug in her cloak, she leaned against the cold stone of the balcony railing and breathed in the briny air, closing her eyes. Behind her, she could hear the two snow cubs playing roughly with each other. They had turned out to be both females. Iris and Clover, she had named them; because she felt this icy world needed a little bit of spring in it.

Dorsa didn't feel like herself; something had changed inside of her. It wasn't just because she was frightened by the vivid dream she'd had and that it had haunted her ever since. It was that she was beginning to feel like she was actually capable of doing such a deed. This frightened her a great deal.

She didn't want to live here. She didn't want to love Cheldon. But she didn't want to hate him either, and she most certainly didn't want to murder him. But it seemed that marrying him was her fate. She opened her eyes and looked down below to where the water crashed on the crags beneath the balcony. She could throw herself over and all would be solved. It wouldn't last long. She probably wouldn't feel much. She'd be saving herself from a horrible life and perhaps saving the Chancellor as well. Even if they lived a long life together, they could never be truly happy. They'd end up making each other miserable because she didn't love him, and he'd soon tire of trying to make her love him. It was better this way. She leaned farther over the ledge, listening to the crashing waves, and shut her eyes, holding her breath, knowing she wouldn't, couldn't really jump.

Then a voice came to her on the wind. She paused and opened her eyes. It was the most beautiful, enchanting voice she had ever heard. It sounded like an angel. She looked avidly around her, desperate to find the source. She looked below, back to the water. It came from the ocean. It called to her. It sang her name, although she couldn't distinguish any coherent words. It was the language of another world.

She wanted to be with that voice. She wanted to find the owner of that voice. If she did, her troubles would all evaporate. Evaporate just like the mist off the ocean in the early morning.

It sang for her to leap. The owner of the voice wanted her to come and join it. Her eyes darted among the wet crags below and latched on to the slightest movement snuggled between two large boulders close to the water's edge. The waves splashed coldly up around the figure, but the creature did not seem affected by the icy waters. After another violent wave swept over the figure and ebbed away, Dorsa locked her eyes on the source of the voice.

The creature sat very stately on the rock. It was a mermaid. Dorsa inhaled sharply; all her worries forgotten. The creature was gazing at her, singing its song. It was a beautiful creature, just as beautiful as its voice. It had a pale complexion with dark wavy hair and dark fathomless eyes. Her fins were a deep plum and glittery. And her eyes held Dorsa captive.

Suddenly, Dorsa wanted to be with this creature, to follow it into the deepest part of the ocean. She knew that if she did, all her troubles wouldn't matter anymore. The mermaid would watch over her and take care of her. She was certain of this, though she didn't know how she knew this. But she knew that, eventually, she would become one with the ocean. She could leave behind all the world's sorrow and plights. The lovely mermaid sang this to her. She called to her.

Dorsa's heart longed to go, and she leaned over the edge of the railing, feeling the cold stone beneath her warm fingers. She would dive outward and miss the crags, and if she didn't, well, that was okay too. She glanced back to Iris and Clover; they tumbled around, oblivious to her. And unable to keep her eyes from the mermaid for long, she fixed them back on the beckoning creature and prepared herself to jump.

★★★★

As the company made their way farther into the valley, they sniffed the apple-perfumed breeze with appreciation. They headed in the straightest fashion toward the large apple tree. Alexa led the company with Sword Bryan and the Prince directly behind her. She rode with poise, her face set in resolution.

"Mmm, I have to have one of those." Hazerk went to grab at one of the scarlet apples dangling from the nearest tree.

Apollos suddenly appeared next to him and whispered, "Don't touch those!"

Hazerk snapped his hand back as if the apple had bitten him. "How come?"

The unicorn tossed his nose in the air. "We don't want to risk anything until we have what we need," he said under his breath.

"Huh?"

"Shhh!" Alexa hissed, twisting in her saddle to scowl at Hazerk with her fiery sapphire eyes.

"Yes," Apollos said, his voice still soft. "We have to be quiet. We can't scare the trees."

"You mean the dryads, right?"

Apollos sniffed and flicked his tail. "Yes."

The company made their way quietly across the valley. They traveled up and down the small knolls, forded the crystal river, and headed up one last hill toward the tree.

The surrounding trees appeared to have noticed their presence, for they began moving more in the soft breeze, their plump apples hanging precariously on their branches. Sunlight streaming through the leaves made shadows and light dance all around the company. The horses seemed to have picked up on their riders' carefulness. They stepped more surefooted and softer, their heads low, eyes alert, and ears swiveling for sounds.

Once they neared the ancient apple tree, they dismounted a couple hundred strides away and paused to gaze at it. It was a gnarled looking tree, but was abundant with scarlet, luscious looking apples and vibrant green leaves. Despite its awkward form, it waved elegantly in the wind.

Gazing ahead with stoic features, Alexa handed her reins unknowingly off to the Prince, who had been standing closest to her. With her dagger strapped on her right thigh, her bow and quiver across her back, and her hand on the hilt of her sword belted at her waist, she strode with confidence toward the tree. The Master Sword was quick on her heels, his features austere. She glanced back at him, said nothing, but looked to Apollos and motioned for him to come as well. The unicorn came swiftly beside the Master Sword, giving Alexa the lead. The others hung back, watching in earnest.

Alexa marched straight up to the tree's nearest branch hanging just above her head. Pursing her lips, she contemplated for a moment and then looked over her shoulder at the Master Sword and Apollos. Bryan had his hand gripped on the hilt of his sword, his features intense, and Apollos looked on encouragingly, imploring her to take an apple. She flashed them a quick, brave grin, knowing it was now or never, and then reached up to grip a plump apple.

The scenery transformed before all their eyes. Just as her fingertips brushed the red skin of the apple, it, along with all the apples on every tree in the valley, shrunk down and transformed back into bright pink and white blossoms. The valley instantly changed from a vibrant red to a delicate pink.

Flabbergasted, Alexa spun around, her mouth agape, and took in the transformed valley. The apple blossoms danced in the breeze, releasing a euphoric aroma. All in the company gazed in wonder. The Head-Master Sword diverted his attention for but a moment, and when he turned back to his charge, he saw something beyond her take form from out of the tree's trunk. He drew his sword and called, "Alexa! Look!" His azure eyes avid and features taut.

Alexa spun, her hand going to her hilt. A creature emerged from within the tree and walked fearlessly toward her. It was undeniably a dryad. Alexa stared, astounded, unable to speak. The dryad was so remarkably beautiful that she doubted her own eyes.

The being had long, straight, shiny, bark-brown hair. Her lips as scarlet as an apple's skin. Her eyes almond-shaped and a dark, fathomless brown. Her skin creamy, tinted the palest rose, and the blush of her cheeks a dark crimson. She wore a shimmering, vivid red dress that flowed down her slender figure to trail behind her on the plush grass. She came to a stop in front of Alexa and smiled.

Alexa released the death grip on her hilt. The Master Sword kept his blade drawn but stood at ease as he watched the exchange.

"Why do you come to this tree and pick one of my apples?" the dryad asked. Her voice was sweet, and Alexa could smell the scent of apples on her.

"We're searching for the Earth-Keeper. We're in need of the pure elemental power that lies within the earth. Do you know what I speak of, blessed dryad?" Alexa replied as politely as she could.

The dryad didn't speak but moved toward her and placed a soft palm on her cheek, and looking into her eyes, said, "You are a witch by half your blood, are you not?"

Alexa looked solemn. "Yes. My name is Alexandra."

The dryad studied her, though without judgment. Then, stepping back, she gestured toward her tree behind her. "This tree is from the start of time. It has grown since the day the soil was first born from the Master of the Earth. I have been its caretaker since that time. I guard and protect the power it holds. I am the Earth-Keeper. Why have you sought me?"

Such a flood of relief and happiness came over Alexa that she nearly shouted in glee. She restrained herself, however, only allowing a wild, grateful grin to spread across her features.

"You understand I cannot just give this power away to anyone?"

"We don't seek the power for any selfish gain. We desperately need it to stop evil from destroying Eetharum. The High Power has asked me to do this," Alexa said with urgency.

"I know of this evil you speak of," the dryad said, sorrow lacing all her features.

"You do?" Alexa paused.

"The earth whispers and cries many things in my ear," she said. Then she looked away from Alexa to Sword Bryan and Apollos, who were standing with tense hope. "You have a great

- 323 -

ally, I see," she said of Apollos, then added, "You, too, have your own keeper. The Master of the Earth is wise." She smiled brightly at Bryan. The Master Sword acknowledged her and bowed his head in reverence, his heart greatly pleased. She motioned for him and Apollos to come and stand with them.

Alexa looked on her with awe. The dryad was so much more than just the Earth-Keeper. This creature was connected intricately with the High Power. There was no doubt in her mind.

Once the four of them stood beneath the boughs of the apple tree, the dryad reached up and touched a blossom, which suddenly was no longer a blossom. The entire tree, along with the rest of the valley, changed back into its original state of plump, scarlet apples. The dryad picked the apple. "Here." She gave the fruit to Alexa.

Alexa took it in astonishment. "You're giving this to me freely?"

"I have no doubt, you who keep company with a unicorn, your blood is not evil, no matter its origin. I've heard the earth's pains, and I feel the Master of the Earth is with us. It's my responsibility to tell you simply to believe he is with you and will not forsake you." She smiled fondly at the stunned group. Then, seeing Alexa's confused expression while staring at the apple in her hand, she said, "Eat it to its core and then take one seed and combine it with the other elements."

"Now?"

"Yes. It won't harm you. It'll only make you feel pleasantly full for hours to come."

Alexa bit into the apple. Her teeth broke the scarlet skin, and sweet, sticky juice ran down her chin. "This is so delicious! I can't describe it," she exclaimed, and then quickly devoured the whole thing.

While she ate, the others spoke of simple things with the dryad. Strangely, it came as naturally as if they were speaking with a dear friend of the weather.

Finishing the apple, Alexa plucked the seeds from the core. She took one and placed it in the vial with the mermaid tears. The other seeds she gathered and then dropped them into the opened palm of the dryad. They all smiled at one another as the task was done; Apollos gave his head a gleeful toss.

"Alexandra, once you have this power, you must do a favor for me," the dryad said.

"Anything."

"Will you promise me that wherever you go, you will grow life there? The kind that is indigenous to the land."

"I'll be able to do that?"

The dryad chuckled merrily. "You'll be able to do many things."

"Then, of course, I'd be pleased to," she promised. Then, looking solemn again, she added, "You are a very exquisite being, next to Apollos. What is your name?"

The dryad flashed a reticent smile and began to move away from them. "You may call me Apple if you wish."

"Please, before you go, could you tell us where the other Elemental Keepers are," Alexa pleaded after her, for the being was quickly becoming aloof and had her hand on the trunk of her tree.

"Good luck, dear Alexandra. Good luck to you as well, her brave keeper, and you, beloved unicorn. If you're meant to find the elements, they'll be revealed to you." With that, she melded into the trunk of the tree and disappeared.

The three companions turned and looked at one another with cheerful countenances.

Sword Bryan grinned, his clear blue eyes twinkling. "Good job, Sand Queen. We're another step closer."

"I couldn't have done better myself," Apollos praised, butting a beaming Alexa affectionately on the arm. She gave the unicorn a tight hug around his neck, and they made their way back to the others, who waited, anxious for the news.

"She knew everything already. I just got lucky," Alexa said merrily.

"I think it was more than just luck," Bryan commented with a smile.

"Right." Alexa pondered that thought. Right, because *she* was the key that was turned to open the door. And, after all, a key cannot turn itself.

They reached the others and told them the good news, and they all expressed their great delight.

"Well, all I want to know is if we can eat these apples now?" Hazerk said good-naturedly while they prepared to mount up.

"I don't see why not. I'd like one, too," Apollos said.

"Great!" Eelyne expressed.

Then, selecting trees other than Apple's, they all gleefully picked armfuls of the juicy fruit. They collected enough to fill their bellies for now and more for later, and even gathered some for their horses; Eelyne made sure to pick a share for the pack mule.

The company then sprawled out on the grass before they reentered the perilous forest and enjoyed the sweet fruit that had tempted them the moment they had stepped foot in the valley.

CHAPTER THIRTY-ONE

Lady Dorsa's heart was as numb as her rosy, wind-bitten cheeks. Struggling in her thick, velvet gown and heavy cloak, she scrambled to push herself up onto the cold, white stone of the balcony. She just *had* to join the singing mermaid perched on the crags, who appeared impervious to the bitter waves crashing all around her.

Dorsa's mind felt erased. Her heart not only felt numb, but it was cold, wrapped in a thick casing of ice, frozen, on the verge of cracking. She had come to this land, her heart unwilling but her mind resolved to do the right thing for her country: marry the Chancellor to provide friendly ties with Shelkite. But her dedication to propriety was losing out to her sensibility. She had tried to occupy her lonely, slowly despairing mind with her pets: her snow cubs, her horse, her falcon. But they were not enough. No, nothing would help her but this enchanting mermaid. She would go to her, and if she died in the fall, it would only be a relief. For not only was she in despair of her lost future, she was evil. And evil did not deserve to live at all. Her vivid thoughts of murder were frightening. She did not understand them, and she could not drown them out. And this mermaid, singing a song in her own tongue, sang of freedom and reprieve.

Dorsa managed to get one of her legs over the railing, her eyes still locked to the icy, dark eyes of the mermaid. Soon her troubles would end. She leaned, and her body swayed, unbalanced. She prepared for the fall.

"My lady, stop!"

A sharp yank on her cloak plucked her away from the railing and she crashed to the balcony floor. Dazed, she glanced around to see the face of Chancellor Cheldon, his brown eyes wide with concern and his mouth set in a tight line. His hands trembled as he assisted her to her feet.

"Close your ears. Close your eyes. Come with me!" He pulled her through the doors leading back into her chamber and slammed them shut, shutting out the bitter cold along with the enthralling song.

For a few agonizing moments, they stood there in the warmth of the chamber staring at one another, Dorsa still not comprehending what had just taken place and the Chancellor trying to recompose himself.

Finally, he spoke, stroking his golden-brown beard with a trembling hand. "I didn't mean to manhandle you. Did I hurt you?"

Numb, Dorsa shook her head, blinking and struggling to return from the trance.

"You just gave me a fright is all. I should've warned you of the merpeople. Do not look at them or listen to their songs. They are cursed, evil, murderous sirens. I cannot tell you how many palace guards I have lost to them…never to be found." He added the last part on emphatically, trying to look her in the eyes for reassurance of her understanding. She did not acknowledge him. "Do you understand, my lady? Maybe you should move to another chamber for a while. One that doesn't have an ocean view."

She sucked in a breath of air. "That won't be necessary. I understand. I have never encountered a creature such as that before, and I'll be guarded from now on. I thank you kindly, Chancellor…for saving me."

"Cheldon," he corrected softly.

She gave him a small, cheerless smile.

There was another moment of silence as he studied her. He then ventured, "Well…I was coming to ask you to join me for tea before we dine for the evening. If you feel up for it, I'd love to have your company. Perhaps we can talk…"

She cleared her throat and forced her mind back into propriety. "Oh yes, of course."

There were several moments of awkward silence as they sipped their tea. Dorsa felt her cold fingers tingle as the warmth of the tea spread through her. She and the Chancellor sat snuggled in warm blankets, each on their own settee in the library of the Ice Palace. It was one of the few rooms that was decorated more warmly, not a cold alabaster stone was visible. The walls and floor were oak. The floors were lined with plush navy rugs, and not a single ice sculpture was present. Tomes lined the walls, giving the room a close, cozy feeling. The main attraction, however, was the overly large and elaborate stone hearth, where just as an impressive fire was snapping furiously. She leaned closer to the heat emanating from it, closing her eyes in peace.

"Lady Dorsa, I want to be forward with you. I hope you don't mind," Cheldon broke the silence, a bit hesitantly.

She looked up from her rare peaceful thoughts to see the Chancellor studying her features carefully. Upon placing her gaze on him, her chest tightened as the compulsion gripped a hold of her. She fought it and tried to push it away, nodding stiffly and not trusting herself to speak.

"I have the feeling—well, rather, I'd like to know…" Cheldon began.

Dorsa's brow furrowed and her jade-colored eyes turned puzzled, but she gestured for him to continue.

"And you can be honest with me; it won't hinder my pride. But I was wondering if…if you are in love with another?" He finished, his brown eyes large and unguarded.

Dorsa was struck into silence for a moment, and in this, her compulsion seized her. A vivid image hit her; one of herself driving a knife through his throat, in this very situation, right where they sat. She could see the bright crimson blood pour from his neck onto her pale hands, and she cringed.

"Forgive me! I wasn't accusing you of any wrong. I merely wanted to be honest with each other," Cheldon blurted.

She quickly composed herself, shaking her sunshine-blonde head. "No, no. It's not that. I—ah—I am afflicted with headaches every so often," she lied. "You did not offend me. You have every right to know where your future bride's heart stands." The Chancellor relaxed, and she continued on, uncaring now where her mouth led her, for her mind had left her completely. "To answer your question—yes. Yes, I had given my heart to another before you proposed this marriage…"

Cheldon's brown eyes lowered, his countenance falling. After a moment, he said, "I don't wish to keep you here as my prisoner. I have held a special place in my heart for you ever since you came to visit years ago when I was a young man. You seem like a rare soul, all purity and honesty…not a single soiled thought in your mind."—Dorsa wanted to cry out in the irony of his words—"But I don't want to keep you here against your will... Although, I hope you'll give me a fighting chance. I don't know who this other man is, or if I can stand up to your ideal, but I hope that you'll learn to love me as you do him." He proclaimed this with such depth, it stunned her to her core.

Her heart cried out to Eelyne to save her. But she was alone, and there was no reply but the throbbing silence. She could not force her heart to let Eelyne go, although she knew she *could* learn to care for the Chancellor. Perhaps, that would turn into something more because she had no choice, despite what Cheldon claimed, even though it wasn't him who had stolen her choice but her mother. Adama would never allow her to come home.

She swallowed and nodded. "Of course, Cheldon."

This elicited a broad grin from him. "Wonderful. Now, I wanted to tell you I have a surprise in the making for you."

She gave him a weak but grateful smile.

★★★★

"Two keys down and three to go."

"Ugh, don't remind me."

"We've been gone a long time and we still have three elements to find. And they could quite possibly be in other countries far from here. Who knows what's going on in the world? Ret could've taken over completely by now."

"Don't be so positive, Warkan, you're making me giddy with hope." Hazerk turned in his saddle to shoot his sarcastic reply back at the stoic-faced warrior bringing up the rear of the company.

"Well, I was just pointing out—"

"Don't forget that part of our mission was to figure out what the keys were. This is just going to take time." Prince Alkin sighed, sounding as if he were trying to convince himself. "I have complete faith in my Shelkite warriors, the Galeon warriors, *and* Lady Evelyn," he added with confidence.

It had been a few days since they had left the orchard. The

company was making their way north through the forest, traveling toward the Kaltraz and Carthorn border. Apollos, as usual, was leading the way down a narrow path among the thick trees, vines, and soft moss. This part of the forest was dense, and Apollos' prismatic horn shimmered with a light that both comforted and guided the companions.

The company kept up a casual conversation to help ease the apprehension the forest pressed on them as they trekked through its heart. The wood was unusually quiet, as if it wanted to listen to their very thoughts, so they were vigilant of their surroundings, on the keen lookout for some of the creatures Levaun had warned them about.

"Have any intuition clues, Alexa?" Eelyne asked with a hopeful tone.

She turned to look nonchalantly at the warrior, "Nope." She wasn't about to let her once again lack of direction affect the elated feeling she'd been nurturing since she'd obtained the earth element. A sense of disappointment rose among the company at her reply. However, she knew they hadn't had their hopes up too much, anyway.

The afternoon passed and turned into evening without a single sight of any creature aside from the colorful birds watching from the branches above.

Right before dusk, Alexa felt something collide with her senses. It was something magical—several strong magical things. She tried to puzzle it out for a few minutes before she said, "Wait a moment."

The sleepy silence of the companions broke, and they halted at her command, noting the familiar, discerning countenance and fervent sparkle in her eyes. She was on to something. They waited anxiously.

"Apollos, do you sense that? It's magic," she said.

"Yes, I do. I've been trying to decide the direction it's coming from." The unicorn held his head high, his eyes wide, and ears pricked. His nose was pointed into the light breeze, his nostrils flaring. "This way," he said, and then turned east, off the narrow path. He slid through the thick branches, the company seemingly crashing along behind him. He paused at a hedge-like wall. They eyed it. It ran north for a long distance and gradually turned east.

"This is the wall Levaun spoke of," Alkin said, dismounting. He walked to it with Apollos and attempted to feel inside the thick vines and branches. The unicorn stuck his nose in and sniffed.

"The magic is coming from the other side," Alexa said, looking up and over to the dusky sky above. The hedge rose to about four times the height of a man.

"Yes," Apollos agreed.

"Do you think the next element is behind there?" Hazerk asked.

Alexa craned her neck about her, trying with all her might to sense out the area. As always, to her frustration, the forest seemed to press in on her senses and clog them. "I can't tell."

"Well, let's see. I can climb that easily," Sword Bryan said and dismounted. He strode over to the wall and scrutinized it. Just as he placed his foot on one of the vines, using it as a foothold, and hoisted himself up, the sound of heavy hoofbeats pounding the earth alerted them. Everyone's head shot up in defense, and the Master Sword leapt down. They pulled out their weapons and looked around for the source of the hoof beats.

From the north, in the clearing alongside the wall, came a figure riding at a gallop toward them. As it neared, they could tell the rider held a crossbow. The warriors, in intense and focused silence, held their weapons ready to strike. Apollos lowered his horn, and Alexa drew her bow.

The intruder barreled closer, and they came to realize the man was not riding the horse. To their astonishment, a large centaur skidded to a halt twenty strides from them.

He was broad and well-muscled, both his human and animal halves. His horse body was tall and proportionate to its seamless joining with his regular-sized human torso. His long and wavy hair was the same coppery coloring as his chestnut body. And his bare chest was so bronzed by the sun, it nearly matched his coat. He clenched his square jaw and studied them with a severe brow and dark, alert eyes.

Stunned but not put off guard, the company held their stance and waited for him to speak.

Holding his weapon at the ready, he demanded, "Who are you? What do you want?"

The company sensed more eyes on them, and they heard the familiar sound of snapping twigs; a half a dozen other centaurs came from the woods, surrounding them, all with their crossbows at the ready.

Alkin, with a quick glance at Apollos, took the unicorn's nod as an okay that the centaurs were good. He told the truth, "I'm Prince Alkin of Shelkite, and these are my warriors. We sensed magic beyond this wall and were about to investigate. We don't mean any harm."

The centaur eyed them with suspicion. Then, glancing at Apollos, he seemed to take Alkin's word for it and lowered his crossbow; the others followed suit. His features still not softening, he said, "I'm Hard Flame; these are *my* warriors." He swept his arm out arrogantly toward the other centaurs. "We're the guardians of the Empress Jadelin and her kingdom."

"Empress?" Alkin looked puzzled. "I don't know of any empress or organized kingdom in Carthorn."

Hard Flame smiled proudly, showing pearly teeth. "That's because it's a secret kingdom."

"Well, not anymore…" Hazerk mumbled behind Alexa. She stifled a snicker.

"It's within this wall?" Alkin asked. The centaur nodded. "There are other creatures? Magical creatures?"

"Yes. Come. It's a sign you're here. I'll take you there. Empress Jadelin will want to meet you. And your unicorn is especially welcome with great surprise and warmth from us all." He raised his hand to his mouth and whistled to the sky.

The company gazed at one another, slightly befuddled at the quick invite and wondering whether it was safe to accept. But with a few hasty glances between Apollos, Alkin, Alexa, and the Master Sword, the decision was made. They agreed; they needed information.

A loud, chilling caw came from above their heads. The company looked up to see four massive griffins. They carried in their beaks, by hefty ropes, a large wooden platform that they lowered to the ground between Hard Flame and the company. The

creatures' wings stirred the wind as they descended, and the
company looked upon the sight with awe.

Hard Flame mounted the platform as soon as it grounded and
turned around to beckon the company, his hooves clomping noisily
on the wooden floor. "We'll take half up now and immediately
return for the rest of you."

Apollos and Alkin, leading Sapharan, boarded the platform.
Alexa waited for Sword Bryan's say. He glanced at her, eyeing her
without thought, and waved a hand for her to come. He then
looked back to Warrior Warkan and said sternly, "Until we rejoin,
you're in charge." The warrior nodded and stayed back with the
rest of the company.

The Master Sword and Alexa led their mounts onto the
platform without a problem. Hard Flame gave the signal. The
griffins nodded and took flight, carefully lifting the platform. The
horses snorted and braced themselves, eyeballing the great
creatures and the disappearing ground all at once. Their masters
moved to soothe them.

Once in flight, Alkin turned to Hard Flame, "Why do you say
it's a sign and invite us so readily?"

"Because we had thought there was only one unicorn left in
this world," he answered pointedly, looking up toward the top of
the wall.

Apollos stepped forward with eagerness. "There's another of
my kind here?" A bright light was in his chocolate eyes.

Hard Flame looked down to the unicorn and smiled. "Yes."

"Oh, Apollos!" Alexa exclaimed with dancing eyes. She
reached out and stroked his withers. Apollos shook his mane in
elation. His eyes gleamed as he looked at the Prince and Bryan.
They smiled. The unicorn raised his head and waited expectantly
as the platform slowly rose above the wall.

Alexa looked down into the enclosed area, and her breath
caught in her throat, for it was painstakingly beautiful. Her eyes
darted to behold everything; her senses barely aware of the light
hand that came to rest on her shoulder. Down below was a vast,
meticulously groomed yard, the grass cut and the bushes trimmed,
a garden admirably arranged in paths all around. Abundant lilac

bushes scented the air so pleasantly, it sent a euphoric sensation through her, and she sighed in appreciation. A small, elegant palace was off in the distance to the northwest. Small cottages, stables, and buildings made up a village to the northeast. It went beyond her sight to see the end of the road leading through the town.

"Why is this secret?" she asked, leaning over the edge for a better look below. Zhan whickered nervously at his mistress.

"Be careful," Bryan whispered in her ear, his fingers closing tighter on her shoulder.

She suddenly became aware of his hand, and a shiver ran through her body. She stepped back from the edge and looked up slightly starry-eyed into the Master Sword's face. He watched her with his intent, beautiful azure eyes whisking protectively over her face, and she stared at him stupidly, feeling her attraction to him rise most unwillingly. He gave her a crooked smile and removed his hand, and she gulped and tore her eyes from him, not understanding, nor wanting to see, the smirk on his handsome face. She looked over to Hard Flame, who, she realized, was answering and had been answering her question while she had been distracted.

"…a haven. After the war, we good creatures wanted a place we would be safe and would not be bothered by humans. Empress Jadelin came after we had established ourselves. But we wanted a leader, someone who was not biased because we have so many kinds here. Although Empress Jadelin *is* human, we found her to be just and good-hearted. So, we set her up as our empress. I'm sure she will be pleased to have visitors of her same kind."

The griffins lowered the platform to land it gently on the grass and waited for them to dismount before taking off again. The occupants filed off, looking around them, taking in the sights and charming smells.

Alexa looked down the road to the small shops and homes. She noted vegetable gardens behind some of the houses. There was also a wooded area inside the wall where a tiny, wooly creature with huge, round eyes was waddling from, carrying a basket of berries. She smiled. The creature spotted her, and its eyes got even larger. Frightened, it scurried away.

Just then, another centaur approached them. His entire body, his human half and horse half, was a sleek dark black. He was just as broad and well-muscled as Hard Flame. His hooves were large and fetlocks lightly feathered. He carried a long-sword strapped across his girth. His face was more handsome than Hard Flame's— by human standards, anyway.

"Night Strider," Hard Flame addressed him. "Tell the Empress she has visitors of her kind and of Estella's."

At that, Night Strider was off in a flash, his big hooves kicking up sod as he took off toward the palace.

The five of them waited most pleasantly for the griffins to return with the rest of their group. They let their horses crop grass while they waited. Alexa watched Zhan with fondness as he tore at the juicy bits of grass, gleeful and stuffing his mouth as full as he could get it. She smiled at the horse and gave him a loving pat and then looked up to see Alkin watching her and grinning. She smiled back; he gave her a wink and looked away upon hearing the griffins return.

She glanced up to see the platform slowly lowering. Hazerk's loud, excited voice boomed about something. She chuckled and glanced at the Master Sword, who stood watching with his arms crossed. He rolled his eyes good-naturedly and then caught her gaze. They looked at each other for a passive moment, his face showing no emotion.

Alexa tossed her senses out and tried to decipher him before she lost the chance. He was content for once. She couldn't feel any sign of bitterness in him at all, albeit she could feel the slight stress and fatigue he was suffering from. But, like a good warrior, he never showed it.

Bryan broke her gaze when the others landed and began filing off. Hazerk and Eelyne were exclaiming about everything. Warkan looked less ornery than usual, and the poor pack mule looked bug-eyed as he dragged Eelyne and Swift Phoenix off the platform.

Back together, they mounted up, and Hard Flame led them toward the palace. The trek was a nice one. They rode through nicely manicured grounds and weaved through both gardens of flowers and food, and passed a large, open, rolling field with a rushing stream slicing through it.

When they reached the palace, their eyes were dazzled, for it looked as if it were made completely out of white marble. It was not large by any standards, but it was a palace, nonetheless. There were ten marble steps leading to the entrance, with marble pillars lining the front terrace and gently sloping ramps on either end, presumably for the centaurs' convenience. Alexa looked up to see several windows and a balcony overlooking the fields. When she returned her eyes to the terrace, a woman was standing in the doorway.

Alexa didn't have to take much of her in to feel suddenly insignificant. If she had to describe her, it would be as beautiful. Alexa didn't usually consider people to be beautiful. When she thought of beautiful, she thought of landscape, or of a well-bred horse, or of the merman and dryad she had met, but this woman was beautiful. She was tall and stately. Alexa could tell just by glancing that the Empress was taller than she was. The woman was slender but with a curvy figure, the pink satin dress she wore complementing her greatly. Her skin was like porcelain, no freckles, and had a pink flush to it. Her lips full and rosy, and her face was not angular but had soft features that made her look kind, with eyes a vivid shade of blue topaz and hair a brilliant shade of sunshine-blonde that lay in long, swooping curls and waves down her back.

Alexa heard the men in the company take in a breath, and she suddenly disliked the Empress. *Even after they saw the dryad?* She wanted to blurt her bitter comment, feeling possessive of the men, especially one in particular. Although, she knew their reaction was because this was a human woman. It was more natural for them to exhibit this response. She wondered if the Master Sword had been one of them who'd taken in a breath, and she tried to decipher him again.

Letting her senses loose, she was hit hard with an intense, jubilant feeling coming from someone else in the group. Surprised and curious, she turned around to see who it was.

Prince Alkin stepped forward and introduced himself. The rest of the company moved forward, up the stairs, past the frozen Alexa. She was trying desperately hard to feel each one out as they passed her. She stood with one foot on the bottom stair, her head cocked toward each man as he walked by. *It's not the Prince or Bryrunan*—that was a relief—*not him either, nope, but he's fascinated by her, no…*

The silent and still heavily cloaked and hooded Kheane stalked by her, and her heart skipped a beat at the connection. Though the ex-assassin showed not a single sign of it on his face or even in his eyes, it was him emitting the elated feeling she was receiving.

Kheane followed the company up to the terrace, standing at the back of them, silent and vigilant as always. Alexa watched the greeting exchange from the bottom of the stairs. She glanced from the ex-assassin to the Empress and back again. With narrowed eyes and brow furrowed, realization dawned on her. This was his lost orphan girl. The woman he was searching for was Jadelin, now an empress. She smiled, her heart happy for him.

"Alexa, stop daydreaming and come say hello to our hostess." Alkin beckoned to her.

She mentally shook her senses free and bounded up the marble stairs to stand next to Kheane in the back. "Hi," she said, peeking around the others and raising a hand to the Empress. It was rather rude of her to greet an empress this way, but Jadelin didn't seem to mind. She smiled.

"Hello, Alexa, I'm Jadelin."

Her voice was pretty, too. *How unfair*, Alexa groused to herself but kept a smile on her face. She stole a glance at Kheane as the others spoke with the Empress. He was already looking at her from the corner of his eye. It startled her to see his dark, coffee-colored eyes discerning her unexpectedly, and she gazed back at the ex-assassin, trying to communicate. *He knows I know something. How on earth does he know that without magical senses?* Kheane gave her a curt nod of confirmation, though there was a sparkle in his eye now. She smiled back knowingly, realizing that if any of the other men had any ideas of sweet-talking this lady, they would not get far if Kheane had anything to do with it.

Empress Jadelin led them into the main entranceway. The

floor was marble as well, and the room opened into a large foyer with a curving stairway up the left side and a gently inclined ramp curving up on the right—for the centaurs. There were pots of sweet-smelling blossoms placed around. The room had a happy aura. Upstairs, Alexa could see yet another balcony with beautifully carved railings overlooking the foyer. A hallway led both right and left.

She looked over her shoulder to see their mounts being led away to the stable by other centaurs and creatures appearing to be the groundskeepers or the stable hands. Zhan's comfort was always one of her first concerns. Once she figured he would be fine, she listened to what the Empress was saying.

"Estella is in the back courtyard. You have to meet her at once. And please don't call me empress. Jadelin is fine. I'm of no royal blood. My mystical friends persist in calling me their empress. But I only ever promised I'd help dictate if they needed an outside opinion. I don't look on them as my subjects at all. They've been so kind to me all my life. They rescued me, actually." She rattled this off incessantly. It was obvious she didn't have company often. "The same as they rescued you, too!" She bent down and lovingly reached out her arms to a long-haired, gray cat that had come bounding into the entranceway to see her. She scooped him up in her arms and cuddled him. The cat purred and rubbed his head on her chin. "Hard Flame found this little guy wandering outside one of the villages near Carthorn's edge and brought him to me—another way to spoil me. I love cats." She smiled. "And don't let Hard Flame fool you. He's a big softy." She grinned wider.

Alexa's earlier jealousy melted upon observing the Empress. She seemed so innocent and kind; she acted as if she had been planning all week to host a gruff and smelly bunch of warriors for the weekend.

Jadelin led them into a grand room with comfortable chairs, settees, and chaise lounges. A small library was there, along with a fire ablaze in a hearth. It all looked very inviting to the weary company. In the back of the room, two sets of double doors stood open. They could see a pleasant courtyard through them. And there, in the courtyard, was a unicorn. She dipped her elegant head into a fountain to drink. Her crystal horn sparkled softly from the last rays of the setting sun; pastel color spots danced across the flagstone path. Her iridescent mane shimmered, and her hooves glistened a light coppery color. She looked identical to Apollos, although, somehow, more feminine.

Apollos was rendered still. He looked on her with eyes that held so much depth. Alexa was certain he felt many things at once. He must have been elated to realize he wasn't the last of his kind. He must have wanted to know what other unicorns were like. Did they act the same as him? Would she be the filly for him? He had a look in his eyes as if he had just come home for the first time in years.

The entire company was still as they watched Apollos' reaction. Finally, Estella raised her head and took in the arrivals. She caught eyes with Apollos, and everyone grinned like idiots, glad for this union, including Jadelin. For she was happy her friend finally had one of her kind here, too.

Estella tossed her shimmering mane. Her eyes were alight, and she whinnied a beautiful musical note. Apollos answered her, and Alexa realized she had never heard him whinny before. Estella gave her mane another playful toss, reared up, and came galloping into the palace through the open doors to meet him. Her hooves barely made a sound on the marble floors. Apollos moved forward to greet her, his neck outstretched. They touched noses, timidly. Then they were talking, although in their own language.

"Let's leave them to get to know one another," Jadelin said happily. "Are you hungry?" she asked as the two unicorns turned and walked through the doors to the courtyard. The company all agreed to food immediately. "Great! I'll let Morning Breeze know we will have more eating with us tonight. She'll be happy. She loves having guests. You'll love the food, I'm sure."

With that, the Empress gently placed the cat on the floor, watched him bound away, and then turned on her heel toward the kitchen supposedly. Then, abruptly, she stopped and turned back, "I'm sorry, I'm so rude. Let me show you to your rooms. You'll stay the night, right? It's getting too late to keep traveling. And I would love to talk. We never have visitors. At least, all the years

I've been here there haven't been many."

The company agreed happily to stay. Beds sounded heavenly, and maybe they could pick Jadelin's thoughts to see if she could help them find the next element. She smiled at their enthusiastic acceptance and led them back to the foyer and up the marble staircase to the second floor. Down the hall to the left, she pointed out small but elegantly decorated rooms for each one of them.

"And don't worry about standing guard here. You're safe. Hard Flame always has a couple of his warriors on duty outside the palace and plenty more outside the wall." Jadelin smiled comfortingly, seeming to guess they were in dire need of a good night's sleep.

The company all sighed simultaneously, relieved upon hearing this. Then, the Empress left them to themselves, saying she would have hot water and supplies sent up for baths. They thanked her profusely.

CHAPTER THIRTY-TWO

"Stop telling us not to call you empress," Prince Alkin gently chided Jadelin later that evening, after the company had washed and eaten.

They were sitting relaxed in front of the hearth in the great room. Everyone was spread out in a plush chair or settee, while Eelyne nosed through the library. Warkan was bobbing off to sleep in his chair—this was after he had finally stopped ogling Jadelin. Alkin and the Empress shared a settee since they were talking the most. Hazerk sat on the other side of the Empress, listening politely, and the two unicorns lay curled up on a soft rug in front of the hearth.

Alexa reclined nonchalantly and in silence, daydreaming on a chaise lounge nearest to Sword Bryan, who sat in a high-backed chair. He had hardly spoken a word all evening. And though he looked comfortable, he sat with his usual stoic poise. He still held his empty mug of ale in his hand.

They had all indulged in a drink and were now at ease for the first time in a long time. Among them, Kheane was the most aloof of the company. He sat in the farthest chair from the Empress, still wrapped in his cloak and never speaking a word to her or anyone else.

"Just plainly your stature, place of residence, and the affection your people show you, prove that you are indeed their empress," Alkin finished his mild scolding.

Jadelin shrugged, "I suppose so. I don't feel that way, though." She smiled, gently brushing off the Prince's assertion.

The company had warmed up to Jadelin and her people, feeling welcomed and comfortable with her. They had already revealed parts of their mission to her in hopes she or her subjects had any helpful information. However, unfortunately, she couldn't think of anything right off that might help them. Though, she promised she would speak to some of the higher-ranking mystical creatures in the morning. She was certain there was something she wasn't thinking of that may be of use to the company. She seemed pleased to be confided in and appealed to for assistance as well as horrified by the reason for their mission. Alexa noted she was sincere through and through, a rare and gentle person.

Alexa pondered Kheane while she lounged, her back warmed by the coals in the fireplace. Why hadn't he said anything to the Empress? He was without a doubt thrilled at the company's serendipitous meeting with his old companion. After all, he had said he was searching for her, wishing to find the woman he loved alive. And here she was, whole and beautiful beyond what he probably remembered, benevolent and regal. Why didn't he reveal himself? Did he worry she wouldn't remember him? With all the time lost, did he think she now loved another? He couldn't think that. It was apparent that Jadelin didn't have a lover, for she kept too close of a relationship with Estella, always stroking the unicorn's silky mane and patting her fondly. Perhaps she should say something to help push Kheane to reveal himself. Alexa never thought of herself as a matchmaker of any kind, but this match had already been made centuries before. It just needed a little nudge to start where it had left off. Right? Nevertheless, she thought better of it. Kheane was choosing, for some reason, not to say anything. The situation was better left up to him since he was the one involved.

Eyes closed and leaning back on the chaise lounge, pretending to dose, Alexa sensed out Kheane's mood, hoping to get a grasp on his hesitance. Maybe he was just biding his time. Her brow furrowed as she caught hold of his anxious mood. Outside, he was calm and as composed as ever, but inside he was a bundle of knotted emotions. Worry, fear, regret, anger, and sadness all tangled within his core, but he was also happy and so full of love for her. Alexa knew he wouldn't be able to keep himself from speaking to her. She couldn't bring herself to imagine what the ex-assassin was going through. He had spent centuries in bloodlust, while Jadelin had spent centuries in pure innocence, hidden away here in this paradise. How could they compare? How could they be compatible? Feeling his pain all too much, Alexa detached her senses from the heartbreaking scene taking place inside the always confident Kheane. She opened her eyes and stole a quick glance at the ex-assassin slumped in his chair. His eyes darted over at her, but she couldn't read his thoughts from the outside, his eyes keenly guarded. She looked away, feeling empathy.

Uninterested in the conversation taking place, she yawned, not bothering to hide it. Bryan looked at her from the corner of his eye, his lips twitching ever-so-slightly into a crooked smile. She stared back at him from the corner of her eye. Then he broke his silence, interrupting the Prince and Jadelin, "We should get some rest." They looked at him a bit surprised, but accordingly.

"Yes, well, I suppose I forgot that you all have been traveling a long time and must be frightfully tired. I just got caught up in the pleasure of finally having some company. Please forgive my rudeness!" Jadelin smiled, somewhat ashamed.

"You have been nothing but kind, dear lady. But my company has a job they must commit to in the morning. We have to keep plugging forward," the Master Sword said, with a protective glance at Alexa.

Alexa turned away and made a disgruntled face. Bryan was acting more and more like a mother hen to her than anything else. Staring at his handsome features dimly lit in the flickering light of the fire, she wondered if he would ever be anything more to her than her Sword-Guard—or, rather, that *she would* be anything more *to him* other than something he was required to watch over. She sighed and clambered to her feet when he stood to leave.

Jadelin broke through Alexa's despondent thoughts as the company gathered into the foyer to go upstairs. She addressed Kheane directly, "You've been silent all night. Is there anything I can get you to make your stay more comfortable?" She stood but a few steps from him, holding her hands out in appeal.

Halting only his step, Kheane didn't let a heartbeat go by before he replied huskily, "No, I'm fine."

The Empress paused, trying to study his eyes deep within his hood. "Oh, well then, can I take your cloak? It's Kheane, right? You must be roasting; it isn't really needed." She regarded the rest of the company, "In fact, how about once you all get upstairs, you can lie out your clothing, and I'll have them washed for you by morning."

"Yes, thank you. That would be kind of you, Jadelin." Alkin gave her a grateful smile.

Jadelin led the company up the stairs, lifting her pink satin gown slightly so she wouldn't trip on the hem as she ascended the marble stairway. Alexa overheard her whisper to Alkin, "Your friend Kheane prefers to be alone, doesn't he? He seems unconcerned with trivial society."

"He likes to keep to himself." Alkin hesitated, looking for the right words. "He's been self-employed, working alone for centuries. He's only now joining back into society; well, just our company. I'm sure there's a lot he must adjust to." They reached the top of the stairway and stopped in the hall.

"Centuries?" The Empress suddenly seemed very interested, her eyes probing.

"Yes. He's of old Alidonian blood," Alkin replied.

"What? So am I!" she exclaimed.

Alexa smiled, knowing this was the revealing point. She glanced back at Kheane as the rest of the company filed awkwardly around to see why Jadelin was so ecstatic.

"Really?" Alkin replied, surprised. "Jadelin is of old Alidonian blood," he explained to the puzzled company.

Alexa watched as each face in the company turned from puzzled to surprised and then to awareness. She didn't have to sense out their feelings to know they were all wondering if this was the woman Kheane had been searching for.

Kheane peaked the stairs last. He seemed not to be paying any attention to the fervent conversation taking place. But Alexa knew better, he wasn't called the Cold Wolf for nothing. He had heard everything, though he still kept his aloof façade. He looked up and locked eyes with the Empress' eager ones. Her hands were clasped together like a child waiting for a present, but his coffee-colored eyes held no emotion and were still guarded heavily.

"You're Alidonian?" Jadelin said, a light in her eyes.

Alexa's brow wrinkled in puzzlement as she realized Jadelin still didn't know who Kheane was. *Maybe she doesn't remember him!*

"Yes, Jadelin, I am," Kheane answered in his low, raspy tone.

The given empress studied his face longer, lingering on his

eyes, trying to imagine the rest of his face within the depths of the
hood. Then, suddenly, with no apparent cause, the beautiful
woman began to tremble from head to toe. Her hands, still clasped,
were held tightly in front of her, bobbing with the shudders. Her
topaz eyes became full of emotion and her mouth clenched as if
she were in pain. The company all gasped and took an obliging
step toward her, thinking she was having a fit of some sort.

"Jadelin? Jadelin, are you okay?" Prince Alkin was at her side,
touching her on the arm.

"It-it's y-you," she stuttered through her teeth. The violent
shakes of her body racked her like she had been left out in a
blizzard.

Kheane, who was the only one of the company not put at
unease by her sudden fit, merely continued to watch her with his
intense gaze.

"Yes," he finally said after a moment. The company all looked
around, slightly confused.

"Are you frightened of him?" Alkin asked. "Do you know
what he is?" Alkin was referring to Kheane being a notorious
assassin. "He won't hurt you. I promise. He's with us."

Jadelin continued to shake, unable to control herself; her long,
sunshine-blonde curls waved with the movement, and her
porcelain skin flushed pink. "No, no." She fought to gain control
of herself and waved the Prince's administering hand away,
ignoring him. Her eyes were only for Kheane. "Oh, Tol—"

"Jade," Kheane cut her off quietly, "that's no longer my
name." He alone seemed to understand the Empress' fit and saw
that it wasn't fear, but out of utter happiness and shock that she
shook.

"Oh!" she exclaimed and flung herself across the space
between them and into his arms, where he awkwardly held her
shaking figure.

The company took in a breath of understanding. No one said a
word while Kheane clumsily patted Jadelin's back while she
clutched him, her head on his shoulder. They weren't a part of this.
They eyed each other.

"We'll leave the two of you. It has been…a long time for you.

More than a few lifetimes of ours. You have plenty to talk about, I'm certain," Alkin finally said.

Jadelin pulled away, tears streaming down her face, and nodded gratefully to the Prince, smiling all the while. "Thank you."

With that, the company left for their rooms. They each paused briefly to watch the two head down the hall side by side toward the door leading onto the balcony.

Alexa stopped at the threshold of her room. She rested her hand on the doorframe, a thoughtful and perhaps wistful look on her face as her eyes followed the two reunited loves. She didn't notice the Master Sword standing but a hair's breadth behind her, watching them as she. After a moment, she comprehended his close presence. She peeked over her shoulder to peer up at him. He gazed at her with such an unfamiliar look in his eyes, it caught her off guard and she couldn't help but let a startled, puzzled look come across her features. She slid through the door and turned around to study him as he hesitated in the threshold, still watching her in the same way.

She came to a quick conclusion as to what the look was. It was uncertainty, with a vague hint of…aching or longing, perhaps? A moment passed, and Bryan didn't speak a word. His brow furrowed as if he seemed to be pondering exactly what it was he wanted to say. She waited with her heart in her throat. This look he was bestowing on her was completely new.

"Alexa," he began.

"Yes." She looked up expectantly from where she had tried to occupy herself with unbuckling her dagger with fumbling fingers. At this, a neutral look stole across the Master Sword's face, confirming a change of mind.

"I'll…be in the room across the hall if you need me. Good night."

"Yes, I know that, Master Sword," she said, trying to conceal her disappointment. He nodded and hurriedly closed the door. "Good night, Bryrunan," she sighed to the shut door. She turned to undress for bed, her heart now in her stomach.

★★★★

Kheane's dark heart had literally almost pumped out of his chest when he had recognized Jadelin on the terrace. It wasn't hard to recognize her; although, she was more beautiful than he remembered. How could it be that he could search for her for centuries, only to find her when he had finally given up? She had become such an obsession with him. She was always something there in the back of his mind, never real, really. Her memory had kept him going. Somehow, he had hung on to the belief she was still alive. At least, that's what he had told himself to get through all the horrible, endless, bloody nights and days. The memory of her was something warm and good he could be comforted in. But deep down he had never really honestly allowed himself to believe she was alive. He had only fooled himself into believing it so he could get through the rest of his days. He had been simply waiting for someone to outsmart him in a fight, or for him to make a fatal wrong move that would end his pathetic existence.

Jadelin had become an unobtainable goddess to him. He held her memory high on a pedestal, embalming everything good about her in the back of his mind, preserving it so he could take it out every so often and patch up the gaping hole in his black heart. He had told himself she was alive and waiting for him just for comfort. And yet, here she was. How shocking it had been to see the very core of his obsession! She was alive, so beautiful, and so innocent…

He was a villain of the worst kind. He had no right to be even in her presence. For he saw that she truly was a goddess in her own way. He had led such a lurid, sinful life. How could she ever accept him? She would be appalled just by his mere appearance.

She hadn't changed, not really. Underneath the façade of an empress, Kheane could still see the strong, determined orphan girl that had stowed away with him. He found he still loved her; he could never stop loving her. The years apart had deepened his love so beyond its normal boundaries it was unfathomable. But with everything he had done, how could he expect for her to feel the same? If she still loved him, it would be more than he deserved. If she didn't, he would be content in knowing she was alive and happy. Yes, he would. He could die content…fulfilled.

He followed Jadelin out onto the balcony. A warm lilac-scented breeze wafted into his hood; his hot face pleasured at the touch. They walked in silence to the balcony's edge. She stopped, placing her hands on the marble railing, looking thoughtfully out at the moonlit rolling fields and the tiny village snuggled amongst the knolls. Kheane watched her as she composed herself.

"I thought I'd lost you," she finally said.

"And I, you," he replied, wishing his voice wasn't so harsh sounding. It sounded like a bear struggling to communicate. There was nothing harsh about *her*. She was so elegant and feminine. He admired the way the pale pink satin gown hugged and flowed silkily down her curves. He noted for the first time that she was barefoot and how delicate her feet and ankles were. She looked over at him with bright eyes, her sunny-blonde curls lifting in the breeze. He could barely catch the sweet scent of her on the gust.

"I never really gave up hope, though," she said, turning to face him, leaning her hip against the rail. Kheane didn't answer. She studied his dark eyes. After a moment, she added, "I remember your eyes. They are the same…once I really looked at them; I knew it was you. I've never forgotten them." Kheane blinked, a small smile reaching his eyes. She smiled back, her teeth as beautiful as pearls. "I guess I didn't recognize you at first because of, well, your hood and cloak. And you're so mysterious now, like you'd rather blend into the wall…but you recognized me right away, didn't you?"

"Yes," he said, inwardly cursing his voice again. She nodded, eyeing him carefully. She didn't speak for a few moments but merely continued to study him. Finally, Kheane spoke, "I searched for you. I looked for days. I thought the storm had taken you…"

She leaned against the rail with her back toward the fields. She crossed her arms, her mouth forming a frown. "I tried to stay with you in the storm, but the waves were too strong for me. I managed to find a piece of jetsam and climbed on. I called for you, but it was no use. Eventually, I floated to shore. I was sick, barely able to move. That's when Estella found me. I don't know why a unicorn would have mercy on a stranger. But she did. She brought me here. And the rest of the creatures took to me kindly. I was very lucky."

She locked eyes with his. "I never forgot you. You were imprinted so deep on my soul. I couldn't forget you. I fretted over losing you, over not knowing if you were alive and okay, over leaving—abandoning you. But the creatures here loved me and claimed I was safer here, and the chances of finding you were close to none. I'm sorry I failed you." Her topaz eyes fell to the floor in remorse, and she hugged herself as if to comfort a pain inside.

"Don't blame yourself. It was uncontrollable circumstances that took us apart. I thought of you every day. It was good that you were here, safe, away from where I was. I haven't led a life I'm proud of. You're better off without that past," Kheane consoled softly.

She looked up. "You say you thought of me."

"Yes. It kept me sane."

"I have waited for you... I have loved you," she whispered. Her eyes held an intense longing, but it was imprisoned in the pain of all the lonely years. Kheane could see this; he knew it himself. She went to wrap her arms around him, and said, "I still love you, my dearest Tol—"

"You shouldn't. Don't call me that," he cut her off, and she stopped, hurt flooding into her eyes.

"You don't love me?" Her gentle face was scrunched in pain and misunderstanding.

"I love you." He couldn't lie, and she flashed him a brilliant smile, the pain vanishing from her face.

"Then let's not be sad any longer. Come here," she pleaded.

"Jade, I'm not the same person. I've done terrible things. You shouldn't even know of them, they are so vile. I'm torn from the inside out, right down to my soul. I don't think there is any way to salvage myself. You couldn't love someone like me."

Jadelin shook her head in disagreement. "You don't believe I should love you, but you still love me. That is something. I don't care what you've done. I will always love you unconditionally."

Kheane shook his head sadly. "You don't—"

"No," she cut him off, an uncharacteristic edge to her voice. "No. *You* don't." Her countenance softened when he looked up to lock eyes with her. She took his hands in hers and said with fervor,

"If I were in your place and you were in mine, would you care for me any less?"

Kheane smiled, his coffee-colored eyes alight, "No."

She returned his smile. "Let's marry. Tomorrow."

"Okay," he simply replied, but his eyes sparkled with a new hope. His heart felt so light, and his soul suddenly was whole again. The gaping hole in it was being filled in. He looked at her longingly. She reached up and gently touched the tip of the scar at the crease in the corner of his eye. She started to remove his obscuring hood. "I don't know if you want to see what's underneath…" he said.

"I've been longing to see this face for centuries." She pushed his hood down.

Kheane waited for her petrified gasp, but she didn't show any emotion at all, except maybe pain, pain for his pain. Her elegant brow furrowed as she traced the reddish scars seared across the left side of his face. Her fingers gently ran down the large, ugly, purple scar from his right eye to his disfigured lips and rested there as she pondered the cause of such a wound. Her eyes lingered on his disfigured nose.

Kheane gently wrapped his fingers around her wrist. She looked back into his eyes; his yearning feelings were mirrored in her face. He hadn't had someone touch him so gently, so lovingly in such a long time. It was an old, comforting feeling, almost nostalgic—one that he longed never to stop. He reached out and touched her soft, porcelain skin, taking her face in his calloused hands. Her big topaz-colored eyes beckoned to his heart and tugged at it in a way nothing ever had. Suddenly, his lips were on hers. She met him with just as much fervor. Her lips were soft and warm. His must feel so coarse and twisted with scarred tissue, but she didn't seem to mind. He was complete with her in his arms, and he didn't doubt she felt the same. He pulled her gently toward himself by the small of her back. She didn't need much encouragement. She wrapped herself around him as snug, as close, as she could get.

"Be near me always," she whispered into his mouth.

He nodded, his mouth busy with the kisses he had longed to give her for centuries. She pulled back all too soon, and he reached for her a bit desperately, not wanting her warmth or healing ever to leave him.

"I ache for you, knowing you've been through so much pain." She gently tugged at his cloak.

"It only gets worse." He gave a coarse laugh. But he removed his cloak, and Jadelin took him in with eyes filled with sorrow.

She took his scarred arms in her small hands, turning his left wrist around to study the bloodied-mouth wolf tattooed on the inside of his forearm. He watched her as she traced the lines of the wolf's head with the tips of her fingers, deep in thought, a frown on her pretty face. She took his other arm and studied the burn wounds that traveled up his elbow and disappeared into his shirt. He watched her reaction, carefully discerning her troubled features. She tugged at his shirt. He sighed and removed it. She covered her mouth as her fears were confirmed. The scar beginning from his right eye traveled all the way down his chin to his torso where it was only one of many scars seared across his muscled chest. The burn wound crawled up his arm and over his shoulder and covered half his back, connecting to more wounds twisting around each other to form some sadistic design buried in his skin. They continued down past the waistband of his trousers.

"See?" he commented, noting her horrified face.

She circled him, trailing her hands over his rough skin. When she came around to face him, she gazed into his eyes with sympathy. "I wish I could have saved you from all the painful things you've been through," she breathed, tears enhancing her watery blue eyes.

Kheane shook his head and smiled, "You have. The worst pain was only that I couldn't be with you."

"I have scars from that, too."

Their lips met once more, and they didn't stop this time.

Chapter Thirty-Three

I t was a good dream. But it was only a dream, too bad because it was a really good one. One that Alexa didn't want to rouse and leave behind to the night. She wanted to keep the story going; it was so pleasant, and he was so handsome... But there was this annoying clunking sound that kept interrupting what he was trying to say to her. Every time he opened his mouth to speak, *clunk, clunk*, was his voice. It didn't make sense. What was he trying to say?

She tossed agitatedly in her half-state of sleep, her brow scrunching in frustration as she fought to keep the dream alive a bit longer. *Clunk, clunk.* She groused in her pillow as she flipped around. *Ah.* The bed was so soft. The softest she had ever had the pleasure of sleeping on. The blankets were so cozy, and her toes were toasty warm, unlike so many nights she had spent shivering on the hard ground in the forest. *Clunk, clunk.* She buried her head into the down pillow, finally waking to consciousness. She flipped over on her back and glared at the closed door where the annoying sound came from. What could the Master Sword possibly want at this hour? *I thought we'd be able to sleep in a bit today.* She groaned and turned over. "Go...a...way...Brry-roo-nan," she mumbled into her pillow with no intent for him to hear. The door creaked open; she ignored it. "What is it, Master Sword?" she groused, louder this time.

"It's me, dearie," a female voice said. Alexa sat up abruptly and rubbed the sleep from her eyes, peering at the doorway to see the centaur Morning Breeze's head peeking in. "Your Head-Master Sword says it's time to rise!" she said brightly.

"So early?" She attempted to clear the fuzzy sleep from her brain but was unwilling to forget her dream.

"Early?" Morning Breeze chuckled, "It's nearly mid-day. You were the only one he let sleep in, dear." She laughed again, her voice like pleasant silver bells.

Alexa raised her eyebrows in surprise, "Oh." She fumbled with the covers as she rose.

Morning Breeze pushed through the door, easily fitting her petite equine body through, and it dawned on Alexa that all the palace doorways were built larger to accommodate the centaurs. She carried a tray of food. It looked like hotcakes.

Alexa's stomach grumbled. "Mmm," she said in appreciation.

"Yes, breakfast. The others have already eaten." She set the tray down at the small desk next to the bed.

Alexa glanced around the room. Pulling at her nightgown, she asked, "Where are my clothes?"

"They're being washed and mended."

"What am I supposed to wear?"

"We have something for you. Don't you worry, dear." Morning Breeze turned her dappled-gray body around, nearly swishing her long, silver tail in Alexa's face when she turned for the door. Once she was through, she had to turn all the way around again to face her. *How awkward*, Alexa observed as she pulled out the chair to the desk and plopped down.

The centaur poked her white-blonde head through the doorway, "Oh, and do hurry with breakfast. We have to get you ready for the wedding. I'm preparing a bath for you now."

Alexa gulped a piece of hotcake down. Staring, befuddled, she said, "Wedding?"

"Yes, the ceremony starts at twilight. Prince Alkin is marrying Kheane and Empress Jadelin. You're to be an honored guest. Now hurry, dear, we have lots to do. To plan a whole wedding in one day!" The friendly centaur threw up her hands as if exasperated; though, she looked excited. "Enjoy." She closed the door.

"Humph," Alexa mumbled to herself as she jammed the scrumptious hotcakes in her mouth. So, Kheane and Jadelin were getting married. How nice. She was honestly happy for them; she was just never one to get overly excited about celebrations such as this. Her main concern was whether Kheane would still continue on with the company. She hoped so. They definitely could use him. She would hate to lose him for the missions' sake…and hers; she enjoyed his flinty company. And she couldn't imagine the elegant Jadelin coming along either. She chuckled at the thought.

Just a few minutes later, there was another knock. She had

finished up her hotcakes and was gulping down her orange juice, something she had never had before, but found it delectable.

"Yes," she answered.

"It's me again, dear," Morning Breeze said as she opened the door. "Are you ready for your bath? We have to size you for your gown, too."

"Gown?" Alexa looked horrified.

"Yes, come on." The centaur beckoned her.

Alexa poked her head out the door to see if the hall was clear. It was. She skipped out, still in her nightgown. Morning Breeze took her wrist and practically drug her down the hall to the bathing room.

"This is going to be fun," the centaur gloated with a broad smile. Alexa stared at her with wide, dubious eyes.

Morning Breeze nearly shoved her through the door, following unnecessarily close behind. Alexa spotted a big tub in the center of the large, circular room, along with two other female centaurs. One was a dark chestnut with long, wavy strawberry-colored hair tied back from her face. The other was a soft, smoky black, with dark hair and black jeweled eyes. She smiled, her pearly teeth standing out prettily.

Like Morning Breeze, all the female centaurs wore corsets to cover their chests. The fashion style was a little racy for Alexa's own personal taste, but the lady centaurs with their elegant human torsos and ample busts pulled it off in a very lovely way. Like all females, they each had their own favorite style of corset and colors they preferred. In fact, the dark chestnut centaur was wearing fingerless gloves that came to her elbows. At this, Alexa found herself oddly contemplating centaur fashions. *I wonder what they do for the winter... jackets... or maybe cloaks that fit their human half but also cover their body like a horse blanket...*

"This is Molasses Tang and Thunder Lily." Morning Breeze interrupted her thoughts. "But you can call them Lass and Lily. Lass is going to measure you, and Lily will help you with all the beautification." Morning Breeze smiled, giving the frozen Alexa a gentle push on the back toward Lass.

"Hello," she said to Lass as the centaur promptly began measuring her figure. Lass smiled in response and stared thoughtfully at Alexa's eyes.

"Hmm, what do you think? I say cobalt. A satin A-line that flows gently down her frame. She is so slender it will complement her perfectly. I think that would be best. Or do you think lavender, Breezie?" Lass asked.

Morning Breeze came over to study Alexa's frame, eye, and hair color. Alexa stared blankly at them, feeling like a horse at auction. *How ironic*, she joked good-naturedly to herself.

"Hmm, I think you're correct with the blue," Morning Breeze said. "Her eyes will glow."

"Right. I'll get started." Lass gave Alexa a gleeful smile and then went directly to a pile of fabric in the corner of the room and began rummaging through it.

Before she could compose her thoughts, someone tugged at her nightgown. Thunder Lily was attempting to undress her. "Hey, um, I can do that myself." She laughed, but there was a hint of appall in her voice she couldn't hide.

"Don't be silly." Lily chuckled.

"Well, I'm off. I have lots to do," Morning Breeze announced. She then trotted out the door, snapping it shut behind her.

"Come on. Off with it," Lily demanded, tugging the nightdress over Alexa's head.

Feeling very much exposed and a little embarrassed at the brash immodesty, Alexa attempted to cover herself.

"Oh, my!" Lily gasped.

"What?" she shot in defense and tried to hide behind the flimsy fabric of the nightgown.

"What in Carthorn! Were you with child?" Lily exclaimed, catching Lass' abrupt attention. The centaur clopped curiously over.

Alexa stared flabbergasted at the two for a moment before she realized what they were talking about. "Oh!" She laughed, "No! I had a knife injury." She took down her protective covering and traced the thick, white scar across her abdomen with her fingers, recalling the intense pain. It still ached at times. After all, it hadn't happened *that* long ago.

"Oh. Well, it gave me a fright. That must have been painful!"

Lily seemed to brush off the shock quickly and began pulling her toward the tub. Lass went back to her sewing.

"I *am* capable of bathing myself," Alexa said as she immersed herself in the warm water. She sunk up to her neck and gave a sigh of pleasure. Lily tugged at her tangled hair, pulling out her long braid and what felt like some hairs, too.

"Yes, yes, of course," Lily merely replied, then poured water on Alexa's head.

Alexa shrugged her shoulders. If they wanted a doll to play with for the day, she supposed she could comply. So, she finally surrendered to their will and allowed them to tug and pull her around for the rest of the afternoon, cleaning and preening her.

She hoped this whole ordeal was part of the company's plans. She had thought they were supposed to be discussing their next mission. Alexa smiled, imagining the Master Sword's agitated face as he was forced to take part in this ceremonial event.

A despondent sigh escaped her at the thought of him. Somehow, she had to extract him from her mind. At present, she was sure he felt something for her. His off demeanor last night had proved it. She could tell it, too, by using her senses. His bitterness was gone, and she could sense at least a fondness for her. But she couldn't discern more than that. He was a puzzling man, composed even on the inside. For some reason, he was fighting his feelings. Thus, it meant he did not *want* to feel that way for her. So, she had to *not* feel that way for him. It just couldn't be. They were worlds apart. He was the Head-Master Sword of Shelkite, and she was merely a foreign commoner. That was the way it was. She sighed unhappily. Oh, but she was losing control of herself! And, unfortunately, she knew it wasn't a fleeting, girlish infatuation. At this point, Alexa could admit she was certainly and so very inconveniently in love with the Master Sword...

★★★★

Dusk arrived. The stars appeared in the smoky purple sky, and a silvery-white crescent moon rose as the last colorful rays of the sun streaked over the treetops on the horizon. A warm breeze whispered through the branches of the lilacs and scented the air pleasantly. The wedding guests all gathered on the lawn of the palace. The guests, of course, were all the creatures of the kingdom. Excitement reverberated in the atmosphere. The creatures were happy their empress had found a husband and were gentle enough to accept him, whoever he was, without hesitation into their kingdom.

Bryan paced restively, waiting for the ceremony to begin. He and the other warriors were all attired in new suits for the occasion. The centaurs had worked tirelessly all morning and through the afternoon to make sure everything was perfect for their empress' wedding. That included making sure the guests were presentable.

The Master Sword never really cared for events like this. But, being a Sword, he was often required to attend these kinds of things. And here, he didn't have much of a choice. He looked over at Prince Alkin, who was waiting in front of the crowd under an arbor laced intricately with flowers and ivy. He looked quite happy, as usual. But the Prince was brought up in this type of lifestyle. It was no bother to him.

Bryan waited at the end of the aisle that had been created through the center of the crowd. It was decorated with white flower petals. The other warriors were already standing by the arbor where the ceremony was to take place. Bryan preferred to wait here for Alexa. He hadn't seen her all day. Being parted from his main obligation put his already annoyed nerves on edge. He had to admit he felt kind of useless without her around to protect. He held his hand on the hilt of his sword as he paced back and forth, staring at his shined boots. It suddenly occurred to him—was that *really* the only reason he felt on edge? Or was he just telling himself that? He came to a halt and glared down at the blades of grass.

New, excited voices caught his attention and jerked him out of his confused thoughts. He looked up and saw two female centaurs conversing excitedly and making their way toward the party. He looked beyond and spotted a human figure trailing them slowly. An unexpected smile crept over his lips as he recognized her. He couldn't help but wonder at his increased heart rate. He tried to suppress it.

Alexa was nearing the crowd, walking in her normal Alexa-type stride, but she was making an attempt at being more graceful; he could tell. His mouth crooked into a smile when she stopped in front of him, giving him a brief, pained look. He raised an eyebrow at her, and she gave him a smug look for a moment before bestowing a radiant smile on him. His breath caught in his throat, and he quickly chided himself. He couldn't help admiring her, as breathtaking as she was to him. Why not? What was the harm in only admiring her?

Her dress flattered her slender figure. It was shiny cobalt, made of sinuous satin. It flowed down her body in a long wave, rippling like blue flames when she shifted her weight. The hem kissed the ground and a short train trailed her. The sleeves were capped and off the shoulders with only a touch of ruffle. The bodice of the gown scooped down low, enhancing the hollow between her humble bust. His eyes lingered there for but a mere second before he raised them to admire the rest of her. He vaguely remembered wishing at one time what she would look like with her hair down. He realized he had gotten his wish. Her raven hair fell to her waist, straight and shiny, and looked as if it might slide like silk between his fingers. The centaurs had pulled some locks softly away from her face and braided them in small, intricate plaits, twisting them around each other in a pleasing design. Snuggled amongst the tiny plaits were small, white blossoms that, when she wasn't looking, he breathed in the scent and discovered they were lilacs. Finally, he let his eyes wander over her face. Her dainty, angular features were rosy—but her cheeks were always rosy. He fondly eyed the light freckles sprinkled across her nose. Her lips were full and pleasingly soft looking, as always. Little wisps of hair had loosened and danced around her brow, and he found himself resisting the urge to brush them from her eyes. Her eyes. His eyes paused there the longest. They shone like two fiery-blue beacons in the night and sparkled like jewels in the sun. Although he had been the victim many times of those bewitching sapphire orbs, he actually stopped breathing for a moment, and realized it only when he sucked in a breath of much-needed oxygen, which in turn made him feel uncomfortable; for she gave him a self-satisfied grin, noting his brief ogling, he was sure. He cleared his throat and pulled himself together, allowing himself only those few brief moments to look at her as a woman and not his ward. Everything was right again, now that she was back under his watchful eye.

"Ready to get this over with, Sand Queen?" He gestured down the aisle toward the rest of the warriors gazing at her expectantly.

"Sure thing, my dearest Sword-Guard," she said with only the slightest touch of mockery in her voice. It had that bitter chocolate sound to it. Something he found he was partial to. She started down the aisle, smiling widely at the creatures greeting her along the way. He walked just a pace behind her, laying his palm ever-so-softly on the small of her back, guiding her down.

"Oh, I almost forgot. I need to tell you we've an idea where to find the fire element," he said off-handedly.

As he expected, she came to a screeching halt and went to whip around to face him. But his hand on the small of her back pressed more firmly and caused her to keep moving toward the front of the crowd full of mystical creatures.

Straining from his push for only a breath, she gave in and kept walking, but whispered fervently, "When did you discover this?"

"Hard Flame gathered all the inhabitants this morning, and we had a conference," he whispered in her ear, bending so close he could smell the intoxicating scent of her. He distantly wished he could just stay there...smelling her forever. How juvenile!

"Without me?"

"I thought you could use some extra rest, with everything you've been through...right? Do you feel better?"

He must have caught her off guard with his unusual consideration, for she paused before answering, "Yes. It was nice. Thank you..." She trailed off but then added eagerly, "So? Where is it?"

He didn't answer immediately, and they came to a halt at the front of the crowd, taking their place next to Warkan, Hazerk, and Eelyne. Kheane and the Prince stood under the arbor, speaking in low tones, Kheane without his concealing cloak tonight.

The warriors surrounded Alexa, and Bryan rolled his eyes in exasperation as they all fought for her attention.

"You look beautiful!" Eelyne's brown eyes sparkled as he

boldly admired her figure in a friendly way.

"Gorgeous, I say, Lil' Sis'." Hazerk gave her bare shoulders a squeeze and a platonic kiss on her brow. Nonetheless, she blushed at his sentiments.

"Wow! You're a girl?" Warkan marveled. Alexa laughed and punched him on the arm; the austere-faced warrior actually laughed in return.

Alkin caught her eye and gave her a wink. She smiled shyly back, and Bryan watched with irritation as the Prince's interested gaze lingered on her longer than necessary.

The crowd hushed as the ceremony was on the verge of starting. But Alexa's attention wasn't deterred for long. She turned to the Master Sword and said earnestly, "So? Tell me."

"Well." He tried to control an idiotic grin from forming on his face for having the chance to bend his head closer to her and whisper once more in her ear. "They almost immediately thought of a place only a day's travel from here, luckily. It's an ancient ruin. It's fabled that an eternal flame deriving from the center of the earth comes out there. An old fortress is built around it, from who knows when. The flame is said to be in caverns beneath."

Being as close to her as he was, he could easily sense the tremor of anticipation zip through her body. She whipped her head to look at him and nearly knocked foreheads with him, but she didn't seem to mind the close quarters, and the Master Sword didn't feel inclined to back up. They stared into each other's eyes, seeming to dare the other to move back a fraction of an inch.

"And the Keepers?" she whispered, her appealing lips barely moving.

"Dragons—supposedly," he replied. He could see the wheels turning beyond her sparkling sapphire eyes as she stared at him but did not *look* at him, her mind miles away.

"The plan?" she finally said, now looking at him.

"Working on that one." His brow furrowed. How could they go up against a dragon?

"I say we wing it."

"You *would* just go in head-on." He sighed, fighting the urge to roll his eyes. Her eyes narrowed, but she gave him a crooked smile.

"Well—"

He cut her off with a finger pressed to his lips, signaling that the ceremony had begun. The Empress had already started down the aisle. Alexa backed away from him as if she had realized there was no reason to be standing so close to him, and he suddenly felt colder.

Distracting his mind, he turned to watch the pretty Jadelin walk toward Kheane. The bride smiled brilliantly. No one person ever looked so happy. Bryan glanced at Kheane and was nearly frightened to see him grinning back at her. It was almost discomforting. He couldn't say why. It wasn't because the ex-assassin's face was maimed. It was probably because a smiling assassin just didn't seem to make sense.

Bryan sighed as the ceremonial vows began. Hopefully, it would be short, and they could move on to the food and drinks part of this celebration.

Later, Alexa bit on a fingernail as she eyed Jadelin from across the lawn. The formal ceremony was over, and all the creatures were mingling, eating, and drinking. They had set up tall torches intermittently in the yard to light up the area; it made it all very cozy. They were the most pleasant and accepting group of people Alexa had been around, more so than some humans she had met. Many of the creatures had started several fun games and had beseeched her and the other warriors to join them, but she declined politely, fearing she would make a fool of herself in the silly gown she was sporting. Right now, for some reason, she was more concerned with how beautiful Jadelin was with her long, sunshine-blonde, wavy locks and elegant, curvy figure, and how plain *she* felt compared to the other woman. But more importantly, why did it matter? Jadelin was married to Kheane. She shouldn't be concerned with what the other men in her company thought of the dazzling empress, meaning whether or not they found her attractive. Alexa just felt strangely possessive of *her* company, of *her* men. She rolled her eyes at her childish thoughts.

The Empress did, without a doubt, look like the epitome of beauty. She wore a cream satin gown with a short train, longer than the one on Alexa's own dress, but still short. Her hair was down and wavy, much longer than Alexa's hair. She wore a garland of blue flowers on her head, and her eyes were the most unique color of blue topaz. Her soft, pale skin was flushed a pretty attractive pink. Her gown had long sleeves but was cut low and flattered her ample bosom. Alexa looked down at her own bosom. She had been surprised at how Lass and Lily had somehow boosted her own humble bust up to make it look half-way luscious. She straightened her shoulders and tried to stand up straighter, sticking out her chest. Someone tapped her on the shoulder. Mortified and hoping that whoever it was hadn't seen what she'd been doing, she spun around and almost knocked poor Prince Alkin's drink out of his hands.

"Whoa, there. Sorry, didn't mean to startle you," he said, a grin on his face.

She smiled awkwardly, wondering if he had noticed her girly fussing. "Oh, no, it's fine." She found her composure.

"Take a walk with me." He gestured toward the path twisting through the courtyard.

"Sure." She shrugged. He held out his arm, and she took it. Well, at least she took it in the way she thought she was supposed to. She had never been taught courtly manners. She was sure the Prince knew this, so she didn't fret over it. He led her down the path and out of the light of the party. They walked silently along the flagged-stoned path for a few minutes before he spoke first.

"The Master Sword tell you about the fire element?" he asked.

"Yes. I've a good feeling."

"A good feeling about dragons?" He laughed, his hazel eyes twinkling.

"Well...I did..." She grinned idiotically back at him; she couldn't help herself. He just drew forth the happiness out of people. It was hard to ignore. He chuckled at her and glanced over his shoulder to peer at something. She followed his gaze. He was looking at Apollos and Estella. They were playing a game of tag or the like with each other in the open field.

"I'm so happy he's found a mate," Alkin said, but he sounded almost sad.

She turned to study the Prince's handsome face. "You're

worried he won't come back to Shelkite?"

Alkin gave her a half-smile wreathed with gloom. "Yes."

"I can understand the loss. He's an exquisite creature and a good friend. I owe him my life," she replied, suddenly feeling what it would be like to be forced to separate from the company someday and go her own way. She shook her head. She couldn't think of that right now. She was so attached to them all.

They circled the fountain and began walking toward the front terrace. They ascended the steps and came to the railing to stop and watch the festivities. "Did Apollos ever tell you his story?" Alkin asked.

"No. I guess he hasn't," Alexa realized.

"Well, I guess there's not much to it. But when he was a colt, he was part of a small herd. He got separated from them one day. He was still young enough that his powers hadn't manifested yet, and he was captured. He was forced to be on display in a circus. This was still before he got his powers, mind you, so he wasn't able to help himself escape. But, one day, a prince of Shelkite came along, my ancestor, and had pity on him and paid for his freedom. Apollos went to find his herd. But he was unable to find any other unicorn, let alone his herd. They'd been slaughtered. So, he went to Shelkite and made it his home. He's served willingly under Shelkite rule ever since. He's my closest companion. I trust him more than anyone, more than my sister, more than the Head-Master Sword, and I trust them more than myself." He smiled.

Alexa looked fondly at the Prince, unsure what to say. Then she said, "I'm sure he'll be able to balance the time between his new love and his duty." She smiled, and Alkin grinned back. He leaned casually against the rail, putting aside any princely demeanor. Alexa leaned her elbows on the railing, still smiling at him, unable to remove her eyes from his hazel ones.

"You're a unique young woman, Alexandra," he said, gazing at her. "I'm glad I've had the pleasure to meet you, travel, and work with you."

She smiled even wider, soaring gleefully from his praise. "Thanks. Shelkite is a lucky country to have a man such as you to rule," she said, in complete honesty. He gave her a crooked smile, his eyes alight.

All of a sudden, she was very aware of how close he was to her. While they had spoken, they had moved closer, their heads bending toward one another, caught up in the conversation. How had she not noticed it two breaths before? She subconsciously leaned away, but Alkin followed her like he was attached to her by a string. She then realized what was about to happen, and her heart fluttered in panic. She stiffened in horror as the Prince leaned in and tilted his head toward her face. A couple options raced through her mind. One: she could back away; two: she could punch him. She rejected both of the options instantaneously. This was a prince! How was she able to turn down a prince without offending him? So, she held stock-still as he gently and tenderly placed his lips on hers. His lips were soft, warm, and light on her mouth. Should she kiss him back? Wouldn't it give him the opposite impression she wanted? If she didn't, would he be offended? The kiss was over before she'd made up her mind. Alkin leaned back and smiled. She returned it with a small, tentative one, her hands fidgeting.

"Come on, let's get back," he finally said. She grinned at him again, mostly relieved she would be leaving this awkward moment. "I think your Sword-Guard is wondering where you are." Alkin gestured at the Master Sword out among the partygoers. Even in the dim light, Alexa could see that Sword Bryan was staring straight at them, an impassive expression across his features. Her breath caught in her throat, and her heart beat even faster. It felt as if it might come right up her chest through her throat. Had he seen them?

Alkin led her down the stairs, back into the boisterous, partying crowd. She followed, feeling rather numb and practically frightened to meet up with her Sword-Guard. Her mind raced as she contemplated making an excuse, claiming she was sick and then running in the opposite direction of the Master Sword. First off, why did she feel this way? It wasn't like Sword Bryan had actually *said* he wanted her himself. There was no way he could be upset with her. *Get a handle on yourself, Alexandra!* she scolded herself as they came closer and closer to the Sword. Besides, she couldn't have turned down the Prince anyway...

Prince Alkin came to a stop next to his friend. They greeted each other in their casual manner, and then both seemed intent on watching a new, rowdier game unfold on the field. Alexa fidgeted uncomfortably next to the Prince. The Master Sword was standing on the other side of Alkin. He appeared to be completely oblivious to her presence.

Then, Alkin did the unthinkable and turned to her. "I'm going to speak with Kheane and Jadelin for a bit. Thank you kindly for the walk, Alexandra." He kissed her cheek and strode off eloquently toward the newlyweds, leaving her *alone* with the Master Sword.

Alexa's throat constricted, and her mouth went dry. She was positive the Sword had seen the happening on the terrace. She didn't want to sense out his feelings. She didn't want to know. An awkward silence stretched between them. Or was it just awkward for her? She desperately needed a drink of water. She couldn't stand the self-inflicted stress anymore. The party was no longer fun. She thought of her soft bed upstairs and longed to remove the wicked, cumbersome gown she wore.

"Um," she said, her voice sounding strange to her ears. Bryan looked over at her for the first time since she had joined him. "I'm tired. I think I'm going to go to bed. Good night." She didn't raise her eyes to look at him. She didn't want to wait and hear his response, or, let alone, get a good look at his face. Was she feeling guilty? Nevertheless, she made the mistake of glancing at him before she turned to leave. And there it was: the thing she'd been fearing. His bright azure eyes stared at her. They practically burned through her. She stood there stunned for a second. It was not an angry stare; it was far from it. It was not even an accusing stare. She didn't know *what* kind of stare it was. All she knew was she didn't like it. It made her feel belittled. How had she allowed him to have this kind of power over her? Giving him her best smug look, she twisted her lips into a vague smile and turned on her heel, lifting her train as she went.

"I'll walk you in," he said with a sigh behind her.

She attempted to make her legs move faster, to leave him in the dust and forget the whole night, but her gown and her downright ridiculous shoes were not allowing her to do anything of the sort. He caught up with her quickly and easily. She stumbled along in the grass, twisting her ankle; she cursed, and he caught her elbow to steady her.

"All right?" he asked with concern.

She endeavored to keep walking, attempting to pull her elbow discreetly from his hand, but a shock of pain shot through her ankle. She growled in frustration and hopped a step, struggling to compose herself. Reluctantly, she stopped trying to flee from him and allowed him to steady her. She leaned pathetically on his arm with a sigh and rubbed her aching ankle. He stood, watching her. She glared up at him, not really understanding why. In all honesty, she was really angry with herself for what had happened, even though it was not her fault...

"Why are you being so nice?" she said, a bit harsher than she intended.

Stunned, his eyes widened in surprise as he gazed into her face. Then, eyes flashing, he said in a curt tone, "I didn't realize I was such a brute."

Alexa snorted. She tested her weight on her foot. It was sore, but not bad. Though, unfortunately, she might need help getting up the stairs.

"It's not very ladylike to snort, you know," he continued, a little scornfully.

She sighed and tried to stand on her own, leaning her weight off his. "Sorry," she mumbled, "I'm just tired. And I want to get this gown off." She made a face at her own pitiful excuses.

"Well, go to bed then," he retorted, his brow furrowing crossly.

"That's where I'm headed. If you'd let me," she snapped and then began limping toward the marble stairway leading up to the unmentionable terrace.

He gave an aggravated groan from behind her. "Here, I'm going to have to help you up the stairs, lest you break your leg...or something worse." He rolled his eyes in exasperation.

He followed her and assisted her up the stairway without another word passing between them. Though, with each step up they took, Alexa could feel his anger and bitterness growing. She didn't have to use her senses to comprehend that. He became quiet. His square jaw locked when he clenched his teeth, and his azure eyes seemed to spit flames. She found herself wondering again why he should care if he had chosen to ignore his feelings for her.

Finally, they made it to her room. It would have made the trip much quicker and easier if he had just picked her up and carried her up the second stairway, but neither of their stubborn minds was going to allow that.

She gimped through her doorway and turned to shut the door in his face, but to her great surprise, he held it open. Her mouth went dry again. He was staring at her the same way he had been in the field. She stared back, more self-assured this time, not willing to allow him to belittle her for this. After all, it was none of his business... Or, was it?

After an absurdly long moment of staring silently at each other, she finally spoke, clearing her throat and composing herself, "Tomorrow we'll discuss the plans, then?" His bright blue eyes softened, and this worried her. He took a step toward her. *Why won't he leave me be?* she agonized.

"No," he stated, "We leave for the ruins."

"What's your plan, then?" she said with less haughtiness.

"I thought you already had one," he replied, more quietly and gently.

"Head-on?"

"Has worked so far."

Then, to her utter surprise, she said, "As long as you're there to get me out of any scrapes." Her own words shocked her, but she didn't allow it to show on her face. She set her features to gaze at him stoically, raising her chin, and eyeing him.

He took another step toward her. She held her ground. He stepped once more. He was close enough to take her in his arms if he wanted. Alexa froze and barely breathed. "That's my general plan," he said softly.

The gentle sound of his voice, bordering on fondness, was so uncharacteristic of him that it jolted her heart and threw it back into a hammering stampede. She suddenly wanted to blurt a confession of not wanting to kiss Alkin and that what she really wanted was *him*. She yearned to throw her arms around his neck, pull him down to her level, and bestow blissful kisses on his face and perfect lips. But she held her composure, uncertain of his intentions.

A pained, unguarded look passed across his features as he gazed at her, but it turned quickly to something else, something more powerful. He stared into her eyes, motionless for a moment, studying her frame of mind. She stared back, softening her own eyes, letting all her guards down. She could beseech him easily with her persuasion power, but she would never do such a thing. Then, seeming to decide of his own accord, the Master Sword leaned his upper body toward her as if he were pondering the same thing as she. His eyes watched hers as he came closer and closer. She waited, tilting her chin toward him as an offering, but kept her eyes firmly on his. She could feel the warmth of him and his light breath on her skin. His fingertips grazed her chin as he was about to take her face gently in his hands. But then, just as she was about to close her eyes, her body quivering, anticipating his touch, something dreadful happened. He clenched his jaw, and a steely look came into his eyes. He backed away. His hand was on the door frame before she could utter imploringly, "Bryrunan."

At the sound of the unused version of his name, he turned to look at her. He didn't look angry for her use of it; his expression looked rather bittersweet, and Alexa gazed at him a bit despairingly, trying desperately to keep her poise. She could see a conflict boiling behind his eyes. He looked regretful as he gazed at her. He glanced briefly down the hall. She didn't need him to explain what he was thinking. She could guess a number of reasons for his final resolve not to go through with what he had been about to. She gave him a sad half-smile, feeling like her heart had just literally cracked. He shut his eyes, trying, seemingly, to clear his mind, and when he opened them, they were heavily guarded once more. He then clenched his jaw and gave her a stiff nod.

"Good night, Bryrunan," she whispered in finality, his name on her tongue sorrowfully sweet.

"Good night, Alexa."

His voice was life-giving. If only she could wallow in its

sound forever. She closed her eyes in pitiful defeat. He crossed the threshold and shut the door behind him. She could hear his boot falls as he walked back down the hallway. Gone. Her chance for his love was gone.

She turned and sighed a sigh pregnant with sorrow. Clenching clammy hands, she rubbed them brusquely on her gown. She would *not* cry. She noted hazily that she was trembling and began to undress for bed, trying to occupy her mind with other thoughts, but she only fought in frustration with the ties on the dress and corset.

The soft bed screamed her name tonight, and she couldn't help but think how nice it would have been to snuggle up against his broad body and fall asleep to his heartbeat, his scent, his strength, to *him*. Oh, how she hoped that Bryrunan wouldn't visit her in her dreams tonight. She needed to let go, for her heart was engulfed in torment. Oh yes, she could easily think of many reasons for him not to kiss her.

CHAPTER THIRTY-FOUR

"**O**ne…two…three," Alexa counted to herself. It was early morning, the day after the ceremony, and no one had yet knocked on her door to wake her. However, she had already risen on her own.

She counted while she washed up and pulled on her form-fitting trousers and lightweight top, greatly relieved at their familiar comfort. She counted as she plopped down on the bed and pulled on her calf-high riding boots, pleased to find her tender ankle nicely supported. She counted as she buckled on her dagger, strapped her sword on, and slid her knife in her boot-flap.

"Four…five…six," she continued as she stood to brush her hair and re-braid it into its usual single plait. In the small mirror, she numbly watched her fingers move the locks in and out of each other. "Seven…eight."

She had made it a game this morning to count each foal that had been born at her home the previous spring and carefully envision each one's characteristics. The basic reason for this exercise was to keep her mind occupied, to keep from thinking of the disastrous previous night. It was the only way she could go downstairs and face the others…to face the Master Sword.

It was a weak solution, but it was working so far. She was staying calm and keeping the memories of the night before at bay. Though, she soon had to stop, because there had been only ten foals. So, she began envisioning what each one would look like now. Since she had left months ago, they were now older and most assuredly bigger and stronger. It was silly, but it was engaging her mind. And after that, if she had to, she would envision all the lambs her family owned. But that would take ages, she thought, sullen.

It may have been silly, but she was now done getting ready for the day. She now had no choice but to leave the room and immerse herself back into the company and all their problems—outward and inward ones.

Though she couldn't stop the thoughts flooding into her brain, she composed herself as she headed down the hall toward the stairway, priming herself to look in the Master Sword's face and not show any sign of emotion. She knew *he* wouldn't have any problem. She knew Bryan was innately responsible and had such a strong control of his personal emotions no one would ever guess how he felt inside. He compartmentalized his feelings very well.

And, if that were not enough, she had to somehow deal with her pending status concerning Prince Alkin. Had it just been a friendly kiss? Or was he expecting something more from her now? She shook her head, pursing her lips, trying to suppress the complicated thoughts. She had more important things to think about. She shouldn't be thinking about men when she was about to meet a dragon in a day's time!

She reached the bottom of the marble stairs to find the front doors opened. Energetic voices drifted in, and stepping out on the terrace, she could see the company along with several centaurs, Estella, and Jadelin gathered on the lawn. The company's mounts were tacked up and ready to go, the pack mule loaded up with fresh goods.

She jogged down the steps, being careful of her iffy ankle. Shading her eyes from the brilliant morning sun, she joined the group and returned their greetings with a confident smile and wave. She didn't even bother looking at either the Master Sword or the Prince directly.

Searching out Zhan, she took his reins from the waiting Eelyne. Zhan greeted her joyously. He gave his mistress a half-whinny, half-whicker and tossed his mane, jubilant. Alexa smiled, her heart lightening a great deal. "Hey, Pal." She took his muzzle in her hands and looked into his milky chocolate eyes. He eyed her back curiously. She grinned at his expression and gave him a kiss on his soft nose. He wiggled his muzzle and raised his head to lip her wetly on the nose, flicking his ears forward. She laughed loudly. Zhan was always excellent medicine for an unhappy heart. "Well, at least *you* want to kiss me," she whispered with an ironic chuckle. Zhan bobbed his head, flipping his mane. She gave him a firm pat on the neck.

Pulling her attention from her buddy, she glanced up in hope to find what the next form of action was. It just so happened she looked right up into Sword Bryan's face, who was standing a few strides away; he had been observing her interaction with Zhan.

Just as she suspected, he stood poised, looking completely impassive as he gazed at her and her horse. After an unnerving moment of locking eyes with her, he turned blankly away to speak to Hard Flame, who had been conversing with the Prince.

Alexa took a deep breath, willing her features to look just as impassive. She could do it. She would just ignore the Prince and him as much as possible. She forced her legs to move forward, fretful in thinking that she had no choice but to speak with them to get mission details. She changed course, however, upon seeing Kheane and Jadelin.

To her surprise, Jadelin wore riding clothes, and she held the reins of a chocolate-colored mare with a silver mane. Kheane stood by her, Blize hanging her head over his shoulder. Alexa approached them for information instead. They greeted her with pleasant expressions.

"Hi. So, what's the plan?" she asked.

"Since the ruins are only a day from here, Hard Flame suggested he and several of his warriors accompany us," Kheane answered, "No one knows what to expect, so it's best to have reinforcements."

Alexa regarded Jadelin with a smile, "You joining us?"

"Yes. I know I don't seem cut out for this kind of stuff. But I'm tougher than everyone thinks," she said with a timid smile.

"Oh, I don't doubt it after hearing your stowaway story." Alexa laughed away the Empress trying to defend herself. Jadelin grinned at Kheane, and he quirked one back. It brought another thought to Alexa's mind, and she addressed Kheane, "I suppose after today you're going to come back to be with Jadelin." Kheane and Jadelin shared a disheartened look, and Kheane shook his head solemnly, surprising Alexa. She raised her eyebrows. "No?"

"I started this mission. I'll finish it. I practically begged to join your company. I'll not back out."

Jadelin added, "He also thinks he needs to do something good to salvage himself. I don't believe in that so much, but I do understand his reasoning." She sighed; it sounded heavy with frustration.

Alexa stared at the newlyweds, perplexed. They had been apart for centuries, not even knowing if the other was alive, and now that they were finally together, they were willing to part because of Kheane's sense of duty. This was far beyond her comprehension. She had underestimated them in a few ways.

Studying her baffled reaction, Kheane and Jadelin smiled at her in a way that made her feel naïve and young, albeit their smiles were wreathed with sorrow. She shook her head and sighed on their behalf, "I don't understand it." She gave them a slight, encouraging smile.

Within a few minutes, the company, as well as Estella, Jadelin, and seven centaur warriors, set out for the ruins. The griffins flew them over the wall, first dividing them into small groups on the platform. This took some time. But once they were all over, the new, bigger company started making its way northeast, led by Hard Flame. The unicorns followed next in the procession.

Alexa distracted herself by watching the two beautiful creatures. They seemed oblivious to all around them; they chatted happily and played nipping games. Though, she was certain they were still vigilant.

After them rode the Prince, Jadelin, and Kheane. Sword Bryan followed directly behind. Alexa, not being allowed to be a long distance from her Sword-Guard, tried to keep her distance from him, nonetheless. She held Zhan back behind Dragon's flank and didn't bother speaking to or looking at the Sword. He didn't bother looking over his shoulder to check on her either, despite that being his normal practice. As usual, the others followed closely behind her. The centaur warriors flanked the entire company and strode silent and stoic, blending into the forest.

Even with a larger number, Alexa didn't feel any safer. But it did alleviate the awkwardness she had worried about concerning the Master Sword and the Prince. Alkin had greeted her happily and had spoken a few times with her, but it was nothing out of the ordinary. This confused and relieved her. He didn't seem any more partial to her than he usually did. This had to be a good sign.

Maybe it had only been a friendly kiss or a spur-of-the-moment reaction.

Then a thought occurred to her. Maybe, without knowing it, she had persuaded him to kiss her. She hadn't remembered turning on the skill she'd often used to get people to do trivial things her way. The persuasion skill had its tight limits; she couldn't *make* someone do something if they really didn't want to. Maybe it was better if she had accidentally persuaded Alkin. Because then he wouldn't have been acting completely on his own accord, so there was the chance he would move on without a second thought. She groaned inwardly, scowling at her thoughts. Now she was making excuses! Of course, he had kissed her of his own will.

She had long since gotten bored with watching the playful unicorns, and this last train of thought eventually led to another, more complex set of estimations. These were the possible explanations for Sword Bryan's odd, but obviously thought out, actions last night. She tried vainly not to think about her very confusing interaction with the Master Sword. For she had gone over it and over it last night as she lay in bed unable to fall asleep.

Now, staring at his poised back as he rode ahead of her, Alexa found herself counting down the reasons he'd decided at the last minute not to kiss her, therefore crushing all hopes she had had of them being together. Her logic for counting the foals that morning was because she had been trying not to count the reasons Bryan *would not* love her. Because she had come to the conclusion that he definitely had strong feelings for her. There was no doubt in her mind about that.

Her reasoning was: One, he was her Sword-Guard. And, therefore, she was his duty and not a lover. It was simple and logical; he was determined not to jeopardize his responsibility. Two, he was a Head-Master Sword and she was merely a commoner. She had thought this many times before, but this argument seemed weak. His personality didn't show he felt superior to her or anyone else. Plus, he had been quite willing to kiss her. If only he was not so stubborn and self-disciplined! Third, some old feelings of betrayal had been aroused by him witnessing Alkin kiss her, so he wasn't willing to let his guard down and allow himself to love her. Lastly, it was Sword Bryan's superior and childhood best friend that had made the first move for her affections, and he now saw her as taboo. From knowing his personality, she knew the Master Sword would never compromise his friend and especially a prince of any country let alone his own. Each of these reasons was probable. Perhaps it was not just one, maybe it was a conglomeration of a few.

Sighing in agitation, Alexa shook the thoughts away. There was no point in lingering on this. She would never know. She tried to sense his feelings out, but all she got was the old, black bog of bitterness he used to have when she'd first met him. She *had* to focus on more important things, like not being the mother to a bunch of abominations created by her uncle. Now that was something to think about! Why was her mind so charged with worries over the Master Sword? He was blatantly ignoring her as much as she was him. The door to that opportunity was locked tight. Something had to be wrong with her brain…

They reached a spacious clearing by dusk. The centaurs promptly set up tall, blazing torches around the circumference. They began unpacking and setting up their tents. The centaurs had supplied tents and cots for the company, and Alexa was thankful for this thoughtful gesture, as each member of the company had their own private tent. The tents were not by any means extravagant; they were small but serviceable. She was extremely relieved she would have some solitude. She didn't feel like huddling up on the ground next to the Master Sword tonight, or Prince Alkin for that matter, albeit Bryan dutifully and stubbornly set his tent up right next to hers.

The camp was set up in efficient time. Alexa had her tent up and cot out in no time. She worked side by side with Bryan as he set up his, though they didn't speak a word to each other. She stole covert glances at him, but she found he looked just as impassive as he had earlier. He never once looked at her. This bothered her a great deal. She realized sadly she had become accustomed to his protective glances, and it worried her that maybe he had suddenly stopped caring.

She fiddled around with fixing her tent, waiting for Bryan to finish his. When he had finally left to join the others, she waited a half a minute before following him. She joined the others by the huge bonfire in the center of the camp. She sat down between Eelyne and Hazerk. The group was preparing for a meal. She stared inattentively into the blazing fire, watching the flames flicker and listening to the wood snap. The heat was immense on her face, but she didn't feel like moving back. Maybe it would burn her freckles off and along with them, her feelings for the Master Sword.

Coming out of her sullen reverie, she looked up to see Apollos gazing at her from across the fire. He was curled up on the ground, his legs tucked up beneath him. Estella was curled up next to him and gazed intently at her, too. Puzzled, Alexa raised her eyebrows quizzically at the two unicorns. They looked suspiciously conniving. Apollos eyed her with his deep, chocolate eyes. Tossing his nose in the air, he gestured toward the Master Sword, who was sitting farther down the circle of warriors in conversation with Hard Flame. She glanced down to the unaware Sword and back to the unicorns. Apollos narrowed his eyes at her, staring at her a bit reproachfully.

She wasn't exactly sure what the clever unicorn was getting at, but she had a good idea he knew something was going on between her and the Master Sword and he wanted her to fix it. Feeling beat, she sighed and nodded her acknowledgment. This seemed to appease both unicorns, and they turned away to enjoy their dinners. Nothing escaped Apollos' keen observations. He had probably noted early on that she and Bryan hadn't been interacting the way they normally did. As she ate, she vaguely wondered why the unicorn thought it was so important for her and the Master Sword to be on good terms. It wasn't like either of them was slacking on their duties. She shrugged it away and tried to immerse herself in the conversation at hand.

"...the ruins are about two or so miles from here. We picked here because it's a good spot to accommodate us all, and it's far enough away it's safe from piquing the dragon's senses," Hard Flame explained to the group.

"You said the legend is that the eternal flame is in caverns beneath the ruins. Is the dragon there, too?" Prince Alkin asked.

"Well, the story claims the fountain of flame is the dragon's hoard. It protects it viciously. So, my assumption is that if the flame is underground, the dragon is very close by."

"Do you or your warriors have any ideas, Hard Flame, on how to breach this?" Alkin asked. The entire group was now paying rapt attention to the conversation.

"I'm afraid I don't have any knowledge of dragon lore. How about you all?" Hard Flame addressed his warriors. They shook their heads in regret. "We'll just be here to help fight if you need us," he said, addressing the Prince again.

"Yes, thank you." Alkin looked grateful but disappointed. He regarded Alexa, peering around Warrior Hazerk, who sat between them, "Have any intuition clues?" he inquired hopefully.

Alexa was suddenly aware of sixteen pairs of eyes on her. This didn't bother her so much as knowing the Master Sword was now gazing inquisitively at her, too. She stared blankly at all the eyes glittering expectantly in the firelight. She swallowed. She had been so preoccupied with all her thoughts of Bryan; the idea hadn't even crossed her mind to search her senses for help on the impending matter. How stupid! Perhaps her situation with Bryan *was* making her disregard her duties. "Ah, I…no," she said, avoiding the Prince's fallen countenance. Then she added, perking up with force, "Eelyne, you must know something about dragons that could help us."

"Yeah, sure." He straightened, and then said a little self-consciously, "Well, I know they have an excellent sense of smell and sight. They can spit fire up to about thirty strides. Of course, they can fly, swift and high. And, like I said before, they can be finicky, and obviously, they are quite vicious. Though, I do know they're easily distracted, which could be to our advantage. Also, if they're guarding something, they won't leave it long, or go far from it, which could be helpful, too… That's all I got…sorry," he ended, somewhat dejectedly.

Everyone was silent for a moment as they processed his information. The unspoken defeat was palpable.

"To help boost my witch intuition, I'll need to see the ruins beforehand. I need to know for sure if it's, in fact, where the fire element is located, and to get a better idea as to how to go about doing this," Alexa stated, regaining her confidence. She had half in mind to just say do it head on, like her and the Master Sword had joked, but now, ironically enough, that seemed almost too private to bring out in the open. As if she were to mention it, it would intimately connect her and her Sword-Guard more than either of them was willing to be connected at the moment. She shook the thought away, squeezing her eyes shut, forcing *him* out of her mind.

"Well then, we shouldn't waste time," Alkin concluded. "Let's scout out the ruins now. That way we can begin right away in the morning." The others agreed.

"All right," Bryan said authoritatively as he stood. "Just a small group should go. Hard Flame, Apollos, Prince Alkin, Alexa, and I will go," he said, and then added on thoughtfully, "Kheane and Estella can come, too. We definitely can use your expertise, Kheane, and two unicorns are better than one." Everyone he had listed nodded in acknowledgment and stood to prepare to leave. "Hurry, so we can get back and get some rest," he stated as they dispersed to go re-tack their horses.

Alexa felt guilty about having to tack up Zhan again. Since they had ridden all day long, he probably needed a rest. Her animal friend spotted her approaching with his tack to retrieve him from his grazing, and he came to her, merely lifting his muzzle to her ear to give a resigned huff of sweet horsy breath in her hair. She smiled in apology and gave him a loving pat, landing another kiss on his nose. With the saddle and bridle in hand, she considered for a moment whether to ride him without tack. She set them down by her tent and then hugged Zhan tightly around his neck. He nuzzled her back. Pulling away, she hopped up onto his sleek back, and his spirits seemed to lift upon realizing she wasn't putting the confining contraptions on him. He danced playfully under her, thinking this was a game. She patted him and then nudged him to join the others. He danced over.

She waited for the rest with Hard Flame and the unicorns. Astride Sapharan, Alkin was the first to join them; the others followed close behind. As he rode up, the Prince eyed Alexa and flashed a wide smile. "You're probably the best woman rider I've ever seen," he commented, an admiring twinkle in his eye. He'd obviously noted that Zhan didn't even wear a halter.

"Thanks. You're pretty good yourself." She smiled coquettishly at him, casting a sly glance at the Master Sword in the process. If he was going to ignore her, she would play that she didn't care. Bryan looked at her with an austere gaze, his clear, azure eyes narrowed irritably. Dragon pulled at his bit grumpily and stomped a hoof. The Sword and his mount seemed to be one entity at times, she thought with no small amount of amusement… at least Bryan was regarding her now.

Apollos gave a loud snort and caught everyone's attention. "Come on, humans, let's go." He motioned for Hard Flame to lead the way, and he and Estella followed. The soft glow emanating from the two unicorns' horns lit the path.

The trek was a short one. It was mostly a quiet one, too. Only Prince Alkin and Alexa spoke to each other, discussing their theories of horse-riding tactics and handling.

Soon, through the darkness and trees, they could see the ancient ruins loom before them. The group became silent as each pondered out ideas in their head. The ruins were merely a crumbling stone castle and its outer buildings lay amongst overgrown vines, trees, and shrubbery. In the dark, it looked somewhat foreboding, but if someone happened to cross it in the day, it might seem like a pleasant place to have a picnic.

Alexa let her senses loose. A race of adrenalin zipped through her body when they made the familiar connection to something old, powerful, and magical. It took her breath away. "This is definitely it," she whispered.

"Good," Alkin responded, pleased.

"There's more than one dragon in the caverns," Apollos asserted, his eyes far away as he, too, sensed out the area. The company replied by moaning in unison.

"How many?"

"Two, maybe three. But I can only sense one that appears to be at its fullest power."

The company had dismounted and were huddled close together in a copse just off the overgrown yard of the dilapidated castle. It looked simple enough from the outside to get in. There had to be an entranceway leading down into the caverns amongst all the rubble. Hopefully, it wasn't blocked off.

Kheane's gruff whisper broke the thoughtful silence, "In my opinion, the best bet is the element of surprise. I don't know much about dragons, but if it sees us coming, well, we'd probably not get anywhere near the element with all our limbs."

Alexa deliberated for another minute before deciding the basics of her tactic. "Warrior Eelyne said they were easily distracted. If we had a diversion on top of surprising them, we might have a chance to escape with the element. After all, we only want a little piece of the element. The dragons might give up chasing us to continue to protect the rest of their hoard."

"True. Estella and I would be good distractions," Apollos volunteered, and Estella bobbed her head, a glint of anticipation in her eyes.

"Are you sure you want to help by being bait, Apollos?" Alkin asked with apprehension. "To even think of unicorns as bait is beyond my comprehension."

The unicorn tossed his head. "I'm not worried about my safety. Estella and I can take care of ourselves. And yes, I want to help. I *need* to help. You'd be foolish to pass it up," he said, a twinkle in his chocolate eyes.

"I suppose you're right. Well, if you're willing…" Alkin resigned, feeling protective over his one-of-a-kind friend.

"Well, the details are vague," Alexa contemplated aloud. "But if we can sneak down into the caverns without alerting them, and Apollos and Estella cause a distraction, I might be able to snatch the fire element and run. How a person snatches flames, I'm not sure. We did have to ask the dryad for the earth element. Though, I'm hoping this fountain of flame is something I can just approach and gather." Everyone nodded in silent accord.

Then, the Master Sword spoke up, his tone holding an icy edge, "Well, it sounds all good and well enough, straightforward as ever. Head-on is probably the best in this case; there's no other way it seems."

An aggrieved tremor shocked through Alexa's heart at his reminding words and tantalizing voice. But he wasn't finished, and he turned on her with a firm look.

"If what you say is true, then anyone can gather the element. I don't see where you're needed to go down into the caverns at all," he stated to a now stunned Alexa.

Her features turned into a dire glare, boring hard into the Master Sword, who held her gaze, austere as ever. She couldn't even form a thought in her mind, she was so furious. What was his game?

The others contemplated this for a second. Then, Alkin said in approval, "Yes, I don't see having her go either."

Alexa's temper got the better of her; she turned on the Prince like an angry cat, "You all can't stop me from going in there. I'm supposed to gather the elements."

"No, you're the one to *use* the elements," Bryan clarified. She opened her mouth to retort angrily back, but he cut her off, "You're not going, and that's final."

She gave a harsh snort. The others in the company watched her in apprehension. "And what? *You're* going down there?" she spit.

"I could," Bryan replied.

"He does have a point, Alexa." Apollos' soft voice tried to console her. "You're too important in the matter of using the elements."

"I'm smart enough to do this. I know how to fight and can take care of myself." Her tone was imploring, but it had a dangerous edge to it. She utterly despised how the Master Sword was taking on such a calm demeanor while basically betraying her. This was her mission! This was her company!

"This is a dragon," Bryan said, his tone frosty, "It doesn't care what you can offer in a fight. It would roast you for its dinner. It can fly. And I don't see you sprouting any angel wings. Its tooth is probably bigger than you. Forget it, girl." His icy blue eyes practically burned right through her.

Why was he doing this to her? She had to do this! He was doing it out of spite; she was positive. She clenched her jaw and scowled at him, crossing her arms. He glared back, unmoving. She then regarded a concerned Prince Alkin. His hazel eyes widened with apprehension. "Tell him he doesn't have to babysit me. I'm mature enough. I can handle this," she said. Alkin looked as if he didn't want to get in the middle of this argument. *Kind of cowardly for a prince.* She stared sourly into his submissive eyes.

"Ha!" Bryan scoffed; she turned her blazing eyes back on the Sword. "Oh, okay, Miss Temper Tantrum," he jeered.

Alexa's mouth gaped in utter indignation. The Master Sword merely stared at her with a slight, smug smile across his lips. She snapped her jaw shut. "I do *not* throw temper tantrums," she seethed through her teeth. Her sapphire eyes bored straight into Bryan's clear, blue obstinate ones. *Well, he isn't ignoring me by any means now!* What bitter irony.

"Like a two-year-old," he replied, his air arrogant.

"I do not!"

"Well…" Bryan snickered and held up his hands to show her obvious display.

Any shards left of Alexa's composure shattered completely. "Well, you," she growled, "you're a chauvinistic, pigheaded, conceited, bossy, great big—"

"Whoa, now," he interrupted her with a casual laugh, but his eyes narrowed, the azure blue darkening dangerously.

His off-handedness maddened her all the more. She wanted nothing more than to punch him right in his smug face. She clenched her fist. But taking a quick glance at the shocked faces of the company, she realized she was making a scene. She quelled her anger, although she glowered once more at the Master Sword before she composed herself. "I guess we'll discuss it in the morning," she said, her teeth clenched.

Bryan shrugged, brushing her off self-importantly.

Alexa looked over at Zhan, who was pulling at some leaves on a nearby tree. She gave a low whistle, and the horse plodded over. Placing her hand on his sleek, white neck, her boiling insides calmed. She looked back at the company, who were now mounting up, and mumbled, "I'm sorry…for my behavior." They all nodded in acceptance, except for the Master Sword, who merely stared at her with penetrating eyes.

Prince Alkin, who was closest to her, gave a tentative smile. "It's all right. I understand why you feel the way you do." She responded with an appreciative half-smile and swung up onto

Zhan.

She grumbled to herself the whole way back to the camp. She had a good feeling Bryan was punishing her for something that was entirely *not* her fault. It had nothing to do with protecting her. She didn't bother acknowledging the Master Sword as they split to go their separate ways.

CHAPTER THIRTY-FIVE

Something felt uncomfortable, and he was cold. With a shiver, Bryan tugged at his coarse blanket. The movement caused his rickety cot to creak. He had a stiff neck, and was vaguely aware that he'd been sleeping on his stomach, his neck cranked to one side, his right arm dangling to the ground. He groaned and shifted, opening his eyes just enough to see that it was dark out, and then closed them again and fell back to sleep.

Next thing he knew, a jarring flapping noise from all around startled him awake. He jerked up, heart pounding. The cot rocked precariously, nearly bucking him to the ground. His sword was in his hand before he was even fully conscious. The flapping vibration persisted, and he looked sleepily around, noting that his tent was waving as if it were in a violent windstorm.

Then it stopped.

Lowering his sword, and well aware of his surroundings now, he realized the situation. Someone had taken a hold of his tent and had shaken it. A small smile escaped his lips along with a whispery, knowing chuckle. He rubbed the sleep from his eyes and sheathed his sword. Bryan had an idea of who it was, and he shook his head in amusement. He had better go out and face her. The Master Sword stepped out into the dark, breezy night.

He could see her willowy silhouette. She held a tacked-up Zhan and had set glare across her features. He felt a twinge of guilt upon seeing her. Though, in spite of his feelings, he groused, "What in the demon's name was that for?"

Alexa shifted her tense stance. "I'm leaving for the ruins. I'm giving you the option to come with me or not," she said, and then in one swift movement, she mounted Zhan. The white horse gave a snort and an excited toss of his head.

Bryan studied her for a moment. She had all her gear mounted on her. Her quiver full of black arrows and bow were strapped across her back, her dagger strapped around her thigh, and the sword he had given her belted to her waist. She stared at him, her countenance level, as she waited for him to respond.

Rubbing his face, a tad exasperated, he sighed. "I thought I told you that you weren't going."

"You said we'd discuss it in the morning. It's morning, and I'm discussing it. I've decided I'm going with or without your permission."

"You'd go alone?"

"Apollos and Estella." She pointed off into the distance to where the two unicorns stood watching their confrontation.

"I never said we'd discuss it," he stated.

"You shrugged. That implies we would."

He stared at her with a blank expression, and thought morosely, *I deserve her anger*. His command for her to stay behind *was* intended for her protection, but the guilty feeling he had derived from it also told him he had done it for other, more bitter and selfish reasons. He had known she would want more than anything to gather the fire element herself. So, he had taken that away, to anger her…purposely. And now he felt guilty. Yet, he still didn't want her in harm's way.

"Okay, then. I'm leaving." She reined Zhan around.

"All right, all right," he said, caving in for probably the first time ever. How was she doing this to him? He was unnervingly vulnerable to her fury. He had slept out his own bitter anger that night.

She turned Zhan back around to face him, a triumphant smile spreading across her features. "Good. Let's go."

Bryan sighed and shook his head in denial of his weakness. "Give me a minute. Wake the others and have them prepare for the dragon just in case." He turned into his tent and readied himself.

By the time he was finished, he could hear the company rousing and the centaurs readying themselves. He stepped outside and went to Dragon, who was tethered on a nearby tree. The horse stretched his neck toward his master and puffed a small breath into Bryan's offered palm. The black stallion's dark eyes gleamed in the low dawn light. The Sword gave his mount an affectionate pat and began tacking him up.

Then, despite all his power to rein in his feelings, Bryan's thoughts washed over him like a tide pulling him down. He had been strongly endeavoring to resist all thoughts and feelings pertaining to Alexa in an affectionate manner. He realized he had been doing this for weeks, but now the situation between the two of them had reached a boiling point. He could no longer deny he had feelings for her, nor could he deny she showed feelings for him as well. Despite all his efforts in the beginning to not even like her, he had fallen completely for her, like she was some kind of seductive sorceress. He laughed ironically at his own thoughts. What if she had bewitched him? But deep down he knew she hadn't. He had been drawn to her the moment he had laid eyes on her; he remembered blatantly resisting it.

Before he had met her, he had sworn off women. He had decided to die an old, lonely warrior if he must. Because of his own bitter resentment toward women, he had foolishly denied his natural partiality to Alexa. He had also resisted her because his sense of duty was so overpowering. Being her Sword-Guard was his first and foremost obligation with her. He couldn't think of her as a lover did. Such thoughts befuddled his mind, his judgment, weakening his ability to do his job. It would be dangerous for her as well as him and the company. But despite his best efforts, it slowly crept over him and ensnared him. His feelings for her had broken out and won over.

The night of the ceremony, he had finally resigned to the fact that he indeed loved her. And allowing himself to delve deeper into his feelings that night, he found he cared more for her than he had cared for anyone else ever. It was a strange, almost liberating feeling to finally allow himself to be okay with this resolve. Then, he had seen her and Alkin kiss on the terrace. By his former keen observations of the two, which he now knew were because of his jealousy, he had known that the Prince felt some kind of attraction to her. But he never thought he would act upon it.

Upon seeing their kiss that night, Bryan had burned with anger and resentment...as well as betrayal. He had wanted nothing more than to march over, yank them apart, and punch his friend and prince square in the face. He was also angry and bitter toward Alexa for allowing Alkin to kiss her. Although, he knew deep down that was the last thing she had wanted. He knew this by her ridged stature when Alkin had touched her and by the way she resisted looking himself in the face. Still, he felt betrayed on some level by her. She had given him signs, or so he thought she had shown him she reciprocated his feelings. He had resented her, but it was for only a short time before he had realized that everything was all his own foolish fault. He had allowed this to happen. He had denied his feelings so far that he had let her slip right through his ignorant hands.

Now, she was out of reach. Bryan would never, could never, cross Prince Alkin. It went against his obligation as just a mere citizen of Shelkite. Even more so, he was the Head-Master Sword and was once Alkin's good friend. So, as always, his self-control and strong sense of duty toward his job won over. He had played his impassive part well. Apart from that one blissful moment when he had decided he didn't care about his duty, or about an irate prince, and he was going to take Alexa for himself despite all. He had been so close. If he had broken the floodgates and had taken her in his arms like he had wanted and had kissed her and had— well, done many things—that would have been it. He wouldn't have been able to stop himself from loving her, and he would've blatantly disregarded his duty to Alkin and Shelkite. But he had had enough resolve to stop before her sweet, offered lips had touched his. Thus, making the distance he knew he had to put between them easier, or so he thought easier.

Yesterday, he had receded back into his old, bitter shell, and he had wanted to punish her despite his knowing that he was really at fault. But today, well, his own mood swings were annoying him; today, he felt guilty, and he would do anything to make her happy and not have her fiery, sapphire eyes bore into him. He just wanted to make sure she came through this safely. He would be there for her, as he had promised.

Bryan had long finished tacking up Dragon. He had mounted and gone to wait by the unicorns, inattentive to their open musings about Alexa and him. His mind was full of his own complex thoughts too much to care what the two conniving unicorns had to say. Alexa was over speaking with the others in last-minute preparations. Bryan could tell Prince Alkin wasn't happy about her going. But he had relented, of course, the softy that he was.

Alexa glanced up and caught eyes with him. Bryan looked away; she was punishing him, and he didn't want to see her spiteful eyes.

After another few minutes, when the rising sun was casting a dusty hew over their surroundings, Alexa rode over to join him and the unicorns. She looked stoic, ready for the business at hand. Bryan had to resolve himself to do the same. Wow, how he was falling to pieces under her power, he reflected bitterly. He couldn't let this jeopardize his job. He met eyes with her again, and their blazing resentment was now replaced with an anticipation that only had to do with the task at hand.

"Ready?" she addressed them all, her voice light.

"Yes. Let's go," he huffed.

They set off down the lightly wooded path, the two unicorns leading the way. The crude plan was the others would follow behind but stay back, to not alert the dragons to their presence. Sword Bryan, Alexa, and the unicorns were hoping to sneak up on the creatures. It would be easier and perhaps safer for all to have only a few steal down into the caverns. Even this plan would be farfetched, except that the unicorns had revealed they could cast an aura about their small party that would mask them from the dragons' senses, at least until the dragons spotted them. After that, well, it would play out. The unicorns would try to distract while Alexa and Bryan would gather the element and run.

The Master Sword tried not to think about how they were going to get out of the caverns alive. It seemed astronomical that they would make it without a scratch. But he tried to think positively; they had two clever unicorns helping them. That had to count for something. And, of course, he was a good warrior, and Alexa was definitely nothing to scoff at when she put her mind to it.

Alexa shifted her quiver of arrows on her back to a more comfortable position. Well, it was over before it had even begun; she determined as they made their way toward the ruins. She wasn't thinking about the dragons. It was her and the Master Sword's potential love she ruminated on, much to her disgust. She couldn't even manage to extricate him from her thoughts even as they marched to face the dragons this very hour.

He rode just a half a stride behind her. Close enough to jump to action if something was to happen to her, but far enough away to make a point that he didn't want to have a conversation with her, let alone look at her. Well, she didn't care. She despised him. She sighed grudgingly at the lie to herself. She couldn't bring herself to hate him, even after he had hurt her so excruciatingly. How could a girl hate any man that had saved her from the certain fate she had almost succumbed to by the warm spring? And she wasn't just merely thinking of her death…

Enough, enough! Alexa squeezed her eyes shut to rid herself of all thought. *High Power, help me!* She pleaded desperately. When she opened them again, she could see the ruins through the branches. Something stole over her, and she allowed herself to be completely consumed by it. It was the lucid mindset she needed to handle the task. She sighed in relief at the freedom from her imprisoning thoughts.

They halted in a thicket just beyond the overgrown yard of the old castle. Alexa and Sword Bryan dismounted in silence and tied Dragon and Zhan near each other on a tree, hiding them from the view of the ruins. The two crept to where the unicorns were peering at the grounds through the branches. They crouched down next to each other, forgetting all their complications and grievances with one another.

After a moment of fervent study, Estella said, "You two humans ready?"

Alexa and Bryan glanced at each other, their eyes briefly and unwillingly scanning the other's face. They each gave a stoic nod.

"Okay," Apollos said in a whisper. "We're going to cast a masking aura. Don't wander too far from us. We'll keep it snug around the four of us. The dragons will be less likely to notice the aura if it's small. They would get suspicious if there was a huge space in their lair where they couldn't sense anything."

Alexa and the Master Sword nodded their understanding, each feeling a twist of nerves in their stomach flare up.

"All right, let's find a way in," Bryan said, risking a glance at Alexa. He was content to see she was already looking at him, impassive as it was.

The two elegant unicorns bobbed their heads, and their horns lit up, glowing lavender. Something warm closed in on Alexa. It was barely noticeable. She couldn't describe it any way other than like a soft blanket being tucked in around her.

"Okay, let's go." Apollos' voice was muffled by the aura.

They moved together, crossing the grassy field and entering the wasted grounds. They searched as quietly and as quickly as they could. There was so much rubble; there wasn't much to see or find.

As the sun rose and warmed their backs, Alexa began to get discouraged. It was possible the entranceway to the caverns had been blocked by the castle's wreckage, and it would be impenetrable. But after some further intense minutes of searching, they found a door. It was snuggled in a grassy knoll behind the ruins, in what would have been the courtyard.

Alexa and the Master Sword quickly dug at the dirt covering the door and pulled at the long grasses to clear the front of it. The unicorns helped by pawing the dirt aside. Once they had the door uncovered, they pulled hard together on the handle. It crossed their minds that once this thing budged, it was going to make an ungodly noise opening. But the unicorns stood close to the door and muffled the sound as it finally gave and popped opened.

Crouched over the gaping entrance in the ground, they all peered in. The old stairway leading down was crumbled into nothing but rubble.

"It looks like an old shelter of some sort," Bryan said, his own voice muted.

"Yes, but it could lead to the caverns. It's hard for me to sense anything with the masking aura," Alexa replied.

"It's a good a start as any," Apollos said.

"No dragon could get down here. It wouldn't fit," Alexa said, thinking the dragons must leave the caverns once in a while. She had a sudden image of a dragon trying to squeeze its large girth through the small door and couldn't help but let a small smile escape her despite everything.

"There might be another exit in the woods," Apollos suggested.

"All right, let's check it out." Alexa swung her legs through the doorway and went to drop into the hole, but the Master Sword put a firm, restraining hand on her shoulder before she could. Her skin tingled pleasantly at his touch, much to her dislike. She gave him a small scowl. He looked at her with a disapproving brow and shook his head.

"Let me or one of the unicorns go first," he said.

"I'll go," Estella said from behind.

Alexa shrugged Bryan's hand off her shoulder and moved out of the way, not bothering to see his reaction as he too moved back to make room for the unicorn's leap.

Estella leaned back on her haunches and launched herself from a standstill through the doorway and down into the dark. They all rushed to the edge and peered in. The unicorn was standing soundly on the ground, not too far below, her body softly glowing, lighting the darkness. She looked up at them expectantly.

"I'll go now," Bryan stated without consulting Alexa.

He sat down in the grass, dangled his legs over the edge and pushed himself off, aiming for a spot clear of rubble. He bent his knees as he fell, preparing for the impact. He hit the rocky ground and stumbled a bit, his feet stinging from the impact. Estella moved aside to make room for him. He looked up at Alexa, who was now dangling her legs over the side. She pushed off, falling in one smooth motion to the floor, and landed with a light thud, crouched and with one hand steadying herself on the ground. She straightened and came to stand by Estella, not regarding Bryan at all as he eyed her a tad regretfully. The three moved aside to make room for Apollos.

Once he was down in, they looked around. Alexa noted the area they were in was small and didn't have much to it. It was cold and damp and had shelves lining the walls. There was a door in the back, and they moved to it. She gave the door a firm jerk, and it opened with a groan. The Master Sword stood with his sword drawn as they peered down the dark passageway. It was narrow, long, and carved from the earth. The humans moved aside and let Estella take the lead into the corridor. Apollos took the rear.

They marched silently down the damp passage, the soft glow

of the unicorns' bodies and horns providing the only light. The path was so narrow, they walked single-file. The only sounds heard were their light, muted footsteps and low, nervous breaths. They soon came to an opening. Surrounding them were stone shelves filled with dusty, rotting objects, along with scattered bones from some creature or two.

Without a second glance, they moved past the unsettling sight and into the passageway leading deeper into the earth. They followed the twisted path for what seemed like hours, but it wasn't. Beginning to sweat, conscious only then that it had gotten extremely hot, they stopped and glanced apprehensively at one another, realizing they must be getting close to the fountain of flame. Alexa swallowed over a lump in her throat, drawing her dagger as she followed close behind the Master Sword.

After a few more bends, they could see a flickering light ahead that wasn't emanating from the unicorns. Moving farther, they heard a roaring, snapping and sizzling noise. Estella stopped, halting Bryan. Alexa bumped into his broad back, and her body seemed to catch fire by the insignificant touch. He glanced over his shoulder at her, his blue eyes deep. She wanted to mutter an apology, but she stubbornly bit her lip instead.

"We're here," Estella barely whispered, craning her neck around to regard them, her gaze piercing. "I'm sure they're just around the next bend. I sense they're asleep."

Alexa's heart began thudding with such ferocity that it nearly hurt. The blood it pumped came whipping into her brain so fast she began to feel lightheaded. She put a hand to her heart to calm it and leaned against the wall, the stone too warm on her back.

Bryan turned and regarded her, his clear, azure eyes pragmatic and wide with concern for her. "You all right?" he whispered. His forehead was creased with worry and sweat gathered at his brow.

"I'm fine. You?" she choked as she struggled to gain control of herself. Sweat trickled down from her hairline; the cavern was like the inside of an oven. They would be baked alive if they stayed long.

"Yes, as much as I can be." He had the urge to reach out and touch her face in reassurance. His hand rose up, but it fell to the hilt of his sword instead.

Alexa eyed him for a second, gathering her bearings. A vague thought crossed her mind that this could be the last time she looked into his penetrating eyes or saw his perfect, square jaw clench in apprehension. But why did it matter? He was not hers anyhow. She came quickly back together at this sobering thought, and she straightened her stance. In a brisk movement, she wiped her hand across her face, attempting to clear the hot, slick sweat gathering there. Her heart began to slow its rapid pace, and her old confidence flooded back.

Bryan waited patiently as she fought to gain her confidence. It was slightly unnerving to see her so unsettled; it wasn't her norm. He fought another urge to take her in his arms, especially when he found it so surprisingly alluring to see that when she had wiped her hand across her face, she had left muddy streaks from her dirt-caked fingers. But he didn't have to resist long, because a steely look came over her features and her stature became rigid. She held her chin up, her sapphire eyes holding a dangerous, haughty spark. *That's more like her.* He glanced with longing at her soft, curving lips, but disregarding him, she placed her palm firmly on his chest and shoved him out of her way. He hadn't realized how close he had been. She pushed past him with a dark look and walked to the bend in the passageway. An unexpected pang thrummed in his chest. He ignored it and followed her, the unicorns at his heels.

They walked around the bend and found that the corridor opened into a high-domed cavern. On their left, the wall of the corridor continued for several strides, then stopped. But its height was to the vaulted ceiling and blocked them from the view of the open cave. On their right, the rocky wall merged and became the perimeter of the cavern.

The heat and light of the blazing flame of the fountain of fire filled the cavern with its intensity. It was brighter than daylight, leaving only scarce shadows flitting.

Alexa crouched down and very stealthily poked her head around the corner of the wall. The Master Sword was at her shoulder; the unicorns stood abreast at his.

CHAPTER THIRTY-SIX

At first, the shock of hounding light blinded Alexa. Her impaired vision gave her a jolt of fear, but she soon recovered and drank in the incredible sight.

In the center of the cavern's stone floor was a wide, circular chasm with water-like flames spewing out of it. The fire was a brilliant conglomeration of colors: white, blue, purple, yellow, orange, red, and pink. It shot high into the air, touching the domed ceiling of the chamber, scorching hot but smokeless.

Alexa noted, with brave resolve, three beasts on the far side of the fountain of flame. Two appeared to be asleep. One of the sleeping beasts was the largest of them. The smallest paced with its back toward her.

Fighting against the immense heat assaulting her face and sweating profusely, she studied the animals, configuring her next move. So far, they seemed unaware of their presence, thanks to the unicorns' masking aura. However, once the beasts spotted them, the sneaking around would be over. The unicorns could make themselves invisible, but they couldn't make the humans so.

Alexa could feel all too well Sword Bryan hovering over her shoulder, his breath hot on her neck and his sweat dripping on her. She forced herself to remain focused and appraise the dragons.

The one pacing was gangly. It reminded her of a yearling colt, not quite full-grown. It was roughly the size of two horses of normal proportions. The full-grown dragon, which she assumed was the mother of the two others, was larger, but not as large as she had imagined a dragon to be. It reminded her of a beast she once saw a rich merchant riding when he came to stay at their inn. The man had called it an elephant. It was an intriguing creature. She had liked it. But this dragon only compared in size and not looks what-so-ever.

The dragons' scales were metallic and iridescent, changing color when the light of the flame touched them. The tones shifted from silvery green to bronze, to a dull blue and black. The reptiles had two ram-like horns curling out of their skulls. Their faces were lizard like, with small, swiveling ears, reminiscent of large mouse ears. Their necks were long and sinuous, their front legs slender but muscular and ending in sharp four-fingered talons. Though their bat-like wings were folded, their span appeared immense. They had rotund girths and muscular haunches, with even nastier looking talons on their hind feet. Their tails matched the length of their body and had sharp, boney spikes protruding all the way down to their tip.

The companions were abnormally quiet as they beheld the scene. Without a signal, they ducked back behind the wall to have a quick conference.

Alexa realized she was panting from the heat, her mouth parched and sticky. She glanced at the unicorns; they seemed unaffected by the heat. They stood cool and collected as always. The Master Sword seemed to be having the same trouble breathing as she. He gulped and wiped away the pouring sweat from his brow and knelt down close to her, where she crouched on the floor against the wall. His intense, azure eyes searched her face earnestly. She gathered her thoughts and whispered to him, "Hear any voices in your head?"

Bryan stared, perplexed, into her red face, studying her darkened eyes, and then snickered in spite of the situation, "No."

Disappointed, she huffed and wiped away the sweat dripping in her eyes. "Humph. I was hoping you were a dragon whisperer because I'm certainly not hearing any unfamiliar voices."

"No new ones aside from what you normally listen to, huh?" Bryan said, with a wicked grin.

"This isn't time to joke," Alexa hissed. "You know what I mean."

Apollos cut in, "I'm not sure if that's how dragon whispering works anyhow."

"Okay, well, how are we doing this?" she retorted and pulled at her damp shirt.

Bryan's faced turned thoughtful, and he sat back on his heels, realizing, upon seeing her annoyed eye, that he was once again invading her space.

They sat in contemplative silence.

Then Estella spoke, "There isn't any way other than to just go for it. Apollos and I will do our best to keep the dragons distracted while you run for the flame."

The two humans nodded, apprehensive.

"I'm not leaving your side," Bryan emphasized, gazing at Alexa with intense features.

She was surprised by his fervor, but she clenched her jaw and nodded with resolution, her eyes steel.

"All right, then," Apollos said.

"Let's stop stalling and just do it." Bryan stood. Alexa followed suit.

For a moment the four of them stared anxiously at one another, the flickering light dancing around them in the chamber. The reality that in just a few moments they could quite possibly be torn to pieces and eaten was powerful.

Apollos stretched his neck out and pressed his muzzle to Alexa's shoulder, his chocolate eyes encouraging and fretful all together. She turned to the unicorn and took his equine head in her hands to gaze fervently into his eyes. "Thank you," she said, and was about to say more, but the unicorn stopped her.

"None of that," he soothed, giving her another affectionate bump.

Alexa turned to Estella and nodded her appreciation. Apollos bobbed his head in encouragement toward the Master Sword, his eyes twinkling with fondness. Bryan nodded to him with a small, tense smile.

Once more, Bryan glanced at Alexa to find her gaze on him intense, a strange, powerful look behind her deep, sapphire eyes. They held only warmth. His heart swelled, and he suddenly wanted to crush her to his chest and smother her with kisses full of regret and farewell. But he wouldn't resort to the fact that they might not see each other again. He returned her gaze with as much depth. And they fell into a silent resolve together. They were a team: she, the warrior guide, and he, her warrior guardian.

Then, tearing their eyes from each other, they marched around the corner into the chamber. Everything that happened after went so quickly it was a surreal blur for the two humans.

The dragons didn't sense them, but the young one on guard

saw them straight away. At first, he was stunned, as still as a statue. His lithe, gangly body poised tall, his head high, and his eyes wild. He looked like a young colt braced for flight, but he would not flee; he would fight. The beast snorted a warning, arousing the others. Then he hissed. His ears flattened, and his eyes narrowed, glistening in anger. His neck outstretched, and he opened his mouth and sent out a blast of hot air and flames. The friends scattered.

Bryan, his sword drawn, gripped Alexa's arm so hard it would leave a bruise and pulled her toward the chasm. The unicorns shot with amazing speed toward the dragons. All three were now fully aware and prepared to fight. With arched bodies, they advanced, hissing and spitting flames.

Alexa and Bryan ran as fast as they could, dodging the spewing flames. Alexa fumbled with the vial, extracting it from her pocket and readying it in her hands as they dashed to the fountain. She wondered vaguely how she was even going to collect the flame. She barely noticed the Master Sword's body bumping and pressing harshly up against hers as they charged as one. He ran with his torso turned from her, his back on her, his sword drawn protectively.

Apollos and Estella were amazing. They dashed around with such speed that it confused the dragons. The reptiles were distracted altogether by the strange, white blurs that shot black bolts of pain at them.

Alexa and Bryan came to a skidding halt at the edge of the chasm. Bryan's grip tightened as Alexa's foot slipped over the rocky precipice. Both gasped for air, breathless from the heat and thrill. The flame lit their faces until their skin shone a brilliant white. The heat was immense; save for the magic in the everlasting flame, they would have ignited and turned to ash.

Alexa's eyes were alight as she gazed transfixed into the fire. "Quickly!" Bryan urged, watching the dragons hiss and snap at the two lethal unicorns.

She reached out, and he held his grip on her with one hand while the other held his sword aloft. She leaned over the edge and opened the vial, and without a second thought, stuck her hand straight into the colorful blaze. They both watched in amazement as the flames swirled and rippled as if she had stuck her hand into a placid pond. The flames shone an even brighter shade of their ever-changing colors and flowed swiftly into the vial like smoke sucked through a pipe. Alexa snapped the lid shut. And before she comprehended it, the Master Sword tugged her with such force away from the ledge that it jerked her entire body into action.

"Apollos! We got it!" Bryan hollered at the top of his lungs as they ran. His interruption caught the dragons' attentions. They turned toward the humans with such fury it sent a jolt of fear straight through both of their hearts. The unicorns were on the creatures in a flash, blocking the vomited flames with powerful magic emitted from their horns.

"Run! Run!" Apollos yelled frantically. "We'll hold them!"

Looking at their friends with love and trepidation, the humans escaped to the corridor as quickly as their legs could carry them. One of the smaller dragons flew and landed with a loud thud behind them. It growled, with a low, accompanying hiss, and spit another flame at the two frightened thieves, but they were just out of its reach; the beast couldn't fit down the passageway. It gave a roar of fury.

The Master Sword and Alexa pushed themselves as hard as they could. Their hearts pumped with a passion to match the dragons' wrath. Adrenalin raced through their limbs, sending them on farther and faster. They sprinted down the dark corridor blind, their breaths short and ragged. Their mouths dry as if stuffed with wool, their lungs burning and windpipes sore, and their minds pregnant with worry for the two left behind.

Racing around another bend, the heat lessened, but their sweat did not. They gripped hands now as they charged down the hall. Their eyes met on occasion, each brimming with small victory and immense fear.

They reached the door and crashed through it. The sunlight flooded the small storage chamber, and the two welcomed its comfort. Releasing Alexa's hand, Bryan regarded her briefly. "I'll go first, then pull you up," he breathed, his eyes wide and his face urgent. Alexa nodded mutely, gulping in an attempt to moisten her throat.

Bryan clambered up the rubble without much difficulty. He scrambled onto the green, weedy ground, flinging his legs out and around so his torso was hanging over the edge. He stretched his arms out to Alexa's reaching fingers. She clambered over the dilapidated stairs until she touched the blessed hands of her guardian. His strong grip closed around her hands, snaking down for a firmer one around her wrists, and then he heaved her up with little effort.

She scrambled onto the ground, momentarily sprawled awkwardly next to the Sword. They quickly got to their feet and upped their pace to a dead run, leaping over the rubble as they went. Alexa tripped, but Bryan caught her in reflex, and they barely missed a stride.

They reached the horses, breathless. The two animals were alert, having somehow sensed the catastrophe underground. They danced where they stood tied and waited impatiently as their masters mounted them. With enthusiastic snorts, the horses didn't even need to be asked to charge into a full-fledged gallop from a dead stand. They sensed the urgency and thrived on it.

The two companions galloped abreast, speaking to their mounts encouragingly. Bryan knew they *must* get within the protection of the rest of the company awaiting them with weapons ready, or else they would have no chance of survival.

Then, with an anxious flutter of his heart, he heard a great roar behind and above them. He glanced over his shoulder to see Apollos and Estella crashing, albeit rather quietly, through the forest to his left. The unicorns looked frantic and glanced every so often up to the sky where the largest of the dragons was lazily circling lower and lower. They must have had exited from another entrance in the forest, as Apollos had surmised.

Bryan urged Dragon for a faster pace. The warhorse dug in with pleasure and upped his speed, his nostrils catching wind of the predator chasing them. "Go! Go!" Bryan all but screamed at Alexa, motioning to the sky. She looked above and spotted the dragon, and fear conquered her face. She glanced at Bryan with wide eyes and then leaned down over Zhan's withers, asking the horse for more speed. He responded with amazing swiftness. He dashed past Dragon as if the warhorse was standing still and sprinted down the treacherous forest lane with agility and purpose.

As Bryan fell behind, he watched Alexa's lean body move in perfect sync with Zhan. They were lengths and lengths ahead now. The dragon was closing in. It seemed to take its time, knowing it had the upper hand in flight. It circled lower and lower, heading for Alexa as if it somehow knew she carried its treasure.

The unicorns were now far ahead of the Master Sword and were leaping into the air as high as they could launch themselves and still hit the ground running. They sent black bolts of light out of their horns in the dragon's direction, each taking every other shot.

Soon, the unicorns were running abreast with Zhan. The great reptile in the sky glided high above, screeching wrathfully when the deadly bolts hit. Then, in an instant, the dragon shot down with the alarm and speed of an experienced predator. It charged straight into the fleeing group.

Bryan let out a choked holler, "No!" But all he could do was watch in helpless horror as he galloped Dragon from way back. Ahead of him, there was a tumbling mass of white and metallic. "Alexa!" he shouted, a piercing fear in his chest. He urged Dragon for more. The game stallion, his black body foaming white with sweat, laid his ears flat and pressed faster.

The tumbling mass grappled. White blurs zipped around, and the silver body flipped violently, giving off a vicious hiss. Then, with a snap, the dragon rose out of the heap, dragging with it a white lump in its talons. It roared in triumph.

Bryan's terrified eyes took a second to focus. For a moment, he thought the creature had one of the unicorns, but he then realized it was not. It was Zhan. "Alexa," he whispered hoarsely as his eyes followed the dragon into the sky.

The unicorns were already up and pursuing, shooting never-ending bolts of death. The Master Sword had never had a crushing so intense in his chest before now. He couldn't breathe. His eyes tore from the scene in the sky to latch on a crumpled figure looming ahead of him. His heart jolted.

Alexa stirred on the ground, dazed and struggling to stand, falling to her knees; but she was alive! The dragon hadn't carried her off with Zhan. The greatest relief flooded over him like a tidal wave.

His mind and body had only moments to react as her stunned figure came upon him. The Master Sword let go of the reins, allowing Dragon to take control; the stallion galloped on obediently. Bryan calculated the distance and speed at which they moved. He leaned down over the left side of the saddle and reached out. The girl was on her knees, her head lolling. And as the stallion sped by, Bryan's desperate hands groped for her. He felt the touch of her and gripped onto whatever it was he had.

His left hand clasped around her thick braid at the base of her neck, and he yanked her up as hard as he could. She came up much easier than he had thought. His right hand gripped her shoulder, and he pulled her swiftly onto his saddle where she lay across her belly in front of him. She was scarcely aware and struggled mildly against his hold. He gazed down at her with soft, intense eyes.

He could now see the others ahead. They had gathered, and the centaurs were sending scores of arrows from their crossbows into the sky toward the livid dragon.

Once he reached the group, he dismounted with speed and agility, dragging a bewildered Alexa with him. Warrior Hazerk was suddenly at his side, gesturing for him to carry her to the closest tent so he could tend to her.

Bryan scarcely noted the flames emitting from the sky, or the vile hissing and growling from the dragon. He gazed down into Alexa's befuddled, dirty, sweaty, bloodied face with such affection he could barely hide it any longer, and carried her into a tent and gently laid her down. He didn't notice a sudden cry from one of his own warriors in the background, nor the surprised exclamations from the rest of the company, nor the sudden, strange silence from the dragon herself.

CHAPTER THIRTY-SEVEN

"You're lucky, Lil' Sis'. It's nothing too serious, just going to have to put up with a sore shoulder and neck, a few minor scratches and bruising."

"And a very bad headache," Alexa groaned. She sat perched on the end of a cot in Hazerk's tent, her head resting in her hand. She had a terrible throbbing behind her temples.

"And it looks as if you might get a black eye marring that cute face of yours—though, the good news is it'll cover up some of those freckles," Hazerk said lightheartedly. She gave him a weak look of exasperation. He then added more solicitously, touching her shoulder, "Just take it easy for the rest of the night. It was a pretty nasty spill."

Alexa looked up into the redhead's kind, amber eyes and noticed for the first time that he had laugh wrinkles. She gave him a weak smile, still trying not to move her ailing head. "Thanks, Hazerk." Her voice was hoarse.

He smiled. "Didn't have to do much." He shrugged and glanced at Bryan, who stood among the others crowded in the tent. "But if the Master Sword hadn't yanked you up by your hair, I figure your neck wouldn't be so sore," he joked, with a wide grin.

Alexa looked up at her Sword-Guard. He gazed at her with his face set impassive, but his azure eyes were tense with worry. Despite all, she decided to give him a break from her ire, and she attempted to muster up a grin at him. He returned her gesture with a weak, crooked smile. He then fidgeted restively and glanced away from her gaze. She wondered at this, but before she could think on it too much, Prince Alkin stepped to her side, demanding her attention.

"I think you should get some rest. You've done a good job today." His comment wasn't only meant for Alexa; it was directed at the rest of them hanging around to clear out. He eyeballed each one of them.

She shrugged and was immediately remorseful for this action. A sharp pain shot through her shoulder and up her neck. She winced. "I'm fine, really," she said when Hazerk rushed to her side. "You all can go. I feel like I'm on display or something," she groused.

"All right," Hazerk snickered. "I'm off. If you need anything, let me know. Take care, Lil' Sis'." With that, he stepped over and planted a friendly kiss on her hairline above her temple. Alexa smiled gratefully at him. He departed.

Jadelin, who had been among the crowd, gave her a concerned look and came to place a quick kiss on her cheek. "Get well." She smiled, but Alexa noticed the Empress' eyes were cheerless. She watched her go, waving off Kheane as he nodded his get well and then followed the Empress out.

"Okay, see you, kiddo." Warkan patted her awkwardly on her good shoulder.

"Yeah," she said, looking after him with dry amusement.

The Prince and the Master Sword were the last in the tent. Her head ached so terribly, she wasn't comprehending much. But after an odd moment of the men standing restively by, she looked up from where she had been resting her head in her hands and realized that Eelyne hadn't been among the inquisitive party. She glanced from the Prince to the Sword, not even caring about her previous sillier concerns of the two men. "Where's Eelyne?" she asked with concern. The two men glanced at each other anxiously. Finally, she caught on that something was awry. "What's going on? Is something wrong? Is he all right? The dragon's dead or gone, right?"

"He's fine, Alexa. We actually have something to tell you," the Prince said with forced enthusiasm. He sat down next to her, the cot creaking noisily at his weight. The Master Sword held his stance over by the tent flap, staring unnervingly at her with a quiet demeanor. Though his brows were gathered in a tense way and his eyes bored into her with a guarded concern, his handsome lips turned down ever-so-slightly.

Alexa, now completely unnerved, flashed her eyes back and forth between the two of them. "Tell me what's going on," she demanded.

"Well, it's really good, actually," the Prince forced another smile. She glared at him, incredulous, but he pressed on. "After you passed out, the Master Sword brought you in here while the rest of us tried to bring down the dragon. It looked optimistic, but Eelyne suddenly started yelling at all of us to stop shooting at her. I guess he somehow connected with her like a dragon whisperer would."

"Really?" Alexa was surprised and impressed and rather pleased. "That's good, then. What're you all worried about? Did she stop attacking? Is she communicating back with Eelyne?"

"Yes, actually." The Prince finally looked sincerely happy; that strange, unnerving anxiety no longer clouding his eyes. "She stopped almost immediately. Eelyne explains it only as if he just plain understands her language and her his. He doesn't *hear* her speak human words, but when she hears him speak, she understands him. He's explained everything to her, and surprisingly and fortunately, she's willing to comply with us."

"That's great!" Alexa's enthusiasm caused her to wince again, which made her to note a pain throbbing near her eye. She lifted her hand to probe the area around her left eye gently. It was very tender with a cut there.

"So, the dragon is assigning one of her two sons to be bound faithfully to Eelyne. He'll be Eelyne's counterpart for life. She can't leave herself because she's bound to guard the fountain of flame and pass on that duty to at least one of her sons. The other of her offspring will come to Eelyne's aid when needed. The dragonling will not travel with us. With Eelyne's whisperer connection with him, it will be able to hear his call." Alkin ended with a broad grin.

"This is good news." Alexa smiled, massaging her shoulder as she looked into the Prince's avid eyes. He studied her features fondly for a second. He sat close. And suddenly, feeling the unsolicited attention as a threat, she glanced away just as he reached up and pushed a lock of her tangled hair out of her eyes.

She raised her gaze, somewhat victoriously, up into the Master Sword's once again impassive countenance. She couldn't help but rub the Prince's sentiments toward her in his face, even if they were unwanted. *He'll be sorry for disregarding me*, she thought, revengeful with all the hurt he had caused. She watched with a haughty glint in her eyes as Bryan's face turned from impassive to rigid and then into a scowl. She glanced away from him, triumphant, and regarded the Prince once more with a coy smile. "I think I'll just rest here a bit. I think if I stand, my head might roll off." She grimaced.

Alkin nodded with a small smile. He gave her a gentle hug, careful of her shoulder, and pressed his warm, soft lips to her forehead. "Rest well." He stood and went to leave, gesturing for the ill-tempered Master Sword to follow.

Alexa attempted to lay herself down into a more comfortable position on the cot and then remembered Zhan. How could she possibly forget to ask about him? She must have hit her head hard. "Hey," she said. The two men halted their exit and looked back at her expectantly. "You caught Zhan, right? Make sure he's comfortable and gets fed, too. Will you, please?" She laid her head back, assured that she needn't worry about the care of her horse.

The two men glanced nervously at each other and didn't speak. And this time she truly understood all the odd, anxious looks in everyone's eyes. She jerked up, ignoring her swimming vision. Fear shot through her whole body. Her eyes bored into their troubled faces frantically. "You got Zhan, right? He's not lost in the forest, is he?" She stood abruptly, ignoring her pain, and rushed to the door, but the men blocked her. She tried to push past, close to a panic. "What's going on? Where's Zhan?" she demanded.

"Alexa, sit down for a second." Alkin held her firmly by the shoulders, restraining her from leaving the tent, forgetting to be careful of her shoulder.

"What do you mean?" she growled, her blue eyes suddenly firing up into spitting flames. Alkin pushed her backward toward the cot. Bryan followed with rueful eyes. She glanced frantically between them. "Tell me what's going on," she commanded. She struggled against Alkin's hold and broke free, only to be stopped abruptly by the Master Sword's iron grip on her good shoulder.

"We were going to wait to tell you…so you could get some rest," Alkin began.

She clenched her jaw, and her stomach gave a violent lurch.

Her throat began to constrict. "Tell me what?" she hissed through her teeth.

Both men looked at her with sad eyes. "Zhan...he didn't survive the dragon's attack. I'm sorry, Alexa," Alkin said, his shoulders slumping, and his hazel eyes fallen.

"What? No!" she cried. There was an abrupt, sharp stab behind her eyes, and unstoppable tears pooled and began spilling down her face. "No, that can't be. We just had a tumble! You can't mean... Oh, Zhan, no!" she wept.

She couldn't breathe. How could she breathe? Her throat had closed up completely. Her lungs burned for air. Her head swam. She felt as if she were going to vomit and faint. She couldn't see clearly, but she didn't care to see the men's sympathetic faces. She pushed past them and raced through the tent flap before they could stop her again, but they didn't try.

She sprinted out into the light and glanced around, frantic and searching, searching adamantly for her friend. Where was he? He must be standing over by the other horses, snacking on some juicy blades of grass. She raced to the tethered horses. He wasn't among them; she choked out another panicked cry. She raced to the other side of the camp, unaware of the company's sorrowful gazes on her. "Zhan! Zhan!" she screamed in panic.

Then she saw him. He lay on the ground near where the company had gathered earlier to hold off the dragon. Her breath caught in the lump in her throat, and she choked on a sob. He looked as if he were sunbathing. He was spread lazily out for a nap in the evening sun was all.

She raced to him and fell to her knees at his neck, where her eyes took in the dreaded realization.

Her hand flew to her mouth. Her eyes glistened with tears as they roved over his still body. His head was outstretched. His limbs lay limply down on the ground. His long, white, glossy tail sprawled over the emerald grass. His mane was still slick with cold sweat as it stuck to his neck.

Alexa laid her palm on her horse's shoulder. It was still warm but cooling. After all, it had only been a short time since the whole ordeal. She leaned down close to him and laid her head on his sweaty neck, diverting her gaze from his wide, lifeless, chocolate-colored eyes. "Oh, my dear, dear Zhan. Where have you gone without me?" she whispered. Tears welled again and rolled down her cheeks to land warm and wet on his cool body. She held him for a long moment, not caring what the others thought of her. Her heart physically ached. She had never realized there could be so much agony imprisoned in a person before. She was broken, and she couldn't find the lost piece. *It's all my fault...if only I'd listened and stayed back, you'd be here still. I'm so, so sorry. I'm sorry...*

After several long minutes, she felt warm hands take her and pull her to her feet. She allowed this to happen only because Zhan's body was cooling faster by the minute, and it didn't feel right. No, it didn't feel right at all.

She comprehended that the hands belonged to Prince Alkin. He guided her away from Zhan to her tent. The Prince attempted to hold her and comfort her. But she didn't want to be comforted. She wanted to be left alone in her pain. She tried to pull away in her sorrow, but Prince Alkin wouldn't allow it. It was aggravating, but she didn't have the mentality to fight him. Dazed, she let him guide her to her own cot. Where he sat down and helped her curl up by his side, guiding her aching head to rest on his shoulder. Her fingers clenched around his arm in a harsh embrace. He soothed her, brushing back her damp hair. And that was where she cried until she had no tears left to release her surmounting pain.

CHAPTER THIRTY-EIGHT

That night everyone felt Alexa's pain in some form or another. Most all had a connection with their mount they couldn't explain. None could imagine what it would be like to be abruptly and irrevocably parted forever. It would be like losing a close loved one.

While Prince Alkin held and comforted Alexa in her tent, and while the sun slowly slipped behind the woodland horizon, Bryan kept company with the horses. He was restless, aggrieved, and annoyed. Aggrieved for Alexa's pain, but also for himself, in that he wished he had been the one to take her in his arms and offer comfort. For that same reason, he was annoyed. He was also angry with his prince and friend. He knew full well he couldn't interfere now, especially now that Alkin's intentions were so apparent. In seeing Alexa's deep sorrow, Bryan couldn't even bring himself to be bitter about her revengeful actions against him. He supposed he deserved them. *How pathetic is that?*

Pacing along the line of tethered warhorses, he stared at the toes of his boots as he marched. Every once in a while, a horse would crane out its neck and nuzzle his sleeve in curiosity. The Sword would then pat the soft nose and continue on with his restive pacing. Coming to the end of the line where Dragon was tied, he paused his march and greeted the stallion. The horse tossed his head and stuck his nose in his master's face and whickered a breath. Bryan breathed in the sweet, grassy-scented breath and smiled for the first time since that morning.

Giving his burly, black horse a firm, loving pat, he looked out over the hills of the forest before him to the setting sun. It glowed a soft orange as the very tip finally sunk away. He sighed, annoyed again, clenched his jaw, and thought about what Alkin's reaction might be if he marched into the tent and pulled Alexa out of his arms and into his own. Bryan snorted in derision at the thought. He could never do that; his duty wouldn't allow it. Though, he was discovering he absolutely hated he had to hide that he loved her and that he couldn't have her. Having her for himself was consuming his thoughts more and more with every passing moment.

He grunted, trying to clear his thoughts, and continued his ill-tempered march. After another minute of brooding, he gave Dragon one last pat. He would go to his tent and sleep. At least there his mind could have a reprieve from the vision of Alkin and Alexa together…as well as the fanciful vision of himself and her making love…

With that, he stalked off to his tent moodily. It took all his will-power and self-discipline when he passed Alexa's not to charge in there and command Alkin to get out. He could hear them together in there still. He ground his teeth and ducked into his tent. Adjusting his sword so he wouldn't lay on it, he plopped down on his cot and cleared his mind of all thought so he could fall asleep in peace. Eventually, his mind drifted, and he fell into a sea of happy nothingness.

Bryan's body twitched in his sleep. He snapped awake, groggily opening his eyes. It was very dark out, late in the night. After midnight, he guessed. Sitting up, he moved stiffly, rubbing his face, and reached for his water pouch to take a long drink. His ears caught a soft sound as he drank. He put the pouch aside and wiped his lips, listening, his innate warrior senses piqued. There should be nothing to concern him; some of the centaurs were on guard as well as the unicorns and even a young dragon. He listened only a moment more before he realized what it was. Alexa was moving on her cot, and it sounded as if she tossed violently around. She either wasn't sleeping well, or she was awake and very uncomfortable. But what could he do? He couldn't go to her. Or could he?

He stood abruptly, almost subconsciously, and was out the flap of his tent before he had time to even think about his actions. He took the few quick strides over to the entrance to her tent. The sound of her tossing and the creak of the cot was now clear. He was about to enter when he froze. He couldn't bring himself to go in. If he went in, he would be working against the duty he held as her Sword-Guard. Could he contend with that? Could he interfere with his prince and friend?

The Master Sword sighed and turned around, very annoyed with his sense of duty. But instead of returning to his tent, he settled to pace restively in front of Alexa's. He took in a deep breath of the cool night air and craned his neck back to gaze into the inky blue sky dotted with thousands of twinkling white lights. He relaxed a little at the heavenly sight, and with a furrowed brow, he pondered vaguely why the stars reminded him strongly of the starry twinkle in Apollos' chocolate-colored eyes. This thought didn't last long, as he was interrupted by another violent shifting sound from Alexa's tent. He glanced there, his eyes troubled with a thousand tangled thoughts.

"Master Sword, there isn't any need for you to be on guard duty."

He spun around at the soft voice coming from behind him. Apollos stood a few strides away, his snowy, velvety coat glowing faintly in the dark. The unicorn was looking at him with a curious, pragmatic gaze.

"Yes, I know. I couldn't sleep," he answered.

Apollos lowered his head, his prismatic horn glinting in the low light left from the hot coals in the fire. The unicorn eyed him thoughtfully and said, "It sounds as if Alexa is having a hard time sleeping, too. I'm afraid her sorrow and aches keep her awake. I wish I could go comfort her."

The Master Sword's brow turned puzzled. The unicorn's words were off compared to what his voice implied. "Then go to her. She'd be grateful," he replied.

The unicorn flipped his mane, shaking his head, a twinkle in his chocolate eyes. "I don't fit in the tent," he said, with no small amount of amusement.

"Oh." Bryan looked away from the unicorn's confusing, penetrating gaze and began pacing again.

Apollos walked over to stand directly in front of the Sword's path. Bryan halted, gazing into the unicorn's equine features, trying to discern what the beautiful creature was attempting to communicate. Apollos gave him a level stare. He stared back. What was the silly unicorn trying to say?

"You, Master Sword, could fit in the tent," Apollos stated, giving him another pragmatic look.

Bryan glanced hesitantly from Apollos to the tent, now realizing exactly what the unicorn wanted of him. Speechless for a second, he opened his mouth as if to make an excuse. But who could argue with Apollos? Instead, Bryan's wide, anxious eyes darted over to Prince Alkin's tent in a silent question.

Apollos bobbed his head, his horn glimmering like the stars, and said, "The affection he shows for Alexa is shallow in comparison to yours. Don't worry about your friend. He'll realize it all in time. You do what you know you must."

With that revelation, Apollos left the suddenly elated Master Sword to himself. All thoughts of duty had dissipated at the unicorn's words. He didn't care what his duty called for. He could handle it, and he would handle it as it came. He didn't even care that he knew he may feel differently about his decision in the morning.

Then, forgetting all self-discipline and reservation, Bryan walked straight over to Alexa's tent and went in. He was through the flap before he could have a second thought. He stopped at the entrance. She lay on her cot, her body huddled and dejected looking. He was rendered still. His heart began to thrum at a quicker pace, and his body warmed at his anticipated rebellion.

Alexa thrashed and jerked around to lie in another position, not even noticing his presence. Her magical senses must be distraught, too. But her movement snapped Bryan into action, and he was at her side in one swift movement. He reached out to her and felt her warm skin brush against his rough hands. She made a noise, startled at the touch, and flinched from the unfamiliar hands. But he hushed her and then gently scooped her up and into his arms, where she gazed hazily into his face. She slurred something inarticulate. But he hushed her again. Her puzzled features softened as she comprehended his intentions, and she let out a long, relieved sigh and snuggled closer, causing his heart to race nervously. He smiled despite himself and then lowered himself, with her in his arms, down on the cot where he stretched out on his back. There was no room for them side by side, so he settled her where she lay on her side next to him, his arm around her.

Alexa snuggled up against him, wrapping one leg around his

and draping an arm across his chest. Her body was warm against his, and without explanation, it was *right*. He couldn't get her close enough. It was as if she was a piece of his body that had been missing, and now it was once again fully intact with her here, this close. Happiness flooded through him. It was strange to even feel that emotion...

Alexa slipped in and out of consciousness, her face nuzzled in his shoulder, her arms still surrounding him, and leg draped over him. Every once in a while, he felt her twitch awake with a strangled sob, and he would tighten his arms around her slight frame. She would bury her face in his chest, wetting his shirt with her tears for a short time before she drifted back off to sleep. Still, she slept more restful with him here. That thought comforted him. He doubted he would be able to sleep at all. He was so wide awake with exhilaration. He knew she wasn't completely aware of the situation, perhaps she wouldn't even remember in the morning. But he didn't care. He just merely cuddled her when she cried and smoothed her raven hair back. It was soft, and in her restlessness, it had come free from her plait. It laid over them like a silky shawl, and he ran his fingers blissfully through it.

He was content, more than content, just to lie there and hold her. Though, he knew he must rise and leave for his own tent before the others rose for the day. He was still uneasy about the rest of the company being aware of their feelings for each other. He especially didn't want Alkin to know. That would come in time. He sighed with the thought, but it wasn't an aggrieved sigh. He couldn't feel such a feeling right now, so he wrapped his arms closer around her and gave her a tender squeeze. She responded readily, snuggling her face into the crook of his neck, sending chills spilling through his body.

His wishful vision of him and her together in a more personal manner roared up again. He remembered how lovely she had looked the night he had almost kissed her...and how he had hopelessly thought he would have liked very much to help her remove that elegant gown from her beautiful frame when she had stated so ruefully that she wanted it off. He smiled at his own memory. Then there was the morning he had found her bathing in the warm spring. Her eyes and skin had glowed, inviting in all his senses… Her figure willowy, elegant, strong…

He had better be careful; he couldn't let his mind wander into such thoughts. It had been a long time since he had held a woman in his arms. And he had never held one in his arms before that he felt this strongly about. But, he chided himself, he couldn't compromise her virtue. She held such a close relationship with Apollos, he couldn't upset that. Not right now. He loved her all the more for her liberty to touch the unicorn without retribution. At the thought, he ran his hand tenderly down the length of her back. The feel of her beneath his palm was exhilarating. She mumbled a soft response.

A smile twitched across his mouth. She shifted again in her sleep, and he turned and pressed his lips gently to her head. He wanted to breathe her in forever. He wanted her closer; pulled her close in frustration and kissed her face fervently, once, twice, three times. His lips touching her temple, he stopped, realizing sheepishly he was getting carried away.

Alexa moved, her face near his. But before she settled, he caught her eyes. She held his gaze for a moment, and he froze. Then a long, pleased sigh escaped her lips, and she nestled her head down. "Bryrunan," she whispered into his neck, her breath soft on his skin, and then she fell into sleep once more.

Her tender touch sent stronger emotions coursing through him. He used to hate people using his birth name, but on her lips, it sounded nice. It passed her mouth like music, and he found he didn't mind her use of it.

Bryan loved her. She had dispelled all his bitterness and brought him back down to earth where he belonged. He decided then and there that he wanted her to be his wife. Somehow, he knew she would want the same. When this mission was over, they would stay together. He smiled at this heartening vision of him and her. Not only them together forever, but their bare, warm skin pressed against each other as they lay entwined in each other's arms…

Then, a sudden shock of horrid realization ran through his body, chilling him to his core. His features froze in dismay and he went rigid. He couldn't be with Alexa. He wasn't allowed to be with her. Despite all his qualms of going against his duty as her Sword-Guard and going against his duty as the company's leader and going against his friendship and his prince, he still couldn't be with her. And this was something that was irrevocable, practically sealed with his blood, completely and undeniably permanent. He couldn't go against it, or else it would mean his life, either by severe punishment or even death. It was his oath as a Master Sword. He had made an irreversible oath to serve Shelkite all his life and with all his blood. The strict oath of a Master Sword was to serve Shelkite in every possible way, and that included he could only marry a woman born of Shelkiten blood, so she could bear Shelkiten children.

Bryan lamented the day he became a Master Sword. The thought of him falling in love ever again, let alone falling for a foreigner, had never crossed his mind when he had taken the oath. He had been so determined to be just a simple warrior for the rest of his days.

He wrapped his arms around Alexa's slender body and ran his hands restlessly from her shoulders along her back. How wonderful her frame felt under his fingers. He did *not* want to give her up. Bryan clenched his jaw at the injustice. He couldn't give her up, especially now when he had allowed himself to succumb to her. There was no going back for his heart, or hers. But he honestly didn't have a choice.

The Master Sword squeezed his eyes shut with the immense sorrow for the loss he knew he had to bear. He didn't want to face it, but there wasn't an option. He wanted this night to last forever, for there would never be another for them. He didn't want to admit the oath's power over him. Curse it! He couldn't think of her in another's arms, but he must not hold her either! He would be forced to return to his passive indifference for both of their wellbeing and continue to be merely her Sword-Guard as he was intended to be. It would be best to suppress his feelings and pretend this never happened…

He pressed a desperate kiss to her forehead, and then another, his eyes alight with indignation, torment, and sorrow. What had he done? Why had he allowed himself to come in here and discover how wonderful it felt to hold her in his arms, only to find that this would be the first and last time?

CHAPTER THIRTY-NINE

Unsettling visions swirled before Alexa's closed eyes. They danced and whirled, causing her sleep to be restless and pointless. All night she drifted in and out of agitated sleep and heartrending consciousness. One minute she would fall into the abyss of sleep, only to awaken suddenly with such a crushing force of loss in her chest that it threatened to suffocate her and drown her in its depth.

Her woe over Zhan's death was so powerful it haunted her dreams and consumed her waking moments of the night. He was now only a memory, forever in the past, never again to awaken so he could make new. She yearned for a sweet oblivion to escape the sorrow and the hole he had left.

Then, sometime during the night, oblivion did come. It came to her in the form of Bryan. Or so she thought it was him. She couldn't be sure, her mind so mangled with distress and dreams so vivid and strong, seeming real one moment and ethereal the next. But Bryan had brought with him an oblivion that numbed her pain unlike anything else could. True, she still had awakened with the same suffocating force, but it had lessened as he stayed deeper into the night and soothed her splintered heart with his comforting kisses and embrace. *Kisses?* She puzzled over this, even in her half-asleep state.

His arms locked around her had chased away the abyss of her pain. Though as the rays of dawn seeped through the flap in her tent, reality and sorrow threatened to intertwine its bitter soul around her again. The Master Sword's warmth and comfort were absent. His presence had been as fleeting as peaceful sleep. If it had even been there at all... Perhaps her mind had created the illusion of his presence to ease her pain. She pondered this in slumber.

But deep down, locked away in a casket, she knew, even in her sleep, that his presence *had* been real. She had wanted him to stay. But why did he leave, taking with him his solace? Would he now return with the dawn? Was he finally succumbing to his feelings for her? Would he now love her as she knew he wanted to?

Alexa tossed on her cot, tangled in her disturbing dreams and thoughts of the Master Sword. The bright morning sun threatened to peel its way behind her closed eyelids, but her mind was not done dreaming. It was exhausted from the restless night, and it yearned for time to recede and wallow in the dark, although its paths of dreams were anything but dulcet oblivion.

She dreamed of Zhan. He galloped joyfully in his pasture back home. The desert sun shone on his satiny back. He leapt merrily over the sandy terrain and raced up the side of a rocky cliff. The Alexa in her dream watched in admiration at his grace. But it turned to horror as she watched him leap splendidly over the cliff and free fall. He flew down, down, to land softly on the ground before her. She reached out to touch him, and he transformed into the white stag.

She stood in the dense forest of Carthorn. The stag with his grand antlers towered above her as if she were only a foot tall. His fierce black eyes gazed at her. Then he spoke, and his voice was like thunder racking the air around her, blowing her hair back in its gust. *Alexandra! The breath of the world dawns from the soil of your blood!*

She jerked awake, and found herself alone, the late morning light glaring through her tent. She rubbed the sleep from her eyes. They were puffy from her tears of the night as well as her wounds. She looked hazily around, trying to absorb everything. She stared, perplexed, at the ground, and then swung her stiff legs out and placed her feet down. Was Zhan really dead? Had the Master Sword really come to comfort her? Why did her dreams turn to the stag's mysterious words?

In thought, she ran her fingers through her tangled, raven mane and reached for her battered brush in her sack. Brushing her hair and braiding it for the day, she pondered the words of the stag: *the breath of the world dawns from the soil of your blood*. She repeated the statement over and over in her head. Sitting and staring baffled at the wall of her tent for a moment, she realized the stag had given her a riddle.

Her brows raised in comprehension. It wasn't a hard one. Slightly excited and pushing aside her inner pain, she worked on its meaning. The breath of the world. What would the breath of the world be? It meant the wind, of course. He was helping her find the wind element. *Okay.* She bit her lip and then chewed a nail. *Dawns...ah...the beginning of the day; the origin...it comes from!* She felt a tinge of glee. She stood and began pacing. Though, she had to stop briefly to collect her bearings, her body sore and stiff. Slowly and gently, she stretched her muscles while she thought. *The wind element comes from the soil of my blood?* She contemplated this confusing idea, a bit cynical.

"Soil...soil...land, of course," she muttered aloud to herself. She licked her lips and took a swig from her water pouch, wiping the excess on her lips away with her sleeve. "Blood, my blood. It's inside me? No. It's my ancestry. The wizards have the element? No, that's not right." She growled in aggravation. The answer was there; it was just barely eluding her. "My father, my home...soil, home. My homeland! The wind element is in Kaltraz. Not just Kaltraz, but Eastern Kaltraz, my home. Dawn, where the sun rises in the east; it has a double meaning. It's in the far east of Kaltraz. That's it!" Alexa bounced on her heels in triumph and promptly regretted it.

It had been so simple. How hadn't she seen the answer before? Well, it was most likely because right after her encounter with the stag, she'd been nearly violated and murdered, and then after, she'd been consumed with thoughts only for the Master Sword...Bryan...how would he act toward her today, after last night?

Trying desperately to forget her sorrow and think only of her newfound bond with her Sword-Guard and her knowledge of the wind element, she decided she would tell the others of her discovery.

She readied herself. But quickly found that even with her determination to forget her pain, it still raised its ugly head. The gaping hollowness in her chest sucked all the good thoughts right into it like a vortex, leaving her feeling sour and low. She sighed in averseness to its power as she stepped outside. She would have to press on, nonetheless, and let the hollow vortex do its evil as she did her job. It wasn't something she could ignore or rid herself of. She would just have to tolerate it while it lasted, much like the aches still emanating from her body.

In the glaring morning sun, she studied the camp. Everyone was mingling around, preparing to depart. Obviously, the Master Sword hadn't rushed them to leave at the crack of dawn like he usually did. It was probably on her account. She was grateful. Plus, as far as they were concerned, they were unsure what their next step was, anyway. She would fix that right now.

"Alexa! You're up. How are you feeling?" Prince Alkin broke from the throng of centaurs and warriors to come to her side.

She smiled at him, remembering his own attempt at comforting her. He had held her and allowed her to cry on his shoulder for a few hours. But, really, she would have rather been left alone or had Bryan there instead. However, she would never say such a thing to the kind prince. "I'm fine, thank you." She forced a smile past the crater in her chest and endeavored not to look over to where Zhan's body had lain motionless the night before.

"I'm glad." His hazel eyes searched her.

She looked at him, her blue eyes soft with appreciation. "Thank you for…for understanding."

The Prince smiled. "Of course."

"I have some good news," she continued, trying to sound upbeat.

Alkin's eyebrows rose. "Really? What?"

"I know where to look for the wind element. If you want, I'll explain it to the company as a whole," she said, struggling to place herself into a business-like mood.

"That's great news," Alkin exclaimed and touched her arm lightly. "Come on." He took her hand and led her to where the rest of the company was gathered around the fire pit.

"Everyone! Alexa knows where to find the wind element," he called, halting all conversation and grabbing everyone's rapt attention.

Alexa searched the many expectant faces and found the one she sought. The Master Sword was on the opposite side of the pit among the centaurs. His view of her had been blocked, and he moved so he could see her better. They met eyes. She took this brief moment to let loose her senses on him. To get a clear reading, it was always best if she looked directly in the other's eyes. She needed to know what he was feeling. She couldn't guess and didn't want to be surprised if he suddenly treated her with indifference.

The Master Sword gazed at her passively, his guarded eyes unwilling to meet hers. She felt like a dagger was thrust into her chest at his avoidance and nearly became overwhelmed with the sudden crushing, entangled emotions of betrayal and sadness, of the undeniable loss of him as well as Zhan. She couldn't take much more. Her soul would crumble to dust soon.

She narrowed her enchanting eyes at him ever-so-slightly, her jaw set hard with inner rage and hurt. The Sword tried to pull away from her dire glare, but she wasn't giving up so easily. She forced her senses on him, magically persuading the reluctant Sword to meet her eyes and hold her deciphering gaze. He resisted, but he bent under her power, swimming in the depths of her eyes. Strangely enough, she could feel powerful and *good* emotions emitting from him. However, they were tangled and bound tightly with anger and sadness. Then, slowly, as she had him ensnared, all his emotions became obscured with the old, bitter, dark sludge. This perplexed her, and she let his fighting gaze go, feeling lost at the confrontations going on inside of him.

Once she released him, he let his passive, azure eyes linger on her a moment longer. But she could read no emotion from him now; he had shut down. She tried to decipher this knowledge with common sense, pushing her bewildered pain aside. Maybe she *had* dreamt of him during the night, and his visit was merely an imaginary vision of her wishes. She looked away from his broad stature, feeling small and child-like. She was like a heart-sick young girl filled with dreams of falling in love with a knight in shining armor. How ironic and sad. She had become what she used to detest in other girls her age, always dreaming of ridiculous romances.

But how could she have imagined that? It was unlike the vivid dream she had had while sleeping in Shelkite's hills. It had to be real. He felt *something* for her; she sensed it. Why wasn't he letting go? Why did he endeavor so hard to close himself off from her? She sighed; she wasn't only upset but confused.

She glanced at the Prince, who still looked fondly at her, his hazel eyes alight. She gazed into his handsome, kind face and pondered. Perhaps the Master Sword knew Alkin held affections for her, too. So, the Sword's hands—and his heart—were figuratively bound. Why should it matter in the long run, though? Unless he was only playing with her...

She nodded a solemn greeting at Bryan and left it at that. She was tiring of this game that involved the senseless interpretation of his emotions. They needed to clear things between them. But that was pointless; considering it was obvious he had no intention of pursuing her. In a strange, heartrending way she understood. They both had a duty, and that was where their relationship ended. That was their unspoken understanding. She left her musings there. She had a job to do and couldn't dwell on it.

The others waited expectantly for her news and had not noticed her brief pause. She forced herself to switch to the business at hand, determined to keep it there, lest she become even more distracted from her mission. So, she promptly immersed herself in the explanation of the discovery of the wind element. They listened with rapt attention as she explained about the white stag. The company expressed their approval at her decipherment of the riddle and agreed that it sounded as if the wind element was in Eastern Kaltraz. It was decided on the spot they would travel there next without delay.

Alexa didn't have to persuade them to continue on with their original plan to stop by her family's inn on the way. She wanted to speak with her father about the mission. Alkin and Bryan wished to hear the wizard's thoughts on Ret, and also wanted his opinion of the elemental usage and maybe a better explanation of it, too.

It was settled. Within the next couple days, they would pack up and head out of Carthorn toward Alexa's home. How comforting that sounded. She was pleased to be going home, even if it was only for a short time. Being home with her family might ease her stress of losing Zhan, among other things.

CHAPTER FORTY

It was late in the night at the Ice Palace; most everyone rested quietly in their chamber. Lady Dorsa slept, though she walked with purpose down the dimly lit corridor, her open eyes unseeing, her thin nightdress barely enough to keep her warm from the draftiness of the palace, but she did not feel the cold. Beneath her soles, her bare feet should have felt the iciness of the stone alabaster floor and the lushness of the soft, elaborate rugs as she moved over them, but they did not. She did not feel the cool, smooth, solid object clutched in the fingers of her left hand.

Her involuntary steps brought her closer and closer to her subconscious' destination. Somewhere in the back of her mind, something aware and terrified screamed for her to wake. But her dream persisted, driven by a dark enchantment she knew nothing about. A curse was on her. It moved her limbs numbly forward, determined to finish its wicked task.

"My lady, what are you doing up at this hour?" a male voice questioned from behind.

Dorsa's consciousness whooshed into effect; she awoke with a start. Her footsteps halted as her mind became aware she was walking. She looked around herself and realized she was standing in the corridor that led away from the kitchens.

"My lady, are you all right?" the voice persisted.

Dorsa glanced down at her hand, comprehending a foreign object there. A knife glinted in the low light cast from the sconces lining the alabaster walls. She bit back a frightened gasp and nearly dropped it. The concerned voice's footsteps started toward her, and she gathered her wits about her. She spun, concealing the kitchen knife behind her back, and looked into the guard's troubled features.

"Oh, I apologize. I'm fine. I—ah, occasionally walk in my sleep. No reason to be alarmed." She forced a cheerful, sheepish smile on her face. The guard stopped a few strides before he reached her, comprehension replacing his troubled countenance.

"I see." He tried to hide a smile.

"I guess I will be off to my chamber now. Thank you kindly for waking me." Dorsa inclined her head with as much civility as she could muster and then darted down the corridor before he could say any more. If nothing else, she would prove to Vtalmay's people she was a courteous person, even if they discovered her to be a complete lunatic.

Practically scurrying down the corridor to her room, she glanced over her shoulder to be sure of her total privacy. She let out a gasp of breath when she was certain she could not be heard. She gazed in shock down at the knife still clutched in her hand. How had it gotten there? How had she gotten in the corridor? She had *never* before walked in her sleep!

She hounded her brain for answers and vaguely remembered what she had dreamed. To her great fear, she realized she had dreamt the very dream she had been for weeks now, the one about murdering the Chancellor in his sleep. She then realized that she had not only just left the kitchen from having taken the knife, but she had started going in the very direction of the Chancellor's room.

"Oh, for the love of Shelkite! Please save me, High Power!" she whispered when she reached her bedroom door. She entered the solitary comfort of her own place and swiftly shut and locked the door behind her and then leaned up against it, panting, her heart racing in fear. She gazed down again at the blade in her hand. It seemed to flicker red, as if with blood. She yelped and tossed it down on the nearest tabletop. But coming to her senses, she realized it was only the reddish reflection from the hot coals that still burned in her fireplace. She began to pace in front of the hearth, her bare feet sinking deep in the lavish rug placed there.

Her thoughts jumbled, she soon comprehended she was chilled and went and retrieved her thick robe and tied it around herself. She then continued her fervent pacing, biting a fingernail. She sat down on the chaise facing the hearth and slipped on her warm stockings that had been lying there, all the while thinking urgently.

What was happening to her? She was becoming utterly consumed by this tidal wave of insanity. It was now a constant fight for her to keep thoughts of murdering the Chancellor away. Was she going insane? Was she just an evil person at heart? She broke down and cried, burying her face in the cushions of the lounge.

"He's a good man. I will not. I cannot..." she mumbled into the cushions. But it seemed that no matter what she desired, her subconscious would do what it wished. She felt cursed. Her compulsion to kill was so strong she feared for Cheldon's life and for her sanity.

Turning to lie on her back and face the high ceiling of the palace, she watched the low light of the fire flicker there. Breathing in a great breath, she collected her thoughts. Slowly her inner being calmed, and her heart settled down to its normal thrumming cadence. She turned on her side, wrapping her robe more snuggly around herself, and stared into the fire. Its warmth dried her tears.

As a child, she had been taught by her father, as well as her mother, that no matter what happened in her life she always had a choice as to how she would react to it.

"A choice," she whispered to herself. "I can choose," she said, with more determination, sitting up. She brushed some long locks of curly hair out of her face and clenched her teeth in resolve. "I have a choice to either let this thought destroy me. Or..."—She glanced over at the snow cubs curled up in their basket by the hearth; they eyed her sleepily— "Or I can fight this. I always have a choice. And I choose not to allow myself to be affected negatively by this dream anymore," she said firmly to the cubs.

They yawned and climbed out of the basket, stretching as they came to her. She reached out her hands and stroked them both, feeling strengthened, inward and outward. She smiled to herself and fell asleep with them cuddling around her on the chaise. As she lay back, her emerald necklace slid down its chain and glinted enchantingly in the coals' feverish light.

★★★★

They had been instructed to stay away from the dragon. Alexa had been warned right after she had explained the riddle.

Apparently, the young male dragon was not safe or tame in any sense. Eelyne was the only human that could approach him without being mauled or eaten. The horses were obviously not allowed close either. Although, the warhorses seemed to know on a prey versus predator level that they didn't want to be near the dragon anyhow. They kept their watchful distance.

Alexa stood with her arms crossed, glaring at the dragon from a distance. She wanted nothing more than to shoot one of her obsidian arrows straight into his soft, beating heart, and was contemplating doing just this, even unknowingly drawing out an arrow and getting so far as to set it, when the Master Sword came up behind her and firmly pushed her bow down. She frowned up into his face, for he had been decisively ignoring her again. Her hard eyes locked on his features. His expression was stern as he shook his head, but his eyes held a spark of empathy. She sighed and lowered her bow, stiffly nodding her understanding, her jaw clenched and eyes aflame. Then, the Sword stalked away to finish packing, without another word or glance back.

As the company prepared to move out, a heartrending lover's goodbye took shape between the newlyweds. Kheane kept his composure well. However, Jadelin fell to pieces. She struggled courageously to contain her racking sobs. Kheane did his best to soothe her, even in his own gloom. Although the Empress knew he had a vow to keep in helping the company and he would soon return to live with her, she couldn't bear the idea of being separated from him again.

Eavesdropping, Alexa heard Jadelin say, her voice fraught with fret, "What if you die?"

In which Kheane replied, "Then, I'll die happy. Something I used to think wouldn't happen."

Alexa felt on Jadelin's behalf that this answer was perhaps not a fair one. But she kept her grumpy opinion to herself.

The company awkwardly endured the quarrel as they gathered their things, tacked the horses, and ate a quick meal. They never saw Kheane speak so many words since he had been with them or look so distraught. He was frightening to look at, even in his most comforting countenance. His raspy voice was lowered in a soothing tone that came across almost menacing, belying his words. His broad body was tense, and his dark eyes held bleak encouragement, his scarred face twisted in agitation. But the Empress seemed impervious to his unavoidable, frightful countenance, something that for sure had struck fear into many of his victims. She seemed to see through all his imperfections to his true intent.

Finally, their parting goodbye ended. Jadelin held herself tall and dignified, though her eyes were still red around the rims. With the conclusion of their goodbye, Prince Alkin approached Jadelin to say his farewell and thank you. She expressed her pleasure at being able to help the company and was only sorry she couldn't help more. Her place was back in her small kingdom. Though, she proposed with great enthusiasm that two of her centaur guards accompany them on the mission. Alkin was pleased she and the centaurs were so willing to help. However, he was a bit hesitant in adding more to their company. It would make it more difficult for them to travel covertly. Still, the extra help would be welcomed. His indecision called for him to summon Alexa and Sword Bryan for their advice.

Alexa had been sitting morosely at the trunk of a great tree, throwing her dagger at the earth. Reluctant, she stood and joined the Prince. The Master Sword stalked over from having been taking his time tacking up Dragon. Apollos followed close in the Sword's steps.

In the end, between the four of them, they decided it would be beneficial for at least one centaur to join their company. Night Strider would travel with them. This pleased the Empress and the centaurs, though they were still regretful they couldn't spare more help. They promised they would arrange to send what little help they could on ahead to the battlements in Galeon. Most of them would stay behind to protect the hidden kingdom, for many of the mystical creatures there were the last of their kind and unable to protect themselves.

Estella was torn in whether she would join the company. The unicorn could, of course, like Apollos, make herself unseen. She would not be a hindrance to the company's stealth, but, in fact, would add to it. However, she was bound greatly to Jadelin, as

Apollos was to Alkin. The unicorn yearned to be with Apollos, too: her own kind. After some debate, Jadelin insisted Estella go with the company, and released the unicorn from any vows to her. Estella was deeply grateful.

With the decisions made and without a single glance at Alexa during the conversation, Bryan went back to his grooming and tacking of Dragon. Alexa turned to return to her spot under the tree to await their departure, but before she did, Prince Alkin clasped her hand and gave it an encouraging squeeze. She glanced impassively down at their joined hands, then raised her eyes to meet his sparkling hazel ones. She returned his squeeze, smiling cheerlessly, and left him to watch her walk away.

While the warriors packed to leave, she sat at the base of the tree in a trance, watching the camp turn back into a vacant valley. She allowed her eyes to wander every once in a while over to the mound of dirt piled high on the other side of the meadow beneath the low-hanging boughs of a maple tree. Her eyes misted over with tears, and she looked away, not being able to bear the thought of leaving Zhan behind forever. She resisted accepting the reality that his body now lay cold and still beneath the ground, where it would eventually become earth itself. She had been grateful when she had discovered the company—either the Prince or Master Sword, more likely—had had Zhan's body buried so she would not have to bear the sight of it again. Surprisingly enough, they had done it with the dragon's help. Eelyne had instructed the creature to dig a hole and to move Zhan in it without any problems. The dragon was willing under Eelyne's command.

A few moments before they were ready to leave, everyone realized Alexa didn't have a mount. She had noted this problem— obviously—from very early on. But she hadn't bothered or cared to discuss it. By this time, the Empress and centaurs had left to return to the kingdom, and the camp was completely packed up, and most of the company was mounted.

Alexa rose from her spot under the tree and came to stand amongst them. All mounted now, they circled her, looking contemplative. In an off-handed manner, she suggested she just walk. She didn't mind walking. But the Master Sword was quick to shoot down that idea. She would slow them down and be more vulnerable to danger. Then someone suggested the pack mule. But the poor animal was already burdened with all their supplies. There wasn't any way he could carry Alexa, too. And no human was daring enough to ask Night Strider to carry her. The centaur was carrying his own supplies. And the company could tell by his defiant countenance that he was very averse to carrying a human, half-blood or not.

Night Strider announced that there were no horses back in the hidden kingdom, either. The mystical creatures didn't have any need for them. Then Prince Alkin suggested she ride double with one of them. He proposed she could either ride with the Master Sword since he was her guardian—Dragon could bear them both without a problem—or she was welcome to ride with him.

Alexa balked at his idea. She didn't want to ride with either of them for more than one reason. First off, riding double was entirely uncomfortable, especially for the distance they had to travel. Second, and most of all, she did not want to have to be in the constant very close proximity to either of them, each for very different reasons.

She glanced by impulse at the Master Sword upon the Prince's suggestion for her to ride with him. Bryan finally looked at her. His features, as always, set austere. But oddly, after two days of avoiding her eyes, he allowed her to hold his gaze. He stared at her a bit unnervingly, his azure eyes full of an unspoken opinion on the matter. She couldn't tell by the clenching of his jaw and his hard set, boring eyes whether he wanted her to come join him on Dragon, or that he would rather her not come near him period. Alexa looked away, not even bothering to use her senses on him to understand. She then spoke up and opposed the idea vehemently.

After another minute of contemplating, Apollos came forward, and to everyone's great surprise, he offered to carry her. No one had even dreamed of asking him or Estella to carry her. It was unheard of to ride a unicorn. They were fiercely independent and divine-like creatures—beyond such things. It surprised no one more than Alexa herself. She should not ride the unicorn; she wasn't worthy of such an honor. But Apollos assured her it didn't bother him to carry her. He would do it willingly.

Still hesitant, she eventually yielded to his insistence that she was welcome to ride him. However, it was under the condition that she didn't use her tack. She agreed readily to this. Though, he did consent to her placing a blanket underneath her seat in order to help ease the discomfort of riding bareback. She would leave her tack behind, set up like an adornment with flowers by Zhan's grave. It would be too much trouble to take along with her.

With all their mundane problems settled, the company continued steadfastly on with their journey.

Those strained events were days behind them now. The company was far from the meadow and traveled steadily northeast toward Kaltraz. It would take several days to get out of the territory of Carthorn. As far as they had traveled at this point, they now only passed the heart of the forest. Ever since they had entered the boundaries of Carthorn, it was as if they had been there years; so much had transpired in their travels and in their hearts. Everyone was anxious to leave.

Riding Apollos was the strangest thing for Alexa, strange but heavenly all together. It was like they glided over the forest floor. She barely felt his smooth gait when he placed his hooves down; they never made a sound. He never stumbled. He never knocked her head on a branch. He slinked smoothly around tight places, much like a cat. His bare back was also peculiarly comfortable compared to a horse's. Her backside didn't even get numb. He was a very comfortable ride. Beneath her thighs, his sleek barrel moved and swayed, much like what she thought riding air would be.

Her senses were heightened to him. She felt every toned muscle of his ripple under her. She sat astride him, tall and confident; her legs wrapped around his barrel as he took her fluidly over the ground. She could feel his power, too. The consistent touch of his body beneath her seemed to cause her to absorb the magical vibes emanating from him. She felt the potent magic he contained, as well as his physical power. It energized her. She could tell that at any given moment he could spring into a gallop that would easily leave any living horse far behind, and it would be nothing to him.

The strangest thing of all, though, was that while she rode him, she was always calm. She ran her hands down his satiny neck and through the silky, iridescent threads of his mane. She couldn't help herself. He had a draw to him that no one could resist. It was like he was a piece of heaven here on earth. It was normal for anyone who had ever laid eyes on a unicorn to have an inexplicable desire to be as close as they were allowed to be to the creature, always wanting to touch and feel a piece of paradise. Few, however, were ever permitted. But Alexa was, and she reveled in it. She didn't understand the draw of unicorns any more than she understood the draw of merpeople on humans, nor any more than she understood magic itself or the High Power. No one did.

The more she touched him, patted him, the calmer she felt. It was magic. She knew this because she had tried to think of her task and worry about the coming days, even think of her lost love on the Master Sword, but she could never dwell on anything negative for long. It just didn't last with him beneath her. The despairing thoughts were always evanescent and quickly replaced with a sense of peace. The hollow vortex in her chest muted, still there, but its power weakened. Did he do this for her sake? Or was this something everyone felt when they touched a unicorn? It didn't matter, really.

At twilight, they stopped for the day and made camp. Alexa dismounted Apollos, and he went his own way while she went hers. She immediately felt all her cares settle back down on her where they thought they belonged. Maybe she could snuggle up next to the unicorn during the night. Would he mind so much? She doubted he would deny her that.

As she helped collect dry wood for the fire, she thought about the last days and how Bryan had acted toward her. At first, he had completely ignored her. They all rode, made camp, slept, rose, and rode again. That was how it went. He had paid her no mind beyond his Sword-Guard duties. Then, slowly, he began acting as if nothing had ever transpired between them. He spoke to her as he'd always had and treated her much the same. This infuriated her. But what could she do? She hated this foolish game he played with her. She was tired of it. She didn't understand it. As much as she had tried to explain his actions away because of his hard-core sense of duty, she found she just did not care anymore about giving him excuses. Wasn't there ever a time when one took their duty too far? Her heartsickness was allowing her temper to get the better of her, obliterating her earlier resolve of tolerance and understanding toward him to ashes.

Alexa remembered vividly that he had once very much wanted to kiss her. She *knew* he had come to her during the night she mourned Zhan, bringing solace to her because he cared. She knew he had feelings for her because he had allowed her to see it in his eyes and actions every so often when he was unguarded. There was no way he could talk himself out of the real reason he had held her in his arms that night and had placed soft, consoling kisses on her brow. Unless she was somehow greatly mistaken on the normal relationship of a Sword-Guard and his charge, this kind of behavior was not the norm, because she was very certain the Head-Master Sword Bryan hadn't ever related to Prince Alkin in this manner when he had been *his* Sword-Guard. She smirked inwardly at the assurance this thought brought her. He couldn't fool her, and she wouldn't allow him to fool himself any longer. She would put an end to this madness, starting right now if she must. Despite her love for him, she was beginning to loathe him for all he had done...or hadn't done.

By the time she had made this staunch revelation to herself, she had collected the firewood and had helped make a snapping fire. She plopped down next to the flame and gazed into it, deep in thought. A large, warm body came to the ground next to her. She glanced over to see Apollos lying with his legs tucked up beneath him and Estella alongside him. He watched her closely, his chocolate eyes discerning. She gave him a half smile and leaned up against his warm, sleek side. He bobbed his head and said nothing. Here she stayed, and let his calming effect spill over her, right down to her toes.

Night Strider had gone out to catch fresh dinner. The rest of the company, after feeding their mounts for the night, joined Alexa and the unicorns around the fire. A few of the men groaned when they lowered themselves to the ground. Everyone was stiff and tired from the long day of riding. At least they had had no trouble with the uncanny forest lately. This was the advantage of having the added company of an extra unicorn and a formidable centaur, not to mention a dragon on call.

Bryan finished brushing Dragon and came to squat by the fire. He looked at Eelyne and Alexa, who refused to regard him even though she knew he was gazing at her. "All right, I think I've given you both a long enough break. We need to get back to practicing your swordsmanship," he said.

Eelyne shifted and grimaced at the thought of not relaxing, but he stood obediently and stretched, preparing for the bout. Alexa didn't move. She continued to lean against Apollos and stare passively into the fire. At her inaction, Bryan merely gave her an amused look. He then stood and went with Eelyne to a designated spot for the bout.

"Okay. Where'd we leave off?" he thought out loud, still regarding both Eelyne and Alexa. "Right. We left off at three on one. But I think I'd rather work on team practices tonight," he said, and then called over to Alexa, "Come on, Sand Queen, let's get moving. We don't have all night to wait on you." His tone was even, but his eyes and features were firm in his command, as if he expected some kind of defiance.

"I'm not going to sword fight tonight, thank you," she said offhandedly. She leaned forward to gaze into the fire, not looking him in the eye.

Bryan stared at her in exasperation. Her curt comment had caught the attention of the rest of the company, and they stopped their conversations to listen.

"There's no doubt that you're getting better with your fighting, but I still think you need to practice. You've a lot to learn. Now, come on," the Master Sword said more sternly. The company watched them with uneasiness, noting the scowl across Alexa's face.

"I don't have to. I don't feel like I need to. If I'll be using the counter-magic, I don't think perfecting my swordsmanship is necessary," she said, her sapphire eyes firing up.

"What do you mean you don't have to?" Bryan growled, "I told you to, so get over here."

"No, Master Sword." She glared at him, defiant, from where she could see his braced, broad stature across the fire pit.

He took a tense step toward her; his jaw clenched at her disobedience. His hand grasped the hilt of his drawn sword so tightly his knuckles showed white, and his azure eyes narrowed dangerously. "You'll do what I say," he said through his teeth.

She had never before heard him use this tone. A flutter of anxiety rose in her chest, but she held fast to her defiance. The whole company seemed to stop breathing as they watched the confrontation with wide eyes.

"Are you going to make me, Sword Bryan?" she challenged, holding his dire glare with her own. "I thought it had just been an off-hand idea to train me. Warrior Eelyne is the one who originally asked for your help. Being my Sword-Guard, you're not required to train me, only to protect me."

Bryan stalked to the edge of the fire to stare down over it at her. Alexa mustered as much courage as she had and stared resolutely back into his formidable face. He looked intimidating and dangerous. Despite her actions, she couldn't help but at that moment feel so very attracted to him in this state. He looked as if he wanted to wallop her head off with his sword; though inexplicable and foolish, she felt ever-so-more drawn to him for it. But she couldn't let her guard down. She had to not only push aside her feelings for him, but she had to find a way to make them completely disappear. It was impossible.

"I gave you that sword so you could learn to protect yourself with it," he said, livid, "Now—"

"Sword Bryan," Alkin cut in, "If Alexa doesn't feel like fighting tonight, I think it's all right if she passes this time."

Bryan snorted a response, his features rebuffed and furious. He was not used to someone blatantly refusing his commands. He clenched his jaw, shot Alexa one last glare that would have knocked her unconscious if it had been physical and turned, stomping back over to where Eelyne stood frozen by his shock. "Come on. Fight me," Bryan commanded.

"Uh, okay," Eelyne stuttered, his eyes wide. He probably feared for his life, having taken in the menacing stance of the

Master Sword and how he held his sword aloft with a death grip on its hilt and a vile spark in his darkened eyes.

Eelyne fidgeted for a moment. Then, with the Master Sword's apparent impatience, he decided he had better obey. So, he threw himself bravely into a match he had no chance of winning.

They fought viciously. Well, the Master Sword fought viciously, apparently taking his frustration out on poor Eelyne. The young warrior had no chance up against the Head-Master Sword. He was certainly learning to defend himself tonight, quickly and efficiently, for the Sword wasn't playing around. Bryan's blows were hard, quick, and precise. His footwork perfect.

Alexa watched the heated match, feeling satisfied. He would have no power over her. He knew how he was playing with her, and she wasn't going to allow him to get away with what he had done to her heart without any punishment. This was his punishment. She wouldn't be compliant to his whims any longer. He had to have known what she was doing, or else he would not have gotten as angry as he had. Or would he have? Alexa sighed. She didn't understand him at all.

She realized she had leaned away from Apollos' side. This must have been why she could think and act in the insolent manner she had intended. She glanced over her shoulder and found the profile of Apollos' equine head inches from her. His big, round, chocolate-colored eye stared right at her, very much reproachfully. He eyeballed her, and she suddenly became ashamed of what she had done. The unicorn huffed out a soft, sweet-smelling breath and shook his head, his penetrating eye still on her. She glanced away, shameful, toward the brooding Master Sword. He was pounding Eelyne in the fight. Alexa could tell the younger warrior was tiring. His defenses weakened. He sweated notably and grimaced whenever Bryan landed a blow. She should go over and give him a reprieve.

By that time, the rabbits Night Strider had caught were skinned and roasting over the open flames. The scent of them filled their small camp. The rest of the company had now long forgotten the argument and were partaking in other conversations.

Overhead, clouds rolled in, and the thick smell of rain was on a warm, mounting breeze. They heard thunder off in the distance.

The company groaned simultaneously. There wasn't room in this small clearing to set up their tents to escape the storm. They would have to huddle under the boughs of the trees and hope they wouldn't get too wet.

The forest was thick in this area, and the trees were broad and tall, with beautiful vines hanging from the branches. This would provide some cover for them, and they were grateful. The ground was mossy and spongy, which would be good to bed on if they could find a space unbroken by the plethora of roots breaking the surface.

By the time they had finished eating and had readied their bedrolls and climbed in for the night, the rain had come. The thunder was soft and the lightning dim. It wouldn't be a harsh storm. The rain merely drizzled. The pattering drops on the forest floor and the quiet rumbling of the distant thunder acted like a lullaby and lulled the exhausted company into a deep, contented sleep, except for Alexa.

She lay awake, troubled. Apollos was on guard duty. He moved silently and vigilantly around the camp. So, she couldn't snuggle up against his warm, sleek body and find comfort there. She didn't dare ask Estella.

She lay on her side, staring at her Sword-Guard's back, feeling every so often the pleasant plop of a warm raindrop on her exposed face. Of course, despite his anger with her, he had stubbornly unrolled his bedroll near hers so he would be protectively close by.

Alexa allowed herself to sigh heavily. She was sorry for her treatment of her Sword-Guard now. How could one love someone so much one second and then seemingly hate them the next and then find their hate replaced with love again? She took a deep breath, inhaling the heavy, moist air, pleased by the wet-soil smell filling her lungs. She felt restless. She needed to think. She needed to walk. She had to get away so she could sort through her feelings.

She sat up and quietly extricated herself from her bedroll. Peering around, she stood and then crept to the edge of the camp, heading for the dark woods. She wouldn't go far. She would go just far enough to where she could feel some solitude and sit and think, gather her senses, and re-collect her magic, for her emotions had somehow scattered them.

She glanced over her shoulder to find Apollos perked up, watching her fixedly from across the camp. His head was high, his tail arched, and his horn glittered in the low light. She stopped and mouthed, "I won't go far. Need to think. Keep your senses on me."

The unicorn was still as a statue for a moment while he considered. Then he lowered his head in acceptance, though his eyes held a sharp warning for her to be careful. She nodded her understanding and crept into the forest where it wrapped itself like a dark shroud around her.

Apollos watched her disappear. But he wasn't the only one watching her disappear into the forest. Bryan had been awake. He hadn't been able to sleep and only been pretending to because he knew Alexa was still up. He glared at her back as she retreated alone into the woods. After he could no longer see her dark silhouette, the Master Sword untangled himself from his bedroll and stood. He would follow her and keep an eye on her and then maybe tell her off, too. She was such a fool-headed girl. Why would she do such a thing? Being her Sword-Guard was becoming more of a difficult task than he had ever imagined, considering how he had come to feel for her as well as her reckless behavior. He threw a glance over his shoulder as he crept into the woods and found Apollos gazing at him. He paused and shook his head in disapproval at the lenient unicorn. The unicorn looked at him with wide, innocent eyes. Bryan softened, and Apollos bobbed his head, thrusting his muzzle outward in a gesture to tell him to get going. Bryan turned to the woods and let the dark swallow him.

CHAPTER FORTY-ONE

Alexa took Apollos' warning to heart and allowed her senses to run rampant while she crept through the forest. Her boot falls fell silent on the mossy ground. She brushed the harsh bark of the trees with her fingertips as she passed by, breathing in the damp air with relish. And lifting her face to the sky, she allowed the light raindrops to runnel softly down and wet it. The forest was quiet and soothing. It didn't seem bothered with the company's trespassing at that time.

Thunder roiled in the distance, and every now and then a strong warm breeze would whip through the branches, bringing with it a kind of ethereal presence.

She found a sheltered spot under a great oak tree and sat down. She leaned against the rough trunk and let her head rest back against it, closed her eyes, and felt out her magical senses, collecting them and reveling in them. Someday she would learn how to control and use them better. She would be powerful…someday.

She sighed. Then slowly, among the healing power of nature, she relaxed. All her troubles dissolved in the rain.

With her eyes closed and her ears and mind focused on the soft noises in the forest around her, her unchecked witch senses latched on to something approaching. Her eyes popped opened. She rose, her back hugging the tree, and drew out her dagger, having purposely left the sword Bryan had given her behind. She peered into the dark woods. Her keen eyesight caught a movement in the distance, approaching from the direction of the camp. Soon, she could see the silhouette of a tall person. She held her breath and clenched the dagger tighter. Her body braced for action.

As the figure moved closer, her senses recognized him before her eyes did. *How ironic.* She knew him well enough to recognize him through her senses, yet she could never figure him out.

The Master Sword paused several strides away. He didn't speak, but Alexa sensed his irritation. She closed her senses off.

She didn't want to feel his bitterness. She didn't feel like deciphering all his complex emotions right now. It was him and thoughts of him she had been trying to escape; now here he was tormenting her. This was a cruel game. Whether he was playing it on purpose or not didn't matter anymore.

Lightning flashed and lit his broad stature for her to see. He saw her, too. His hand rested on the hilt of his sword, his face impassive. *Why does he still play the austere part of the Head-Master Sword in only my presence? It's wasted on me.* She sighed and returned her dagger back to its sheath at her thigh.

"Come to give me a thrashing, my precious Sword-Guard?" she asked, her tone more than a little sour.

"Maybe. You definitely deserve it," he huffed. "You shouldn't run off like this, especially after dark. How many times have I told you that?"

"Not enough." She raised her chin and kept her stature tall and confident.

"You're so infuriating." He stalked toward her, lessening the distance between them to barely a step. In the darkness, his angry eyes sought out her face.

"And you're not?" she spat.

He took a half a step back. "What are you doing out here?"

"Thinking. I just needed to get away and clear my mind."

"Get away? Get away from what? You could be eaten out here." He ran his hand through his tangled hair.

Alexa pursed her lips and stared him down. "From you."

"Me?" he scoffed. "What for?"

She clenched her fists and growled. He watched her with a bewildered expression and still stood rather close. This annoyed her even more. She didn't want him near her, and releasing her pent-up frustration, she gave him a brusque shove on his chest. He pushed her hands off himself with a glare.

"I don't understand you." Her eyes were aflame now, and her witch temper was taking hold of her. All her hurt and confusion were bubbling to the surface. She feared she wouldn't be able to control her anger.

"What isn't there to understand? I wanted you to practice tonight like we've done almost every night," he said, indignant. "It

- 439 -

doesn't warrant you running off and putting yourself in danger."

"No, no." Alexa began to pace, her eyes troubled. She ran her fingers into the crown of her hair, pulling locks loose from her tight braid, giving her a slightly crazed look.

The Sword stood back and watched her closely as she paced and huffed; it being very clear that she was holding more anger back. With her jaw tense and her fists clenched, she nearly trembled from head to boot.

"Just—just please leave me alone before I lose my temper!" she groaned after a minute, turning to regard him with a sharp look.

"*Before* you lose your temper?" he snorted, and allowed himself to give her a wry, crooked smile.

She stopped her pacing to glare in exasperation at him. He could see her clearly now that his sight had adjusted to the dark. Her eyes looked dangerous and bewitching, and he suddenly felt a light, unnatural chill spill through his body. He held up his hands in surrender and gave her a boyish grin; his own anger dissipating upon seeing her in such a stressed state. Bryan didn't budge at her request, though. He merely stood there, watching her. He was willing to wait out whatever was bothering her so they could return to camp. Perhaps she was mourning Zhan or stressed over the mission—so he told himself.

Alexa, so busy mumbling to herself, pacing, and trying to hold in her horrible temper, didn't notice that the Master Sword had calmed and now gazed at her with a deeper perception. After another minute, she glanced up as if surprised to see him still there and narrowed her eyes. "I'm not going back with you. I can take care of myself."

"Yes, you will. I'm not leaving without you," he said, his tone soft.

"I want to collect myself first."

"What's going on?" he finally asked, but deep down, in a place he kept locked, he knew exactly what was going on. It had taken him to calm down before he could see what was distressing her. He just didn't want to address the impending, painful subject… Everything would be best if she thought him indifferent.

Then they could altogether avoid proclaiming their feelings, thus avoiding the desolation of their unpermitted love.

She eyed him begrudgingly, like a harassed cat. *I've fallen in love with you, and for some reason, you won't love me...* But she couldn't bring herself to say it. Instead, she said, "I'm just sick of...the game."

"Game? What game?" he asked with a stubborn air, though his voice held no malice.

"Nothing. Never mind. I'm just a silly girl." She waved him away and bit a fingernail.

"Sometimes, but—" he started, in an attempt to lighten the mood, but he stopped upon seeing her resentful, sapphire eyes turn on him.

Alexa paced again, faster and faster. She wanted to run; to run far away from him until her lungs burned and her mind was utterly cleared of him. He was playing the game again. As if he had no idea there was something between them. How wicked of him to think he could fool her! It was all so mystifying and heartrending to believe he cared one moment, only to find out the next he didn't. Then again, perhaps she had *really*, honestly fooled herself into thinking he loved her...

"Alexa," Bryan began; his voice held the tone of an adult soothing a child. It irritated her. "We've forgotten our pact. We need to be on good terms...in order to accomplish this mission."

She snapped her head up to regard him flatly. She hated to admit to herself that she had been half hoping he was going to declare his love for her. How stupid to think that! Her jaw tensed and her eyes glossed over with suppressed tears. She fought them, not trusting herself to speak, and trained herself to bestow an uncivil look on him.

Bryan took her silence as an okay for him to continue. "There are good reasons to explain...my behavior," he faltered, but pressed on as her unreadable eyes bored into him, "I haven't been the best Sword-Guard to you." Her countenance changed to a quizzical hurt and her mouth curved ever-so-slightly, but she didn't speak, her troubled eyes fathomless and dark. "I have sworn a duty to you and to Shelkite, and on many levels, I have failed."

"You have not," she murmured, lowering her eyes, her anger

dissipating.

"I can't allow anything to compromise my responsibility. Anything that would jeopardize my obligation to you puts your success at severe risk. I would like to renew my promise to you." He paused and came to stand closer.

He regarded her tenderly, his aloof words belying his eyes. She didn't move away. He was so close to her she could almost feel the heat from his skin. He smelled enduringly of campfire smoke and woods.

"There's no need to renew any promise. You've never failed me. You've given your best from the start," she said, her voice soft as she looked up into his face to land her eyes on his intent ones. He parted his lips as if he had decided to speak some sudden truth, but paused, studying her face, her lips. She ached for his touch, but his countenance was conflicted; his whole being acted as if he wanted to be nearer to her than he was allowing himself. His eyes held a forgone yearning and he leaned closer to her, his eyes on her mouth. Alexa's breath stopped as she waited for his touch; she could just barely feel his soft exhale on her skin, but to her once again dismay, his brow furrowed, and he pulled away.

"Our connection," he continued huskily—She looked away sorry—"Can't be personal." He fought to set his features, and something in her chest slipped to the depths of defeat. "I am solely your Sword-Guard; that's where our connection begins and ends." His inflection grew firm, "When this is finished, we will part as only Master Sword and charge."

She gazed at him with lost eyes. He swallowed and looked away. So, this was how it was to be. She finally understood. Their feelings were banned. Their love was never to be. It would only be a hindrance to him, to her...to the mission. He was plucking it from its very new and tender roots. If he would not love her, she couldn't make him. And he was right; they both had a responsibility to concentrate on. She nodded numbly in resignation.

"Alexa." Bryan suddenly looked sorry, an untypical expression of him; it didn't suit him. His clear, azure eyes were sad and regretful. His lips moved to speak again, but she jerked her head to silence him, pursing her mouth. He had said all she wanted to hear. She needed no more from him. He clenched his jaw and nodded in silent accord. He also had to bear with his statement now that it was voiced.

"Fine then, dear Sword-Guard." Her voice was brittle. "I'll be from here on out a more dutiful charge of yours." She gave a slight, mocking bow at the waist. And straightening, she added with sarcasm, "Though, I shall still admire your gallantry from afar in agonizing solitude." Bryan gave her a wry look; an amused glimmer came into his eye at her dramatization. She continued, "Perhaps someday when you're a crusty old Sword, sick of attending all the dreary councils and the repugnant parties with dull ladies, you will think back on me with some nostalgia…and regret," she ended quite bitterly.

"Alexa…" Bryan sighed. He felt as if he was going against the grain of fate by lying to her. But he must—he must, for her own good!

"Master Sword." She silenced him with another sour smile. "I've heard all that I need to. You made it clear; we are guardian and charge only. Pact?" She held out her hand brusquely. He glanced down at it, unsure of her sincerity. Then, resolutely, he gripped her hand and gave it a firm shake. They both broke their grasp, neither able to bear the touch of the other.

Alexa knew all her hopes of their love had been slaughtered with that handshake. Even though Bryan's eyes said differently, he had never said outright that he cared for her in any way other than as his charge. To Alexa, this decision of forbidding their feelings was all the worse because it was an absolute conscious rejection.

They stood in silence for a moment, listening to the sound of the soft thunder and the gentle tap, tap of the drops of rain on the leaves. The damp wind rustled the treetops, bringing with it a consoling atmosphere.

Bryan moved awkwardly to speak, "You must understand that I do ca—"

She silenced him with her hand, staring, avid, into the dark of the forest to the left. "Something is near. And it's not friendly," she whispered, her eyes anxious and alert.

The Master Sword's broad stature tensed into defense mode.

He drew his sword, coming to stand even closer. Alexa already had her dagger in her hand. She cursed herself for leaving her bow behind. What had she been thinking?

The creature approached. The two still couldn't discern it, but Alexa could sense it clearly. It was a creature of stealth, a predatory animal, but it also had a mystical nature. She adjusted her slender fingers around the hilt of her dagger for a snugger grip.

"I think I see som—" Bryan began, but a ferocious snarl gulped his words, and the creature was on them before they could distinguish it. It charged out from behind a nearby tree and hammered straight into Alexa, knocking her into the Master Sword. Then, just as swiftly, it bounded back off into the dark.

Befuddled for a moment, they scrambled to collect themselves.

"What is it?" Bryan asked, grasping Alexa's arm a bit hard and dragging her right up next to him. He held his sword drawn in the direction the creature had disappeared in.

Alexa had her dagger drawn in the hand opposite of the arm he held. She squirmed against his bruising hold. "I'm not sure. But you need to allow me to fight! It's large whatever it is, and you can't fight it on your own."

He released her. And they stood back to back, peering into the dark, scanning the forest, fervent.

This time the creature gave them a warning. Straight to the right of them, it let out a low growl. They snapped around to face it and found themselves mere lengths away from an enormous hellhound staring them down. They inhaled a shocked breath in unison and uttered a curse.

Hellhounds were much larger and meaner than their distant cousins, the howlers, and much more dog-like. Unlike the howlers' repulsive hairless bodies, hellhounds sported shaggy, smoke-gray coats. This one could have been considered cute if it weren't for its red eyes and deadly glare.

The hound crouched down and inched toward the two companions, its shoulder blades protruding like blades.

Locked in its alert eye, Bryan and Alexa braced themselves for action.

"What is it?" the Sword whispered through his lips. He had never seen a creature like this.

"Hellhound. They're smart. Be careful," she whispered in warning. "To our benefit, they hunt alone... I think..." she added, and it crept toward them, showing its pristine, white fangs. It eyed them one at a time, apparently trying to decide which one of them to take out first.

It decided on Bryan.

The hound sat back on its haunches and launched itself into the air straight at the Master Sword. Bryan was quick, but not quick enough for this animal's predatory instinct. Its massive bulk crashed into him, knocking him to the ground faster than Alexa could react; yet, miraculously, he kept a hold of his weapon.

In a brief scramble, for she had been knocked aside, Alexa jumped forward and plunged her dagger into the hip of the hellhound. It howled and spun, plowed right over her, knocking her to the ground, denying her a chance to free her dagger.

Bryan jumped to his feet and charged the creature.

Scarcely aware her face had been trampled into the dirt, Alexa leapt up to help, with only her hands now, but she wasn't about to surrender.

Bryan made wide swipes at the darting hound. It dashed closer each time, attempting to take a chomp out of the Master Sword. Alexa raced toward them and skidded to a stop, realizing she still had a knife in the hidden flap in her boot. She reached down and pulled it out. Bryan landed a few blows with his sword, but the hound only became angrier as it got bloodier. She approached them, holding her knife aloft.

"Stay back!" Bryan hollered at her. The hound snarled and bit down onto his sword, its teeth making an appalling sound on the weapon. Bryan jerked his sword as hard as he could, and the creature came away with a mouth gushing scarlet.

Trying to make herself useful, Alexa took aim and threw her knife with all the strength she had. It flew straight and hard, but the hellhound suddenly darted, and the knife buried itself into a harmless spot in its flesh.

Now, she was completely unarmed.

The hellhound then seemed to decide, upon her determined

attacks, that she was more of a threat than it had anticipated, and it dashed around Bryan to bite his ankles and incapacitate him. The Master Sword's boots protected him from the brunt of the teeth's damage, but the creature jerked its massive head and he crashed to the ground. Then, showing uncanny intelligence, it left Bryan in his temporary weak state to charge after Alexa as if in a game.

It leapt on top of her; the boulder-like heaviness of its shaggy body plowed her right to the earth. She hit the damp ground hard; the wind knocked out of her lungs, and she gasped for air, unable to react when the hellhound bit down on her left arm. Once she had breath, she cried out in pain, but the creature began dragging her away with startling speed.

Bryan jumped to his feet and chased them down, frantic.

Alexa squirmed and thrashed, but the more she jerked, the deeper the hound's teeth went. She thought her arm might tear right off. The hellhound dragged her at a pace much faster than she thought possible, though she could see the Master Sword charging after them, fear apparent across his features. As he neared them, the creature halted at a creek's edge and thrashed his head side to side, tossing Alexa like a rag and disorienting her. When the shaking came to an abrupt stop, the hound released her arm.

Bryan was close, but he had paused, his sword at the ready. Alexa could smell and feel the hound's putrid breath on her face. It stood possessively over her, snarling at the Master Sword, daring him to approach.

"Alexa, are you okay?" Bryan asked, his azure eyes fretful and peering anxiously into her dirtied face.

"Yes," she croaked, "he just twisted my arm a bit. No real damage."

"He's playing games with us. He could have killed me back there but chose not to. Now he *wants* me to attempt to rescue you again."

Alexa rolled her eyes up to look into the hellhound's face. It looked as if it was enjoying itself; its tail even wagged as it hovered over her like a dog with a toy, while it leveled a challenging gaze on Bryan.

"Be ready," Bryan said, and then he charged. The hellhound

pounced on Alexa, grabbing her shoulder, and began dragging her again. But this time the Master Sword was quicker and more precise. His sword came down hard on the creature's neck, severing it and barely missing Alexa as she rolled out of the way.

Bryan fell to her side, dropping his sword, and braced her as she tried to sit up. "Are you sure you're not hurt?" he asked in earnest as he checked her over, his hands a bit prying, and without thought, his anxious fingers brushed her hair from her face.

She nodded, rubbing her injured shoulder, and then prodding her arm. Though it had felt like the teeth had pierced her skin, she found they hadn't. The hound had only been playing with them. But that wouldn't have lasted long. He would have soon killed them both.

"Are you bleeding?" Bryan persisted.

"I don't think so." She looked herself over. No blood. The blood from the hellhound's mouth was on her, but unlike howlers' blood, it wasn't poisonous. Overall, she was just a bit rumpled and dirty from being trampled and drug.

"You have some claw scratches on your arm, but they aren't bad," Bryan said inspecting them.

"Are you hurt?" She looked him over.

"No," he said, and then went to the creek and wet the sleeve of his overcoat.

Alexa rose and walked, rather more easily than she thought she might, over to a nearby weeping willow. Its slender leaves draped over the creek and formed a kind of curtain around her where she sat down, her back against its stocky trunk. Bryan came to her, having cleansed his sword, and took a seat beside her, handing her his overcoat with the wet sleeve.

"For your face," he said. She nodded, grateful, and took the coat and wiped her face. He shook his head with disapproval at her. "When will you learn not to run off?" She shrugged, not meeting him in the eye. "What would you have done if I hadn't been here?"

"I would've managed."

He gave her a skeptical look.

"And if not, you would've been rid of a lot of trouble." Her tone frank, though soft.

After a moment of quiet, he let out a reluctant sigh. "No. My troubles would've just begun…at losing my charge."

She paused her cleansing and looked up to meet his eyes, wondering if his statement was more personal than what he implied. But he held an impassive gaze, as was his stubborn way.

They sat for several minutes in companionable silence, listening to the now calm nighttime sounds arising all around them.

Deep in her thoughts, with a clear and relaxed mind, Alexa heard the Master Sword heave another sigh beside her; one she would have called aggrieved. She moved her sapphire eyes to look at him in question and was quite stunned to see him studying her with a strange, conflicted expression across his features, and she realized he was rather needlessly close to her. He gazed at her with a thoughtful brow, and then his azure eyes turned unguarded and peaceful, as if he had suddenly made some sort of resolve inside.

Her breath caught in her throat when he reached up and brushed away leftover smudges of dirt from her face with his fingertips and said softly, "That hellhound made me panic." She stared at him, entranced, and he let his thumb trace over her lips, which parted in surprise. His eyes lingered on her mouth, mesmerized it seemed.

She studied his face, bewildered, feeling shivers run through her at this unexpected touch. His eyes flicked up to meet hers; they were unmistakably full of longing. Then, as if without thought, he leaned in and placed his lips softly on hers. She returned his tentative kiss. He pulled back and glanced at her as if he questioned his actions. When she didn't protest, he kissed her again, more fervent this time. She responded the same, falling back to lie in the plush moss as he hovered over her, his insistent, warm mouth still on hers.

Hesitant, she reached up to touch his face and damp locks of hair. He kissed her deeper, slipping his tongue over hers. She grasped his hair tighter, entangling it in her fingers. His hand was at her jaw, and it ran down the sensitive skin of her neck to clutch her shoulder. His palm was rough, but his touch wasn't. *Oh man, he kisses even better than he handles a sword*, she thought, beside herself. Then, to her confusion, he stopped and pulled away. *He's the most aggravating person I've ever met.* She tried to control her frustration, but he had just gotten done telling her they could be nothing more to each other than business, and then he had kissed her, and now this again...

With a conflicted countenance, he traced his fingers down her chin, giving her a sad smile and letting his hand fall into his lap, despondent. He leaned back and looked up at the clearing night sky. The rain clouds were drifting away, leaving the sky a midnight blue and unspoiled.

Alexa sat up and faced him. "What is it, Bryrunan?"

At the sound of his given name, his eyes snapped back to hers, an unmistakable yearning glowing inside them again. He leaned into her, and she came in to meet him. He rested his forehead against hers, his demeanor still troubled. She could feel his breath on her, and she waited anxiously for his lips to touch hers again, but they didn't. Puzzled, she leaned away from his strange embrace to study his features better.

His usual impassive façade had completely melted down, and he looked rather dejected. His normally bright azure eyes were darkened and wreathed with gloom, his handsome lips turned down in a frown. He gazed sadly at her, and she was rendered still at the sight of him. She knew now without a doubt that he truly cared for her, and she was speechless.

"Alexa, the truth is..." he said, his voice husky. She waited, holding her breath. His words seemed to trip over his tongue as if part of him didn't want them said, "I want you to marry me...but it isn't possible."

CHAPTER FORTY-TWO

Dumbfounded, Alexa leaned back and stared at him in astonishment. That wasn't exactly what she'd been expecting. It surpassed all she had wanted, demanded, from him. Her mood brightened a great deal, hope poured into her wrinkled soul, and her wry humor came back tenfold. She snorted an uncontrolled chuckle, and Bryan's eyes narrowed in defense.

Giving him a crooked smile, she said in a wry tone, "You could at least ask me and not tell me. You may be in command of me in some ways, Master Sword, but definitely not in who I decide to marry."

Bryan ran an agitated hand through his tousled hair. He seemed lost for words and vulnerable, his broad body slumped where he sat. Alexa found this nearly irresistible; she had never seen him in such a dismal state, and she regarded him warmly, her sapphire eyes bright and hopeful. She moved closer to him, close enough to where her senses were completely engulfed by him, and he didn't move away. He simply watched her with soft, unguarded eyes. And then peering beseechingly into his face, she whispered, "So, all this time that you've been disregarding me and confusing me was only you not allowing your dedication to your duty yield to your feelings?"

"Yes and no," he answered, solemn. "There is something else…"

But she silenced him with her eyes and said without hesitation, "I love you, Bryrunan." He looked at her with a bittersweet expression. "I have for a while now, ever since we made that ridiculous pact. I want you more than anything I've ever wanted. I *would* marry you," she declared, her eyes searching his face in earnest.

Bryan's heart swelled with elation a thousand times its size, despite his distress. "I've tried to resist you for many reasons ever since I first saw you, but I can't. I can't deny that I love you any longer."

Alexa's lips quirked into a sweet smile, and she yearned to reach out and take his coarse, unshaven face in her hands and taste his mouth again. However, the dismayed look in his eyes brought her reaching hands to a puzzled halt.

"You don't understand. I said it's impossible for us to marry. I'm bound by my oath as a Master Sword. I would be disgraced and exiled if I were to break it. I can only marry a Shelkiten woman. It was impulsive of me to accept the offer to become a Sword. I didn't even want it. I never realized I'd fall in love with anyone again, let alone a Kaltrazian enchantress." His mouth curved into a humorous smile, though it was bound with sorrow.

Finally, Alexa fully comprehended his logic for everything he had done. He was such a loyal and rational person. It all made sense now. He was isolating himself from her for good reason: to protect both of them. Buried in the back of her mind, she remembered hearing of the strict Master Sword's oath Melea had explained to her. She lowered her eyes, feeling lost, sad, and trodden. She couldn't have him still. This was utterly unfair. Her body felt torn asunder. Her soul fell, rumpled.

"I know," he said at seeing her fallen countenance. "That's why I've distanced myself. It's for both our sakes."

Then, with an unexpected fire blaze up in her eyes, she gazed at him with fierce hope, "We could be lovers."

"In secret?" He was skeptical and looked at her askance.

"Yes." Her sapphire eyes were as light as the morning sky.

"That's not really fair to either of us," he said, his blue eyes dark and full of distress.

"What do you mean? We'd be together."

"Alexa, you have to be rational. Over time, we'd tire of it."

"Rational? You're too rational. When is love rational? We wouldn't tire of it. Not if we really loved each other."

"You don't see." He shook his head.

"We could travel to each other. I'd come to Shelkite to be with you—"

"To stay for how long?" he cut her off bitterly. "People would suspect. We'd be found out, and your honor would be ruined."

"I could visit for short periods. I'd tell whoever asked that I was just passing through to visit relatives in the west. I'd tell my family that I'm visiting a friend. I don't care about my honor." She nearly pleaded with him now. She was losing him, and it was more painful this time; because now, she truly knew how much he did care.

"You always traveling?" he said, skeptical and resisting the urge to brush a lock of hair from her face. He mustn't touch her again, lest he couldn't stop. "I could never come to Kaltraz. You know that, right? My duty ties me to Shelkite. I travel the countryside sometimes for months at a time. And when I'm at the castle, I always have some kind of business to attend to." He dropped his blue eyes away from her face as if he couldn't bear to look at her because of the pain he inflicted on her.

"So?" she shot. Her persistent resolve pulled his eyes back to her face. He looked bewildered, amused, and pleased all at once. "I'd come to you when I could. Who cares if anyone discovered us?" she said, adamant. She *would* be with him. She would let nothing keep them apart.

The Master Sword gave her a cheerless half-smile. "And you don't see how this would wear on us? We'd become an obligation to each other. You always traveling, alone and in danger, always at *my* beckoning."

"It wouldn't be like that," she retorted, her eyes sparking up flames at his unrelenting resistance.

"It wouldn't be at first. Then, eventually, it would come to that. Trust me…" He sighed, feeling frustrated himself. "I refuse to use you. If we can't be together lawfully, then we shouldn't allow ourselves to be together at all. It'll save much pain later." He lifted his hand as if to brush her cheek in reassurance, but he made it fall short.

They sat silently facing one another, close, but neither reached out to the other. Alexa because she realized he was unwilling, and Bryan because he feared if he did, he wouldn't be able to resist anymore and hold to what he knew was the right thing for them both.

After a moment, he spoke, still trying desperately to convince her and make her understand, "Don't you want a home and a husband that can be with you always? Would we do this until the day we died? And what about children? Don't you want children?"

Alexa's pondering eyes shot up to his downcast face. "Yes, of course. But I'd give up all that to be with you," she said earnestly, almost frantically.

He sighed, a bit exasperated, trying to stay resolved in his decision. "You say that now. You'd change your mind."

"Stop making excuses! No, I wouldn't. I'm a very determined girl," she said, her brow set in a firm line.

Bryan ground his teeth in frustration and breathed out. "All right. So, what if we did become lovers, despite the difficulties, and then you became with child? You would be ostracized. I wouldn't do that to you," he said, his tone forceful, his own eyes now ablaze at her foolish stubbornness.

"There are herbs to prevent me from conceiving," she countered.

Bryan sighed and smiled forlornly at her. "You have a solution for everything."

Alexa gave him a weak smile and then said, "It sounds as if you'd feel I was the obligation."

"You'd never be an obligation," he said with frustration. "It's just that we can't be with each other in a way that will be easy. It'll be hard on us and perhaps detrimental to us in the future," he explained, beseeching her to understand and be logical. He searched her face, struggling against his desire to reach out to her.

"Prince Alkin is kind. Don't you think he'll allow this for you? He wouldn't force his power over me," she said.

Bryan pursed his lips. "It's part of the oath. The other Swords would become angry and malcontent. And don't think that I haven't noticed how Alkin feels for you. He won't be so thrilled to grant me permission to marry a woman he cares for. He may be kind, but he's still a man. And he can do as he wishes. I know him enough to believe he's capable of begrudging someone."

Alexa pondered the oath and tried to think of another way around the Master Sword's stubborn way of thought. Then she suddenly remembered Melea and how in love the servant was with the Master Sword. She felt a twinge of guilt. "I'd forgotten."

"What?"

"Melea. She loves you."

Bryan sighed and rolled his eyes. "I suspected it. It doesn't matter. She'll find someone new. You shouldn't care; it's not her I care for."

Alexa raised her eyes, perplexed. "Why shouldn't I? You've been spending all this time convincing me we shouldn't be together."

He gave her a boyish grin, then it faded, and he cocked his head, raising his eyebrows at her. "Now, *you* tell me that you were only playing games by acting coquettish with the Prince and Kheane," he demanded gently, his eyes intent.

She merely grinned at him, a little sheepish. "I only ever wanted you." And all his qualms melted away.

Deep in their troubles and falling into thoughtful silence, the two loves hadn't noticed when the stars had come out to sparkle in all their grandeur. Or when the moon's silvery rays started spilling down through the branches to cast eerie, white shadows all around them. They looked around and saw a quiet woodland paradise. The curtain of the willow shielded them, and the forest was content, for now, and seeming to request that the two new loves be left undisturbed.

"Well, I could just bewitch you and have you anyway," Alexa finally broke the silence. Bryan turned his gaze back on her from where he had been observing the woods.

"I was afraid you'd already done that." He smiled nervously, eyeing her enthralling eyes.

She cast a crooked grin at him and shook her head. There was another moment of silence, and Alexa studied him as he once again looked out into the intriguing forest around them, lost deep in his thoughts. She loved his steadfastness, his loyalty, and even his infuriating rationality and stubbornness. And, oh, how she loved that face with his strong square jaw, high cheekbones, and bright azure eyes. She loved his tousled dark hair and his broad, well-muscled body, and how she loved, *loved* to watch him sword fight. He was irresistible on all accounts, and she wanted him for always. She bit her bottom lip and couldn't resist any longer. She leaned toward him, reaching out to him, touching the edge of his jaw with her fingertips, wishing she could dispel the conflict in his heart.

He turned to look at her, surprise across his face. She smiled coyly at him, her eyes twinkling in the white light of the moon. He gave her a sad, crooked smile, and her heart started beating like she'd run a mile. Her breath came short and quick as he held her gaze intensely with his shining blue eyes. She could see in them that he had lost the battle he was fighting with himself. He hesitated, lightly touching her fingers resting on his face. Then he gathered her face in his own hands and placed his mouth on hers, kissing her determinedly.

There were several moments of blissful, fervent kisses on both their parts, along with feelings of regret for all the time they had lost in resisting one another. But they couldn't think of that now, or their uncertain future...

Bryan pulled away from her soft lips and mumbled quietly in her mouth with a regretful groan, "Alexandra, your lips are as foolishly reckless as you are. How much I've kept myself from..." He landed a few quick, ardent kisses on her face, his eyes showing the torment of his oath. And breaking away, he studied her for a moment, still fighting the battle inside against his rationality. He loved every part of this girl, no matter how infuriating she was at times. He loved her courage, her spirit, even her recklessness. Bryan gazed into her face for only a moment more before he could no longer contain his desire. He had her back in his arms in one quick motion, wrapping his arms around her waist, pulling her up close to him. She didn't protest, and he didn't care anymore about resisting. She had ended up convincing *him*, and it was done.

Her willowy body pressed against his when she tilted her chin, offering her lips to his. He placed his yearning mouth on hers like he had imagined so many times, and she responded to his touch like straw to flames. She liberated him from all his responsibilities, and he allowed himself to become utterly unconstrained, reveling in the rare sensation.

Alexa's lips were warm and luscious, her touch invigorating. She clung to him as if she could make up for the time she'd lost in not having the privilege to touch him. Everywhere she brushed, he was aware of her heightened magical power racing into him. His skin simmered with the alien feeling. Her body shuddered and melted beneath his hands, and he melded with her. He thrived from the realization that she was finally in his arms.

He wanted to touch her, to know it was real. And touch her he did. He drew her firm body close to his, pressing his lips beseechingly on hers, tasting her sweet tongue on his. And intertwining his fingers into her hair, he drew her deeper into his kiss and heart. His body ached for more. His hands desperately wanted to discover more of her. She was so lithe, warm, and lovely. He wanted her under him, where he could feel her smooth, bare skin touch his, so they could wrap themselves around each other and become one permanently. Though he knew it couldn't be that way now, he craved for that day. He just wanted her ever closer and yearned for the day her soul would become a piece of his for always.

Alexa saw Bryan as high above her—like a god—and here he was loving *her*. His kisses were so sweet and ardent—intoxicating. His lips were full and precise in their ever-changing charm as they whisked over her throat and features. Thrill after blissful thrill fell from her head to her toes every time she realized it was really him finally pulling her closer to embrace and kiss her. She ran her hands over his shoulders as her lips reveled in the taste of him. The muscles in his arms were taut as he drew her close. Through his shirt, she could feel the firm outline of his torso. When his fingers brushed her skin and his light breaths tickled her neck, she thought she might fall straight into heaven…or hell.

He gently lowered her to lie back on the ground, and she laced her fingers around his strong neck and clung to him, still drinking in and returning his fierce, insistent kisses. His light hands brushed dangerously along her thighs, seemingly shooting enough flames through her to ignite the fabric between them. He was exquisite, inside and out, and she wanted more of him, all of him…

Taking his unshaven chin in her hands, she kissed him with deep, solid affection. Her heart beat as if a thousand horses galloped through her veins. She could sense his own rapid heartbeats, and she drowned rapturously in the certainty of his love.

Holding his exquisite body dangerously close to hers, he

hovered over her, his lips making a sweet trail from her neckline to her ear. Breathless, she peppered his pleased features with gentle kisses. He had finally surrendered himself to her; victory was hers. She had desired him above all else in the world, and now she would never give him up from this moment.

She traced her fingers perilously along his trouser waistline, feeling the warmth of his skin on her fingertips. They both sensed the tense desire within the other. But Bryan pulled slightly away, though he still kissed her tenderly. She froze in apprehension. "We should stop," he groaned reluctantly into her mouth. She relaxed. "You need Apollos too much right now to hinder your relationship," he explained hoarsely, his mouth going from her lips to land a soft kiss on her forehead. He paused, his azure eyes searching out hers. She gazed into his handsome face, a bit starry-eyed.

"I understand," she replied, her voice soft. He grinned at her, flashing his perfect teeth.

There was a moment of silence between them, and they studied each other as if they couldn't believe what they had just done. They had fallen down into a mysterious new world.

"So, I take it you've chosen to be lovers?" she asked.

"More like surrendering. Since there's no other way to be with you," he answered in all honesty.

"In secret, then?"

"Yes."

"Forever?"

"For as long as you wish." He brushed aside a loose lock of her raven hair that had fallen in her eyes. He found her so enchantingly pretty.

"Then," she said, contemplative, "that will be until my death."

He gave her a small, cheerless smile, looking unsure and forlorn. He watched her features for a moment more when he saw them turn from determined to distressed. "What is it?" he asked, his brow puzzled.

She bit her lip; her bright sapphire eyes were round with a dreaded realization, and she glanced away from his intent gaze. He waited.

"I just realized something," she began, looking out to the

moonlit forest around them, unable to look him in the eyes. "I will outlive you by almost two hundred years."

Bryan's heart plummeted to his feet, and his breath caught in his throat. He swallowed, trying to get his bearings as he let this reality sink in. He stared at her, unclenching and clenching his jaw in thought. She turned her eyes back to him. All her earlier fervor had dissipated. Her eyes looked frightened, and he couldn't help but want to take her again in his arms and kiss all the trouble away. Wordlessly, he bent down and pressed a gentle and reassuring kiss to her forehead.

"I won't live to the age that my father will, only being half-blood, but I'll live a long time," she said, morose and glancing away again from his sympathetic eyes. This was possibly the first time she wished she weren't a witch...

"Well," he started, his voice quiet and hesitant, "Then, maybe you could find someone...after I'm gone, that you could marry. Unless, of course, you change your mind, and we just...go our separate ways." He nearly had to choke out the words, but he had to say them. She wasn't something he could capture and bridle and hoard away for only his pleasure.

A determined look came into her blue eyes, and she sat up taller, looking him in the eye again. "No. I will have you. I'll endure...somehow...when that time comes. I won't give you up while I can have you."

Bryan gave her a cheerless smile. "Fate isn't too charitable to us is it?"

Alexa snorted in derision, her fiery spirit resurfacing. "Fate? I don't believe in fate or destiny. I think something, like the High Power, prods us and guides us. But ultimately, we decide what we're going to do with the circumstances, and we decide our own future."

"How do you explain us? I kept resisting, and I know you tried to forget about your feelings, too. But we couldn't ignore *us*, no matter how we tried. And what about the naiad giving your name, isn't that destiny?"

"I could have fought the Shelkiten warriors when they came for me. Could've said no and ran away. I could have still chosen to turn around and go back home even after I met with the Prince…but I didn't. Kaltraz is in danger. It's my home. What kind of person would turn their back on their country and allow people to suffer? It was *my* choice to do this. Sometimes, we just have to listen to the quiet, persistent prodding we feel inside, and then everything will fall into place from the choices we make from there. You'll see. It's more like providence, guidance. Nothing is forcing us to do anything, though we have to be willing to accept the consequences from our choices."

He chuckled and reached out to her and pulled her into an affectionate hug. She snuggled into his chest, breathing in his scent. He rested his chin on her head and breathed her in, too. He heaved a sigh. "You're smarter than you act at times," he teased, and then added with sincerity, "And brave." He gave her a soft kiss, which she returned. "At least I won't have to endure losing you because of old age," he said.

She pulled away to look thoughtfully up at him. "You talk as if I might leave you. Do you think I'm a silly, scatterbrained girl? That I'll someday bore of you, and I'll take off, forgetting all about you like a broken toy?" she asked, her eyes narrowed in defense.

He sighed again. "I just don't think you realize what a difficult situation we're getting ourselves into." His eyes searched her face unhappily.

"Don't worry your handsome head about that." She smiled good-naturedly at him. "Just concern yourself with being my Sword-Guard and leading the company right now."

He glanced away from her avid face in thought, his brow creasing in concern, his blue eyes troubled and unguarded. Alexa allowed herself to sense out his emotions.

"You're thinking about what will happen when we finally meet up with Ret, aren't you?" she asked.

He looked at her, troubled. "Yes."

"Don't be anxious, my beloved Sword-Guard, my uncle won't turn me into a breathing corpse that bears abominations. I won't allow that to happen. I promise. We'll all make it through this okay. This is where I choose my own fate."

He gave her a small smile and shook his head in amused disbelief. "You're not lacking in confidence or courage that's for sure." He hugged her and kissed her one last time, savoring it, for he knew they had to be heading back to camp.

She grinned up at him as he stood. "Never been a problem."

He shook his head, giving her an amused, crooked smile. "Come on, girl, we need to get sleep." He wrapped his arm around her shoulders when she stood.

He began walking with her back toward the camp. There was a moment of silence between them where they both reveled in the midnight paradise the forest had created for them. They looked wistfully back at the weeping willow tree they had sheltered under. It alone appeared like a haven, as its long, slender leaves swayed gently in the night breeze.

Carthorn was truly an enchanting place, angry and aspiring to destroy one moment, and then a blissful haven for lovers the next. Maybe Carthorn and its strange magic and hidden presences had condoned their love from its ire and had allowed them this time to finally come together the way they should have months ago. Perhaps the willow's dryad had tenderly protected them from the forest's dangers, in memory of two lost, forbidden loves. Maybe fate was charitable to them, after all.

"Oh," he broke the silence, "Could you just try a little harder to be indifferent toward Alk—Prince Alkin," he corrected himself and looked at her warily, raising an eyebrow.

A knowing smile spread across her face. "Yes, I'll try." She shot him a sly, teasing glance, and he gave her a warning look. Then she added more seriously, "How are we to act now?"

He shrugged, and a crooked smile tugged at his lips. "Well, let's just refrain from making love in front of the company, shall we?" He wrapped an arm around her shoulder as they walked.

She laughed merrily and marveled in the warmth of his embrace, her witch and human senses dazzled and consumed by him. The sensation of him was everywhere, dancing on the wind, and she was determined to keep it that way.

ABOUT THE AUTHOR

Alicia grew up loving the outdoors, reading, writing, and riding horses—and not much has changed! Today, she enjoys reading, spending time with her family (and pets!), hanging out with horses, and archery. She has a Certificate in Horse Management from Michigan State University and a Bachelor of Arts in English and Creative Writing from Southern New Hampshire University. Currently, she is writing *PINNACLE OF MAGIC*, **VOLUME II**. Visit her Facebook page (*Remnants of Magic, Vol. I*), Instagram (*aliciarchapin*), and website for more info: http://aliciarchapinbooks.wixsite.com/author

ACKNOWLEDGMENTS

I have a throng of people I'd like to acknowledge for their love, friendship, and support, without which I would have never been able to finish this novel or tackle the next. Foremost, I'd like to thank my parents, Jim and Diane, and my sister Erica for supporting every endeavor I've ever pursued with loving enthusiasm. Of course, I can't forget some of my first readers, Victoria Perkins and Brandy Everson, whose excitement over my work was so infectious it gave me the push I needed. I'm also exceedingly grateful to Cristina Kautsky, who helped me iron out so many wrinkles, and to whom I extend heartfelt thanks for all her edits and hard work. I extend a huge thanks to Jessica Malkin as well, whose proofreading was invaluable. I'd like to thank my grandmothers, Jacqueline Chapin and Donna Clark, and my Great Aunt Marj Shooter for their steadfast encouragement in all areas of my life. And, always, thanks to my God, my Savior, the High Power, who somehow made all the puzzle pieces fit together. And lastly but certainly not least, a thousand thank yous to all my lovely readers! My one wish is for you to snuggle up some rainy day and get lost in my story. And if you have enjoyed it, please consider leaving a review. Many happy days to you!